GRIMM'S HOUSEHOLD TALES

THE BRITISH LIBRARY

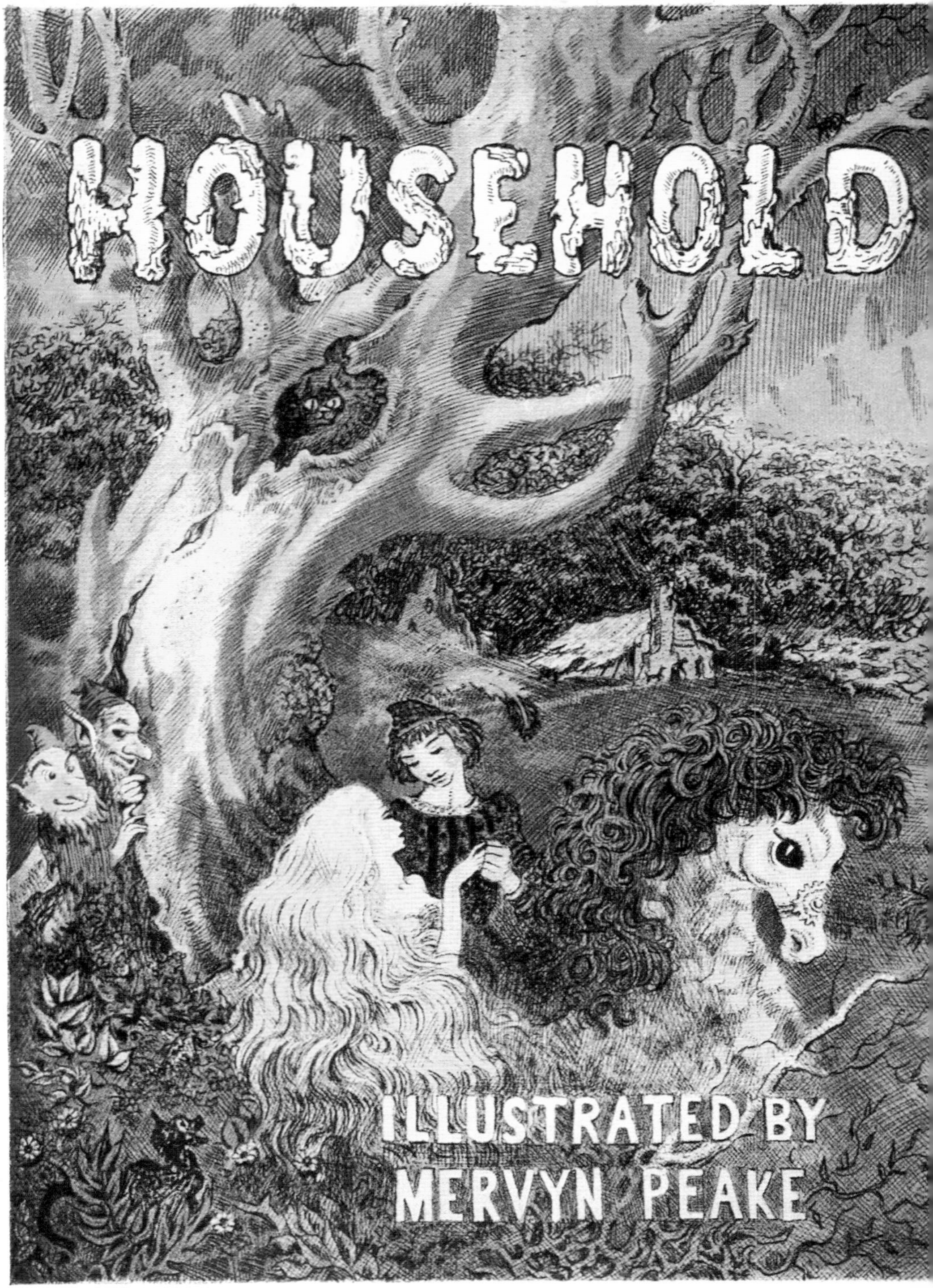
HOUSEHOLD
ILLUSTRATED BY
MERVYN PEAKE

TALES

BY THE BROTHERS

GRIMM

EYRE & SPOTTISWOODE · LONDON

The Queen Bee (p.52)

The Many-Furred Creature (p.104)

Snow-White and the Seven Dwarfs (p.287)

Ashputtel, or Cinderella (p.296)

INTRODUCTION

I first came across *Household Tales* in 1977, when I was given a copy for an eleventh birthday present. I was already familiar by then, of course, with the fairy stories of the Grimms, but I knew them mainly through sanitised modern re-tellings. This book, I soon realised, was something altogether different. For a start, its gorgeous cover showed a pair of fey-looking sweethearts and a large-eyed, curly-maned horse, and though at first glance this image seemed very much in the harmless Disney tradition, to study the illustration with the sharp and patient eyes of childhood was to notice subtle suggestions of menace – to spot the hissing black cats in the shadows, the ruined cottage in the distance, the pair of gleeful goblins leering at the sweethearts from a hollow tree.

The artwork was Mervyn Peake's, the cover a cropped version of the original title page designed by him for an edition of *Household Tales* by Eyre & Spottiswoode, thirty years before. It also appears as the title page in this brand new edition, in which all of Peake's illustrations to the anthology, monochrome and colour, are displayed for the first time since that publication of 1946. Peake's essentially gothic imagination made him an ideal interpreter of the stories collected by the Grimms, for, as I began to suspect on my first reading, and appreciate much more fully now, they are folk tales rather than fairy tales, with nothing cosy about them at all. In fact, with their recurring cast of vulnerable characters – neglected children, 'simpletons', cashiered soldiers, faithful dogs and labouring horses past their best and facing the chop - they offer a quite terrifying glimpse of the brutalities and uncertainties of peasant life.

But childhood, of course, can also be a brutal and uncertain experience, and it isn't hard to see why these stories' preoccupation with injustice and sacrifice, with harsh punishments and outrageous rewards, might speak so meaningfully to younger readers. And though the tales are full of violence, it's usually the bloodless violence of infantile extremes. In 'The Seven Ravens' a little girl blithely cuts off a finger in order to use it as a key to the locked door of her brothers' prison. In 'The Wolf and the Seven Little Kids' a mother slices open the belly of the slumbering wolf who has just gobbled up her children, and fills him with stones instead; he subsequently tumbles down a well and drowns. Peake's art brings these stories to life in all their power, strangeness and beauty. He conveys the terror of lonely quests - for example in his depiction of 'Our Lady's Child', a small ragged figure making her uneasy way through a wilderness of blasted trees. He captures the comedy and horror of physical transformation – as in his illustration to 'The Nose Tree', which shows a bemused peasant whose enchanted proboscis is extending itself into the far distance of a mountainous landscape. I don't recall being troubled either by the grotesqueries of these stories or by the expressive precision which which Peake responded to them; on the contrary, I found the extravagance of the narratives something to relish. I do, however, remember grieving over 'A Sad Story about a Snake', in which a kind serpent befriends a child, only to be unjustly killed by the child's startled mother. It's one of the few tales in the collection that has no magical resolution - which is perhaps why it so upset me. At eleven, already on the journey out of childhood, I was beginning to understand that enchantment has its limits, that unfairness cannot always be magicked away.

And I was starting to understand, too, the power of books for the people who read and love them. My edition of *Household Tales* still has the plate I pasted into it in 1977, which declares importantly that *This book belongs to Sarah A. Waters*; I like to look at that, remembering my younger reading self. I've returned to the stories and their illustrations many times over the years, finding new details and meanings in their odd and lovely landscapes. For me, the Grimms' tales will always be at their best when accompanied by the pictures of Mervyn Peake. It's wonderful to see them brought together again in this glorious edition.

Sarah Waters
2011

CONTENTS

CONTENTS

THE THREE SONS OF FORTUNE

A FATHER once called his three sons before him, and he gave to the first a cock, to the second a scythe, and to the third a cat. "I am already aged," said he, "my death is nigh, and I have wished to take

7

thought for you before my end ; money I have not, and what I now give you seems of little worth, but all depends on your making a sensible use of it. Only seek out a country where such things are still unknown, and your fortune is made."

After the father's death the eldest went away with his cock, but wherever he came the cock was already known ; in the towns he saw him from a long distance, sitting upon the steeples and turning round with the wind, and in the villages he heard more than one crowing ; no one would show any wonder at the creature, so that it did not look as if he would make his fortune by it.

At last, however, it happened that he came to an island where the people knew nothing about cocks, and did not even understand how to divide their time. They certainly knew when it was morning or evening, but at night, if they did not sleep through it, not one of them knew how to find out the time.

" Look ! " said he, " what a proud creature ! it has a ruby-red crown upon its head, and wears spurs like a knight ; it calls you three times during the night, at fixed hours, and when it calls for the last time, the sun soon rises. But if it crows by broad daylight, then take notice, for there will certainly be a change of weather."

The people were well pleased ; for a whole night they did not sleep, and listened with great delight as the cock at two, four, and six o'clock, loudly and clearly proclaimed the time. They asked if the creature were for sale, and how much he wanted for it ? " About as much gold as an ass can carry," answered he. " A ridiculously small price for such a precious creature ! " they cried unanimously, and willingly gave him what he had asked.

When he came home with his wealth his brothers were astonished, and the second said, " Well, I will go forth and see whether I cannot get rid of my scythe as profitably." But it did not look as if he would, for labourers met him everywhere, and they had scythes upon their shoulders as well as he.

At last, however, he chanced upon an island where the people knew nothing of scythes. When the corn was ripe there, they took cannon out to the fields and shot it down. Now this was rather an uncertain affair ; many shot right over it, others hit the ears instead of the stems and shot them away, whereby much was lost, and besides all this it made a terrible noise. So the man set to work and mowed it down so quietly and quickly that the people opened their mouths with astonishment. They agreed to give him what he wanted for the scythe, and he received a horse laden with as much gold as it could carry.

And now the third brother wanted to take his cat to the right man. He fared just like the others ; so long as he stayed on the mainland there was nothing to be done. Every place had cats, and there were so many of them that new-born kittens were generally drowned in the ponds.

At last he sailed over to an island, and it luckily happened that no cats had ever yet been seen here, and that the mice had got the upper hand so much that they danced upon the tables and benches whether the master were at home or not. The people complained bitterly of the plague ; the King himself in his palace did not know how to secure himself against them ; mice squeaked in every corner, and gnawed whatever they could lay hold of with their teeth. But now the cat began her chase and soon cleared a couple of rooms, and the people begged the King to buy the wonderful beast for the country. The King willingly gave what was asked, which was a mule laden with gold, and the third brother came home with the greatest treasure of all.

The cat made herself merry with the mice in the royal palace, and killed so many that they could not be counted. At last she grew warm with the work and thirsty, so she stood still, lifted up her head and cried, " Mew ! mew ! " When they heard this strange cry, the King and all his people were frightened, and in their terror ran all at once out of the palace. Then the King took counsel what was best to be done ; at last it was determined to send a herald to the cat, and demand that she should leave the palace, or if not, she was to expect that force would be used against her. The councillors said, " Rather will we let ourselves be plagued with the mice, for to that misfortune we are accustomed, than give up our lives to such a monster as this." A noble youth, therefore, was sent to ask the cat " whether she would peaceably quit the castle ? " But the cat, whose thirst had become still greater, merely answered, " Mew ! mew ! " The youth understood her to say, " Most certainly not ! most certainly not ! " and took this answer to the King. " Then," said the councillors, " she

9

shall yield to force." Cannon were brought out, and the palace was soon in flames. When the fire reached the room where the cat was sitting, she sprang safely out of the window ; but the besiegers did not leave off until the whole palace was shot to the ground.

THE NOSE-TREE

DID you ever hear the story of the three poor soldiers, who, after having fought hard in the wars, set out on their road home, begging their way as they went ?

They had journeyed on a long way, sick at heart with their bad luck at thus being turned loose on the world in their old days ; when one evening they reached a deep gloomy wood, through which lay their road. Night came fast upon them, and they found that they must, however unwillingly, sleep in this wood ; so, to make all safe as they could, it was agreed that two should lie down and sleep, while a third sat up and watched, lest wild beasts should break in and tear them to pieces. When he was tired he was to wake one of the others, and sleep in his turn ; and so on with the third, so as to share the work fairly among them.

The two who were to rest first soon lay down and fell fast asleep ; and the other made himself a good fire under the trees, and sat down by its side to keep watch. He had not sat long before, all on a sudden, up came a little dwarf in a red jacket. " Who is there ? " said he. " A friend," said the soldier. " What sort of a friend ? " " An old broken soldier," said the other, " with his two comrades, who have nothing left to live on ; come, sit down and warm yourself." " Well, my worthy fellow," said the little man, " I will do what I can for you ; take this and show it to your comrades in the morning." So he took out an old cloak and gave it to the soldier ; telling him, that whenever he put it over his shoulders anything that he wished for would be done for him. Then the little man made a bow and walked away.

The second soldier's turn to watch soon came, and the first laid him down to sleep ; but the second man had not sat by himself long before up came the dwarf in the red jacket again. The soldier treated him in as friendly a way as his comrade had done, and the little man gave him a purse, which he told him would be always full of gold, let him draw as much as he would out of it.

Then the third soldier's turn to watch came ; and he also had little Red-jacket for his guest, who gave him a wonderful horn, that drew crowds around it whenever it was played, and made every one forget his business to come and dance to its beautiful music.

In the morning each told his story, and showed the gift he had got from the elf ; and as they all liked each other very much, and were old friends, they agreed to travel together to see the world, and, for a while, only to make use of the wonderful purse. And thus they spent their time very joyously ; till at last they began to be tired of this roving life, and thought they should like to have a home of their own. So the first soldier put his old cloak on, and wished for a fine castle. In a moment it stood before their eyes : fine gardens and green lawns spread round it, and flocks of sheep, and goats, and herds of oxen were grazing about ; and out of the gate came a grand coach with three dapple-grey horses, to meet them and bring them home.

All this was very well for a time, but they found it would not do to stay at home always ; so they got together all their rich clothes, and jewels, and money, and ordered their coach with three dapple-grey horses, and set out on a journey to see a neighbouring king. Now

this king had an only daughter, and as he saw the three soldiers
travelling in such grand style, he took them for kings' sons, and so
gave them a kind welcome.   One day, as the second soldier was walking with the princess, she saw that he had the wonderful purse in his
hand.   Then she asked him what it was, and he was foolish enough to
tell her,—though, indeed, it did not much signify what he said, for
she was a fairy, and knew all the wonderful things that the three
soldiers brought.   Now this princess was very cunning and artful;
so she set to work and made a purse, so like the soldier's that no one
would know one from the other; and then she asked him to come and

see her, and made him drink some wine that she had got ready for him, and which soon made him fall fast asleep. Then she felt in his pocket, and took away the wonderful purse, and left the one she had made in its place.

The next morning the soldiers set out home ; and soon after they reached their castle, happening to want some money, they went to their purse for it, and found something in it ; but to their great sorrow, when they had emptied it, none came in the place of what they took. Then the cheat was soon found out ; for the second soldier knew where he had been, and how he had told the story to the princess, and he guessed that she had played him a trick. "Alas !" cried he, "poor wretches that we are, what shall we do ?" "Oh !" said the first soldier, "let no grey hairs grow for this mishap : I will soon get the purse back." So he threw his cloak across his shoulders; and wished himself in the princess's chamber.

There he found her sitting alone, telling up her gold, that fell around her in a shower from the wonderful purse.

But the soldier stood looking at her too long ; for she turned round, and the moment she saw him she started up and cried out with all her force, "Thieves ! thieves !" so that the whole court came running in, and tried to seize on him. The poor soldier now began to be dreadfully frightened in his turn, and thought it was high time to make the best of his way off ; so, without thinking of the ready way of travelling that his cloak gave him, he ran to the window, opened it, and jumped out ; and unluckily, in his haste, his cloak caught and was left hanging, to the great joy of the princess, who knew its worth.

The poor soldier made the best of his way home to his comrades on foot, and in a very downcast mood ; but the third soldier told him to keep up his heart, and took his horn and blew a merry tune. At the first blast a countless troop of foot and horse came rushing to their aid, and they set out to make war against their enemy. Then the king's palace was besieged, and he was told that he must give up the purse and cloak, or that not one stone should be left upon another. And the king went into his daughter's chamber and talked with her ; but she said, "Let me try first if I cannot beat them some way or another." So she thought of a cunning scheme to overreach them ; and dressing herself out as a poor girl, with a basket on her arm, she set out by night with her maid and went into the enemy's camp, as if she wanted to sell trinkets.

In the morning she began to ramble about, singing ballads so beautifully that all the tents were left empty, and the soldiers ran round in crowds, and thought of nothing but hearing her sing. Amongst the rest came the soldier to whom the horn belonged, and as soon as she saw him she winked to her maid, who slipped slyly through the crowd, and went into his tent where it hung, and stole it away. This done they both got safely back to the palace, the besieging army went away, the three wonderful gifts were all left in the hands of the princess, and the three soldiers were as penniless and forlorn as when little Red-jacket found them in the wood.

Poor fellows! they began to think what was now to be done. " Comrades," at last said the second soldier, who had had the purse, " we had better part ; we cannot live together, let each seek his bread as well as he can." So he turned to the right, and the other two went to the left, for they said they would rather travel together. Then on the second soldier strayed till he came to a wood (now this was the same wood where they had met with so much good luck before), and he walked on a long time till evening began to fall, when he sat down tired beneath a tree, and soon fell asleep.

Morning dawned, and he was greatly delighted, at opening his eyes, to see that the tree was laden with the most beautiful apples. He was hungry enough, so he soon plucked and ate first one, then a second, then a third apple. A strange feeling came over his nose ; when he put the apple to his mouth something was in the way. He felt it— it was his nose, that grew and grew till it hung down to his breast. It did not stop there—still it grew and grew. " Heavens ! " thought he. " When will it have done growing ? " And well might he ask, for by this time it reached the ground as he sat on the grass,—and thus it kept creeping on, till he could not bear its weight or raise himself up ; and it seemed as if it would never end, for already it stretched its enormous length all through the wood, over hill and dale.

Meanwhile his comrades were journeying on, till on a sudden one of them stumbled against something. " What can that be ? " said the other. They looked, and could think of nothing that it was like but a nose. " We will follow it and find its owner, however," said

14

they. So they traced it up, till at last they found their poor comrade, lying stretched along under the apple-tree.

What was to be done? They tried to carry him, but in vain. They caught an ass that was passing, and raised him upon its back; but it was soon tired of carrying such a load. So they sat down in despair, when before long up came their old friend the dwarf with the red jacket. "Why, how now, friend?" said he, laughing: "well, I must find a cure for you, I see." So he told them to gather a pear from another tree that grew close by, and the nose would come right again. No time was lost ; and the nose was soon brought to its proper size, to the poor soldier's joy.

"I will do something more for you yet," said the dwarf ; "take some of those pears and apples with you ; whoever eats one of the apples will have his nose grow like yours just now ; but if you give him a pear, all will come right again. Go to the princess, and get her to eat some of your apples ; her nose will grow twenty times as long as yours did : then look sharp, and you will get what you want from her."

Then they thanked their old friend very heartily for all his kindness ; and it was agreed that the poor soldier, who had already tried the power of the apple, should undertake the task. So he dressed himself up as a gardener's boy, and went to the king's palace, and said he had apples to sell, so fine and so beautiful as were never seen there before. Every one that saw them was delighted, and wanted to taste ; but he said they were only for the princess ; and she soon sent her maid to buy his stock. They were so ripe and rosy that she soon began eating ; and had not eaten above a dozen before she too began to wonder what ailed her nose, for it grew and grew down to the ground, out at the window, and over the garden, and away, nobody knows where.

Then the king made known to all his kingdom, that whoever would heal her of this dreadful disease should be richly rewarded. Many tried, but the princess got no relief. And now the old soldier dressed himself up very sprucely as a doctor, and said he would cure her. So he chopped up some of the apple, and, to punish her a little more, gave her a dose, saying he would call to-morrow and see her again. The morrow came, and, of course, instead of being better, the nose had been growing on all night as before ; and the poor princess was in a dreadful fright. So the doctor then chopped up a very little of the pear and gave her, and said he was sure that would do good, and he would call again the next day. Next day came, and the nose was to be sure a little smaller, but yet it was bigger than when the doctor first began to meddle with it.

Then he thought to himself, " I must frighten this cunning princess a little more before I shall get what I want from her " ; so he gave

her another dose of the apple, and said he would call on the morrow. The morrow came, and the nose was ten times as bad as before. "My good lady," said the doctor, "something works against my medicine, and is too strong for it ; but I know by the force of my art what it is : you have stolen goods about you, I am sure ; and if you do not give them back, I can do nothing for you." But the princess denied very stoutly that she had anything of the kind. "Very well," said the doctor, "you may do as you please, but I am sure I am right, and you will die if you do not own it." Then he went to the king, and told him how the matter stood. "Daughter," said he,

" send back the cloak, the purse, and the horn, that you stole from the rightful owners."

Then she ordered her maid to fetch all three, and gave them to the doctor, and begged him to give them back to the soldiers ; and the moment he had them safe he gave her a whole pear to eat, and the nose came right. And as for the doctor, he put on the cloak, wished the king and all his court a good day, and was soon with his two brothers ; who lived from that time happily at home in their palace, except when they took an airing to see the world, in their coach with the three dapple-grey horses.

———————

THE GOOD BARGAIN

THERE was once a peasant who had driven his cow to the fair, and sold her for seven thalers. On the way home he had to pass a pond, and already from afar he heard the frogs crying, " Aik, aik, aik, aik." " Well," said he to himself, " they are talking without rhyme or reason, it is seven that I have received, not eight." When he got to the water, he cried to them, " Stupid animals that you are ! Don't you know better than that ? It is seven thalers and not eight." The frogs, however, stood to their " aik, aik, aik, aik." " Come, then, if you won't believe it, I can count it out to you," and he got his money out of his pocket and counted out the seven thalers, always reckoning four and twenty groschen to a thaler. The frogs, however, would not pay any attention to his reckoning, but still cried, " aik, aik, aik, aik." " What," cried the peasant quite angry, " since you are determined to know better than I, count it yourselves," and threw all the money into the water to them. He stood still and wanted to wait until they were done and had brought him his own again, but the frogs maintained their opinion and cried continually " aik, aik, aik, aik." and besides that, did not throw the money out again. He still waited a long while until evening came on and he was forced to go home. Then he abused the frogs and cried, "You water-splashers, you thick-heads, you goggle-eyes, you have great mouths and can screech till you hurt one's ears, but you cannot count seven thalers ! Do you think I'm going to stand here till you get done ? " And with that he went away, but the frogs still cried, " aik, aik, aik, aik," after him till he went home quite angry.

After a while he bought another cow, which he killed, and he made the calculation that if he sold the meat well he might gain as much as the two cows were worth, and have the skin into the bargain. When therefore he got to the town with the meat, a great troop of dogs were gathered together in front of the gate, with a large greyhound at the head of them, which jumped at the meat, snuffed at it, and barked, " Wow, wow, wow." As there was no stopping him, the peasant said to him. " Yes, yes, I know quite well that thou art saying, ' wow, wow, wow,' because thou wantest some of the meat ; but I should fare badly if I were to give it to thee." The dog, however, answered nothing but " wow, wow." " Wilt thou promise not to devour it all then, and wilt thou go bail for thy companions ? " " Wow, wow, wow," said the dog. " Well, if thou insistest on it, I will leave it for thee ; I know thee well, and know who is thy master ; but this I tell thee, I must have my money in three days or else it will go ill with thee ; thou must just bring it out to me." Thereupon he unloaded the meat and turned back again, the dogs fell upon it and loudly barked, " wow, wow."

The countryman, who heard them from afar, said to himself, " Hark, now they all want some, but the big one is responsible to me for it."

When three days had passed, the countryman thought, " To-night my money will be in my pocket," and was quite delighted. But no one would come and pay it. " There is no trusting any one now," said he ; and at last he lost patience, and went into the town to the butcher and demanded his money. The butcher thought it was a joke, but the peasant said, " Jesting apart, I will have my money ! Did not the great dog bring you the whole of the slaughtered cow

three days ago ? " Then the butcher grew angry, snatched a broom-
stick and drove him out. " Wait a while," said the peasant, " there
is still some justice in the world ! " and went to the royal palace and
begged for an audience. He was led before the King, who sat there
with his daughter, and asked him what injury he had suffered.
" Alas ! " said he, " the frogs and the dogs have taken from me what
is mine, and the butcher has paid me for it with the stick," and he
related at full length all that had happened. Thereupon the King's
daughter began to laugh heartily, and the King said to him, " I
cannot give you justice in this, but you shall have my daughter to wife
for it,—in her whole life she has never yet laughed as she has just done
at thee, and I have promised her to him who could make her laugh.
Thou mayst thank God for thy good fortune ! "

" Oh," answered the peasant, " I will not have her, I have a wife
already, and she is one too many for me ; when I go home, it is just
as bad as if I had a wife standing in every corner." Then the King
grew angry, and said, " Thou art a boor." " Ah, Lord King,"
replied the peasant, " what can you expect from an ox, but beef ? "
" Stop," answered the King, " thou shalt have another reward. Be
off now, but come back in three days, and then thou shalt have five
hundred counted out in full."

When the peasant went out by the gate, the sentry said, " Thou
hast made the King's daughter laugh, so thou wilt certainly receive
something good." " Yes, that is what I think," answered the peasant ;
" five hundred are to be counted out to me." " Hark thee," said the
soldier, " give me some of it. What canst thou do with all that
money ? " " As it is thou," said the peasant, " thou shalt have two
hundred ; present thyself in three days' time before the King, and let
it be paid to thee." A Jew, who was standing by and had heard the
conversation, ran after the peasant, held him by the coat, and said,
" Oh, wonder ! what a luck-child thou art ! I will change it for
thee, I will change it for thee into small coins, what dost thou want
with the great thalers ? " " Jew," said the countryman, " three
hundred canst thou still have ; give it to me at once in coin, in three
days from this, thou wilt be paid for it by the King." The Jew was
delighted with the profit, and brought the sum in bad groschen, three
of which were worth two good ones. After three days had passed,

according to the King's command, the peasant went before the King. " Pull his coat off," said the latter, " and he shall have his five hundred." " Ah ! " said the peasant, " they no longer belong to me ; I presented two hundred of them to the sentinel, and three hundred the Jew has changed for me, so by right nothing at all belongs to me." In the meantime the soldier and the Jew entered and claimed what they had gained from the peasant, and they received the blows strictly counted out. The soldier bore it patiently and knew already how it tasted ; but the Jew said sorrowfully, " Alas, alas, are these the heavy thalers ? " The King could not help laughing at the peasant, and as all his anger was gone, he said, " As thou has already lost thy reward before it fell to thy lot, I will give thee something in the place of it. Go into my treasure chamber and get some money for thyself, as much as thou wilt." The peasant did not need to be told twice, and stuffed into his big pockets whatsoever would go in. Afterwards he went to an inn and counted over his money. The Jew had crept after him and heard how he muttered to himself, " That rogue of a king has cheated me after all, why could he not have given me the money himself, and then I should have known what I had ? How can I tell now if what I have had the luck to put in my pockets is right or not ? " " Good heavens !." said the Jew to himself, " that man is speaking disrespectfully of our lord the King, I will run and inform, and then I shall get a reward, and he will be punished as well."

When the King heard of the peasant's word he fell into a passion, and commanded the Jew to go and bring the offender to him. The Jew ran to the peasant, " You are to go at once to the lord King in the very clothes you have on." " I know what's right better than that," answered the peasant, " I shall have a new coat made first. Dost thou think that a man with so much money in his pocket is to go there in his ragged old coat ? " The Jew, as he saw that the peasant would not stir without another coat, and as he feared that if the King's anger cooled, he himself would lose his reward, and the peasant his punishment, said, " I will out of pure friendship lend thee a coat for the short time. What will people not do for love ! " The peasant was contented with this, put the Jew's coat on, and went off with him.

The King reproached the countryman because of the evil speaking of which the Jew had informed him. " Ah," said the peasant, " what a Jew says is always false—no true word ever comes out of his mouth ! That rascal there is capable of maintaining that I have his coat on."

"What is that?" shrieked the Jew. "Is the coat not mine? Have I not lent it to thee out of pure friendship, in order that thou mightest appear before the lord King?" When the King heard that, he said, "The Jew has assuredly deceived one or the other of us, either myself or the peasant," and again he ordered something to be counted out to him in hard thalers. The peasant, however, went home in the good coat, with the good money in his pocket, and said to himself, "This time I have hit it !"

THE PACK OF RAGAMUFFINS

The cock once said to the hen, " It is now the time when the nuts are ripe, so let us go to the hill together and for once eat our fill before the squirrel takes them all away." " Yes," replied the hen, " come, we will have some pleasure together." Then they went away to the hill, and as it was a bright day they stayed till evening. Now I do not know whether it was that they had eaten till they were too fat, or whether they had become proud, but they would not go home on foot, and the cock had to build a little carriage of nut-shells. When it was ready, the little hen seated herself in it and said to the cock, " Thou canst just harness thyself to it." " I like that !" said the cock, " I would rather go home on foot than let myself be harnessed to it ; no, that is not our bargain. I do not mind being coachman and sitting on the box, but drag it myself I will not."

As they were thus disputing, a duck quacked to them, " You thieving folks, who bade you go to my nut-hill? Wait, you shall suffer for it !" and ran with open beak at the cock. But the cock also was not idle, and fell boldly on the duck, and at last wounded her

so with his spurs that she begged for mercy, and willingly let herself be harnessed to the carriage as a punishment. The little cock now seated himself on the box and was coachman, and thereupon they went off in a gallop, with " Duck, go as fast as thou canst." When they had driven a part of the way they met two foot-passengers, a pin and a needle. They cried " Stop ! stop ! " and said that it would soon be as dark as pitch, and then they could not go a step further, and that it was so dirty on the road, and asked if they could not get into the earriage for a while. They had been at the tailor's public-house by the gate, and had stayed too long over the beer. As they were thin people, who did not take up much room, the cock let them both get in, but they had to promise him and his little hen not to step on their feet. Late in the evening they came to an inn, and as they did not like to go further by night, and as the duck also was not strong on her feet, and fell from one side to the other, they went in. The host at first made many objections, his house was already full, besides he thought they could not be very distinguished persons ; but at last, as they made pleasant speeches, and told him that he should have the egg which the little hen had laid on the way, and should likewise keep the duck, which laid one every day, he at length said that they might stay the night. And now they had themselves well served, and feasted and rioted. Early in the morning, when day was breaking, and every one was asleep, the cock awoke the hen, brought the egg, pecked it open, and they ate it together, but they threw the shell on the hearth. Then they went to the needle which was still asleep, took it by the head and stuck it into the cushion of the landlord's chair, and put the pin in his towel, and at last without more ado they flew away over the heath. The duck who liked to sleep in the open air and had stayed in the yard heard them going away, made herself merry and found a stream, down which she swam, which was a much quicker way of travelling than being harnessed to a carriage. The host did not get out of bed for two hours after this ; he washed himself and wanted to dry himself, then the pin went over his face and made a red streak from one ear to the other. After this he went into the kitchen and wanted to light a pipe, but when he came to the hearth the egg-shell darted into his eyes. " This morning everything attacks my head," said he, and angrily sat down on his grandfather's chair, but he quickly started up again and cried, " Woe is me," for the needle had pricked him still worse than the pin, and not in the head. Now he was thoroughly angry, and suspected the guests who had come so late the night before, and when he went and looked about for them, they were gone. Then he made a vow to take no more ragamuffins into his house, for they consume much, pay for nothing, and play mischievous tricks into the bargain by way of gratitude.

THE SEVEN RAVENS

THERE was once a man who had seven sons, and still he had no daughter, however much he wished for one. At length his wife again gave him hope of a child, and when it came into the world it was a girl. The joy was great, but the child was sickly and small, and had to be privately baptized on account of its weakness. The father sent one of the boys in haste to the spring to fetch water for the baptism. The other six went with him, and as each of them wanted to be first to fill it, the jug fell into the well. There they stood and did not know what to do, and none of them dared to go home. As they still did not return, the father grew impatient, and said, " They have certainly forgotten it for some game, the wicked boys ! " He became afraid that the girl would have to die without being baptized, and in his anger cried, " I wish the boys were all turned into ravens." Hardly was the word spoken before he heard a whirring of wings over his head in the air, looked up and saw seven coal-black ravens flying away. The parents could not recall the curse, and however sad they were at the loss of their seven sons, they still to some extent comforted themselves with their dear little daughter, who soon grew strong and every day became more beautiful. For a long time she did not know that she had had brothers, for her parents were careful not to mention them before her, but one day she accidentally heard some people saying of herself, " that the girl was certainly beautiful, but that in reality she was to blame for the misfortune which had befallen her seven brothers." Then she was much troubled, and went to her father and mother and asked if it was true that she had had brothers, and what had become of them ? The parents now dared keep the secret no longer, but said that what had befallen her brothers was the will of Heaven, and that her birth had only been the innocent cause. But the maiden laid it to heart daily, and thought she must deliver her brothers. She had no rest or peace until she set out secretly, and went forth into the wide world to trace out her brothers and set them free, let it cost what it might. She took nothing with her but a little ring belonging to her parents as a keepsake, a loaf of bread against hunger, a little pitcher of water against thirst, and a little chair as a provision against weariness.

And now she went continually onwards, far, far, to the very end of the world. Then she came to the sun, but it was too hot and terrible, and burned little children. Hastily she ran away, and ran to the moon, but it was far too cold, and also awful and malicious, and when it saw the child, it said, " I smell, I smell the flesh of men." On this she ran swiftly away, and came to the stars, which were kind and good to her, and each of them sat on its own particular little chair. But the morning star arose, and gave her the leg-bone of a chicken, and said, " If thou hast not that drumstick thou canst not open the Glass Mountain, and in the Glass Mountain are thy brothers."

The maiden took the drumstick, wrapped it carefully in a cloth, and went onwards again until she came to the Glass Mountain. The door was shut, and she thought she would take out the drumstick ; but when she undid the cloth, it was empty, and she had lost the good star's present. What was she now to do ? She wished to rescue her brothers, and had no key to the Glass Mountain. The good sister took a knife, cut off one of her little fingers, put it in the door, and succeeded in opening it. When she had gone inside, a little dwarf came to meet her, who said, " My child, what are you looking for ? " " I am look-ing for my brothers, the seven ravens," she replied. The dwarf said, " The lord ravens are not at home, but if you will wait here until they come, step in." Thereupon the little dwarf carried the ravens' dinner in, on seven little plates and in seven little glasses, and the little sister ate a morsel from each plate, and from each little glass she took a sip, but in the last little glass she dropped the ring which she had brought away with her.

Suddenly she heard a whirring of wings and a rushing through the air, and then the little dwarf said, " Now the lord ravens are flying home." Then they came, and wanted to eat and drink, and looked for their little plates and glasses. Then said one after the other, " Who has eaten something from my plate ? Who has drunk out of my little glass ? It was a human mouth." And when the seventh came to the bottom of the glass, the ring rolled against his mouth. Then he looked at it, and saw that it was a ring belonging to his father and mother, and said, " God grant that our sister may be here, and then we shall be free." When the maiden, who was standing behind the door watching, heard that wish, she came forth, and on this all the ravens were restored to their human form again. And they embraced and kissed each other, and went joyfully home.

OLD SULTAN

A FARMER once had a faithful dog called Sultan, who had grown old, and lost all his teeth, so that he could no longer hold anything fast. One day the farmer was standing with his wife before the house-door, and said, " To-morrow I intend to shoot Old Sultan, he is no longer of any use."

His wife, who felt pity for the faithful beast, answered, " He has served us so long, and been so faithful, that we might well give him his keep."

" Eh ! what ? " said the man. " You are not very sharp. He has not a tooth left in his mouth, and not a thief is afraid of him ; now he may be off. If he has served us, he has had good feeding for it."

The poor dog, who was lying stretched out in the sun not far off, had heard everything, and was sorry that the morrow was to be his last day. He had a good friend, the wolf, and he crept out in the evening into the forest to him, and complained of the fate that awaited him. " Hark ye, gossip," said the wolf, " be of good cheer, I will help you out of your trouble. I have thought of something. To-morrow, early in the morning, your master is going with his wife to make hay, and they will take their little child with them, for no one will be left behind in the house. They are wont during work-time to lay the child under the hedge in the shade; you lay yourself there too, just as if you wished to guard it. Then I will come out of the wood, and carry off the child. You must rush swiftly after me as if you would seize it again from me. I will let it fall, and you will take it back to its parents who will think that you have saved it, and will be far too grateful to do you any harm ; on the contrary, you will be in high favour, and they will never let you want for anything again."

The plan pleased the dog, and it was carried out just as it was arranged. The father screamed when he saw the wolf running across the field with his child, but when Old Sultan brought it back then he was full of joy, and stroked him and said, " Not a hair of yours shall be hurt, you shall eat my bread free as long as you live." And to his wife he said, " Go home at once and make Old Sultan some bread-sop that he will not have to bite, and bring the pillow out of my bed, I will give him that to lie upon."

Henceforward Old Sultan was as well off as he could wish to be.

Soon afterwards the wolf visited him, and was pleased that every-thing had succeeded so well. " But, gossip," said he, " you will just wink an eye if when I have a chance I carry off one of your master's fat sheep." " Do not reckon upon that," answered the dog ; " I will remain true to my master ; I cannot agree to that." The wolf, who thought that this could not be spoken in earnest, came creeping about in the night and was going to take away the sheep. But the farmer, to whom the faithful Sultan had told the wolf's plan, caught him and dressed his hide soundly with the flail. The wolf had to pack off, but he cried out to the dog, " Wait a bit, you scoundrel, you shall pay for this."

The next morning the wolf sent the boar to challenge the dog to come out into the forest so that they might settle the affair. Old Sultan could find no one to stand by him but a cat with only three legs, and as they went out together the poor cat limped along, and at the same time stretched out her tail into the air with pain.

The wolf and his friend were already on the spot appointed, but when they saw their enemy coming they thought that he was bringing a sword with him, for they mistook the outstretched tail of the cat for one. And when the poor beast hopped on its three legs, they could only think every time that it was picking up a stone to throw at them. So they were both afraid ; the wild boar crept into the under-wood and the wolf jumped up a tree.

The dog and the cat, when they came up, wondered that there was no one to be seen. The wild boar, however, had not been able to hide himself altogether ; and one of his ears was still to be seen. Whilst the cat was looking carefully about, the boar moved his ear ; the cat, who thought it was a mouse moving there, jumped upon it and bit it hard. The boar made a fearful noise and ran away, crying out, " The guilty one is up in the tree." The dog and cat looked up and saw the wolf, who was ashamed of having shown himself so timid and made friends with the dog again.

THE MOUSE, THE BIRD, AND THE SAUSAGE

ONCE on a time a mouse, a bird, and a sausage became companions, kept house together, lived well and happily with each other, and wonderfully increased their possessions. The bird's work was to fly every day into the forest and bring back wood. The mouse had to carry water, light the fire, and lay the table, but the sausage had to cook.

He who is too well off is always longing for something new. One day, therefore, the bird met with another bird, on the way, to whom it related its excellent circumstances and boasted of them. The other bird, however, called it a poor simpleton for its hard work, but said that the two at home had good times. For when the mouse had made her fire and carried her water, she went into her little room to rest until they called her to lay the cloth. The sausage stayed by the pot, saw that the food was cooking well, and, when it was nearly time for dinner, it rolled itself once or twice through the broth or vegetables and then they were buttered, salted, and ready. When the bird came home and laid his burden down, they sat down to dinner, and after they had had their meal, they slept their fill till next morning, and that was a splendid life.

Next day the bird, prompted by the other bird, would go no more into the wood, saying that he had been servant long enough, and had been made a fool of by them, and that they must change about for once, and try to arrange it in another way. And, though the mouse and the sausage also begged most earnestly, the bird would have his way, and said it must be tried. They cast lots about it, and the lot fell on the sausage who was to carry wood, the mouse became cook, and the bird was to fetch water.

What happened ? The little sausage went out towards the wood, the little bird lighted the fire, the mouse stayed by the pot and waited alone until little sausage came home and brought wood for next day. But the little sausage stayed so long on the road that they both feared something was amiss, and the bird flew out a little way in the air to meet it. Not far off, however, it met a dog on the road who had fallen on the poor sausage as lawful booty, and had seized and swallowed it. The bird charged the dog with an act of barefaced robbery, but it was in vain to speak, for the dog said he had found forged letters on the sausage, on which account its life was forfeited to him.

The bird sadly took up the wood, flew home, and related what he had seen and heard. They were much troubled, but agreed to do their best and remain together. The bird therefore laid the cloth, and the mouse made ready the food, and wanted to dress it, and to get into the pot as the sausage used to do, and roll and creep amongst the vegetables to mix them ; but before she got into the midst of them she was scalded, and lost her skin and hair and life in the attempt.

When the bird came to carry up the dinner, no cook was there. In its distress the bird threw the wood here and there, called and searched, but no cook was to be found ! Owing to his carelessness the wood caught fire, so a conflagration ensued, the bird hastened to fetch water, and then the bucket dropped from his claws into the well, and he fell down with it, and could not recover himself, but had to drown there.

THE LITTLE PEASANT

THERE was a certain village wherein no one lived but really rich peasants, and just one poor one, whom they called the little peasant. He had not even so much as a cow, and still less money to buy one, and yet he and his wife did so wish to have one. One day he said to her, " Hark you, I have a good thought, there is our friend the carpenter, he shall make us a wooden calf, and paint it brown, so that it look like any other, and in time it will certainly get big and be a cow." The woman also liked the idea, and their friend the carpenter cut and planed the calf, and painted it as it ought to be, and made it with its head hanging down as if it were eating.

Next morning when the cows were being driven out, the little peasant called the cow-herd in and said, " Look, I have a little calf there, but it is still small and has still to be carried." The cow-herd said, " All right," and took it in his arms and carried it to the pasture and set it among the grass. The little calf always remained standing like one which was eating, and the cow-herd said, " It will soon run alone, just look how it eats already ! " At night when he was going to drive the herd home again, he said to the calf, " If thou canst stand there and eat thy fill, thou canst also go on thy four legs ; I don't care to drag thee home again in my arms." But the little peasant stood at his door, and waited for his little calf, and when the cow-herd drove the cows through the village, and the calf was missing, he inquired where it was. The cow-herd answered, " It is still standing out there eating. It would not stop and come with us." But the little peasant

said, " Oh, but I must have my beast back again." Then they went back to the meadow together, but some one had stolen the calf, and it was gone. The cow-herd said, " It must have run away." The peasant, however, said, " Don't tell me that," and led the cow-herd before the Mayor, who for his carelessness condemned him to give the peasant a cow for the calf which had run away.

And now the little peasant and his wife had the cow for which they had so long wished, and they were heartily glad, but they had no food for it, and could give it nothing to eat, so it soon had to be killed. They salted the flesh, and the peasant went into the town and wanted to sell the skin there, so that he might buy a new calf with the proceeds. On the way he passed by a mill, and there sat a raven with broken wings, and out of pity he took him and wrapped him in the skin. As, however, the weather grew so bad and there was a storm of rain and wind, he could go no further, and turned back to the mill and begged for shelter. The miller's wife was alone in the house, and said to the peasant, " Lay thyself on the straw there," and gave him a slice of bread with cheese on it. The peasant ate it, and lay down with his skin beside him, and the woman thought, " He is tired and has gone to sleep." In the meantime came the parson ; the miller's wife received him well, and said, " My husband is out, so we will have a feast." The peasant listened, and when he heard about feasting he was vexed that he had been forced to make shift with a slice of bread with cheese on it. Then the woman served up four different things, roast meat, salad, cakes, and wine.

Just as they were about to sit down and eat, there was a knocking outside. The woman said, " Oh, heavens ! It is my husband ! " She quickly hid the roast meat inside the tiled stove, the wine under the pillow, the salad on the bed, the cakes under it, and the parson in the cupboard in the entrance. Then she opened the door for her husband, and said, " Thank heaven, thou art back again ! There is such a storm, it looks as if the world were coming to an end." The miller saw the peasant lying on the straw, and asked, " What is that fellow doing there ? " " Ah," said the wife, " the poor knave came in the storm and rain, and begged for shelter, so I gave him a bit of bread and cheese, and showed him where the straw was." The man said, " I have no objection, but be quick and get me something to eat." The woman said, " But I have nothing but bread and cheese." " I am contented with anything," replied the husband, " so far as I am concerned, bread and cheese will do," and looked at the peasant and said, " Come and eat some more with me." The peasant did not require to be invited twice, but got up and ate. After this the miller saw the skin in which the raven was, lying on the ground, and asked, " What hast thou there ? " The peasant answered, " I have a soothsayer inside it." " Can he foretell anything to me ? " said the miller. " Why not ? " answered the peasant, " but he only says four things, and the fifth he keeps to himself." The miller was curious, and said, " Let him foretell something for once." Then the peasant pinched the raven's head, so that he croaked and made a noise like krr, krr. The miller said, " What did he say ? " The peasant answered, " In

34

the first place, he says that there is some wine hidden under the pillow." "Bless me!" cried the miller, and went there and found the wine. "Now go on," said he. The peasant made the raven croak again, and said, "In the second place, he says that there is some roast meat in the tiled stove." "Upon my word!" cried the miller, and went thither, and found the roast meat. The peasant made the raven prophesy still more, and said, "Thirdly, he says that there is some salad on the bed." "That would be a fine thing!" cried the miller, and went there and found the salad. At last the peasant pinched the raven once more till he croaked, and said, "Fourthly, he says that there are some cakes under the bed." "That would be a fine thing!" cried the miller, and looked there, and found the cakes.

And now the two sat down to the table together, but the miller's wife was frightened to death, and went to bed and took all the keys with her. The miller would have liked much to know the fifth, but the little peasant said, "First, we will quickly eat the four things, for the fifth is something bad." So they ate, and after that they bargained how much the miller was to give for the fifth prophesy, until they agreed on three hundred thalers. Then the peasant once more pinched the raven's head till he croaked loudly. The miller asked, "What did he say?" The peasant replied, "He says that the Devil is hiding outside there in the cupboard in the entrance." The miller said, "The Devil must go out," and opened the house-door; then the woman was forced to give up the keys, and the peasant unlocked the cupboard. The parson ran out as fast as he could, and the miller said, "It was true; I saw the black rascal with my own eyes." The peasant, however, made off next morning by daybreak with the three hundred thalers.

At home the small peasant gradually launched out; he built a beautiful house, and the peasants said, "The small peasant has certainly been to the place where golden snow falls, and people carry the gold home in shovels." Then the small peasant was brought before the Mayor, and bidden to say from whence his wealth came. He answered, "I sold my cow's skin in the town, for three hundred thalers." When the peasants heard that, they too wished to enjoy this great profit, and ran home, killed all their cows, and stripped off their skins in order to sell them in the town to the greatest advantage.

The Mayor, however, said, " But my servant must go first." When she came to the merchant in the town, he did not give her more than two thalers for a skin, and when the others came, he did not give them so much, and said, " What can I do with all these skins ? "

Then the peasants were vexed that the small peasant should have thus overreached them, wanted to take vengeance on him, and accused him of this treachery before the Mayor. The innocent little peasant was unanimously sentenced to death, and was to be rolled into the water, in a barrel pierced full of holes. He was led forth, and a priest was brought who was to say a mass for his soul. The others were all obliged to retire to a distance, and when the peasant looked at the priest, he recognized the man who supped with the miller's wife. He said to him, " I set you free from the cupboard, set me free from the barrel." At this same moment up came, with a flock of sheep, the very shepherd who as the peasant knew had long been wishing to be Mayor, so he cried with all his might, " No, I will not do it ; if the whole world insists on it, I will not do it ! " The shepherd hearing that, came up to him, and asked, " What art thou about ? What is it that thou wilt not do ? " The peasant said, " They want to make me Mayor, if I will but put myself in the barrel, but I will not do it." The shepherd said, " If nothing more than that is needful in order to be Mayor, I would get into the barrel at once." The peasant said, " If thou wilt get in, thou wilt be Mayor." The shepherd was willing, and got in, and the peasant shut the top down on him ; then he took the shepherd's flock for himself, and drove it away. The parson went to the crowd, and declared that the mass had been said. Then they came and rolled the barrel towards the water. When the barrel began to roll, the shepherd cried, " I am quite willing to be Mayor." They believed no otherwise than that it was the peasant who was saying this, and answered, " That is what we intend, but first thou shalt look about thee a little down below there," and they rolled the barrel down into the water.

After that the peasants went home, and as they were entering the village, the small peasant also came quietly in, driving a flock of sheep and looking quite contented. Then the peasants were astonished, and said, " Peasant, from whence comest thou ? Hast thou come out of the water ? " " Yes, truly," replied the peasant, " I sank deep, deep down, until at last I got to the bottom ; I pushed the bottom out of the barrel, and crept out; and there were pretty meadows on which a number of lambs were feeding, and from thence I brought this flock away with me." Said the peasants, " Are there any more there ? " " Oh, yes," said he, " more than I could do anything with." Then the peasants made up their minds that they too would fetch some sheep for themselves, a flock apiece, but the Mayor said, " I come first." So they went to the water together, and just then there were some small fleecy clouds in the blue sky, which are called little lambs, and they were reflected in the water, whereupon the peasants cried, " We already see the sheep down below ! " The Mayor pressed forward and said, " I will go down first, and look about me, and if things promise well I'll call you." So he jumped in ; splash ! went the water ; he made a sound as if he were calling them, and the whole crowd plunged in after him as one man. Then the entire village was dead, and the small peasant, as sole heir, became a rich man.

THE BREMEN TOWN-MUSICIANS

A CERTAIN man had a donkey, which had carried the corn-sacks to the mill faithfully for very many long years, but his strength was going, and he was growing more and more unfit for work. Then his master began to consider how he might best save his keep ; but the donkey, seeing that no good wind was blowing, ran away and set out on the road to Bremen. "There," he thought, "I can surely be town-musician." When he had walked some distance, he found a hound lying on the road, gasping like one who had run till he was tired. "What are you gasping so for, you big fellow ? " asked the donkey.

"Ah," replied the hound, "as I am old, and daily grow weaker, and no longer can hunt, my master wanted to kill me, so I took to flight ; but now how am I to earn my bread ? "

"I tell you what," said the donkey, "I am going to Bremen, and shall be town-musician there ; go with me and engage yourself also as a musician. I will play the lute, and you shall beat the kettledrum."

The hound agreed, and on they went.

Before long they came to a cat, sitting on the path, with a face like three rainy days ! "Now then, old shaver, what has gone askew with you ? " asked the donkey.

"Who can be merry when his neck is in danger ? " answered the cat. "Because I am now getting old, and my teeth are worn to stumps, and I prefer to sit by the fire and spin, rather than hunt about after mice, my mistress wanted to drown me, so I ran away. But now good advice is scarce. Where am I to go ? "

"Go with us to Bremen. You understand night-music, so you can be a town-musician."

The cat thought well of it, and went with them. After this the three fugitives came to a farm-yard, where the cock was sitting upon the gate, crowing with all his might. "Your crow goes through and through one," said the donkey. "What is the matter ? "

"I have been foretelling fine weather, because it is the day on which Our Lady washes the Christ-child's little shirts, and wants to dry them," said the cock ; "but guests are coming for Sunday, so the housewife has no pity, and has told the cook that she intends to eat me in the soup to-morrow, and this evening I am to have my head cut off. Now I am crowing at full pitch while I can."

"Ah, but red-comb," said the donkey, "you had better come away with us. We are going to Bremen ; you can find something better than death everywhere : you have a good voice, and if we make music together it must have some quality ! "

The cock agreed to this plan, and all four went on together. They could not, however, reach the city of Bremen in one day, and in the evening they came to a forest where they meant to pass the night. The donkey and the hound laid themselves down under a large tree, the cat and the cock settled themselves in the branches ; but the cock flew right to the top, where he was most safe. Before he went to sleep he looked round on all the four sides, and thought he saw in the distance a little spark burning ; so he called out to his companions that there must be a house not far off, for he saw a light. The donkey said, " If so, we had better get up and go on, for the shelter here is bad." The hound thought that a few bones with some meat on would do him good too !

So they made their way to the place where the light was, and soon saw it shine brighter and grow larger, until they came to a well-lighted robber's house. The donkey, as the biggest, went to the window and looked in.

" What do you see, my grey-horse ? " asked the cock. " What do I see ? " answered the donkey. " A table covered with good things to eat and drink, and robbers sitting at it enjoying themselves." " That would be the sort of thing for us," said the cock. " Yes, yes ; ah, how I wish we were there ! " said the donkey.

Then the animals took counsel together how they should manage to drive away the robbers, and at last they thought of a plan. The donkey was to place himself with his fore-feet upon the window-ledge, the hound was to jump on the donkey's back, the cat was to climb upon the dog, and lastly the cock was to fly up and perch upon the head of the cat.

When this was done, at a given signal, they began to perform their music together : the donkey brayed, the hound barked, the cat mewed, and the cock crowed ; then they burst through the window into the room, so that the glass clattered ! At this horrible din, the robbers sprang up, thinking no otherwise than that a ghost had come in, and fled in a great fright out into the forest. The four companions now sat down at the table, well content with what was left, and ate as if they were going to fast for a month.

As soon as the four minstrels had done, they put out the light, and each sought for himself a sleeping-place according to his nature and to what suited him. The donkey laid himself down upon some straw in the yard, the hound behind the door, the cat upon the hearth near the warm ashes, and the cock perched himself upon a beam of the roof ; and being tired with their long walk, they soon went to sleep.

When it was past midnight, and the robbers saw from afar that the light was no longer burning in their house, and all appeared quiet, the captain said, " We ought not to have let ourselves be frightened out of our wits ; " and ordered one of them to go and examine the house.

The messenger finding all still, went into the kitchen to light a candle, and, taking the glistening fiery eyes of the cat for live coals, he held a lucifer-match to them to light it. But the cat did not understand the joke, and flew in his face, spitting and scratching. He was dreadfully frightened, and ran to the back-door, but the dog, who lay there, sprang up and bit his leg ; and as he ran across the yard by the straw-heap, the donkey gave him a smart kick with its hind foot. The cock, too, who had been awakened by the noise, and had become lively, cried down from the beam, " Cock-a-doodle-doo ! "

Then the robber ran back as fast as he could to his captain, and said, " Ah, there is a horrible witch sitting in the house, who spat on me and scratched my face with her long claws ; and by the door stands a man with a knife, who stabbed me in the leg ; and in the yard there lies a black monster, who beat me with a wooden club ; and above, upon the roof, sits the judge, who called out, ' Bring the rogue here to me ! ' so I got away as well as I could."

After this the robbers did not trust themselves in the house again ; but it suited the four musicians of Bremen so well that they did not care to leave it any more. And the mouth of him who last told this story is still warm.

MOTHER HOLLE

THERE was once a widow who had two daughters—one of whom was pretty and industrious, whilst the other was ugly and idle. But she was much fonder of the ugly and idle one, because she was her own daughter ; and the other, who was a step-daughter, was obliged to do all the work, and be the Cinderella of the house. Every day the poor girl had to sit by a well, in the highway, and spin and spin till her fingers bled.

Now it happened that one day the shuttle was marked with her blood, so she dipped it in the well, to wash the mark off ; but it dropped out of her hand and fell to the bottom. She began to weep, and ran to her step-mother and told her of the mishap. But she scolded her sharply, and was so merciless as to say, " Since you have let the shuttle fall in, you must fetch it out again."

So the girl went back to the well, and did not know what to do ; and in the sorrow of her heart she jumped into the well to get the shuttle. She lost her senses ; and when she awoke and came to herself again, she was in a lovely meadow where the sun was shining and many thousands of flowers were growing. Along this meadow she went, and at last came to a baker's oven full of bread, and the bread cried out, " Oh, take me out ! take me out ! or I shall burn ; I have been baked a long time ! " So she went up to it, and took out all the loaves one after another with the bread-shovel. After that she went on till she came to a tree covered with apples, which called out to her, " Oh, shake me ! shake me ! we apples are all ripe ! " So she shook the tree till the apples fell like rain, and went on shaking till they were all down, and when she had gathered them into a heap, she went on her way.

At last she came to a little house, out of which an old woman peeped ; but she had such large teeth that the girl was frightened, and was about to run away.

But the old woman called out to her, " What are you afraid of, dear child ? Stay with me ; if you will do all the work in the house properly, you shall be the better for it. Only you must take care to make my bed well, and to shake it thoroughly till the feathers fly— for then there is snow on the earth. I am Mother Holle."

As the old woman spoke so kindly to her, the girl took courage and agreed to enter her service. She attended to everything to the satisfaction of her mistress, and always shook her bed so vigorously that the feathers flew about like snow-flakes. So she had a pleasant life with her ; never an angry word, and boiled or roast meat every day.

She stayed some time with Mother Holle, and then she became sad. At first she did not know what was the matter with her, but found at length that it was home-sickness : although she was many thousand times better off here than at home, still she had a longing to be there. At last she said to the old woman, " I have a longing for home ; and however well off I am down here, I cannot stay any longer ; I must go up again to my own people." Mother Holle said, " I am pleased that you long for your home again, and as you have served me so truly I myself will take you up again." Thereupon she took her by the hand, and led her to a large door. The door was opened, and just as the maiden was standing beneath the doorway a heavy shower of golden rain fell, and all the gold remained sticking to her, so that she was completely covered over with it.

" You shall have that because you are so industrious," said Mother Holle, and at the same time she gave her back the shuttle which she had let fall into the well. Thereupon the door closed, and the maiden found herself up above upon the earth, not far from her mother's house.

And as she went into the yard the cock was standing by the well-side, and cried—

" *Cock-a-doodle-doo !*
Your golden girl's come back to you ! "

So she went in to her mother, and as she arrived thus covered with gold, she was well received, both by her and her sister.

The girl told all that had happened to her ; and as soon as the mother heard how she had come by so much wealth she was very anxious to obtain the same good luck for the ugly and lazy daughter. She had to seat herself by the well and spin ; and in order that her shuttle might be stained with blood she stuck her hand into a thorn bush and pricked her finger. Then she threw her shuttle into the well, and jumped in after it.

44

She came, like the other, to the beautiful meadow and walked along the very same path. When she got to the oven the bread again cried, " Oh, take me out ! take me out ! or I shall burn ; I have been baked a long time ! " But the lazy thing answered, " As if I had any wish to make myself dirty ! " and on she went. Soon she came to the apple-tree which cried, " Oh, shake me ! shake me ! we apples are all ripe ! " But she answered, " I like that ! one of you might fall on my head," and so went on.

When she came to Mother Holle's house she was not afraid, for she she had already heard of her big teeth, and she hired herself to her immediately.

The first day she forced herself to work diligently, and obeyed Mother Holle when she told her to do anything, for she was thinking of all the gold that she would give her. But on the second day she began to be lazy, and on the third day still more so, and then she would not get up in the morning at all. Neither did she make Mother Holle's bed as she ought, and did not shake it so as to make the feathers fly up. Mother Holle was soon tired of this, and gave her notice to leave. The lazy girl was willing enough to go and thought that now the golden-rain would come. Mother Holle led her too to the great door ; but while she was standing beneath it, instead of the gold a big kettleful of soot was emptied over her. " That is the reward of your service," said Mother Holle, and shut the door.

So the lazy girl went home ; but she was quite covered with soot, and the cock by the well-side, as soon as he saw her, cried out—

" Cock-a-doodle-doo !
Your sooty girl's come back to you ! "

But the soot stuck fast to her, and could not be got off as long as she lived.

THE ELVES

A SHOEMAKER, by no fault of his own, had become so poor that at last he had nothing left but leather for one pair of shoes. So in the evening, he cut out the shoes which he wished to begin to make the next morning, and as he had a good conscience, he lay down quietly in his bed, commended himself to God, and fell asleep. In the morning, after he had said his prayers, and was just going to sit down to work, the two shoes stood quite finished on his table. He was astounded, and did not know what to say to it. He took the shoes in his hands to observe them closer, and they were so neatly made that there was not one bad stitch in them, just as if they were intended for a princess. Soon after, too, a buyer came in, and as the shoes pleased him so well, he paid more for them than was customary, and, with the money, the shoemaker was able to purchase leather for two pairs of shoes. He cut them out at night, and next morning was about to set to work with fresh courage ; but he had no need to do so, for, when he got up, they were already made, and buyers also were not wanting, who gave him money enough to buy leather for four pairs of shoes. The following morning, too, he found the four pairs made ; and so it went on constantly, what he cut out in the evening was finished by the morning, so that he soon had his honest independence again, and at last became a wealthy man. Now it befell that one evening not long before Christmas, when the man had been cutting out, he said to his wife before going to bed, " What think you if we were to stay up to-night to see who it is that lends us this helping hand ? " The woman liked the idea, and lighted a candle, and then they hid themselves in a corner of the room, behind some clothes which were hanging up there, and watched. When it was midnight two pretty little naked men came, sat down by the shoemaker's table, took all the work which was cut out before them and began to stitch, and sew and hammer so skilfully and so quickly with their little fingers that the shoemaker could not turn away his eyes for astonishment. They did not stop until all was done and stood finished on the table, and then they ran quickly away.

Next morning the woman said, " The little men have made us rich, and we really must show that we are grateful for it. They run about so, and have nothing on, and must be cold. I'll tell thee what I'll do : I will make them little shirts, and coats, and vests, and trousers, and knit both of them a pair of stockings, and do thou, too, make them two little pairs of shoes." The man said, " I shall be very glad to do it " ; and one night, when everything was ready, they laid their presents all together on the table instead of the cut-out work, and then concealed themselves to see how the little men would behave. At midnight they came bounding in, and wanted to get to work at once, but as they did not find any leather cut out, but only the pretty little shirts and coats, they were at first astonished, and then they showed intense delight. They dressed themselves with the greatest rapidity, putting the pretty clothes on, and singing,

" *Now we are so fine to see,*
Why should we longer cobblers be ? "

Then they danced and skipped and leapt over chairs and benches. At last they danced out of doors. From that time forth they came no more, but as long as the shoemaker lived all went well with him, and all his undertakings prospered.

SECOND STORY

THERE was once a poor servant-girl, who was industrious and cleanly, and swept the house every day, and emptied her sweepings on the great heap in front of the door. One morning when she was just going back to her work, she found a letter on this heap, and as she could not read, she put her broom in the corner, and took the letter to her master and mistress, and behold it was an invitation from the elves, who asked the girl to hold a child for them at its christening. The girl did not know what to do, but at length, after much persuasion, and as they told her that it was not right to refuse an invitation of this kind, she consented. Then three elves came and conducted her to a hollow mountain, where the little folks lived. Everything there was small, but more elegant and beautiful than can be described. The baby's mother lay in a bed of black ebony ornamented with pearls,

the coverlets were embroidered with gold, the cradle was of ivory, the bath of gold. The girl stood as godmother, and then wanted to go home again, but the little elves urgently entreated her to stay three days with them. So she stayed, and passed the time in pleasure and gaiety, and the little folks did all they could to make her happy. At last she set out on her way home. Then first they filled her pockets quite full of money, and after that they led her out of the mountain again.

When she got home she wanted to begin her work, and took the broom, which was still standing in the corner, in her hand and began to sweep. Then some strangers came out of the house, who asked her who she was, and what business she had there? And she had not, as she thought, been three days with the little men in the mountains, but seven years, and in the meantime her former masters had died.

THIRD STORY

A CERTAIN mother's child had been taken away out of its cradle by the elves, and a changeling with a large head and staring eyes, which would do nothing but eat and drink, laid in its place. In her trouble she went to her neighbour, and asked her advice. The neighbour said that she was to carry the changeling into the kitchen, set it down on the hearth, light a fire, and boil some water in two egg-shells. This would make the changeling laugh, and if he laughed, all would be over with him. The woman did everything that her neighbour bade her. When she put the egg-shells with water on the fire, the imp said,

" *Though I am old as the oldest tree,*
  Cooking in an eggshell never did I see."

And he began to laugh at it. Whilst he was laughing, suddenly came a host of little elves who brought the right child, set it down on the hearth, and took the changeling away with them.

HANS AND HIS WIFE GRETTEL

In a certain village there once lived Hans and his wife, and the wife was so idle that she would never work at anything ; whatever her husband gave her to spin, she did not get done, and what she did spin she did not wind, but let it all remain entangled in a heap. If the man scolded her, she was always ready with her tongue, and said, " Well, how should I wind it, when I have no reel ? Just you go into the forest and get me one." " If that is all," said the man, " then I will go into the forest, and get some wood for making reels." Then the woman was afraid that if he had the wood he would make her a reel of it, and she would have to wind her yarn off, and then begin to spin again. She bethought herself a little, and then a lucky idea occurred to her, and she secretly followed the man into the forest, and when he had climbed into a tree to choose and cut the wood, she crept into the thicket below where he could not see her, and cried,

> " *Bend not the bough,*
> *He who bends it shall die !*
> *Reel not the reel,*
> *He who reels it shall die !* "

The man listened, laid down his axe for a moment, and began to consider what that could mean. " Hullo," he said at last, " what can that have been ; my ears must have been singing, I won't alarm myself for nothing." So he again seized the axe, and began to hew, then again there came a cry from below :

> " *Bend not the bough,*
> *He who bends it shall die !*
> *Reel not the reel,*
> *He who reels it shall die !* "

He stopped, and felt afraid and alarmed, and pondered over the circumstances. But when a few moments had passed, he took heart again, and a third time he stretched out his hand for the axe and began to cut. But someone called out a third time, and said loudly,

> " *Bend not the bough,*
> *He who bends it shall die !*
> *Reel not the reel,*
> *He who reels it shall die !* "

That was enough for him, and all inclination had departed from him, so he hastily descended the tree, and set out on his way home. The woman ran as fast as she could by bye-ways so as to get home first. So when he entered the parlour, she put on an innocent look as if nothing had happened, and said, " Well, have you brought a nice piece of wood for reels ? " " No," said he, " I see very well that winding won't do," and told her what had happened to him in the forest, and from that time forth left her in peace about it. Nevertheless after some time, the man again began to complain of the disorder of the house. " Wife," said he, " it is really a shame that the spun yarn should lie all there entangled ! " " I'll tell you what," said she, " as we still don't come by any reel, go you up into the loft, and I will stand down below, and will throw the yarn up to you, and you will throw it down to me, and so we shall get a skein after all." " Yes, that will do," said the man. So they did that, and when it was done, he said, " The yarn is in skeins, now it must be boiled." The woman was again distressed ; she certainly said, " Yes, we will boil it next morning early," but she was secretly contriving another trick.

Early in the morning she got up, lighted a fire, and put the kettle on, only instead of the yarn, she put in a lump of tow, and let it boil. After that she went to the man who was still lying in bed, and said to him, " I must just go out, you must get up and look after the yarn which is in the kettle on the fire, but you must be at hand at once ; mind that, for if the cock should happen to crow, and you are not attending to the yarn, it will become tow." The man was willing and took good care not to loiter. He got up as quickly as he could, and went into the kitchen. But when he reached the kettle and peeped in, he saw to his horror nothing but a lump of tow. Then the poor man was as still as a mouse, thinking he had neglected it and was to blame, and in future left Grettel to get on with her spinning as fast as she pleased and no faster.

THE QUEEN BEE

Two king's sons once went out in search of adventures, and fell into a wild, disorderly way of living, so that they never came home again. The youngest, who was called Simpleton, set out to seek his brothers, but when at length he found them they mocked him for thinking that he with his simplicity could get through the world, when they two could not make their way, and yet were so much cleverer. They all three travelled away together, and came to an ant-hill. The two elder wanted to destroy it, to see the little ants creeping about in their terror, and carrying their eggs away, but Simpleton said, " Leave the creatures in peace, I will not allow you to disturb them." Then they went onwards and came to a lake on which a great number of ducks were swimming. The two brothers wanted to catch a couple and roast them, but Simpleton would not permit it, and said, " Leave the creatures in peace, I will not suffer you to kill them." At length they came to a bee's nest, in which there was so much honey that it ran out of the trunk of the tree where it was. The two wanted to make a fire beneath the tree, and suffocate the bees in order to take away the honey, but Simpleton again stopped them and said, " Leave the creatures in peace, I will not allow you to burn them." At length the two brothers arrived at a castle where stone horses were standing in the stables, and no human being was to be seen, and they went through all the halls until, quite at the end, they came to a door in which were three locks. In the middle of the door, however, there was a little pane, through which they could see into the room. There they saw a little grey man, who was sitting at a table. They called him, once, twice, but he did not hear ; at last they called him for the third time, when he got up, opened the locks, and came out. He said nothing, however, but conducted them to a handsomely-spread table, and when they had eaten and drunk, he took each of them to a bed-room. Next morning the little grey man came to the eldest, beckoned to him, and conducted him to a stone table, on which were inscribed three tasks, by the performance of which the castle could be delivered. The first was that in the forest, beneath the moss, lay the princess's pearls, a thousand in number, which must be picked up, and if by

sunset one single pearl was wanting, he who had looked for them would be turned to stone. The eldest went thither, and sought the whole day, but when it came to an end, he had only found one hundred, and what was written on the table came to pass, and he was changed into stone. Next day, the second brother undertook the adventure ; it did not, however, fare much better with him than with the eldest ; he did not find more than two hundred pearls, and was changed to stone. At last the turn came to Simpleton also, who sought in the moss. It was, however, so hard to find the pearls, and he got on so slowly, that he seated himself on a stone and wept. And while he was thus sitting, the King of the ants whose life he had once saved, came with five thousand ants, and before long the little creatures had got all the pearls together and laid them in a heap. The second task, however, was to fetch out of the lake the key of the King's daughter's bed-chamber. When Simpleton came to the lake, the ducks which he had saved, swam up to him, dived down, and brought the key out of the water. But the third was the most difficult ; from amongst the three sleeping daughters of the King was the youngest and dearest to be sought out. They, however, resembled each other exactly, and were only to be distinguished by their having eaten different sweetmeats before they fell asleep : the eldest a bit of sugar ; the second a little syrup ; and the youngest a spoonful of honey. Then the Queen of the bees, which Simpleton had protected from the fire, came and tasted the lips of all three, and at last she remained sitting on the mouth that had eaten honey, and thus the King's son recognized the right princess. Then the enchantment was at an end ; everything was released from sleep, and those who had been turned to stone received once more their natural forms. Simpleton married the youngest and sweetest princess, and after her father's death became King, and his two brothers received the two other sisters.

CLEVER GRETTEL

THERE was once a cook named Grettel, who wore shoes with red rosettes, and when she walked out with them on, she turned herself this way and that, and thought, " You certainly are a pretty girl ! " And when she came home she drank, in her gladness of heart, a draught of wine, and as wine excites a desire to eat, she tasted the best of whatever she was cooking until she was satisfied, and said, " The cook must know what the food is like."

It came to pass that the master one day said to her, " Grettel, there is a guest coming this evening ; prepare me two fowls very daintily." " I will see to it, master," answered Grettel. She killed two fowls, scalded them, plucked them, put them on the spit, and towards evening set them before the fire, that they might roast. The fowls began to turn brown, and were nearly ready, but the guest had not yet arrived. Then Grettel called out to her master, " If the guest does not come, I must take the fowls away from the fire, but it will be a sin and a shame if they are not eaten directly, when they are juicest." The master said, " I will run myself, and fetch the guest." When the master had turned his back, Grettel laid the spit with the fowls on one side, and thought, " Standing so long by the fire there, makes one hot and thirsty ; who knows when they will come ? Meanwhile, I will run into the cellar, and take a drink." She ran down, set a jug, said, " God bless it to thy use, Grettel," and took a good drink, and took yet another hearty draught.

Then she went and put the fowls down again to the fire, basted them, and drove the spit merrily round. But as the roast meat smelt so good, Grettel thought, " Something might be wrong, it ought to be tasted ! " She touched it with her finger, and said, " Ah, how good fowls are ! It certainly is a sin and a shame that they are not eaten directly ! " She ran to the window, to see if the master was not coming with his guest, but she saw no one, and went back to the fowls and thought, " One of the wings is burning ! I had better take it off and eat it." So she cut it off, ate it, and enjoyed it, and when she had done, she thought, " the other must go down too, or else master will observe that something is missing." When the two wings

were eaten, she went and looked for her master, and did not see him.
It suddenly occurred to her, " Who knows ? They are perhaps not

coming at all, and have turned in somewhere." Then she said, "Hallo, Grettel, enjoy yourself, one fowl has been cut into, take another drink, and eat it up entirely ; when it is eaten you will have some peace, why should God's good gifts be spoilt ? " So she ran into the cellar again, took an enormous drink and ate up the one chicken in great glee. When one of the chickens was swallowed down, and still her master did not come, Grettel looked at the other and said, " Where one is, the other should be likewise, the two go together ; what's right for the one is right for the other ; I think if I were to take another draught it would do me no harm." So she took another hearty drink, and let the second chicken rejoin the first.

When she was just in the best of the eating, her master came and cried, " Haste thee, Grettel, the guest is coming directly after me ! " " Yes, sir, I will soon serve up." answered Grettel. Meantime the master looked to see that the table was properly laid, and took the great knife, wherewith he was going to carve the chickens, and sharpened it on the steps. Presently the guest came, and knocked politely and courteously at the house-door. Grettel ran, and looked to see who was there, and when she saw the guest, she put her finger to her lips and said, " Hush ! hush ! get away as quickly as you can, if my master catches you it will be the worse for you ; he certainly did ask you to supper, but his intention is to cut off your two ears. Just listen how he is sharpening the knife for it ! " The guest heard the sharpening, and hurried down the steps again as fast as he could. Grettel was not idle ; she ran screaming to her master, and cried, " You have invited a fine guest ! " " Eh, why, Grettel ? What do you mean ? " " Yes," said she, " he has taken the chickens which I was just going to serve up, off the dish, and has run away with them ! " " That's a nice trick ! " said her master, and lamented the fine chickens. " If he had but left me one, so that something remained for me to eat." He called to him to stop, but the guest pretended not to hear. Then he ran after him with the knife still in his hand, crying, " Just one, just one," meaning that the guest should leave him just one chicken, and not take both. The guest, however, thought otherwise—that he was to give up one of his ears, and ran as if fire were burning under him, in order to take them both home with him.

A KING had a daughter who was beautiful beyond all measure, but so proud and haughty withal that no suitor was good enough for her. She sent away one after the other, and ridiculed them as well.

Once the King made a great feast and invited thereto, from far and near, all the young men likely to marry. They were all marshalled in a row according to their rank and standing ; first came the kings, then the grand-dukes, then the princes, the earls, the barons, and the gentry. Then the King's daughter was led through the ranks, but to every one she had some objection to make ; one was too fat, " The wine-cask," she said. Another was too tall, " Long and thin has little in." The third was too short, " Short and thick is never quick." The fourth was too pale, " As pale as death." The fifth too red, " A fighting-cock." The sixth was not straight enough, " A green log dried behind the stove."

So she had something to say against every one, but she made herself especially merry over a good king who stood quite high up in the row, and whose chin had grown a little crooked. " Well," she cried and laughed, " he has a chin like a thrush's beak ! " and from that time he got the name of King Thrushbeard.

But the old King, when he saw that his daughter did nothing but mock the people, and despised all the suitors who were gathered there, was very angry, and swore that she should have for her husband the very first beggar that came to his doors.

A few days afterwards a fiddler came and sang beneath the windows trying to earn a small alms. When the King heard him he said, " Let him come up." So the fiddler came in, in his dirty, ragged clothes, and sang before the King and his daughter, and when he had ended he asked for a trifling gift. The King said, " Your song has pleased me so well that I will give you my daughter there, to wife."

The King's daughter shuddered, but the King said, " I have taken an oath to give you to the very first beggar-man, and I will keep it." All she could say was in vain ; the priest was brought, and she had to let herself be wedded to the fiddler on the spot. When that was done the King said, " Now it is not proper for you, a beggar-woman, to stay any longer in my palace, you may just go away with your husband."

The beggar-man led her out by the hand, and she was obliged to walk away on foot with him. When they came to a large forest she asked,

O whose is this forest so thick and so fine ?

And the echo answered :

It is King Thrushbeard's and might have been thine.

" Ah, unhappy girl that I am, if I had but taken King Thrush-beard ! "

Afterwards they came to a meadow, and she asked again,

O whose is this meadow so green and so fine ?

And the echo answered :

It is King Thrushbeard's and might have been thine.

" Ah, unhappy girl that I am, if I had but taken King Thrush-beard ! "

Then they came to a large town, and she asked again,

O whose is this city so great and so fine ?

And the echo answered :

It is King Thrushbeard's and might have been thine.

" Ah, unhappy girl that I am, if I had but taken King Thrush-beard ! "

" It does not please me," said the fiddler, " to hear you always wishing for another husband ; am I not good enough for you ? " At last they came to a very little hut, and she said, " Oh, goodness ! what a small house ; to whom does this miserable, mean hovel belong ? " The fiddler answered, " That is my house and yours, where we shall live together."

She had to stoop in order to go in at the low door. " Where are the servants ? " said the King's daughter. " What servants ? " answered the beggar-man ; " you must yourself do what you wish to have done. Just make a fire at once, and set on water to cook my supper, I am quite tired." But the King's daughter knew nothing about lighting fires or cooking, and the beggar-man had to lend a hand himself to get anything fairly done. When they had finished their scanty meal

they went to bed ; but he forced her to get up quite early in the morning in order to look after the house.

For a few days they lived in this way as well as might be, and finished all their provisions. Then the man said, " Wife, we **cannot** go on any longer eating and drinking here and earning nothing. You must weave baskets." He went out, cut some willows, and brought them home. Then she began to weave, but the tough willows wounded her delicate hands.

" I see that this will not do," said the man ; " you had better spin, perhaps you can do that better." She sat down and tried to spin, but the hard thread soon cut her soft fingers so that the blood ran down. " See," said the man, " you are fit for no sort of work ; I have made a bad bargain with you. Now I will try to make a business with pots and earthenware ; you must sit in the market-place and sell the ware." " Alas," thought she, " if any of the people from my father's kingdom come to the market and see me sitting there, selling, how they will mock me ? " But it was of no use, she had to yield unless she chose to die of hunger.

For the first time she succeeded well, for the people were glad to buy the woman's wares because she was good-looking, and they paid her what she asked ; many even gave her the money and left the pots with her as well. So they lived on what she had earned as long as it lasted, then the husband bought a lot of new crockery. With this she sat down at the corner of the market-place, and set it out round about her ready for sale. But suddenly there came a drunken hussar galloping along, and he rode right amongst the pots so that they were all broken into a thousand bits. She began to weep, and did not know what to do for fear. " Alas ! what will happen to me ? " cried she ; " what will my husband say to this ? "

She ran home and told him of the misfortune. " Who would seat herself at a corner of the market-place with crockery ? " said the man ; " leave off crying, I see very well that you cannot do any ordinary work, so I have been to our King's palace and have asked whether they cannot find a place for a kitchen-maid, and they have promised me to take you ; in that way you will get your food for nothing."

The King's daughter was now a kitchen-maid, and had to be at the cook's beck and call, and do the dirtiest work. In both her pockets she fastened a little jar, in which she took home her share of the leavings, and upon this they lived.

It happened that the wedding of the King's eldest son was to be celebrated, so the poor woman went up and placed herself by the door of the hall to look on. When all the candles were lit, and people, each more beautiful than the other, entered, and all was full of pomp and splendour, she thought of her lot with a sad heart, and cursed the pride and haughtiness which had humbled her and brought her to so great poverty.

The smell of the delicious dishes which were being taken in and out reached her, and now and then the servants threw her a few morsels of them : these she put in her jars to take home.

All at once the King's son entered, clothed in velvet and silk, with gold chains about his neck. And when he saw the beautiful woman standing by the door he seized her by the hand, and would have danced with her ; but she refused and shrank with fear, for she saw that it was King Thrushbeard, her suitor whom she had driven away with scorn. Her struggles were of no avail, he drew her into the hall ; but the string by which her pockets were hung broke, the pots fell down, the soup ran out, and the scraps were scattered all about. And when the people saw it, there arose general laughter and derision, and she was so ashamed that she would rather have been a thousand fathoms below the ground. She sprang to the door and would have run away, but on the stairs a man caught her and brought her back ; and when she looked at him it was King Thrushbeard again. He said to her kindly, " Do not be afraid, I and the fiddler who has been living with you in that wretched hovel are one. For love of you I disguised myself so ; and I also was the hussar who rode through your crockery. This was all done to humble your proud spirit, and to punish you for the insolence with which you mocked me."

Then she wept bitterly and said, " I have done great wrong, and am not worthy to be your wife." But he said, " Be comforted, the evil days are past ; now we will celebrate our wedding." Then the maids-in-waiting came and put on her the most splendid clothing, and her father and his whole court came and wished her happiness in her marriage with King Thrushbeard, and the joy now began in earnest. I wish you and I had been there too.

OUR LADY'S CHILD

HARD by a great forest dwelt a wood-cutter with his wife, who had an only child, a little girl of three years old. They were, however, so poor that they no longer had daily bread, and did not know how to get food for her. One morning the wood-cutter went out sorrowfully to his work in the forest, and while he was cutting wood, suddenly there stood before him a tall and beautiful woman with a crown of shining stars on her head, who said to him, " I am the Virgin Mary, mother of the child Jesus. Thou art poor and needy, bring thy child to me, I will take her with me and be her mother, and care for her." The wood-cutter obeyed, brought his child, and gave her to Our Lady, who took her up to heaven with her. There the child fared well, ate sugar-cakes, and drank sweet milk, and her clothes were of gold, and the little angels played with her. And when she was fourteen years of age, Our Lady called her one day and said, " Dear child, I am about to make a long journey, so take into thy keeping the keys of the thirteen doors of heaven. Twelve of these thou mayest open, and behold the glory which is within them, but the thirteenth, to which this little key belongs, is forbidden thee. Beware of opening it, or thou wilt bring misery on thyself." The girl promised to be obedient, and when Our Lady was gone, she began to examine the dwellings of the kingdom of heaven. Each day she opened one of them, until she had made the round of the twelve. In each of them sat one of the Apostles in the midst of a great light, and she rejoiced in all the magnificence and splendour, and the little angels who always accompanied her rejoiced with her. Then the forbidden door alone remained, and she felt a great desire to know what could be hidden behind it, and said to the angels, " I will not quite open it, and I will not go inside it, but I will unlock it so that we can just see a little through the opening." " Oh, no," said the little angels, " that would be a sin. For Our Lady has forbidden it, and it might easily cause thy unhappiness." Then she was silent, but the desire in her heart was not stilled, but gnawed there and tormented her, and let her have no rest. And once when the angels had all gone out, she thought, " Now I am quite alone, and I could peep in. If I do it, no one will ever know." She sought out the key, and when she had got it in her hand, she put it in the lock, and when she had put it in, she turned it round as well. Then the door sprang open, and she saw there the Trinity sitting in fire and splendour. She stayed there awhile, and looked at everything in amazement ; then she touched the light a little with her finger, and her finger became quite golden. Immediately a great fear fell on her. She shut the door violently, and ran away. Her terror too would not quit her, let her do what she might, and her heart beat continually and would not be still ; the gold too stayed on her finger, and would not go away, though she rubbed it and washed it over and over.

It was not long before Our Lady came back from her journey. She called the girl before her, and asked to have the keys of heaven back. When the maiden gave her the bunch, Our Lady looked into her eyes and said, " Hast thou not opened the thirteenth door also ? " " No," she replied. Then she laid her hand on the girl's heart, and felt how it beat and beat, and saw right well that she had disobeyed her order and had opened the door. Then she said once again, " Art thou certain thou has not done it ? " " Yes," said the girl for the second time. Then she perceived the finger which had become golden from touching the fire of heaven, and saw well that the child had sinned, and said for the third time, " Hast thou not done it ? " " No," said the girl for the third time. Then said Our Lady, " Thou hast not obeyed me, and besides that thou hast lied, thou art no longer worthy to be in heaven."

Then the girl fell into a deep sleep, and when she awoke she lay on the earth below, and in the midst of a wilderness. She wanted to cry out, but she could bring forth no sound. She sprang up and wanted to run away, but whithersoever she turned herself, she was continually held back by thick hedges of thorns through which she could not break. In the desert, in which she was imprisoned, there stood an old hollow tree, and this had to be her dwelling-place. Into this she crept when night came, and here she slept. Here, too, she found a shelter from storm and rain, but it was a miserable life and bitterly did she weep when she remembered how happy she had been in heaven, and how the angels had played with her. Roots and wild berries were her only food, and for these she sought as far as she could go. In the autumn she picked up the fallen nuts and leaves, and carried them

into the hole. The nuts were her food in winter, and when snow and ice came, she crept amongst the leaves like a poor little animal that she might not freeze. Before long her clothes were all torn, and one bit of them after another fell off her. As soon, however, as the sun shone warm again, she went out and sat in front of the tree, and her long hair covered her on all sides like a mantle. Thus she sat year after year, and felt the pain and misery of the world. One day, when the trees were once more clothed in fresh green, the King of the country was hunting in the forest, and followed a roe, and as it had fled into the thicket which shut in this bit of the forest, he got off his horse, tore the bushes asunder, and cut himself a path with his sword. When he had at last forced his way through, he saw a wonderfully beautiful maiden sitting under the tree ; and she sat there and was entirely covered with her golden hair down to her very feet. He stood still and looked at her full of surprise, then he spoke to her and said, " Who art thou ? Why art thou sitting here in the wilderness ? " But she gave no answer, for she could not open her mouth. The King continued, " Wilt thou go with me to my castle ? " Then she just nodded her head a little. The King took her in his arms, carried her to his horse, and rode home with her, and when he reached the royal castle he caused her to be dressed in beautiful garments, and gave her all things in abundance. Although she could not speak, she was still so beautiful and charming that he began to love her with all his heart, and it was not long before he married her.

After a year or so had passed, the Queen brought a son into the world. Thereupon Our Lady appeared to her in the night when she lay in her bed alone, and said. " If thou wilt tell the truth and confess that thou didst unlock the forbidden door, I will open thy mouth and give thee back thy speech, but if thou perseverest in thy sin, and deniest obstinately, I will take thy new born child away with me." Then the Queen was permitted to answer, but she remained hard, and said, " No, I did not open the forbidden door " ; and Our Lady took the new-born child from her arms and vanished with it. Next morning, when the child was not to be found, it was whispered among the people that the Queen had killed her own child. She heard all this and could say nothing to the contrary, but the King would not believe it, for he loved her so much.

E

When a year had gone by the Queen again bore a son, and in the night Our Lady again came to her, and said, " If thou wilt confess that thou openedst the forbidden door, I will give thee thy child back and untie thy tongue ; but if thou continuest in sin and deniest it, I will take away with me this new child also." Then the Queen again said, " No, I did not open the forbidden door " ; and Our Lady took the child out of her arms, and went away with him. Next morning, when this child also had disappeared, the people declared quite loudly that the Queen had killed him, and the King's councillors demanded that she should be brought to justice. The King, however, loved her so dearly that he would not believe it, and commanded the councillors under pain of death not to say any more about it.

The following year the Queen gave birth to a beautiful little daughter, and for the third time Our Lady appeared to her in the night and said, "Follow me." She took the Queen by the hand and led her to Heaven, and showed her there her two eldest children, who smiled at her and were playing with the ball of the world. When the Queen rejoiced thereat, Our Lady said, " Is thy heart not yet softened ? If thou wilt own that thou didst open the forbidden door, I will give thee back thy two little sons." But the third time the Queen answered, " No, I did not open the forbidden door." Then Our Lady let her sink down to earth once more, and took from her likewise her third child.

Next morning, when the loss was reported abroad, all the people cried loudly, " The Queen is a murderess ! She must be judged," and the King was no longer able to restrain his councillors. Thereupon a trial was held, and as she could not answer, and defend herself, she was condemned to be burnt alive. The wood was got together, and when she was fast bound to the stake, the hard ice of pride melted, her heart was moved by repentance, and she thought, " If only I could confess before my death that I opened the door ! " Then her voice came back to her, and she cried out loudly, " Yes, Mary, I did it " ; and straightway rain fell from the sky and extinguished the flames of fire, and a light broke forth above her, and Our Lady descended with the two little sons by her side, and the new-born daughter in her arms. She spoke kindly to her, and said, " He who repents his sin and confesses it, is at once forgiven." Then she gave her the three children, untied her tongue, and granted her happiness for her whole life.

RUMPELSTILTSKIN

ONCE there was a miller who was poor, but who had a beautiful daughter. Now it happened that he had to go and speak to the King, and in order to make himself appear important he said to him, " I have a daughter who can spin straw into gold." The King said to the miller, " That is an art which pleases me well ; if your daughter is as clever as you say, bring her to-morrow to my palace, and I will try what she can do."

And when the girl was brought to him he took her into a room which was quite full of straw, gave her a spinning-wheel and a reel, and said, " Now set to work, and if by to-morrow morning early you have not spun this straw into gold during the night, you must die." Thereupon he himself locked up the room, and left her in it alone. So there sat the poor miller's daughter, and for her life could not tell what to do ; she had no idea how straw could be spun into gold, and she grew more and more miserable, until at last she began to weep.

But all at once the door opened, and in came a little man, and said, " Good evening, Mistress Miller ; why are you crying so ? " " Alas ! " answered the girl, " I have to spin straw into gold, and I do not know how to do it." " What will you give me," said the manikin, " If I do it for you ? " " My necklace," said the girl. The little man took the necklace, seated himself in front of the wheel, and sang :

" Round about, round about, lo and behold !
Reel away, reel away, straw into gold,"

and " whirr, whirr, whirr," three turns, and the reel was full ; then he put another on, and whirr, whirr, whirr, three times round, and the second was full too. And so it went on until the morning, when all the straw was spun, and all the reels were full of gold. By daybreak the King was already there, and when he saw the gold he was astonished and delighted, but his heart became only more greedy. He had the miller's daughter taken into another room full of straw, which was much larger, and commanded her to spin that also in one night if she valued her life. The girl knew not how to help herself, and was crying, when the door again opened, and the little man appeared, and said, " What will you give me if I spin the straw into gold for you ? " " The ring on my finger," answered the girl. The little man took the ring, again began to turn the wheel, and by morning had spun all the straw into glittering gold.

The King rejoiced beyond measure at the sight, but still he had not gold enough ; and he had the miller's daughter taken into a still larger room full of straw, and said, " You must spin this, too, in the course of this night ; but if you succeed, you shall be my wife." " Even if she be a miller's daughter," thought he, " I could not find a richer wife in the whole world."

When the girl was alone the dwarf came again for the third time, and said, " What will you give me if I spin the straw for you this time also ? " " I have nothing left that I could give," answered the girl. " Then promise me, if you should become Queen, your first child." " Who knows whether that will ever happen ? " thought the miller's daughter ; and, not knowing how else to help herself in this strait, she promised the little man what he wanted, and for that he once more spun the straw into gold.

And when the King came in the morning, and found all as he had wished, he took her in marriage, and the pretty miller's daughter became a Queen.

A year after, she had a beautiful child, and she never gave a thought to the dwarf. But suddenly he came into her room, and said, " Now give me what you promised." The Queen was horror-struck, and offered the dwarf all the riches of the kingdom if he would leave her the child. But the dwarf said, " No, something that is living is dearer to me than all the treasures in the world." The the Queen began to weep and cry, so that he pitied her. " I will give you three days' time," said he, " if by that time you find out my name, then shall you keep your child."

So the Queen thought the whole night of all the names that she had ever heard, and she sent a messenger over the country to inquire, far and wide, for any other names that there might be. When the manikin came the next day, she began with Caspar, Melchior, Balthazar, and said all the names she knew, one after another ; but to every one the little man said, " That is not my name." On the second

day she had inquiries made in the neighbourhood as to the names of
the people there, and she repeated to the dwarf the most uncommon
and curious. "Perhaps your name is Shortribs, or Sheepshanks, or
Laceleg?" but he always answered, "That is not my name."

On the third day the messenger came back again, and said, " I have not been able to find a single new name, but as I came to a high mountain at the end of the forest, where the fox and the hare bid each other good night, there I saw a little house, and before the house a fire was burning, and round about the fire quite a ridiculous little man was jumping : he hopped upon one leg, and shouted—

> " ' *To-day I'll stew and then I'll bake,*
> *To-morrow I shall the Queen's child take,*
> *How lucky it is that nobody knows,*
> *My name is Rumpelstiltskin.'* "

You may think how glad the Queen was when she heard the name ! And when soon afterwards the little man came in, and asked, " Now, Mistress Queen, what is my name ? " at first she said, " Is your name Conrad ? " " No." " Is your name Nicholas ? " " No."

" Perhaps your name is Rumpelstiltskin ? "

" The devil has told you that ! the devil has told you that ! " cried the little man, and in his anger he plunged his right foot so deep into the earth that his whole leg went in ; and then in rage he pulled at his left leg so hard with both hands that he tore himself in two.

THE HUT IN THE FOREST

A poor wood-cutter lived with his wife and three daughters in a little hut on the edge of a lonely forest. One morning as he was about to go to his work, he said to his wife, " Let my dinner be brought into the forest to me by my eldest daughter, or I shall never get my work done, and in order that she may not miss her way," he added, " I will take a bag of millet with me and strew the seeds on the path." When, therefore, the sun was just above the centre of the forest, the girl set out on her way with a bowl of soup, but the field-sparrows, and wood-sparrows, larks and finches, blackbirds and siskins had picked up the millet long before, and the girl could not find the track. Then trusting to chance, she went on and on, until the sun sank and night began to fall. The trees rustled in the darkness, the owls hooted, and she began to be afraid. Then in the distance she perceived a light which glimmered between the trees. " There ought to be some people living there, who can take me in for the night," thought she, and went up to the light. It was not long before she came to a house the windows of which were all lighted up. She knocked, and a rough voice from the inside, cried, " Come in." The girl stepped into the dark entrance, and knocked at the door of the room. " Just come in," cried the voice, and when she opened the door, an old grey-haired man was sitting at the table, supporting his face with both hands, and his white beard fell down over the table almost as far as the ground. By the stove lay three animals, a hen, a cock, and a brindled cow. The girl told her story to the old man, and begged for shelter for the night. The man said,

> " *Pretty little hen,*
> *Pretty little cock,*
> *And pretty brindled cow,*
> *What say you to that ? "*

" Duks," answered the animals, and that must have meant, " We are willing," for the old man said, " Here you shall have shelter and food, go to the fire, and cook us our supper." The girl found in the kitchen abundance of everything, and cooked a good supper, but had no thought of the animals. She carried the full dishes to the table, seated herself by the grey-haired man, ate and satisfied her hunger. When she had had enough, she said, " But now I am tired, where is there a bed in which I can lie down, and sleep ? " The animals replied,

> " *Thou hast warmed thyself here,*
> *Thou hast eaten our bread,*
> *But cared nothing for us ;*
> *Go seek for thy bed."*

Then said the old man, " Just go upstairs, and thou wilt find a room with two beds, shake them up, and put white linen on them, and then

I, too, will come and lie down to sleep." The girl went up, and when she had shaken the beds and put clean sheets on, she lay down in one of them without waiting any longer for the old man. After some time, however, the grey-haired man came, took his candle, looked at the girl and shook his head. When he saw that she had fallen into a sound sleep, he opened a trap-door, and let her down into the cellar.

Late at night the wood-cutter came home, and reproached his wife for leaving him to hunger all day. "It is not my fault," she replied, " the girl went out with your dinner, and must have lost herself, but she is sure to come back to-morrow." The wood-cutter, however, arose before dawn to go into the forest, and requested that the second daughter should take him his dinner that day. " I will take a bag with lentils," said he ; " the seeds are larger than millet, the girl will see them better, and can't lose her way." At dinner-time, therefore, the girl took out the food, but the lentils had disappeared. The birds of the forest had picked them up as they had done the day before, and had left none. The girl wandered about in the forest until night, and then she too reached the house of the old man, was told to go in, and begged for food and a bed. The man with the white beard again asked the animals,

> " Pretty little hen,
> Pretty little cock,
> And pretty brindled cow,
> What say you to that ? "

The animals again replied " Duks," and everything happened just as it had happened the day before. The girl cooked a good meal, ate and drank with the old man, and did not concern herself about the animals, and when she inquired about her bed they answered,

> " Thou hast warmed thyself here,
> Thou hast eaten our bread,
> But thought nothing of us ;
> Go seek for thy bed."

When she was asleep the old man came, looked at her, shook his head, and let her down into the cellar.

On the third morning the wood-cutter said to his wife, " Send our youngest child out with my dinner to-day, she has always been good and obedient, and will stay in the right path, and not run about after every wild humblebee, as her sisters did." The mother did not want to do it, and said, " Am I to lose my dearest child as well ? "

" Have no fear,' he replied, " the girl will not go astray ; she is too prudent and sensible ; besides I will take some peas with me, and strew them about. They are still larger than lentils, and will show her the way." But when the girl went out with her basket on her arm, the wood-pigeons had already got all the peas in their crops, and she did not know which way she was to turn. She was full of sorrow and never ceased to think how hungry her father would be, and how her good mother would grieve, if she did not go home. At length when it grew dark, she saw the light and came to the house in the forest. She begged quite prettily to be allowed to spend the night there, and the man with the white beard once more asked his animals,

> " *Pretty little hen,*
> *Pretty little cock,*
> *And pretty brindled cow,*
> *What say you to that ?* "

" Duks," said they. Then the girl went to the stove where the animals were lying, and petted the cock and hen, and stroked their smooth feathers with her hand, and caressed the brindled cow between her horns, and when, in obedience to the old man's orders, she had made ready some good soup, and the bowl was placed upon the table, she said, " Am I to eat as much as I want, and the good animals to have nothing ? Outside is food in plenty, I will look after them first." So she went and brought some barley and strewed it for the cock and hen, and a whole armful of sweet-smelling hay for the cow. " I hope you will like it, dear animals," said she, " and you shall have a refreshing draught in case you are thirsty." Then she fetched in a bucketful of water, and the cock and hen jumped on to the edge of it and dipped their beaks in, and then held up their heads as the birds do when they drink, and the brindled cow also took a hearty draught. When the animals were fed, the girl seated herself at the table by the old man, and ate what he had left. It was not long before the cock and the hen began to thrust their heads beneath their wings, and the eyes of the cow likewise began to blink. Then said the girl, " Ought we not to go to bed ? "

> " *Pretty little hen,*
> *Pretty little cock,*
> *And pretty brindled cow,*
> *What say you to that ?* "

The animals answered " Duks,"

> " *Thou hast eaten with us,*
> *Thou hast drunk with us,*
> *Thou hast had kind thought for all of us,*
> *We wish thee good-night.*"

Then the maiden went upstairs, shook the feather-beds, and laid clean sheets on them, and when she had done it the old man came and lay down on one of the beds, and his white beard reached down to his feet. The girl lay down on the other, said her prayers, and fell asleep.

She slept quietly till midnight, and then there was such a noise in the house that she awoke. There was a sound of cracking and splitting in every corner, and the doors sprang open, and beat against the walls. The beams groaned as if they were being torn out of their joints, it seemed as if the staircase were falling down, and at length there was a crash as if the entire roof had fallen in. As, however, all grew quiet once more, and the girl was not hurt, she stayed quietly lying where she was, and fell asleep again. But when she woke up in the morning with the brilliancy of the sunshine, what did her eyes behold ? She was lying in a vast hall, and everything around her shone with royal splendour ; on the walls, golden flowers grew up on a ground of green silk, the bed was of ivory and the canopy of red velvet, and on a chair close by was a pair of shoes embroidered with pearls. The girl believed that she was in a dream, but three richly clad attendants came in, and asked what orders she would like to give ? " If you will go," she replied, " I will get up at once and make ready some soup for the old man, and then I will feed the pretty little hen, and the cock, and the beautiful brindled cow." She thought the old man was up already, and looked round at his bed ; he, however, was not lying in it, but a stranger. And while she was looking at him, and becoming aware that he was young and handsome, he awoke, sat up in bed, and said, " I am a King's son, and was bewitched by a wicked witch and made to live in this forest as an old grey-haired man ; no one was allowed to be with me but my three attendants in the form of a cock, a hen, and a brindled cow. The spell was not to be broken until a girl came to us whose heart was so good that she showed herself full of love, not only towards mankind, but towards animals—and that thou hast done, and by thee at midnight we were set free, and the old hut in the forest was changed back again into my royal palace." And when they had arisen, the King's son ordered the three attendants to set out and fetch the father and mother of the girl to the marriage feast. " But where are my two sisters ? " inquired the maiden. " I have locked them in the cellar, and to-morrow they shall be led into the forest, and shall live as servants to a charcoal-burner, until they have grown kinder, and do not leave poor animals to suffer hunger."

THE LITTLE FOLK'S PRESENTS

A TAILOR and a goldsmith were travelling together, and one evening when the sun had sunk behind the mountains, they heard the sound of distant music, which became more and more distinct. It sounded strange, but so pleasant that they forgot all their weariness and stepped quickly onwards. The moon had already arisen when they reached a hill on which they saw a crowd of little men and women who had taken each other's hands, and were whirling round in the dance with the greatest pleasure and delight.

They sang to it most charmingly, and that was the music which the travellers had heard. In the midst of them sat an old man who was rather taller than the rest. He wore a parti-coloured coat, and his iron-grey beard hung down over his breast. The two remained standing full of astonishment, and watched the dance. The old man made a sign that they should enter, and the little folks willingly opened their circle. The goldsmith, who had a hump, and like all hunchbacks was brave enough, stepped in ; the tailor felt a little afraid at first and held back, but when he saw how merrily all was going he plucked up his courage and followed. The circle closed again directly, and the little folks went on singing and dancing with the wildest leaps. The old man, however, took a large knife which hung to his girdle,

whetted it, and when it was sufficiently sharpened he looked round at the strangers. They were terrified, but they had not much time for reflection, for the old man seized the goldsmith and with the greatest speed shaved the hair of his head clean off, and then the same thing happened to the tailor. But their fear left them when, after he had finished his work, the old man clapped them both on the shoulder in a friendly manner, as much as to say they had behaved well to let all that be done to them willingly and without any struggle. He pointed with his finger to a heap of coals which lay at one side, and signified to the travellers by his gestures that they were to fill their pockets with them. Both of them obeyed, although they did not know of what use the coals would be to them, and then they went on their way to seek a shelter for the night. When they had got into the valley, the clock of the neighbouring monastery struck twelve and the song ceased. In a moment all had vanished, and the hill lay in solitude in the moonlight.

The two travellers found an inn, and covered themselves up on their straw-beds with their coats, but in their weariness forgot to take the coals out of them before doing so. A heavy weight on their limbs awakened them earlier than usual. They felt in the pockets, and could not believe their eyes when they saw that they were not filled with coals, but with pure gold ; happily, too, the hair of their heads and beards was there again as thick as ever.

They had now become rich folks, but the goldsmith, who, in accordance with his greedy disposition, had filled his pockets better, was as rich again as the tailor. A greedy man, even if he has much, still wishes to have more, so the goldsmith proposed to the tailor that they should wait another day and go out again in the evening in order to bring back still greater treasures from the old man on the hill. The tailor refused, and said, " I have enough and am content ; now I shall be a master, and marry my dear object (for so he called his sweetheart), and I am a happy man." But he stayed another day to please him. In the evening the goldsmith hung a couple of bags over his shoulders that he might be able to stow away a great deal, and took the road to the hill. He found, as on the night before, the little folks at their singing and dancing, and the old man again shaved him clean and signed to him to take some coal away with him. He was not slow about sticking as much into his bags as would go, went back quite delighted, and covered himself over with his coat. " Even if the gold does weigh heavily," said he, " I will gladly bear that," and at last he fell asleep with the sweet anticipation of waking in the morning an enormously rich man.

When he opened his eyes, he got up in haste to examine his pockets, but how amazed he was when he drew nothing out of them but black coals, and that howsoever often he put his hands in them. " The gold I got the night before is still there for me," thought he, and went and brought it out, but how shocked he was when he saw that it likewise had again turned into coal. He smote his forehead with his dusty black hand, and then he felt that his whole head was bald and smooth, as was also the place where his beard should have been. But his misfortunes were not yet over ; he now remarked for the first time that in addition to the hump on his back, a second, just as large, had grown in front on his breast. Then he recognized the punishment of his greediness, and began to weep aloud. The good tailor, who was wakened by this, comforted the unhappy fellow as well as he could, and said, " Thou hast been my comrade in my travelling time ; thou shalt stay with me and share in my wealth." He kept his word, but the poor goldsmith was obliged to carry the two humps as long as he lived, and to cover his bald head with a cap.

HANS MARRIED

THERE was once on a time a young peasant named Hans, whose uncle wanted to find him a rich wife. He therefore seated Hans behind the stove, and had it made very hot. Then he fetched a pot of milk and plenty of white bread, gave him a bright newly-coined farthing in his hand, and said, " Hans, hold that farthing fast, crumble the white bread into the milk, and stay where you are, and do not stir from that spot till I come back." " Yes," said Hans, " I will do all that." Then the wooer put on a pair of old patched trousers, went to a rich peasant's daughter in the next village, and said, " Won't you marry my nephew Hans—you will get an honest and sensible man who will suit you ? " The covetous father asked, " How is it with regard to his means ? Has he bread to break ? " " Dear friend," replied the wooer, " my young nephew has a snug berth, a nice bit of money in hand, and plenty of bread to break, besides he has quite as many patches as I have " (and as he spoke, he slapped the patches on his trousers, but in that district small pieces of land were called patches also). " If you will give yourself the trouble to go home with me, you shall see at once that all is as I have said." Then the miser did not want to lose this good opportunity, and said, " If that is the case, I have nothing further to say against the marriage."

So the wedding was celebrated on the appointed day, and when the

young wife went out of doors to see the bridegroom's property, Hans took off his Sunday coat and put on his patched smock-frock and said, " I might spoil my good coat." Then together they went out and wherever a boundary line came in sight, or fields and meadows were divided from each other, Hans pointed with his finger and then slapped either a large or a small patch on his smock-frock, and said, " That patch is mine, and that too, my dearest, just look at it," meaning thereby that his wife should not stare at the broad land, but look at his garment, which was his own.

THE TWELVE HUNTSMEN

THERE was once a King's son who was betrothed to a maiden whom he loved very much. And when he was sitting beside her and very happy, news came that his father lay sick unto death, and desired to see him once again before his end. Then he said to his beloved, " I must now go and leave thee, I give thee a ring as a remembrance of me. When I am King, I will return and fetch thee." So he rode away, and when he reached his father the King was dangerously ill, and near his death. He said to him, " Dear son, I wished to see thee once again before my end, promise me to marry as I wish," and he named a certain King's daughter who was to be his wife. The son was in such trouble that he did not think what he was doing, and said, " Yes, dear father, your will shall be done," and thereupon the King shut his eyes, and died.

When therefore the son had been proclaimed King, and the time of mourning was over, he was forced to keep the promise which he had given his father, and caused the King's daughter to be asked in marriage, and she was promised to him. His first betrothed heard of this, and fretted so much about his faithlessness that she nearly died. Then her father said to her, " Dearest child, why art thou so sad ? Thou shalt have whatsoever thou wilt." She thought for a moment and said, " Dear father, I wish for eleven girls exactly like myself in face, figure, and size." The father said, " If it be possible, thy desire shall be fulfilled," and he caused a search to be made in his whole kingdom, until eleven young maidens were found who exactly resembled his daughter in face, figure, and size.

When they came to the King's daughter, she had twelve suits of huntsmen's clothes made, all alike, and the eleven maidens had to put on the huntsmen's clothes, and she herself put on the twelfth suit. Thereupon she took leave of her father, and rode away with them, and rode to the court of her former betrothed, whom she loved so dearly. Then she inquired if he required any huntsmen, and if he would take the whole of them into his service. The King looked at her and did not know her, but as they were such handsome fellows, he said " Yes," and that he would willingly take them, and now they were the King's twelve huntsmen.

The King, however, had a lion which was a wondrous animal, for he knew all concealed and secret things. It came to pass that one evening he said to the King, " Thou thinkest thou hast twelve huntsmen ? " " Yes," said the King, " they are twelve huntsmen." The lion continued, " Thou art mistaken, they are twelve girls." The King said, " That cannot be true ! How wilt thou prove that to me ? " " Oh, just let some peas be strewn in thy ante-chamber," answered the lion, " and then thou wilt soon see it. Men have a firm step, and when they walk over peas none of them stir, but girls trip and skip, and drag their feet, and the peas roll about." Then King was well pleased with the counsel, and caused the peas to be strewn.

There was, however, a servant of the King's who favoured the huntsmen, and when he heard that they were going to be put to this test he went to them and repeated everything, and said, " The lion wants to make the King believe that you are girls." Then the King's daughter thanked him, and said to her maidens, " Put on some strength, and step firmly on the peas." So next morning when the King had the twelve huntsmen called before him, and they came into the ante-chamber where the peas were lying, they stepped so firmly on them, and had such a strong, sure walk, that not one of the peas either rolled or stirred. Then they went away again, and the King said to the lion, " Thou hast lied to me, they walk just like men." The lion said, " They have got to know that they were going to be put to the test, and have assumed some strength. Just let twelve spinning-wheels be brought into the ante-chamber some day, and they will go to them and be pleased with them, and that is what no man would do." The King liked the advice, and had the spinning-wheels placed in the ante-chamber.

But the servant, who was well disposed to the huntsmen, went to them, and disclosed the project. Then when they were alone the King's daughter said to her eleven girls, " Put some constraint on yourselves, and do not look round at the spinning-wheels." And next morning when the King had his twelve huntsmen summoned, they went through the ante-chamber, and never once looked at the spinning-wheels. Then the King again said to the lion, " Thou hast deceived

me, they are men, for they have not looked at the spinning-wheels."
The lion replied, " They have learnt that they were going to be put to
the test, and have restrained themselves." The King, however, would
no longer believe the lion.

The twelve huntsmen always followed the King to the chase, and his
liking for them continually increased. Now it came to pass that once
when they were out hunting, news came that the King's betrothed was
approaching. When the true bride heard that, it hurt her so much
that her heart was almost broken, and she fell fainting to the ground.
The King thought something had happened to his dear huntsman, ran
up to him, wanted to help him, and drew his glove off. Then he saw
the ring which he had given to his first bride, and when he looked in
her face he recognized her. Then his heart was so touched that he
kissed her, and when she opened her eyes he said, " Thou art mine,
and I am thine, and no one in the world can alter that." He sent a
messenger to the other bride, and entreated her to return to her own
kingdom, for he had a wife already, and a man who had just found an
old dish did not require a new one. Thereupon the wedding was
celebrated, and the lion was again taken into favour, because after all
he had told the truth.

FREDERICK AND CATHERINE

THERE was once on a time a man who was called Frederick and a
woman called Catherine, who had married each other and lived
together as young married folks. One day Frederick said, " I will
now go and plough, Catherine ; when I come back, there must be
some roast meat on the table for hunger, and a fresh draught for
thirst." " Just go, Frederick," answered Kate, " just go, I will have

all ready for you." Therefore when dinner-time drew near she got a sausage out of the chimney, put it in the frying-pan, put some butter to it, and set it on the fire. The sausage began to fry and to hiss, Catherine stood beside it and held the handle of the pan, and had her own thoughts as she was doing it. Then it occurred to her, " While the sausage is getting done thou couldst go into the cellar and draw beer." So she set the frying-pan safely on the fire, took a can, and went down into the cellar to draw beer. The beer ran into the can **and Kate** watched it, and then she thought, " Oh, dear ! The dog upstairs is not fastened up, it might get the sausage out of the pan. Well thought of." And in a trice she was up the cellar-steps again, but the Spitz had the sausage in its mouth already, and trailed it away on the ground. But Catherine, who was not idle, set out after it, and chased it a long way into the field ; the dog, however, was swifter than Catherine and did not let the sausage journey easily, but skipped over the furrows with it. " What's gone is gone ! " said Kate, and turned round, and as she has run till she was weary, she walked quietly and comfortably, and cooled herself. During this time the beer was still running out of the cask, for Kate had not turned the tap. And when the can was full and there was no other place for it, it ran into the cellar and did not stop until the whole cask was empty. As soon as Kate was on the steps she saw the mischance. " Good gracious ! " she cried. " What shall I do now to stop Frederick knowing it ! " She thought for a while, and at last she remembered that up in the garret was still standing a sack of the finest wheat flour from the last fair, and she would fetch that down and strew it over the beer. " Yes," said she, " he who saves a thing when he ought, has it afterwards when he needs it," and she climbed up to the garret and carried the sack below, and threw it straight down on the can of beer, which she knocked over, and Frederick's draught swam also in the cellar. " It is all right," said Kate, " where the one is the other ought to be also," and she strewed the meal over the whole cellar. When it was done she was heartily delighted with her work, and said, " How clean and wholesome it does look here ! " At mid-day home came Frederick : " Now, wife, what have you ready for me ? " " Ah, Freddy," she answered, " I was frying a sausage for you, but whilst I was drawing the beer to drink with it, the dog took it away out of the pan, and whilst

I was running after the dog, all the beer ran out, and whilst I was drying up the beer with the flour, I knocked over the can as well, but be easy, the cellar is quite dry again." Said Frederick, " Kate, Kate, you should not have done that ! to let the sausage be carried off and the beer run out of the cask, and throw out all our flour into the bargain ! " " Indeed, Frederick, I did not know that, you should have told me." The man thought, " If my wife is like this, I must look after things more." Now he had got together a good number of thalers which he changed into gold, and said to Catherine, " Look, these are counters for playing games ; I will put them in a pot and bury them in the stable under the cow's manger, but mind you keep away from them, or it will be the worse for you." Said she, " Oh, no, Frederick, I certainly will not go." And when Frederick was gone some pedlars came into the village who had cheap earthen-bowls and pots, and asked the young woman if there was nothing she wanted to bargain with them for ? " Oh, dear people," said Catherine, " I have no money and can buy nothing, but if you have any use for yellow counters I will buy of you." " Yellow counters, why not ? But just let us see them." " Then go into the stable and dig under the cow's manger, and you will find the yellow counters. I am not allowed to go there." The rogues went thither, dug and found pure gold. Then they laid hold of it, ran away, and left their pots and bowls behind in the house. Catherine thought she must use her new things, and as she had no lack in the kitchen already without these, she knocked the bottom out of every pot, and set them all as ornaments on the paling which went about the house. When Frederick came and saw the new decorations, he said, " Catherine, what have you been about ? " " I have bought them, Frederick, for the counters which were under the cow's manger. I did not go there myself, the pedlars had to dig them out for themselves." " Ah, wife," said Frederick, " what have you done ? Those were not counters, but pure gold, and all our wealth ; you should not have done that." " Indeed, Frederick," said she, " I did not know that, you should have warned me."

Catherine stood for a while and bethought herself ; then she said, " Listen, Frederick, we will soon get the gold back again, we will run after the thieves." " Come, then," said Frederick, " we will try it ;

but take with you some butter and cheese that we may have something to eat on the way." "Yes, Frederick, I will take them." They set out, and as Frederick was the better walker, Catherine followed him. "It is to my advantage," thought she, "when we turn back I shall be a little way in advance." Then she came to a hill where there were deep ruts on both sides of the road. "There one can see," said Catherine, "how they have torn and skinned and galled the poor earth, it will never be whole again as long as it lives," and in her heart's compassion she took her butter and smeared the ruts right and left, that it might not be so hurt by the wheels, and as she was thus bending down in her charity, one of the cheeses rolled out of her pocket down the hill. Said Catherine, "I have made my way once up here, I will not go down again; another may run and fetch it back." So she took another cheese and rolled it down. But the cheese did not come back, so she let a third run down, thinking, "Perhaps they are waiting for company, and do not like to walk alone." As all three stayed away she said, "I do not know what that can mean, but it may perhaps be that the third has not found the way, and has gone wrong, I will just send the fourth to call it." But the fourth did no better than the third. Then Catherine was angry, and threw down the fifth and sixth as well, and these were her last. She remained standing for some time watching for their coming, but when they still did not come, she said, "Oh, you are fine folks to send hunting each other, you stay a good long time away! Do you think I will wait any longer for you? I shall go my way, you may run after me; you have younger legs than I." Catherine went on and found Frederick, who was standing waiting for her because he wanted something to eat. "Now just let us have what you have brought with you," said he. She gave him the dry bread. "Where is the butter and all the cheeses?" asked the man. "Ah, Freddy," said Catherine, "I smeared the cart-ruts with the butter and the cheeses will come soon; one ran away from me, so I sent the others after to call it." Said Frederick, "You should not have done that, Catherine, to smear the butter on the road, and let the cheeses run down the hill!" "Really, Frederick, you should have told me." Then they ate the dry bread together, and Frederick said, "Catherine, did you make the house safe when you came away?" "No, Frederick, you should have told me to do it before." "Then go home again, and make the house safe before we go any farther, and bring with you something else to eat. I will wait here for you." Catherine went back and thought, "Frederick wants something more to eat, he does not like butter and cheese, so I will take with me a handkerchief full of dried pears and a pitcher of vinegar for him to drink." Then she bolted the upper half of the door fast, but unhinged the lower door, and took it on her back, believing that when she had placed the door in security the house must be well taken care of. Catherine took her time on the way, and thought, "Frederick will rest himself so much the longer." When she had once more got up to him she said, "Here is the house-door for you, Frederick, and now you can take care of the house yourself." "Oh, heavens," said he, "what a wise wife I have! She takes the under-door off the hinges that everything may run in, and bolts the upper one. It is now too late to go back home again, but since you have brought the door here, you shall just carry it farther." "I will carry the door, Frederick, but the dried pears and the vinegar will be too heavy for me; I will hang them on the door; it can carry them."

And now they went into the forest, and sought the thieves, but did not find them. At length as it grew dark they climbed into a tree and resolved to spend the night there. Scarcely, however, had they settled down among the leaves than the rascals arrived who carry away with them what does not want to go, and find things before they are lost. They sat down under the very tree in which Frederick and Catherine were sitting, lighted a fire, and were about to share their booty. Frederick got down on the other side and collected some stones together. Then he climbed up again with them, and wished to throw them at the thieves and kill them. The stones, however, did not hit them, and the robbers cried, "It will soon be morning, the wind is shaking down the fir cones." Catherine still had the door on her back, and as it pressed heavily on her, she thought it was the fault of the dried pears, and said, "Frederick, I must throw the pears down." "No, Catherine, not now," he replied, "they might betray us." "Oh, but, Frederick, I must! They weigh me down far too much." "Do it, then, and be hanged!" Then the dried pears rolled down between the branches, and the rascals below said, "The leaves are falling."

A short time afterwards, as the door was still heavy, Catherine said, "Ah, Frederick, I must pour out the vinegar," "No, Catherine, you must not, it might betray us." "Ah, but, Frederick, I must, it weighs me down far too much." "Then do it and be hanged!" So she emptied out the vinegar, and it besprinkled the robbers. They said amongst themselves, "The dew is already falling." At length Catherine thought, "Can it really be the door which weighs me down so?" and said, "Frederick, I must throw the door down." "No, not now, Catherine, they will discover us." "Oh, but, Frederick, I must. It weighs me down far too much." "Oh, no, Catherine, do hold it fast." "Ah, Frederick, I am letting it fall!" "Let it go, then, for heaven's sake!" Then it fell down with a violent clatter, and the robbers below cried, "The devil is coming down the tree!" and they ran away and left everything behind them. Early next morning, when the two came down they found all their gold again, and carried it home.

When they were once more at home, Frederick said, "And now, Catherine, you, too, must be industrious and work." "Yes, Frederick, I will soon do that, I will go into the field and cut corn." When Catherine got into the field, she said to herself, "Shall I eat before I reap, or shall I sleep before I reap? Oh, I will eat first." Then Catherine ate and eating made her sleepy, and she began to cut, and half in a dream, cut all her clothes to pieces, her apron, her gown, and her shift. When Catherine awoke again after a long sleep she was lying there half-naked, and said to herself, "Is it I, or is it not I? Alas, it is not I." In the meantime night came, and Catherine ran into the village, knocked at her husband's window, and cried, "Frederick! Frederick!"

"What is the matter?" "I should very much like to know if Catherine is in?" "Yes, yes," replied Frederick, "she must be in and asleep by now."

Said she, "'Tis well, then I am certainly at home already," and ran away.

CAT AND MOUSE IN PARTNERSHIP

A CERTAIN cat had made the acquaintance of a mouse, and had said so much to her about the great love and friendship she felt for her, that at length the mouse agreed that they should live and keep house together. " But we must make a provision for winter, or else we shall suffer from hunger," said the cat, " and you, little mouse, cannot venture everywhere, or you will be caught in a trap some day." The good advice was followed, and a pot of fat was bought, but they did not know where to put it. At length, after much consideration, the cat said, " I know no place where it will be better stored up than in the church, for no one dares take anything away from there. We will set it beneath the altar, and not touch it until we are really in need of it." So the pot was placed in safety, but it was not long before the cat had a great longing for it, and said to the mouse, " I want to tell you something, little mouse ; my cousin has brought a little son into the world, and has asked me to be godmother ; he is white with brown spots, and I am to hold him at the christening. Let me go out to-day, and you look after the house by yourself." " Yes, yes," answered the mouse, " by all means go, and if you get anything very good, think of me, I should like a drop of sweet red christening wine too." All this, however, was untrue ; the cat had no cousin, and had not been asked to be godmother. She went straight to the church, stole to the pot of fat, began to lick at it, and licked the top of the fat off. Then she took a walk upon the roofs of the town, looked out for opportunities, and then stretched herself in the sun, and licked her lips whenever she thought of the pot of fat, and not until it was evening did she return home. " Well, here you are again," said the mouse, " no doubt you have had a merry day." " All went off well," answered the cat. " What name did they give the child ? " " Top off ! " said the cat quite coolly. " Top off ! " cried the mouse, " that is a very odd and uncommon name, is it a usual one in your family ? " " What does it signify," said the cat, " it is not worse than Crumb-stealer, as your god-children are called."

Before long the cat was seized by another fit of longing. She said to the mouse. " You must do me a favour, and once more manage the house for a day alone. I am again asked to be godmother, and, as the child has a white ring round its neck, I cannot refuse." The good mouse consented, but the cat crept behind the town walls to the church, and devoured half the pot of fat. " Nothing ever seems so good as what one keeps to oneself," said she, and was quite satisfied with her day's work. When she went home the mouse inquired, " And what was this child christened ? " " Half-done," answered the cat. " Half-done ! What are you saying ? I never heard the name in my life, I'll wager anything it is not in the calendar ! "

The cat's mouth soon began to water for some more licking. " All good things go in threes," said she, " I am asked to stand godmother again. The child is quite black, only it has white paws, but with that exception, it has not a single white hair on its whole body ; this only happens once every few years, you will let me go, won't you ? " " Top-off ! Half-done ! " answered the mouse, " they are such odd names, they make me very thoughtful." " You sit at home," said the cat, " in your dark-grey fur coat and long tail, and are filled with fancies, that's because you do not go out in the daytime." During the cat's absence the mouse cleaned the house, and put it in order, but the greedy cat entirely emptied the pot of fat. " When everything is eaten up one has some peace," said she to herself, and well filled and fat she did not return home till night. The mouse at once asked what name had been given to the third child. " It will not please you more than the others," said the cat. " He is called All-gone." " All-gone," cried the mouse, " that is the most suspicious name of all ! I have never seen it in print. All-gone ; what can that mean ? " and she shook her head, curled herself up, and lay down to sleep.

From this time forth no one invited the cat to be god-mother, but when the winter had come and there was no longer anything to be found outside, the mouse thought of their provision, and said, " Come, cat, we will go to our pot of fat which we have stored up for ourselves— we shall enjoy that." " Yes," answered the cat, " you will enjoy it as much as you would enjoy putting that dainty tongue of yours out of the window." They set out on their way, but when they arrived, the pot of fat certainly was still in its place, but it was empty. " Alas ! " said the mouse, " now I see what has happened, now it comes to light ! You are a true friend ? You have eaten it all when you were standing godmother. First top off, then half done, then—" " Will you hold your tongue," cried the cat, " one word more, and I will eat you too." " All gone " was already on the poor mouse's lips ; scarcely had she spoken it before the cat sprang on her, seized her, and swallowed her down. Alas, that is the way of the world.

THE GOLDEN BIRD

In the olden time there was a king, who had behind his palace a beautiful pleasure-garden in which there was a tree that bore golden apples. When the apples were getting ripe they were counted, but on the very next morning one was missing. This was told to the King, and he ordered that a watch should be kept every night beneath the tree.

The King had three sons, the eldest of whom he sent, as soon as night came on, into the garden ; but when midnight came he could not keep himself from sleeping, and next morning again an apple was gone.

The following night the second son had to keep watch, it fared no better with him ; as soon as twelve o'clock had struck he fell asleep, and in the morning an apple was gone.

Now it came to the turn of the third son to watch ; and he was quite ready, but the King had not much trust in him, and thought he would be of less use even than his brothers ; but at last he let him go. The youth lay down beneath the tree, but kept awake, and did not let sleep master him. When it struck twelve, something rustled through the air, and in the moonlight he saw a bird coming whose feathers were all shining with gold. The bird alighted on the tree, and had just plucked off an apple, when the youth shot an arrow at him. The bird flew off, but the arrow had struck his plumage, and one of his golden feathers fell down. The youth picked it up, and the next morning took it to the King and told him what he had seen in the night. The King called his council together, and every one declared that a feather like this was worth more than the whole kingdom. " If the feather is so precious," declared the King, " one alone will not do for me ; I must and will have the whole bird ! "

The eldest son set out ; ne trusted to his cleverness, and thought that he would easily find the Golden Bird. When he had gone some distance he saw a Fox sitting at the edge of a wood, so he cocked his gun and took aim at him. The Fox cried, " Do not shoot me ! and in return I will give you some good counsel. You are on the way to the Golden Bird ; and this evening you will come to a village in which stand two inns opposite to one another. One of them is lighted up brightly, and all goes on merrily within, but do not go into it ; go rather into the other, even though it seems a bad one." "How can such a silly beast give wise advice ? " thought the King's son, and he pulled the trigger. But he missed the Fox, who stretched out his tail and ran quickly into the wood.

So he pursued his way, and by evening came to the village where the two inns were ; in one they were singing and dancing ; the other had a poor, miserable look. "I should be a fool, indeed," he thought, "if I were to go into the shabby tavern, and pass by the good one." So he went into the cheerful one, lived there in riot and revel, and forgot the bird and his father, and all good counsels.

When some time had passed, and the eldest son for month after month did not come back home, the second set out, wishing to find the Golden Bird. The Fox met him as he had met the eldest, and gave him the good advice of which he took no heed. He came to the two inns, and his brother was standing at the window of the one from which came the music, and called out to him. He could not resist, but went inside and lived only for pleasure.

Again some time passed, and then the King's youngest son wanted to set off and try his luck, but his father would not allow it. "It is of no use," said he, "he will find the Golden Bird still less than his brothers, and if a mishap were to befall him he knows not how to help himself ; he is a little wanting at the best." But at last, as he had no peace, he let him go.

Again the Fox was sitting outside the wood, and begged for his life, and offered his good advice. The youth was good-natured, and said, "Be easy, little Fox, I will do you no harm." "You shall not repent it," answered the Fox ; "and that you may get on more quickly, get up behind my tail." And scarcely had he seated himself when the Fox began to run, and away he went over stock and stone till his hair whistled in the wind. When they came to the village the youth got off ; he followed the good advice, and without looking round turned into the little inn, where he spent the night quietly.

The next morning, as soon as he got into the open country, there sat the Fox already, and said, "I will tell you further what you have to do. Go on quite straight, and at last you will come to a castle,

in front of which a whole regiment of soldiers is lying, but do not trouble yourself about them, for they will all be asleep and snoring. Go through the midst of them straight into the castle, and go through all the rooms, till at last you will come to a chamber where a Golden Bird is hanging in a wooden cage. Close by, there stands an empty gold cage for show, but beware of taking the bird out of the common cage and putting it into the fine one, or it may go badly with you." With these words the Fox again stretched out his tail, and the King's son seated himself upon it, and away he went over stock and stone till his hair whistled in the wind.

When he came to the castle he found everything as the Fox had said. The King's son went into the chamber where the Golden Bird was shut up in a wooden cage, whilst a golden one stood hard by ; and the three golden apples lay about the room. " But," thought he, " it would be absurd if I were to leave the beautiful bird in the common and ugly cage," so he opened the door, laid hold of it, and put it into the golden cage. But at the same moment the bird uttered a shrill cry. The soldiers awoke, rushed in, and took him off to prison. The next morning he was taken before a court of justice, and as he confessed everything, was sentenced to death.

The King, however, said he would grant him his life on one condition—namely, if he brought him the Golden Horse which ran faster than the wind ; and in that case he should receive, over and above, as a reward, the Golden Bird.

The King's son set off, but he sighed and was sorrowful, for how was he to find the Golden Horse ? But all at once he saw his old friend the Fox sitting on the road. " Look you," said the Fox, " this happened because you did not heed to me. However, be of good courage. I will give you my help, and tell you how to get to the Golden Horse. You must go straight on, and you will come to a castle, where in the stable stands the horse. The grooms will be lying in front of the stable ; but they will be asleep and snoring, and you can quietly lead out the Golden Horse. But of one thing you must take heed ; put on him the common saddle of wood and leather, and not the golden one, which hangs close by, else it will go ill with you. Then the Fox stretched out his tail, the King's son seated himself upon it, and away he went over stock and stone until his hair whistled in the wind.

Everything happened just as the Fox had said ; the prince came to the stable in which the Golden Horse was standing, but just as he was going to put the common saddle upon him, he thought, " It will be a shame to such a beautiful beast, if I do not give him the good saddle which belongs to him by right." But scarcely had the golden saddle touched the horse than he began to neigh loudly. The grooms awoke, seized the youth, and threw him into prison. The next morning he was sentenced by the court to death ; but the King promised to grant him his life, and the Golden Horse as well, if he could bring back the beautiful princess from the Golden Castle.

With a heavy heart the youth set out ; yet luckily for him he soon found the trusty Fox. " I ought only to leave you to your ill-luck," said the Fox, " but if I pity you, and will help you once more out of your trouble. This road takes you straight to the Golden Castle, you will reach it by eventide ; and at night when everything is quiet the beautiful princess goes to the bathing-house to bathe. When she enters it, run up to her and give her a kiss, then she will follow you, and you can take her away with you ; only do not allow her to take leave of her parents first, or it will go ill with you."

Then the Fox stretched out his tail, the King's son seated himself

G

ɪ] on it, and away the Fox went, over stock and stone, till his hair whistled in the wind.

When he reached the Golden Castle it was just as the Fox had said. He waited until midnight, when everything lay in deep sleep, and the beautiful princess was going to the bathing-house. Then he sprang out and gave her a kiss. She said that she would like to go with him, but she asked him pitifully, and with tears, to allow her first to take leave of her parents. At first he withstood her prayer, but when she wept more and more, and fell at his feet, he at last gave in. But no sooner had the maiden reached the bedside of her father than he and all the rest in the castle awoke, and the youth was laid hold of and put into prison.

The next morning the King said to him, " Your life is forfeited, and you can only find mercy if you take away the hill which stands in front of my windows, and prevents my seeing beyond it ; and you must finish it all within eight days. If you do that you shall have my daughter as your reward."

The King's son began, and dug and shovelled without leaving off, but when after seven days he saw how little he had done, and how all his work was as good as nothing, he fell into great sorrow and gave up all hope. But on the evening of the seventh day the Fox appeared and said, " You do not deserve that I should take any trouble about you ; but just go away and lie down to sleep, and I will do the work for you."

The next morning when he awoke and looked out of the window the hill had gone. The youth ran, full of joy, to the King, and told him that the task was fulfilled, and whether he liked it or not, the King had to hold to his word and give him his daughter.

So the two set forth together, and it was not long before the trusty Fox came up with them. " You have certainly got what is best," said he, " but the Golden Horse also belongs to the maiden of the Golden Castle." " How shall I get it ? " asked the youth. " That I will tell you," answered the Fox ; " first take the beautiful maiden to the King who sent you to the Golden Castle. There will be unheard-of rejoicing ; they will gladly give you the Golden Horse, and will bring it out to you. Mount it as soon as possible, and offer your hand to all in farewell ; last of all to the beautiful maiden. And as soon as you have taken her hand swing her up on to the horse, and gallop away, and no one will be able to bring you back, for the horse runs faster than the wind."

All was brought to pass successfully, and the King's son carried off the beautiful princess on the Golden Horse.

The Fox did not remain behind, and he said to the youth, " Now I will help you to get the Golden Bird. When you come near to the castle where the Golden Bird is to be found, let the maiden get down, and I will take her into my care. Then ride with the Golden Horse into the castle-yard ; there will be great rejoicing at the sight, and they will bring out the Golden Bird for you. As soon as you have the cage in your hand gallop back to us, and take the maiden away again."

When the plan had succeeded, and the King's son was about to ride home with his treasures, the Fox said, " Now you shall reward me for my help." " What do you require for it ? " asked the youth. " When you get into the wood yonder, shoot me dead, and chop off my head and feet."

" That would be fine gratitude," said the King's son. " I cannot possibly do that for you."

The Fox said, " If you will not do it I must leave you, but before I go away I will give you a piece of good advice. Be careful about two things. Buy no gallows' meat, and do not sit at the edge of any well." And then he ran into the wood.

The youth thought, " That is a wonderful beast, he has strange whims ; who is going to buy gallows'-meat ? and the desire to sit at the edge of a well has never yet seized me."

He rode on with the beautiful maiden, and his road took him again through the village in which his two brothers had remained. There was a great stir and noise, and, when he asked what was going on, he was told that two men were going to be hanged. As he came nearer to the place he saw that they were his two brothers, who had been playing all kinds of wicked pranks, and had squandered all their wealth. He inquired whether they could not be set free. " If you will pay for them," answered the people ; " but why should you waste your money on wicked men, and buy them free." He did not think twice about it, but paid for them, and when they were set free they all went on their way together.

They came to the wood where the Fox had first met them, and, as it was cool and pleasant within it, whilst the sun shone hotly, the two brothers said, " Let us rest a little by the well, and eat and drink." He agreed, and whilst they were talking he forgot himself, and sat down upon the edge of the well without foreboding any evil. But the two brothers threw him backwards into the well, took the maiden, the Horse, and the Bird, and went home to their father. " Here we bring you not only the Golden Bird," said they ; " we have won the Golden Horse also, and the maiden from the Golden Castle." Then was there great joy ; but the Horse would not eat, the Bird would not sing, and the maiden sat and wept.

But the youngest brother was not dead. By good fortune the well was dry, and he fell upon soft moss without being hurt, but he could not get out again. Even in this strait the faithful Fox did not leave him : it came and leapt down to him, and upbraided him for having forgotten its advice. " But yet I cannot give it up so," he said ; " I will help you up again into daylight." He bade him grasp his tail and keep tight hold of it ; and then he pulled him up.

" You are not out of all danger yet," said the Fox. " Your brothers were not sure of your death, and have surrounded the wood with watchers, who are to kill you if you let yourself be seen." But a poor man was sitting upon the road, with whom the youth changed clothes, and in this way he got to the King's palace.

No one knew him, but the Bird began to sing, the Horse began to eat, and the beautiful maiden left off weeping. The King, astonished, asked, " What does this mean ? " Then the maiden said, " I do not know, but I have been so sorrowful and now I am so happy ! I feel as if my true bridegroom had come." She told him all that had happened, although the other brothers had threatened her with death if she were to betray anything.

The King commanded that all people who were in his castle should be brought before him ; and amongst them came the youth in his ragged clothes ; but the maiden knew him at once and fell upon his neck. The wicked brothers were seized and put to death, but he was married to the beautiful maiden and declared heir to the King.

But how did it fare with the poor Fox ? Long afterwards the King's son was once again walking in the wood, when the Fox met him and said, " You have everything now that you can wish for, but there is never an end to my misery, and yet it is in your power to free me," and again he asked him with tears to shoot him dead and to chop off his head and feet. So he did it, and scarcely was it done when the Fox was changed into a man, and was no other than the brother of the beautiful princess, who at last was freed from the magic charm which had been laid upon him. And now nothing more was wanting to their happiness as long as they lived.

———————

THE ROGUE AND HIS MASTER

A CERTAIN man, named John, was desirous that his son should learn some trade, and he went into the church to ask the Priest's opinion as to what would be best. Just then the Clerk was standing near the altar and he cried out—" A thief, a rogue ! " At these words the man went away and told his son he must learn to be a rogue for so the Priest had said. So they set out and asked one man and another whether he was a rogue till at the end of the day they entered a large forest, and there they found a little hut with an old woman in it. John says, " Do you know of a man who is acquainted with thieving ? " " You can learn that here quite well," says the woman, " my son is a master of it." So he speaks with the son, and asks if he knows thieving really well ? The master-thief says, " I will teach him well. Come back when a year is over, and then if you recognize your son, I will take no payment at all for teaching him ; but if you don't know him, you must give me two hundred thalers."

The father goes home again, and the son learns witch-craft and thieving, thoroughly. When the year is out, the father is full of

anxiety to know how he is to contrive to recognize his son. As he is thus going about in his trouble, he meets a little dwarf, who says, "Man, what ails you, that you seem to be in such trouble?"

"Oh," says John, "a year ago I placed my son with a master-thief who told me I was to come back when the year was out, and that if I then did not know my son when I saw him, I was to pay two hundred thalers; but if I did know him I was to pay nothing, and now I am afraid of not knowing him and can't tell where I am to get the money." Then the dwarf tells him to take a small basket of bread with him, and to stand beneath the chimney. "There on the cross-beam is a basket, out of which a little bird is peeping, and that is your son."

John goes thither, and throws a little basket full of black bread in front of the basket with the bird in it, and the little bird comes out, and looks up. "Hullo, my son, art thou here?" says the father, and the son is delighted to see his father, but the master-thief says, "A witch must have helped you, or how could you have known your son?" "Father, let us go," said the youth.

Then the father and son set out homeward. On the way a carriage comes driving by. Hereupon, the son says to his father, "I will change myself into a large greyhound, and then you can earn a great deal of money by me." Then the gentleman calls from the carriage, "My man, will you sell your dog?" "Yes," says the father. "How much do you want for it?" "Thirty thalers." "Eh, man, that is a great deal, but as it is such a very fine dog I will have it." The gentleman takes it into his carriage, but when they have driven a little farther the dogs springs out of the carriage through the window, and goes back to his father, and is no longer a greyhound.

They go home together. Next day there is a fair in the neighbouring town, so the youth says to his father, "I will now change myself into a beautiful horse, and you can sell me; but when you have sold me, you must take off my bridle, or I cannot become a man again." Then the father goes with the horse to the fair, and the master-thief comes and buys the horse for a hundred thalers, but the father forgets, and does not take off the bridle. So the man goes home with the horse, and puts it in the stable. When the maid crosses the threshold, the horse says, "Take off my bridle, take off my bridle." Then the maid stands still, and says, "What, canst thou speak?" So she goes and takes the bridle off, and the horse becomes a sparrow, and flies out at the door, and the wizard becomes a sparrow also, and flies after him. Then they come together and cast lots, but the master loses, and betakes himself to the water and is a fish. Then the youth also becomes a fish, and they cast lots again, and the master loses. So the master changes himself into a cock, and the youth becomes a fox, and bites the master's head off, and he died and has remained dead to this day.

THE MANY-FURRED CREATURE

THERE was once on a time a King who had a wife with golden hair, and she was so beautiful that her equal was not to be found on earth. It came to pass that she lay ill, and as she felt that she must soon die, she called the King and said, " If thou wishest to marry again after my death, take no one who is not quite as beautiful as I am, and who has not just such golden hair as I have : this thou must promise me." And after the King had promised her this she closed her eyes and died.

For a long time the King could not be comforted, and had no thought of taking another wife. At length his councillors said, " There is no help for it, the King must marry again, that we may have a Queen." And now messengers were sent about far and wide, to seek a bride who equalled the late Queen in beauty. In the whole world, however, none was to be found, and even if one had been found, still there would have been no one who had such golden hair. So the messengers came home as they went.

Now the King had a daughter who was just as beautiful as her dead mother, and had also the same golden hair, and as she grew up the King saw how like she was to his lost wife. He told the counsellors that he wished to marry his daughter to the oldest councillor, and that she should be Queen. When the oldest councillor heard this, he was delighted, but the daughter was frightened by the resolve of the King : still, she hoped yet to turn him from his intention. So she said to him. " Before I fulfil your wish I must first have three dresses, one as golden as the sun, one as silvery as the moon, and one as bright as the stars ; besides this, I wish for a mantle of a thousand different kinds of fur and hair joined together, and one of every kind of animal in your kingdom must give a bit of his skin for it." But she thought, " To get that will be quite impossible, and thus I shall divert my father from his unkind intentions." The King, however, did not give it up, and the cleverest maidens in his kingdom had to weave the three dresses, one as golden as the sun, one as silvery as the moon, and one as bright as the stars, and his huntsmen had to catch one of every kind of animal in the whole of his kingdom, and take from it a piece of its skin, and out of these was made a mantle of a thousand different kinds

of fur. At length, when all was ready, the King caused the mantle to be brought, spread it out before her, and said, " The wedding shall be to-morrow."

When, therefore, the King's daughter saw that there was no longer any hope of turning her father's heart, she resolved to run away from him. In the night whilst every one was asleep, she got up, and took three different things from her treasures, a golden ring, a golden spinning-wheel, and a golden reel. The three dresses of the sun, moon, and stars she put into a nutshell, put on her mantle of all kinds of fur, and blackened her face and hands with soot. Then she commended herself to God, and went away, and walked the whole night until she reached a great forest. And as she was tired, she got into a hollow tree, and fell asleep.

The sun rose, and she slept on, and she was still sleeping when it was full day. Then it so happened that the King to whom this forest belonged, was hunting in it. When his dogs came to the tree, they snuffed, and ran barking round about it. The King said to the huntsmen, " Just see what kind of wild beast has hidden itself in there." The huntsmen obeyed his order, and when they came back they said, " A wondrous beast is lying in the hollow tree ; we have never before seen one like it. Its skin is fur of a thousand different kinds, but it lying asleep." Said the King, " See if you can catch it alive, and then fasten it on the carriage, and we will take it with us." When the huntsmen laid hold of the maiden, she awoke full of terror, and cried to them, " I am a poor child, deserted by father and mother ; have pity on me, and take me with you." Then said they, " Allerleirauh, thou wilt be useful in the kitchen, come with us, and thou canst sweep up the ashes." So they put her in the carriage, and took her home to the royal palace. There they pointed out to her a closet under the stairs, where no daylight entered, and said, " Furry, there canst thou live and sleep." Then she was sent into the kitchen, and she carried wood and water, swept the hearth, plucked the fowls, picked the vegetables, raked the ashes, and did all the dirty work.

Allerleirauh lived there for a long time in great wretchedness. Alas, fair princess, what is to become of thee now ! It happened, however, that one day a feast was held in the palace, and she said to the cook, " May I go up-stairs for a while, and look on ? I will place myself outside the door." The cook answered, "Yes, go, but you must be back here in half-an-hour to sweep the hearth." Then she took her oil-lamp, went into her den, put off her fur-dress, and washed the soot off her face and hands, so that her full beauty once more came to light. And she opened the nut, and took out her dress which shone like the sun, and when she had done that she went up to the festival, and every one made way for her, for no one knew her, and thought no otherwise than that she was a king's daughter. The King came to meet her, gave his hand to her, and danced with her, and thought in his heart, "My eyes have never yet seen any one so beautiful!" When the dance was over she curtsied, and when the King looked round again she had vanished, and none knew whither. The guards who stood outside the palace were called and questioned, but no one had seen her.

She had, however, run into her little den, had quickly taken off her dress, made her face and hands black again, put on the fur-mantle, and again was Allerleirauh. And now when she went into the kitchen, and was about to get to her work and sweep up the ashes, the cook said, "Leave that alone till morning, and make me the soup for the King; I, too, will go upstairs awhile, and take a look; but let no hairs fall in, or in future thou shalt have nothing to eat." So the cook went away, and Allerleirauh made the soup for the King, and made bread soup and the best she could, and when it was ready she fetched her golden ring from her little den, and put it in the bowl in which the soup was served. When the dancing was over, the King had his soup brought and ate it, and liked it so much that it seemed to him he had never tasted better. But when he came to the bottom of the bowl, he saw a golden ring lying, and could not conceive how it could have got there. Then he ordered the cook to appear before him. The cook was terrified when he heard the order, and said to Allerleirauh, "Thou hast certainly let a hair fall into the soup, and if thou hast, thou shalt be beaten for it." When he came before the King the latter asked who had made the soup? The cook replied, "I made it." But the King said, "That is not true, for it was much better than usual, and cooked differently." He answered, "I must acknowledge that I did not make it, it was made by the many furred-creature." The King said, "Go and bid it come up here."

When Allerleirauh came, the King said, " Who art thou ? " " I am a poor girl who no longer has any father or mother." He asked further, " Of what use art thou in my palace ? " She answered, " I am good for nothing but to have boots thrown at my head." He continued, " Where didst thou get the ring which was in the soup ? " She answered, " I know nothing about the ring." So the King could learn nothing, and had to send her away again.

After a while, there was another festival, and then, as before, Allerleirauh begged the cook for leave to go and look on. He answered, " Yes, but come back again in half-an-hour, and make the King the bread soup which he so much likes." Then she ran into her den, washed herself quickly, and took out of the nut the dress which was as silvery as the moon, and put it on. Then she went up and was like a princess, and the King stepped forward to meet her, and rejoiced to see her once more, and as the dance was just beginning they danced it together. But when it was at end, she again disappeared so quickly that the King could not observe where she went. She, however, sprang into her den, and once more made herself a furry animal, and went into the kitchen to prepare the bread soup. When the cook had gone up-stairs, she fetched the little golden spinning-wheel, and put it in the bowl so that the soup covered it. Then it was taken to the King, who ate it, and liked it as much as before, and had the cook brought, who this time likewise was forced to confess that Allerleirauh had prepared the soup. Allerleirauh again came before the King, but she answered that she was good for nothing else but to have boots thrown at her head, and that she knew nothing at all about the little golden spinning-wheel.

When, for the third time, the King held a festival, all happened just as it had done before. The cook said, " Faith, furry-skin, thou art a witch, and always puttest something in the soup which makes it so good that the King likes it better than that which I cook," but as she begged so hard, he let her go up at the appointed time. And now she put on the dress which shone like the stars, and thus entered the hall. Again the King danced with the beautiful maiden, and thought that she never yet had been so beautiful. And whilst she was dancing, he contrived, without her noticing it, to slip a golden ring on her finger, and he had given orders that the dance should last a very long time. When it was ended, he wanted to hold her fast by her hands, but she tore herself loose, and sprang away so quickly through the crowd that she vanished from his sight. She ran as fast as she could into her den beneath the stairs, but as she had been too long, and had stayed more than half-an-hour she could not take off her pretty dress, but only threw over it her fur-mantle, and in her haste she did not make herself quite black, but one finger remained white. Then Alleleirauh ran into the kitchen, and cooked the bread soup for the King, and as the cook was away, put her golden reel into it. When the King found the reel at the bottom of it, he caused Allerleirauh to be summoned, and then he espied the white finger, and saw the ring which he had put on it during the dance. Then he grasped her by the hand, and held her fast, and when she wanted to release herself and run away, her fur-mantle opened a little, and the star-dress shone forth. The King clutched the mantle and tore it off. Then her golden hair shone forth, and she stood there in full splendour, and could no longer hide herself. And when she had washed the soot and ashes from her face, she was more beautiful than any one who had ever been seen on earth. But the King said, "Thou art my dear bride, and we will never more part from each other." Thereupon the marriage was solemnized, and they lived happily until their death.

THE WOLF AND THE SEVEN LITTLE KIDS

THERE was once on a time an old goat who had seven little kids, and loved them with all the love of a mother for her children. One day she wanted to go into the forest and fetch some food. So she called all seven to her and said, " Dear children, I have to go into the forest, be on your guard against the wolf; if he come in, he will devour you all—skin, hair and all. The wretch often disguises himself, but you will know him at once by his rough voice and his black feet." The kids said, " Dear mother, we will take good care of ourselves ; you may go away without any anxiety." Then the old one bleated, and went on her way with an easy mind.

It was not long before some one knocked at the house-door and cried, " Open the door, dear children ; your mother is here, and has brought something back with her for each of you." But the little kids knew that it was the wolf, by the rough voice ; " We will not open the door," cried they, " thou art not our mother. She has a soft, pleasant voice but thy voice is rough ; thou art the wolf ! " Then the wolf went away to a shopkeeper and bought himself a great lump of chalk, ate this and made his voice soft with it. Then he came back, knocked at the door of the house, and cried, " Open the door, dear children, your mother is here and has brought something back with her for each of you." But the wolf had laid his black paws against the window, and the children saw them and cried, " We will not open the door, our mother has not black feet like thee : thou art the wolf ! " Then the wolf ran to a baker and said, " I have hurt my feet, rub some dough over them for me." And when the baker had rubbed his feet over, he ran to the miller and said, " Strew some white meal over my feet for me." The miller thought to himself, " The wolf wants to deceive some one," and refused ; but the wolf said, " If thou wilt not do it, I will devour thee." Then the miller was afraid, and made his paws white for him. Truly, men are like that.

So now the wretch went for the third time to the house-door, knocked at it and said, " Open the door for me, children, your dear little mother has come home, and has brought every one of you something back from the forest with her." The little kids cried,

" First show us thy paws that we may know if thou art our dear little mother." Then he put his paws in through the window, and when the kids saw that they were white, they believed that all he said was true, and opened the door. But who should come in but the wolf! They were terrified and wanted to hide themselves. One sprang under the table, the second into the bed, the third into the stove, the fourth into the kitchen, the fifth into the cupboard, the sixth under the washing-bowl, and the seventh into the clock-case. But the wolf found them all, and used no great ceremony ; one after the other he swallowed them down his throat. The youngest in the clock-case was the only one he did not find. When the wolf had satisfied his appetite he took himself off, laid himself down under a tree in the green meadow outside, and began to sleep. Soon afterwards the old goat came home again from the forest. Ah ! what a sight she saw there ! The house-door stood wide open. The table, chairs, and benches were thrown down, the washing-bowl lay broken to pieces, and the quilts and pillows were pulled off the bed. She sought her children, but they were nowhere to be found. She called them one after another by name, but no one answered. At last, when she came to the youngest, a soft voice cried, " Dear mother, I am in the clock-case." She took the kid out, and it told her that the wolf had come and had eaten all the others. Then you may imagine how she wept over her poor children.

At length in her grief she went out, and the youngest kid ran with her. When they came to the meadow, there lay the wolf by the tree and snored so loud that the branches shook. She looked at him on every side and saw that something was moving and struggling in his gorged body. " Ah, heavens," said she, " is it possible that my poor children whom he has swallowed down for his supper, can be still alive ? " Then the kid had to run home and fetch scissors, and a needle and thread, and the goat cut open the monster's stomach, and hardly had she made one cut, than one little kid thrust its head out, and when she had cut farther, all six sprang out one after another, and were all still alive, and had suffered no injury whatever, for in his greediness the monster had swallowed them down whole. What rejoicing there was ! Then they embraced their dear mother, and jumped like a tailor at his wedding. The mother, however, said, " Now go and look

for some big stones, and we will fill the wicked beast's stomach with them while he is still asleep." Then the seven kids dragged the stones thither with all speed, and put as many of them into his stomach as they could get in ; and the mother sewed him up again in the greatest haste, so that he was not aware of anything and never once stirred.

When the wolf at length had had his sleep out, he got on his legs, and as the stones in his stomach made him very thirsty, he wanted to go to a well to drink. But when he began to walk and to move about the stones in his stomach knocked against each other and rattled. Then cried he,

> " What rumbles and tumbles
> Against my poor bones ?
> Not little kids, I think,
> But only big stones."

And when he got to the well and stooped over the water and was just about to drink, the heavy stones made him fall in and there was no help, but he had to drown miserably. When the seven kids saw that, they came running to the spot and cried aloud, " The wolf is dead ! The wolf is dead ! " and danced for joy round about the well with their mother.

BROTHER AND SISTER

LITTLE brother took his little sister by the hand and said, " Since our mother died we have had no happiness ; our step-mother beats us every day, and if we come near her she kicks us away with her foot. Our meals are the hard crusts of bread that are left over ; and the little dog under the table is better off, for she often throws it a nice bit. May Heaven pity us. If our mother only knew ! Come, we will go forth together into the wide world."

They walked the whole day over meadows, fields, and stony places ; and when it rained the little sister said, " Heaven and our hearts are weeping together." In the evening they came to a large forest, and they were so weary with sorrow and hunger and the long walk, that they lay down in a hollow tree and fell asleep.

The next day when they awoke, the sun was already high in the sky, and shone down hot into the tree. Then the brother said, " Sister, I am thirsty ; if I knew of a little brook I would go and just take a drink ; I think I hear one running." The brother got up and took the little sister by the hand, and they set off to find the brook.

But the wicked step-mother was a witch, and had seen how the two children had gone away, and had crept after them privily, as witches do creep, and had bewitched all the brooks in the forest.

Now when they found a little brook leaping brightly over the stones, the brother was going to drink out of it, but the sister heard how it said as it ran, " Who drinks of me will be a tiger ; who drinks of me will be a tiger." Then the sister cried, " Pray, dear brother, do not drink, or you will become a wild beast, and tear me to pieces." The brother did not drink, although he was so thirsty, but said, " I will wait for the next spring."

When they came to the next brook the sister heard this also say, " Who drinks of me will be a wolf ; who drinks of me will be a wolf." Then the sister cried out, " Pray, dear brother, do not drink, or you will become a wolf, and devour me." The brother did not drink, and said, " I will wait until we come to the next spring, but then I must drink, say what you like ; for my thirst is too great."

And when they came to the third brook the sister heard how it said as it ran, " Who drinks of me will be a roebuck ; who drinks of me will be a roebuck." The sister said, " Oh, I pray you, dear brother, do not drink, or you will become a roebuck, and run away from me." But the brother had knelt down at once by the brook, and had bent down and drunk some of the water, and as soon as the first drops touched his lips he lay there a young roebuck.

And now the sister wept over her poor bewitched brother, and the little roe wept also, and sat sorrowfully near to her. But at last the girl said, " Be quiet, dear little roe, I will never, never leave you."

Then she untied her golden garter and put it round the roebuck's neck, and she plucked rushes and wove them into a soft cord. With this she tied the little beast and led it on, and she walked deeper and deeper into the forest.

And when they had gone a very long way they came at last to a little house, and the girl looked in ; and as it was empty, she thought,

" We can stay here and live." Then she sought for leaves and moss to make a soft bed for the roe ; and every morning she went out and gathered roots and berries and nuts for herself, and brought tender grass for the roe, who ate out of her hand, and was content and played round about her. In the evening, when the sister was tired, and had said her prayer, she laid her head upon the roebuck's back : that was her pillow, and she slept softly on it. And if only the brother had had his human form it would have been a delightful life.

For some time they were alone like this in the wilderness. But it happened that the King of the country held a great hunt in the forest. Then the blasts of the horns, the barking of dogs, and the merry shouts of the huntsmen rang through the trees, and the roebuck heard all, and was only too anxious to be there. " Oh," said he to his sister, " let me be off to the hunt, I cannot bear it any longer ; " and he begged so much that at last she agreed. " But," said she to him, " come back to me in the evening ; I must shut my door for fear of the rough huntsmen, so knock and say, ' My little sister, let me in ! ' that I may know you ; and if you do not say that, I shall not open the door." Then the young roebuck sprang away ; so happy was he and so merry in the open air.

The King and the huntsmen saw the pretty creature, and started after him, but they could not catch him and when they thought that they surely had him, away he sprang through the bushes and could not be seen. When it was dark he ran to the cottage, knocked, and said, " My little sister, let me in." Then the door was opened for him, and he jumped in, and rested himself the whole might through upon his soft bed.

The next day the hunt went on afresh, and when the roebuck again heard the bugle-horn, and the ho ! ho ! of the huntsmen, he had no peace, but said, " Sister, let me out, I must be off." His sister opened the door for him, and said, " But you must be here again in the evening and say your pass-word."

When the King and his huntsmen again saw the young roebuck with the golden collar, they all chased him, but he was too quick and nimble for them. This went on for the whole day, but at last by the evening the huntsmen had surrounded him, and one of them wounded him a little in the foot, so that he limped and ran slowly. Then a

hunter crept after him to the cottage and heard how he said, " My little
sister, let me in," and saw that the door was opened for him, and was
shut again at once. The huntsman took notice of it all, and went to
the King and told him what he had seen and heard. Then the King
said, " To-morrow we will hunt once more."

The little sister, however, was dreadfully frightened when she saw
that her fawn was hurt. She washed the blood off him, laid herbs
on the wound, and said, " Go to your bed, dear roe, that you may get
well again." But the wound was so slight that the roebuck, next
morning, did not feel it any more. And when he again heard the
sport outside, he said, " I cannot bear it, I must be there ; they shall
not find it so easy to catch me." The sister cried, and said, " This
time they will kill you, and here am I alone in the forest and forsaken
by all the world. I will not let you out." " Then you will have me
die of grief," answered the roe ; " when I hear the bugle-horns I feel

as if I must jump out of my skin." Then the sister could not do other-wise, but opened the door for him with a heavy heart, and the roebuck, full of health and joy, bounded into the forest.

When the King saw him, he said to his huntsmen, " Now chase him all day long till night-fall, but take care that no one does him any harm."

As soon as the sun had set, the King said to the huntsmen, " Now come and show me the cottage in the wood ; " and when he was at the door, he knocked and called out, " Dear little sister, let me in." Then the door opened, and the King walked in, and there stood a maiden more lovely than any he had ever seen. The maiden was frightened when she saw, not her little roe, but a man come in who wore a golden crown upon his head. But the King looked kindly at her, stretched out his hand, and said, " Will you go with me to my palace and be my dear wife ? " " Yes, indeed," answered the maiden, " but the little roe must go with me, I cannot leave him." The King said, " It shall stay with you as long as you live, and shall want nothing." Just then he came running in, and the sister again tied him with the cord of rushes, took it in her own hand, and went away with the King from the cottage.

The King took the lovely maiden upon his horse and carried her to his palace, where the wedding was held with great pomp. She was now the Queen, and they lived for a long time happily together ; the roebuck was tended and cherished, and ran about in the palace-garden.

But the wicked step-mother, because of whom the children had gone out into the world, thought all the time that the sister had been torn to pieces by the wild beasts in the wood, and that the brother had been shot for a roebuck by the huntsmen. Now when she heard that they were so happy, and so well off, envy and hatred rose in her heart and left her no peace, and she thought of nothing but how she could bring them again to misfortune. Her own daughter, who was as ugly as night, and had only one eye, grumbled at her and said, " A Queen ! that ought to have been my luck." " Only be quiet," answered the old woman, and comforted her by saying, " when the time comes I shall be ready."

As time went on, the Queen had a pretty little boy, and it happened that the King was out hunting ; so the old witch took the form of the chamber-maid, went into the room where the Queen lay, and said to her, " Come, the bath is ready ; it will do you good, and give you fresh strength ; make haste before it gets cold."

The daughter also was close by ; so they carried the weakly Queen into the bath-room, and put her into the bath ; then they shut the door and ran away. But in the bath-room they had made a fire of such deadly heat that the beautiful young Queen was soon suffocated.

When this was done the old woman took her daughter, put a night-cap on her head, and laid her in bed in place of the Queen. She gave her too the shape and the look of the Queen, only she could not make good the lost eye. But in order that the King might not see it, she was to lie on the side on which she had no eye.

In the evening when he came home and heard that he had a son he was heartily glad, and was going to the bed of his dear wife to see how she was. But the old woman quickly called out, " For your life leave the curtains closed ; the Queen ought not to see the light yet, and must have rest." The King went away, and did not find out that a false Queen was lying in the bed.

But at midnight, when all slept, the nurse, who was sitting in the nursery by the cradle, and who was the only person awake, saw the door open and the true Queen walk in. She took the child out of the cradle, laid it on her arm, and nursed it. Then she shook up its pillow, laid the child down again, and covered it with the little quilt. And she did not forget the roebuck, but went into the corner where it lay, and stroked its back. Then she went quite silently out of the door again. The next morning the nurse asked the guards whether any one had come into the palace during the night, but they answered, " No, we have seen no one."

She came thus many nights and never spoke a word : the nurse always saw her, but she did not dare to tell any one about it.

When some time had passed in this manner, the Queen began to speak in the night, and said—

> " *How fares my child ? how fares my deer ?*
> *O twice more only shall I come here.*"

The nurse did not answer, but when the Queen had gone again, went to the King and told him all. The King said, " Ah, heavens ! what is this ? To-morrow night I will watch by the child." In the evening he went into the nursery, and at midnight the Queen again appeared and said—

" *How fares my child ? how fares my deer ?*
O once more only shall I come here."

And she nursed the child as she wont to do before she disappeared. The King dared not speak to her, but on the next night he watched again. Then she said—

" *How fares my child ? how fares my deer ?*
O never again shall I come here."

Then the King could not restrain himself ; he sprang towards her, and said, " You can be none other than my dear wife." She answered, " Yes, I am your dear wife," and at the same moment she received life again, and by God's grace became fresh, rosy, and full of health.

Then she told the King the evil deed which the wicked witch and her daughter had been guilty of towards her. The King ordered both to be led before the judge, and judgment was delivered against them. The daughter was taken into the forest where she was torn to pieces by wild beasts, but the witch was cast into the fire and miserably burnt. And as soon as she was burnt the roebuck changed his shape, and received his human form again, so the sister and brother lived happily together all their lives.

THE TURNIP

THERE were once two brothers who both served as soldiers ; one of them was rich, and the other poor. Then the poor one, to escape from his poverty, put off his soldier's coat, and turned farmer. He dug and hoed his bit of land, and sowed it with turnip-seed. The seed came up, and one turnip grew there which became large and vigorous, and visibly grew bigger and bigger, and seemed as if it would never stop growing, so that it might have been called the princess of turnips, for never was such an one seen before, and never will such an one be seen again.

At length it was so enormous that by itself it filled a whole cart, and two oxen were required to draw it, and the farmer had not the least idea what he was to do with the turnip or whether it would be a fortune to him or a misfortune. At last he thought, "If thou sellest it, what wilt thou get for it that is of any importance, and if thou eatest it thyself, why the small turnips would do thee just as much good; it would be better to take it to the King, and make him a present of it."

So he placed it on a cart, harnessed two oxen, took it to the palace, and presented it to the King. "What strange thing is this?" said the King. "Many wonderful things have come before my eyes, but never such a monster as this! From what seed can this have sprung, or are you a luck-child and have met with it by chance?" "Ah, no!" said the farmer, "no luck-child am I. I am a poor soldier, who because he could no longer support himself hung his soldier's coat on a nail and took to farming land. I have a brother who is rich and well known to you, Lord King, but I, because I have nothing, am forgotten by every one."

Then the King felt compassion for him, and said, "Thou shalt be raised from thy poverty, and shalt have such gifts from me that thou shalt be equal to thy rich brother." Then he bestowed on him much gold, and lands, and meadows, and herds, and made him immensely rich, so that the wealth of the other brother could not be compared with his. When the rich brother heard what the poor one had gained for himself with one single turnip, he envied him, and thought in every way how he also could get hold of a similar piece of luck. He would, however, set about it in a much wiser way, and took gold and horses and carried them to the King, and made certain the King would give him a much larger present in return. If his brother had got so much for one turnip, what would he not carry away with him in return for such beautiful things as these? The King accepted his present, and said he had nothing to give him in return that was more rare and excellent than the great turnip. So the rich man was obliged to put his brother's turnip in a cart and have it taken to his home. When there he did not know on whom to vent his rage and anger, until bad thoughts came to him, and he resolved to kill his brother. He hired murderers, who were to lie in ambush, and then he went to his brother and said, "Dear brother, I know of a hidden treasure, we will dig it up together, and divide it between us." The other agreed to this, and accompanied him without suspicion. While they were on their way, however, the murderers fell on him, bound him, and would have hanged him to a tree. But just as they were doing this, loud singing and the sound of a horse's feet were heard in the distance. On this their hearts were filled with terror, and they pushed their prisoner head first into the sack, hung it on a branch, and took to flight. He, however, worked up there until he had made a hole in the sack through which he could put his head. The man who was coming by was no other than a travelling student, a young fellow who rode on his way through the wood joyously singing his song. When he who was aloft saw that some one was passing below him, he cried, " Good day ! You have come at a lucky time." The student looked round on every side, but did not know whence the voice came. At last he said, " Who calls me ? " Then an answer came from the top of the tree, " Raise your eyes ; here I sit aloft in the Sack of Wisdom. In a short time have I learnt great things ; compared with this all schools are a jest ; in a very short time I shall have learnt everything, and shall descend wiser than all other men. I understand the stars, and the signs of the zodiac, and the tracks of the winds, the sand of the sea, the healing of illness, and the virtues of all herbs, birds, and stones. If you were once within it you would feel what noble things issue forth from the Sack of Knowledge."

The student, when he heard all this, was astonished, and said, " Blessed be the hour in which I have found thee ! May not I also enter the sack for a while ? " He in the sack replied as if unwillingly, " For a short time I will let you get into it, if you reward me and give me good words : but you must wait an hour longer, for one thing remains which I must learn before I do it." When the student had waited a while he became impatient, and begged to be allowed to get in at once, his thirst for knowledge was so very great. So he who was above pretended at last to yield, and said, " In order that I may come forth from the house of knowledge you must let it down by the rope, and then you shall enter it." So the student let the sack down, untied it, and set him free, and then cried, " Now draw me up at once," and was about to get into the sack. " Stop ! " said the other, " that won't do," and took him by the head and put him upside down into the sack, fastened it, and drew the disciple of wisdom up the tree by the rope. Then he swung him in the air and said, " How goes it

with thee, my dear fellow? Behold, already thou feelest wisdom coming, and art gaining valuable experience. Keep perfectly quiet until thou becomest wiser." Thereupon he mounted the student's horse and rode away, but in an hour's time sent some one to let the student out again.

THE PEASANT'S WISE DAUGHTER

THERE was once a poor peasant who had no land, but only a small house, and one daughter. Then said the daughter, " We ought to ask our lord the King for a bit of newly-cleared land." When the King heard of their poverty, he presented them with a bit of land, which she and her father dug up, and intended to sow with a little corn and grain of that kind. When they had dug nearly the whole of the field, they found in the earth a mortar made of pure gold. " Listen," said the father to the girl, " as our lord the King has been so gracious and presented us with the field, we ought to give him this mortar in return for it." The daughter, however, would not consent to this, and said, " Father, if we give the mortar without having the pestle as well, we shall have to get the pestle, so you had much better say nothing about it." He would not, however, obey her, but took the mortar and carried it to the King, said that he had found it in the cleared land, and asked if he would accept it as a present. The King took the mortar, and asked if he had found nothing besides that? " No," answered the countryman. Then the King said that he must now bring him the pestle. The peasant said they had not found that, but he might just as well have spoken to the wind ; he was put in prison, and was to stay there until he produced the pestle. The servants had daily to carry him bread and water, which is what people get in prison, and they heard how the man cried out continually, " Ah ! if I had but listened to

my daughter! Alas, alas, if I had but listened to my daughter!"
Then the servants went to the King and told him how the prisoner was
always crying, " Ah! if I had but listened to my daughter!" and
would neither eat nor drink. So he commanded the servants to bring
the prisoner before him, and then the King asked the peasant why
he was always crying, " Ah! if I had but listened to my daughter!"
and what it was that his daughter had said. " She told me that I
ought not to take the mortar to you, for I should have to produce the
pestle as well." " If you have a daughter who is as wise as that, let
her come here." She was therefore obliged to appear before the
King, who asked her if she really was so wise, and said he would set
her a riddle, and if she could guess that, he would marry her. She at
once said yes, she would guess it. Then said the King, " Come to me
not clothed, not naked, not riding, not walking, not in the road, and
not out of the road, and if thou canst do that I will marry thee." So
she went away, put off everything she had on, and then she was not
clothed, and took a great fishing net, and seated herself in it and
wrapped it entirely round and round her, and then she was not naked,
and she hired an ass, and tied the fisherman's net to its tail, so that it
was forced to drag her along, and that was neither riding nor walking.
The ass had also to drag her in the ruts, so that she only touched the
ground with her great toe, and that was neither being in the road nor
out of the road. And when she arrived in that fashion, the King
said she had guessed the riddle and fulfilled all the conditions. Then
he ordered her father to be released from the prison, took her to wife,
and gave into her care all the royal possessions.

Now when some years had passed, the King was once drawing up
his troops on parade, when it happened that some peasants who had
been selling wood stopped with their waggons before the palace ; some
of them had oxen yoked to them, and some horses. There was one
peasant who had three mares, one of them that day had had a young
foal, and it ran away and lay down between two oxen which were in
front of the waggon. When the peasants came together, they began
to dispute, to beat each other and make a disturbance, and the peasant
with the oxen wanted to keep the foal, and said one of the oxen had
given birth to it, and the other said his mare had had it, and that it was
his. The quarrel came before the King, and he gave the verdict that

the foal should stay where it had been found, and so the peasant with the oxen, to whom it did not belong, got it. Then the other went away, and wept and lamented over his foal. Now he had heard how gracious his lady the Queen was because she herself had sprung from poor peasant folks, so he went to her and begged her to see if she could not help him to get his foal back again. Said she, " Yes, I will tell thee what to do, if thou wilt promise me not to betray me. Early to-morrow morning, when the King parades the guard, place thyself there in the middle of the road by which he must pass, take a great fishing-net and pretend to be fishing ; go on fishing too, and empty out the net as if thou hadst got it full "—and then she told him also what he was to say if he was questioned by the King. The next day, therefore, the peasant stood there, and fished on dry ground. When the King passed by, and saw that, he sent his messenger to ask what the stupid man was about ? He answered, " I am fishing." The messenger asked how he could fish when there was no water whatever there ? The peasant said, " It is as easy for me to fish on dry land as it is for an ox to have a foal." The messenger went back and took the answer to the King, who ordered the peasant to be brought to him and told him that this was not his own idea, and he wanted to know whose it was ? The peasant must confess that at once. The peasant, however, would not do so, and said always, God forbid he should ! the idea was his own. They laid him, however, on a heap of straw, and beat him and questioned him so long that at last he admitted that he had got the idea from the Queen.

When the King reached home again, he said to his wife, " Why hast thou behaved so falsely to me ? I will not have thee any longer for a wife ; thy time is up, go back to the place from whence thou camest—to thy peasant's hut." One favour, however, he granted her ; she might take with her the one thing that was dearest and best in her eyes ; and thus was she dismissed. She said, " Yes, my dear husband, if you command this, I will do it," and she embraced him and kissed him, and said she would take leave of him. Then she ordered a powerful sleeping draught to be brought, to drink farewell to him ; the King took a long draught, but she took only a little. He soon fell into a deep sleep, and when she perceived that, she called a servant and took a fair white linen cloth and wrapped the King in it, and the servant was forced to carry him into a carriage that stood before the door, and she drove with him to her own little house. She laid him in her own little bed, and he slept one day and one night without awakening, and when he awoke he looked round and said, " Well-a-day, where am I ? " He called his attendants, but none of them were there. At length his wife came to his bedside and said, " My dear lord and King, you told me I might bring away with me from the palace that which was dearest and most precious in my eyes—I have nothing more precious and dear than yourself, so I have brought you with me." Tears rose to the King's eyes and he said, " Dear wife, thou shalt be mine and I will be thine," and he took her back with him to the royal palace and was married again to her, and at the present time they are very likely still living.

JORINDA AND JORINGEL

THERE was once an old castle in the midst of a large and thick forest, and in it an old woman who was a witch dwelt all alone. In the day-time she changed herself into a cat or a screech-owl, but in the evening she took her proper shape again as a human being. She could lure wild beasts and birds to her, and then she killed and boiled and roasted them. If any one came within one hundred paces of the castle he was obliged to stand still, and could not stir from the place until she bade him be free. But whenever an innocent maiden came within this circle, she changed her into a bird, and shut her up in a wicker-work cage, and carried the cage into a room in the castle. She had about seven thousand cages of rare birds in the castle.

Now, there was once a maiden who was called Jorinda, who was fairer than all other girls. She and a handsome youth named Joringel had promised to marry each other. They were still in the days of betrothal, and their greatest happiness was being together. One day in order that they might be able to talk together in quiet they went for a walk in the forest. " Take care," said Joringel, " that you do not go too near the castle."

It was a beautiful evening ; the sun shone brightly between the trunks of the trees into the dark green of the forest, and the turtle-doves sang mournfully upon the young boughs of the birch-trees.

Jorinda wept now and then : she sat down in the sunshine and was sorrowful. Joringel was sorrowful too ; they were as sad as if they were about to die. Then they looked around them, and were quite at a loss, for they did not know by which way they should go home. The sun was still half above the mountain and half set.

Joringel looked through the bushes, and saw the old walls of the castle close at hand. He was horror-stricken and filled with deadly fear. Jorinda was singing—

> " *My little bird, with the necklace red,*
> *Sings sorrow, sorrow, sorrow,*
> *He sings that the dove must soon be dead,*
> *Sings sorrow, sor—— jug, jug, jug.*"

Joringel looked for Jorinda. She was changed into a nightingale, and sang " jug, jug, jug." A screech-owl with glowing eyes flew three times round about her, and three times cried " to-whoo, to-whoo, to-whoo ! "

Joringel could not move : he stood there like a stone, and could neither weep nor speak, nor move hand or foot.

The sun had now set. The owl flew into the thicket, and directly afterwards there came out of it a crooked old woman, yellow and lean, with large red eyes and a hooked nose, the point of which reached to her chin. She caught the nightingale, and took it away in her hand, muttering :

> *Till the prisoner's fast,*
> *And her doom is cast,*

128

There stay, O stay!
When the charm is round her
And the spell has bound her,
Hie away, away!

Joringel could neither speak nor move from the spot ; the nightingale was gone. At last the woman came back, and said in a hollow voice, " Greet thee, Zachiel. If the moon shines on the cage, Zachiel, let him loose at once." Then Joringel was freed. He fell on his knees before the woman and begged that she would give him back his Jorinda, but she said that he should never have her again, and went away. He called, he wept, he lamented, but all in vain, " Ah, what is to become of me ? "

Joringel went away, and at last came to a strange village ; there he kept sheep for a long time. He often walked round and round the castle, but not too near to it. At last he dreamt one night that he found a star-blue flower, in the middle of which was a beautiful large pearl ; that he picked the flower and went with it to the castle, and that everything he touched with the flower was freed from enchantment ; he also dreamt that by means of it he recovered his Jorinda.

In the morning, when he woke, he began to seek over hill and dale if he could find such a flower. He sought until the ninth day, and then, early in the morning, he found the star-blue flower. In the middle of it there was a large dew-drop, as big as the finest pearl.

Day and night he journeyed with this flower to the castle. When he was within a hundred paces of it he was not held fast, but walked on to the door. Joringel was full of joy ; he touched the door with the flower, and it sprang open. He walked in through the courtyard, and listened for the sound of the birds. At last he heard it. He went on and found the room from whence it came, and there the witch was feeding the birds in the seven thousand cages.

When she saw Joringel she was angry, very angry, and scolded at him, but she could not come within two paces of him. He did not take any notice of her, but went and looked at the cages with the birds ; but there were many hundred nightingales, how was he to find his Jorinda again ?

Just then he saw the old woman quietly take away a cage with a bird in it, and go towards the door.

Swiftly he sprang towards her, touched the cage with the flower, and also the old woman. She could now no longer bewitch any one ;

and Jorinda was standing there, clasping him round the neck, and she was as beautiful as ever!

THE SHOES THAT WERE DANCED TO PIECES

THERE was once upon a time a King who had twelve daughters, each one more beautiful than the other. They all slept together in one chamber, in which their beds stood side by side, and every night when they were in them the King locked the door, and bolted it. But in the morning when he unlocked the door, he saw that their shoes were worn out with dancing, and no one could find out how that had come to pass. Then the King caused it to be proclaimed that whosoever could discover where they danced at night, should choose one of them for his wife and be King after his death, but that whosoever came forward and had not discovered it within three days and nights, should have forfeited his life. It was not long before a King's son presented himself, and offered to undertake the enterprise. He was well received, and in the evening was led into a room adjoining the princesses' sleeping-chamber. His bed was placed there, and he was to observe where they went and danced, and in order that they might do nothing secretly or go away to some other place, the door of their room was left open.

But the eyelids of the prince grew heavy as lead, and he fell asleep, and when he awoke in the morning, all twelve had been to the dance, for their shoes were standing there with holes in the soles. On the second and third nights it fell out just the same, and then his head was struck off without mercy. Many others came after this and undertook the enterprise, but all forfeited their lives. Now it came to pass that a poor solider, who had a wound, and could serve no longer, found himself on the road to the town where the King lived. There he met an old woman, who asked him where he was going. " I hardly know myself," answered he, and added in jest, " I had half a mind to discover where the princesses danced their shoes into holes, and thus become King." " That is not so difficult," said the old woman, " you must not drink the wine which will be brought to you at night, and must pretend to be sound asleep." With that she gave him a little cloak, and said, " If you put on that, you will be invisible, and then you can steal after the twelve." When the soldier had received this good advice, he went into the thing in earnest, took heart, went to the King, and announced himself as a suitor. He was as well received as the others, and royal garments were put upon him. He was conducted that evening at bed-time into the ante-chamber, and as he was about to go to bed, the eldest came and brought him a cup of wine, but he had tied a sponge under this chin, and let the wine run down into it, without drinking a drop. Then he lay down and when he had lain a while, he began to snore, as if in the deepest sleep. The twelve princesses heard that, and laughed, and the eldest said, " He, too, might as well have saved his life." With that they got up, opened wardrobes, presses, cupboards, and brought out pretty dresses ; dressed themselves before the mirrors, sprang about, and rejoiced at the prospect of the dance. Only the youngest said, " I know not how it is ; you are very happy, but I feel very strange ; some misfor- tune is certainly about to befall us." " Thou art a goose, who art always frightened," said the eldest. " Hast thou forgotten how many Kings' sons have already come here in vain ? I had hardly any need to give the soldier a sleeping-draught, in any case the clown would not have awakened." When they were all ready they looked carefully at the soldier, but he had closed his eyes and did not move or stir, so they felt themselves quite secure. The eldest then went to her bed and tapped it ; it immediately sank into the earth, and one after the other they descended through the opening, the eldest going first. The soldier, who had watched everything, tarried no longer, put on his little cloak, and went down last with the youngest. Half-way down the steps, he just trod a little on her dress ; she was terrified at that, and cried out, " What is that ? who is pulling at my dress ? " " Don't be so silly ! " said the eldest, " you have caught it on a nail." Then they went all the way down, and when they were at the bottom, they were standing in a wonderfully pretty avenue of trees, all the leaves of which were of silver and shone and glistened. The soldier thought, " I must carry a token away with me," and broke off a twig from one of them, on which the tree cracked with a loud report. The youngest cried out again, " Something is wrong, did you hear the crack ? " But the eldest said, " It is a gun fired for joy, because we have got rid of our prince so quickly." After that they came into an avenue where all the leaves were of gold, and lastly into a third where they were of bright diamonds ; he broke off a twig from each, which made such a crack each time that the youngest started back in terror, but the eldest still maintained that they were salutes. They went on and came to a great lake whereon stood twelve little boats, and in every boat sat a handsome prince, all of whom were waiting for the twelve, and each took one of them with him, but the soldier seated himself by the youngest. Then her prince said, " I can't tell why the boat is so much heavier to-day ; I shall have to row with all my strength, if I am to get it across." " What should cause that," said the youngest, " but the warm weather ? I feel very warm too." On the opposite side of the lake stood a splendid, brightly-lit castle, from whence resounded the joyous music of trumpets and kettle-drums. They rowed over there, entered, and each prince danced with the girl he loved, but the soldier danced with them unseen, and when one of them had a cup of wine in her hand he drank it up, so that the cup was empty when she carried it to her mouth ; the youngest was alarmed at this, but the eldest always made her be silent. They danced there till three o'clock in the morning when all the shoes were danced into holes, and they were forced to leave off ; the princes rowed them back again over the lake, and this time the soldier seated himself by the eldest. On the shore they took leave of their princes, and promised to return the following night. When they reached the stairs the soldier ran on in front and lay down in his bed, and when the twelve had come up slowly and wearily, he was already snoring so loudly that they could all hear him, and they said, " So far as he is concerned, we are safe." They took off their beautiful dresses, laid them away, put the worn-out shoes under the bed, and lay down. Next morning the soldier was resolved not to speak, but to watch the wonderful goings on, and again went with them. Then everything was done just as it had been done the first time, and each time they danced until their shoes were worn to pieces. But the third time he took a cup away with him as a token. When the hour had arrived for him to give his answer, he took the three twigs and the cup, and went to the King, but the twelve stood behind the door, and listened for what he was going to say. When the King put the question. " Where have my twelve daughters danced their shoes to pieces in the night ? " he answered, " In an underground castle with twelve princes," and related how it had come to pass, and brought out the tokens. The King then summoned his daughters, and asked them if the soldier had told the truth, and when they saw that they were betrayed, and that falsehood would be of no avail, they were obliged to confess all. Thereupon the King asked which of them he would have to wife? He answered, " I am no longer young, so give me the eldest." Then the wedding was celebrated on the self-same day, and the kingdom was promised him after the King's death. But the princes were bewitched for as many days as they had danced nights with the twelve.

HANS IN LUCK

HANS had served his master for seven years, so he said to him, " Master, my time is up ; now I should be glad to go back home to my mother ; give me my wages." The master answered, " You have served me faithfully and honestly ; as the service was so shall the reward be ; " and he gave Hans a piece of gold as big as his head. Hans pulled his handkerchief out of his pocket, wrapped up the lump in it, put it on his shoulder, and set out on the way home.

As he went on, always putting one foot before the other, he saw a horseman trotting quickly and merrily by on a lively horse. " Ah ! " said Hans quite loud, " what a fine thing it is to ride ! There you sit as on a chair ; you stumble over no stones, you save your shoes, and get on, you don't know how."

The rider, who had heard him, stopped and called out, " Hollo ! Hans, why do you go on foot, then ? "

"I must," answered he, "for I have this lump to carry home; it is true that it is gold, but I cannot hold my head straight for it, and it hurts my shoulder."

"I will tell you what," said the rider, "we will exchange: I will give you my horse, and you can give me your lump."

"With all my heart," said Hans, "but I can tell you, you will have to crawl along with it."

The rider got down, took the gold, and helped Hans up; then gave him the bridle tight in his hands and said, "If you want to go at a really good pace, you must click your tongue and call out, 'Jup! Jup!'"

Hans was heartily delighted as he sat upon the horse and rode away so bold and free. After a little while he thought that it ought to go faster, and he began to click with his tongue and call out, "Jup! Jup!" The horse put himself into a sharp trot, and before Hans knew where he was, he was thrown off and lying in a ditch which separated the field from the highway. The horse would have gone off too if it had not been stopped by a countryman, who was coming along the road and driving a cow before him.

Hans got his limbs together and stood up on his legs again, but he was vexed, and said to the countryman, "It is a poor joke, this riding, especially when one gets hold of a mare like this, that kicks and throws one off, so that one has a chance of breaking one's neck. Never again will I mount it. Now I like your cow, for one can walk quietly behind her, and have, over and above, one's milk, butter and cheese every day without fail. What would I not give to have such a cow." " Well," said the countryman, " if it would give you so much pleasure, I do not mind giving the cow for the horse." Hans agreed with the greatest delight ; the countryman jumped upon the horse, and rode quickly away.

Hans drove his cow quietly before him, and thought over his lucky bargain. " If only I have a morsel of bread—and that can hardly fail me—I can eat butter and cheese with it as often as I like ; if I am thirsty, I can milk my cow and drink the milk. Good heart, what more can I want ? "

When he came to an inn he made a halt, and in his great content ate up what he had with him—his dinner and supper—and all he had, and with his last few farthings had half a glass of beer. Then he drove his cow onwards along the road to his mother's village.

As it drew nearer mid-day, the heat was more oppressive, and Hans found himself upon a moor which it took about an hour to cross. He felt it very hot and his tongue clave to the roof of his mouth with thirst. " I can find a cure for this," thought Hans ; " I will milk the cow now and refresh myself with the milk." He tied her to a withered tree, and as he had no pail he put his leather cap underneath ; but try as he would, not a drop of milk came. And as he set himself to work in a clumsy way, the impatient beast at last gave him such a blow on his head with its hind foot, that he fell on the ground, and for a long time could not think where he was.

By good fortune a butcher just then came along the road with a wheel-barrow, in which lay a young pig. " What sort of a trick is this ? " cried he, and helped the good Hans up. Hans told him what had happened. The butcher gave him his flask and said, " Take a drink and refresh yourself. The cow will certainly give no milk, it is an old beast ; at the best it is only fit for the plough, or for the butcher." " Well, well," said Hans, as he stroked his hair down on his head, " who would have thought it ? Certainly it is a fine thing when one can kill a beast like that at home ; what meat one has ! But I do not care much for beef, it is not juicy enough for me. A young pig like that now is the thing to have ; it tastes quite different ; and then there are the sausages ! "

"Hark ye, Hans," said the butcher, " out of love for you I will exchange, and will let you have the pig for the cow." " Heaven repay you for your kindness ! " said Hans as he gave up the cow, whilst the pig was unbound from the barrow, and the cord by which it was tied was put in his hand.

Hans went on, and thought to himself how everything was going just as he wished ; if he did meet with any vexation it was immediately set right. Presently there joined him a lad who was carrying a fine white goose under his arm. They said good morning to each other, and Hans began to tell of his good luck, and how he had always made such good bargains. The boy told him that he was taking the goose to a christening-feast. " Just lift her," added he, and laid hold of her by the wings ; " how heavy she is—she has been fattened up for the last eight weeks. Whoever has a bit of her when she is roasted will have to wipe the fat from both sides of his mouth." " Yes," said Hans, as he weighed her in one hand, " she is a good weight, but my pig is no bad one."

Meanwhile the lad looked suspiciously from one side to the other, and shook his head. " Look here," he said at length, " it may not be all right with your pig. In the village through which I passed, the Mayor himself had just had one stolen out of its sty. I fear—I fear that you have got hold of it there. They have sent out some people and it would be a bad business if they caught you with the pig ; at the very least, you would be shut up in the dark hole."

The good Hans was terrified. " Goodness ! " he said, " help me out of this fix ; you know more about this place than I do, take my pig and leave me your goose." " I shall risk something at that game," answered the lad, " but I will not be the cause of your getting into trouble." So he took the cord in his hand, and drove away the pig quickly along a by-path.

The good Hans, free from care, went homewards with the goose under his arm. " When I think over it properly," said he to himself, " I have even gained by the exchange : first there is the good roast-meat, then the quantity of fat which will drip from it, and which will give me dripping for my bread for a quarter of a year, and lastly the beautiful white feathers ; I will have my pillow stuffed with them, and then indeed I shall go to sleep without rocking. How glad my mother will be ! "

As he was going through the last village, there stood a scissors-grinder with his barrow ; as his wheel whirred he sang—

> " *I sharpen scissors and quickly grind,*
> *My coat blows out in the wind behind.*"

Hans stood still and looked at him ; at last he spoke to him and said, " All's well with you, as you are so merry with your grinding." " Yes," answered the scissors-grinder, " the trade has a golden foundation. A real grinder is a man who as often as he puts his hand into his pocket finds gold in it. But where did you buy that fine goose ? "

" I did not buy it, but exchanged my pig for it."

" And the pig ? "

" That I got for a cow."

" And the cow ? "

" I took that instead of a horse."

" And the horse ? "

" For that I gave a lump of gold as big as my head."

" And the gold ? "

" Well, that was my wages for seven years' service."

" You have known how to look after yourself each time," said the grinder. " If you can only get on so far as to hear the money jingle in your pocket whenever you stand up, you will have made your fortune."

" How shall I manage that ? " said Hans. " You must be a grinder, as I am ; nothing particular is wanted for it but a grindstone, the rest finds itself. I have one here ; it is certainly a little worn, but you need not give me anything for it but your goose ; will you do it ? "

" How can you ask ? " answered Hans. " I shall be the luckiest fellow on earth ; if I have money whenever I put my hand in my pocket, what need I trouble about any longer ? " and he handed him the goose and received the grindstone in exchange. " Now," said the grinder, as he took up an ordinary heavy stone that lay by him, " here is a strong stone for you into the bargain ; you can hammer well upon it, and straighten your old nails. Take it with you and keep it carefully."

Hans loaded himself with the stones, and went on with a contented heart; his eyes shone with joy. "I must have been born with a caul," he cried; "everything I want happens to me just as if I were a Sunday-child."

Meanwhile, as he had been on his legs since daybreak, he began to feel tired. Hunger also tormented him, for in his joy at the bargain by which he got the cow he had eaten up all his store of food at once. At last he could only got on with great trouble, and was forced to stop every minute; the stones, too, weighed him down dreadfully. Then he could not help thinking how nice it would be if he had not to carry them just then.

He crept like a snail to a well in a field, and there he thought that he would rest and refresh himself with a cool draught of water, but in order that he might not injure the stones in sitting down, he laid them carefully by his side on the edge of the well. Then he sat down on it, and was about to stoop and drink, when he made a slip, pushed against the stones, and both of them fell into the water. When Hans saw them with his own eyes sinking to the bottom, he jumped for joy, and then knelt down, and with tears in his eyes thanked God for having shown him this favour also, and delivered him in so good a way, and without his having any need to reproach himself, from those heavy stones which had been the only things that troubled him.

"There is no man under the sun so fortunate as I," he cried out. With a light heart and free from every burden he now ran on until he was with his mother at home.

THE GOOSE-GIRL

THERE was once upon a time an old Queen whose husband had been dead for many years, and she had a beautiful daughter. When the princess grew up she was betrothed to a prince who lived at a great distance. When the time came for her to be married, and she had to journey forth into the distant kingdom, the aged Queen packed up for her many costly vessels of silver and gold, and trinkets also of gold and silver ; and cups and jewels, in short, everything which appertained to a royal dowry, for she loved her child with all her heart. She likewise sent her maid in waiting, who was to ride with her, and hand her over to the bridegroom, and each had a horse for the journey, but the horse of the King's daughter was called Falada, and could speak. So when the hour of parting had come, the aged mother went into her bedroom, took a small knife and cut her finger with it until it bled, then she held a white handkerchief to it into which she let three drops of blood fall, gave it to her daughter and said, " Dear child, preserve this carefully, it will be of service to you on your way."

So they took a sorrowful leave of each other ; the princess put the piece of cloth in her bosom, mounted her horse, and then went away to her bridegroom. After she had ridden for a while she felt a burning thirst, and said to her waiting-maid, " Dismount, and take my cup which thou hast brought with thee for me, and get me some water from the stream, for I should like to drink." " If you are thirsty," said the waiting-maid, " get off your horse yourself, and lie down and drink out of the water, I don't choose to be your servant." So in her great thirst the princess alighted, bent down over the water in the stream and drank, and was not allowed to drink out of the golden cup. Then she said, " Ah, Heaven ! " and the three drops of blood answered, " If thy mother knew this, her heart would break." But the King's daughter was humble, said nothing, and mounted her horse again. She rode some miles further, but the day was warm, the sun scorched her, and she was thirsty once more, and when they came to a stream of water, she again cried to her waiting-maid, " Dismount, and give me some water in my golden cup," for she had long ago forgotten the girl's ill words. But the waiting-maid said still more haughtily,

" If you wish to drink, drink as you can, I don't choose to be your maid." Then in her great thirst the King's daughter alighted, bent over the flowing stream, wept and said, " Ah, Heaven ! " and the drops of blood again replied, " If thy mother knew this, her heart would break." And as she was thus drinking and leaning right over the stream, the handkerchief with the three drops of blood fell out of her bosom, and floated away with the water without her observing it, so great was her trouble. The waiting-maid, however, had seen it, and she rejoiced to think that she had now power over the bride, for since the princess had lost the drops of blood, she had become weak and powerless. So now when she wanted to mount her horse again, the one that was called Falada, the waiting-maid said, " Falada is more suitable for me, and my nag will do for thee," and the princess had to be content with that. Then the waiting-maid, with many hard words, bade the princess exchange her royal apparel for her own shabby clothes ; and at length she was compelled to swear by the clear sky above her, that she would not say one word of this to any one at the royal court, and if she had not taken this oath she would have been killed on the spot. But Falada saw all this, and observed it well.

The waiting-maid now mounted Falada, and the true bride the bad horse, and thus they travelled onwards, until at length they entered the royal palace. There were great rejoicings over her arrival, and the prince sprang forward to meet her, lifted the waiting-maid from her horse, and thought she was his consort. She was conducted upstairs, but the real princess was left standing below. Then the old King looked out of the window and saw her standing in the courtyard, and how dainty and delicate and beautiful she was, and instantly went to the royal apartment, and asked the bride about the girl she had with her who was standing down below in the courtyard, and who she was ? " I picked her up on my way for a companion ; give the girl something to work at, that she may not stand idle." But the old King had no work for her, and knew of none, so he said, " I have a little boy who tends the geese, she may help him." The boy was called Conrad, and the true bride had to help him to tend the geese. Soon afterwards the false bride said to the young King, " Dearest husband, I beg you to do me a favour." He answered, " I will do so most willingly." " Then send for the knacker, and cut off the head of the

horse on which I rode here, for it vexed me on the way. In reality, she was afraid that the horse might tell how she had behaved to the King's daughter. Then she succeeded in making the King promise that it should be done, and the faithful Falada was to die ; this came to the ears of the real princess, and she secretly promised to pay the knacker a piece of gold if he would perform a small service for her. There was a great dark-looking gateway in the town, through which morning and evening she had to pass with the geese : would he be so good as to nail up Falada's head on it, so that she might see him again, more than once. The knacker's man promised to do that, and cut off the head, and nailed it fast beneath the dark gateway.

Early in the morning, when she and Conrad drove out their flock beneath this gateway, she said in passing,

" *Falada, Falada, hanging high* . . ."

Then the head answered,

" *Princess, Princess, passing by.*
Alas, alas ! if thy mother knew it,
Sadly, sadly her heart would rue it."

Then they went still further out of the town, and drove their geese into the country. And when they had come to the meadow, she sat down and unbound her hair which was like pure gold, and Conrad saw it and delighted in its brightness, and wanted to pluck out a few hairs. Then she said,

" *Blow, breezes, blow !*
Let Conrad's hat go !
Blow breezes, blow !
Let him after it go
O'er hills, dales and rocks
Away be it whirled
Till the silvery locks
Are all combed and curled."

And there came such a violent wind that it blew Conrad's hat far away across country, and he was forced to run after it. When he came back she had finished combing her hair and was putting it up again, and he could not get any of it. Then Conrad was angry, and would not speak to her, and thus they watched the geese until the evening, and then they went home.

Next day when they were driving the geese out through the dark gateway, the maiden said,

> " *Falada, Falada, hanging high* . . ."

Falada answered,

> " *Princess, Princess, passing by.*
> *Alas, alas ! if thy mother knew it,*
> *Sadly, sadly her heart would rue it.*"

And she sat down again in the field and began to comb out her hair, and Conrad ran and tried to clutch it, so she said in haste,

> " *Blow, breezes, blow !*
> *Let Conrad's hat go !*
> *Blow breezes, blow !*
> *Let him after it go*
> *O'er hills, dales and rocks*
> *Away be it whirled*
> *Till the silvery locks*
> *Are all combed and curled.*"

Then the wind blew, and blew his little hat off his head and far away, and Conrad was forced to run after it, and when he came back, her hair had been put up a long time, and he could get none of it, and so they looked after their geese till evening came.

But in the evening after they had got home, Conrad went to the old King, and said, " I won't tend the geese with that girl any longer ! " " Why not ? " inquired the aged King. " Oh, because she vexes me the whole day long." Then the old King commanded him to relate what it was that she did to him. And Conrad said, " In the morning when we pass beneath the dark gateway with the flock, there is a sorry horse's head on the wall and she says to it,

> " *Falada, Falada, hanging high* . . ."

And the head replies,

> " *Princess, Princess, passing by.*
> *Alas, alas ! if thy mother knew it,*
> *Sadly, sadly her heart would rue it.*"

And Conrad went on to relate what happened on the goose pasture, and how when there he had to chase his hat.

The aged King commanded him to drive his flock out again next day, and as soon as morning came, he placed himself behind the dark gateway, and heard how the maiden spoke to the head of Falada, and then he too went into the country, and hid himself in the thicket in the meadow. There he soon saw with his own eyes the goose-girl and the goose-boy bringing their flock, and how after a while she sat down and unplaited her hair, which shone with radiance. And soon she said

> " *Blow, breezes, blow !*
> *Let Conrad's hat go !*
> *Blow breezes, blow !*
> *Let him after it go*
> *O'er hills, dales and rocks*
> *Away be it whirled*
> *Till the silvery locks*
> *Are all combed and curled.*"

Then came a blast of wind and carried off Conrad's hat, so that he had to run far away, while the maiden quietly went on combing and plaiting her hair, all of which the King observed. Then, quite unseen, he went away, and when the goose-girl came home in the evening, he called her aside, and asked why she did all these things. " I may not tell you that, and I dare not lament my sorrows to any human being, for I have sworn not to do so by the heaven which is above me ; if I had not done that, I should have lost my life." He urged her and left her no peace, but he could draw nothing from her. Then said he, " If thou wilt not tell me anything, tell thy sorrows to the iron-stove there," and he went away. Then she crept into the iron-stove, and began to weep and lament, and emptied her whole heart, and said, " Here am I deserted by the whole world, and yet I am a King's daughter, and a false waiting-maid has by force brought me to such a pass that I have been compelled to put off my royal apparel, and she has taken my place with my bridegroom, and I have to perform menial service as a goose-girl. If my mother did but know that, her heart would break."

The aged King, however, was standing outside by the pipe of the stove, and was listening to what she said, and heard it. Then he came back again, and bade her come out of the stove. And royal garments were placed on her, and it was marvellous how beautiful she was ! The aged King summoned his son, and revealed to him that he had got the false bride who was only a waiting-maid, but that the true one was standing there, as the sometime goose-girl. The young King rejoiced with all his heart when he saw her beauty and youth, and a great feast was made ready to which all the people and all good friends were invited. At the head of the table sat the bridegroom with the King's daughter at one side of him, and the waiting-maid on the other, but the waiting-maid was blinded, and did not recognize the princess in her dazzling array. When they had eaten and drunk and were merry, the aged King asked the waiting-maid as a riddle, what a person deserved who had behaved in such and such a way to her master, and at the same time related the whole story, and asked what sentence such an one merited ? Then the false bride said, " She deserves no better fate than to be stripped entirely naked, and put in a barrel which is studded inside with pointed nails, and two white horses should be harnessed to it, which will drag her along through one street after another till she is dead." " It is thou," said the aged King, " and thou hast pronounced thine own sentence, and thus shall it be done unto thee." And when the sentence had been carried out, the young King married his true bride, and both of them reigned over their kingdom in peace and happiness.

THE THREE FEATHERS

THERE was once on a time a King who had three sons, of whom two were clever and wise, but the third did not speak much, and was simple, and was called the Simpleton. When the King had become old and weak, and was thinking of his end, he did not know which of his sons should inherit the kingdom after him. Then he said to them, " Go forth, and he who brings me the most beautiful carpet shall be King after my death." And that there should be no dispute amongst them, he took them outside his castle, blew three feathers in the air, and said, " You shall go as they fly." One feather flew to the east, the other to the west, but the third flew straight up and did not fly far, but soon fell to the ground. And now one brother went to the right, and the other to the left, and they mocked Simpleton, who was forced to stay where the third feather had fallen. He sat down and was sad, then all at once he saw that there was a trap-door close by the feather. He raised it up, found some steps, and went down them, and then he came to another door, knocked at it, and heard somebody inside calling,

> " Little green maiden small,
> Hopping hither and thither ;
> Hop to the door,
> And quickly see who is there."

The door opened, and he saw a great, fat toad sitting, and round about her a crowd of little toads. The fat toad asked what he wanted ? He answered, " I should like to have the prettiest and finest carpet in the world." Then she called a young one and said,

> " Little green maiden small,
> Hopping hither and thither,
> Hop quickly and bring me
> The great box here."

The young toad brought the box, and the fat toad opened it, and gave Simpleton a carpet out of it, so beautiful and so fine, that on the earth above, none could have been woven like it. Then he thanked her, and ascended again. The two others had, however, looked on their youngest brother as so stupid that they believed he would find and bring nothing at all. " Why should we give ourselves a great deal of trouble to search ? " said they, and got some coarse handkerchiefs from the first shepherd's wives whom they met, and carried them home to the King. At the same time Simpleton also came back, and brought his beautiful carpet, and when the King saw it he was astonished, and said, " If justice be done, the kingdom belongs to the youngest." But the two others let their father have no peace, and said that it was impossible that Simpleton, who in everything lacked understanding, should be King, and entreated him to make a new agreement with them. Then the father said, " He who brings me the most beautiful ring shall inherit the kingdom," and led the three brothers out, and blew into the air three feathers, which they were to follow. Those of the two eldest again went east and west, and Simpleton's feather flew straight up, and fell down near the door into the earth. Then he went down again to the fat toad, and told her that he wanted the most beautiful ring. She at once ordered her great box to be brought, and gave him a ring out of it, which sparkled with jewels, and was so beautiful that no goldsmith on earth would have been able to make it. The two eldest laughed at Simpleton for going to seek a golden ring. They gave themselves no trouble, but knocked the nails out of an old carriage-ring, and took it to the King ; but when Simpleton produced his golden ring, his father again said; " The kingdom belongs to him." The two eldest did not cease from tormenting the King until he made a third condition, and declared that the one who brought the most beautiful woman home, should have the kingdom. He again blew the three feathers into the air, and they flew as before.

Then Simpleton without more ado went down to the fat toad, and said, " I am to take home the most beautiful woman ! " " Oh," answered the toad, " the most beautiful woman ! She is not at hand at the moment, but still thou shalt have her." She gave him a yellow turnip which had been hollowed out, to which six mice were harnessed. Then Simpleton said quite mournfully, " What am I to do with that ? " The toad answered, " Just put one of my little toads into it." Then he seized one at random out of the circle, and put her into the

yellow coach, but hardly was she seated inside it than she turned into a wonderfully beautiful maiden, and the turnip into a coach, and the six mice into horses. So he kissed her, and drove off quickly with the horses, and took her to the King. His brothers came afterwards; they had given themselves no trouble at all to seek beautiful girls, but had brought with them the first peasant women they chanced to meet.

When the King saw them he said, "After my death the kingdom belongs to my youngest son." But the two eldest deafened the King's ears afresh with their clamour, "We cannot consent to Simpleton's being King," and demanded that the one whose wife could leap through a ring which hung in the centre of the hall should have the preference. They thought, "The peasant women can do that easily; they are strong enough, but the delicate maiden will jump herself to death." The aged King agreed likewise to this. Then the two peasant women jumped, and jumped through the ring, but were so stout that they fell and their coarse arms and legs broke in two. And then the pretty maiden whom Simpleton had brought with him, sprang and sprang through as lightly as a deer, and all opposition had to cease. So he received the crown, and has ruled wisely for a length of time.

THE POOR MAN AND THE RICH MAN

IN olden times, when the Lord himself still used to walk about on this earth amongst men, it once happened that he was tired and overtaken by the darkness before he could reach an inn. Now there stood on the road before him two houses facing each other; the one large and beautiful, the other small and poor. The large one belonged to a rich man, and the small one to a poor man.

Then the Lord thought, "I shall be no burden to the rich man, I will stay the night with him." When the rich man heard some one knocking at his door, he opened the window and asked the stranger what he wanted. The Lord answered, " I only ask for a night's lodging."

Then the rich man looked at the traveller from head to foot, and as the Lord was wearing common clothes, and did not look like one who had much money in his pocket, he shook his head, and said, " No, I cannot take you in, my rooms are full of herbs and seeds ; and if I were to lodge every one who knocked at my door, I might very soon go begging myself. Go somewhere else for a lodging," and with this he shut down the window and left the Lord standing there.

So the Lord turned his back on the rich man, and went across to the small house and knocked. He had hardly done so when the poor man opened the little door and bade the traveller come in. " Pass the night with me, it is already dark," said he ; " you cannot go any further to-night." This pleased the Lord, and he went in. The poor man's wife shook hands with him, and welcomed him, and said he was to make himself at home and put up with what they had got ; they had not much to offer him, but what they had they would give him with all their hearts. Then she put the potatoes on the fire, and while they were boiling, she milked the goat, that they might have a little milk with them. When the cloth was laid, the Lord sat down with the man and his wife, and he enjoyed their coarse food, for there were happy faces at the table. When they had had supper and it was bed-time, the woman called her husband apart and said, " Hark you, dear husband, let us make up a bed of straw for ourselves to-night, and then the poor traveller can sleep in our bed and have a good rest, for he has been walking the whole day through, and that makes one weary." " With all my heart," he answered. " I will go and offer it to him ; " and he went to the stranger and invited him, if he had no objection, to sleep in their bed and rest his limbs properly. But the Lord was unwilling to take their bed from the two old folks ; however, they would not be satisfied, until at length he did it and lay down in their bed, while they themselves lay on some straw on the ground.

Next morning they got up before daybreak, and made as good a breakfast as they could for the guest. When the sun shone in through the little window, and the Lord had got up, he again ate with them, and then prepared to set out on his journey.

But as he was standing at the door he turned round and said, " As you are so kind and good, you may wish three things for yourselves and I will grant them."   Then the man said, " What else should I wish for but eternal happiness, and that we two, as long as we live, may be healthy and have every day our daily bread ; for the third wish, I do not know what to have."   And the Lord said to him, " Will you wish for a new house instead of this old one ? "   " Oh, yes," said the man ; " If I can have that, too, I should like it very much."   And the Lord fulfilled his wish, and changed their old house into a new one, again gave them his blessing, and went on.

The sun was high when the rich man got up and leaned out of his window and saw, on the opposite side of the way, a new clean-looking house with red tiles and bright windows where the old hut used to be. He was very much astonished, and called his wife and said to her, " Tell me, what can have happened ? Last night there was a miserable little hut standing there, and to-day there is a beautiful new house. Run over and see how that has come to pass."

So his wife went and asked the poor man, and he said to her, " Yesterday evening a traveller came here and asked for a night's lodging, and this morning when he took leave of us he granted us three wishes—eternal happiness, health during this life and our daily bread as well, and, besides this, a beautiful new house instead of our old hut."

When the rich man's wife heard this, she ran back in haste and told her husband how it had happened.   The man said, " I could tear myself to pieces ! If I had but known that ! The traveller came to our house too, and wanted to sleep here, and I sent him away." " Quick ! " said his wife, " get on your horse. You can still catch the man up, and then you must ask to have three wishes granted you."

The rich man followed the good counsel and galloped away on his horse, and soon came up with the Lord.   He spoke to him softly and pleasantly, and begged him not to take it amiss that he had not let him in directly ; he was looking for the front-door key, and in the mean-time the stranger had gone away, if he returned the same way he must come and stay with him.   " Yes," said the Lord ; " if I ever come back again, I will do so."   Then the rich man asked if he might not wish for three things too, as his neighbour had done ?   " Yes," said the Lord, he might, but it would not be to his advantage, and he had better not wish for anything ; but the rich man thought that he could easily ask for something which would add to his happiness, if he only knew that it would be granted. So the Lord said to him, " Ride home, then, and three wishes which you shall form, shall be fulfilled."

The rich man had now gained what he wanted, so he rode home, and began to consider what he should wish for. As he was thus thinking he let the bridle fall, and the horse began to caper about, so that he was continually disturbed in his meditations, and could not collect his thoughts at all. He patted its neck, and said, " Gently, Lisa," but the horse only began new tricks. Then at last he was angry, and cried quite impatiently, " I wish your neck was broken ! " Directly he had said the words, down the horse fell on the ground, and there it lay dead and never moved again. And thus was his first wish fulfilled. As he was miserly by nature, he did not like to leave the harness lying there; so he cut it off, and put it on his back ; and now he had to go on foot. " I have still two wishes left," said he, and comforted himself with that thought.

And now as he was walking slowly through the sand, and the sun was burning hot at noon-day, he grew quite hot-tempered and angry. The saddle hurt his back, and he had not yet any idea what to wish for. " If I were to wish for all the riches and treasures in the world," said he to himself, " I should still think of all kinds of things besides later on, I know that, beforehand. But I will manage so that there is nothing at all left me to wish for afterwards." Then he sighed and said, " Ah, if I were but that Bavarian peasant, who likewise had three wishes granted to him, and knew quite well what to do, and in the first place wished for a great deal of beer, and in the second for as much beer as he was able to drink, and in the third for a barrel of beer into the bargain."

Many a time he thought he had found it, but then it seemed to him to be, after all, too little. Then it came into his mind, what an easy life his wife had, for she stayed at home in a cool room and enjoyed herself. This really did vex him, and before he was aware, he said, " I just wish she was sitting there on this saddle, and could not get off it, instead of my having to drag it along on my back." And as the last word was spoken, the saddle disappeared from his back, and he

saw that his second wish had been fulfilled. Then he really did feel
warm. He began to run and wanted to be quite alone in his own room
at home, to think of something really large for his last wish. But

when he arrived there and opened the parlour-door, he saw his wife sitting in the middle of the room on the saddle, crying and complaining and quite unable to get off it. So he said, " Do bear it, and I will wish for all the riches on earth for thee, only stay where thou art." She, however, called him a fool, and said, " What good will all the riches on earth do me, if I am to sit on this saddle ? Thou hast wished me on it, so thou must help me off." So whether he would or not, he was forced to let his third wish be that she should be quit of the saddle, and able to get off it, and immediately the wish was fulfilled. So he got nothing by it but vexation, trouble, abuse, and the loss of his horse ; but the poor people lived happily, quietly, and piously until their happy death.

THE GOLDEN GOOSE

THERE was a man who had three sons, the youngest of whom was called Dummling,* and was despised, mocked, and put down on every occasion.

It happened that the eldest wanted to go into the forest to hew wood, and before he went his mother gave him a beautiful sweet cake and a bottle of wine in order that he might not suffer from hunger or thirst.

When he entered the forest there met him a little grey-haired old man who bade him good-day, and said, " Do give me a piece of cake out of your pocket, and let me have a draught of your wine ; I am so hungry and thirsty." But the prudent youth answered, " If I give you my cake and wine, I shall have none for myself ; be off with you," and he left the little man standing and went on.

* Simpleton.

But when he began to hew down a tree, it was not long before he made a false stroke, and the axe cut him in the arm, so that he had to go home and have it bound up. And this was the little grey man's doing.

After this the second son went into the forest, and his mother gave him, like the eldest, a cake and a bottle of wine. The little old grey man met him likewise, and asked him for a piece of cake and a drink of wine. But the second son, too, said with much reason, " What I give you will be taken away from myself; be off! " and he left the little man standing and went on. His punishment, however, was not delayed ; when he had made a few strokes at the tree he struck himself in the leg, so that he had to be carried home.

The Dummling said, " Father, do let me go and cut wood." The father answered, " Your brothers have hurt themselves with it, leave it alone, you do not understand anything about it." But Dummling begged so long that at last he said, " Just go then, you will get wiser by hurting yourself." His mother gave him a cake made with water and baked in the cinders, and with it a bottle of sour beer.

When he came to the forest the little old grey man met him likewise, and greeting him, said, " Give me a piece of your cake and a drink out of your bottle ; I am so hungry and thirsty." Dummling answered, " I have only cinder-cake and sour beer ; if that pleases you, we will sit down and eat." So they sat down, and when Dummling pulled out his cinder-cake, it was a fine sweet cake, and the sour beer had become good wine. So they ate and drank, and after that the little man said, " Since you have a good heart, and are willing to divide what you have, I will give you good luck. There stands an old tree, cut it down, and you will find something at the roots." Then the old man took leave of him.

Dummling went and cut down the tree, and when it fell there was a goose sitting in the roots with feathers of pure gold. He lifted her up, and taking her with him, went to an inn where he thought he would stay the night. Now the host had three daughters, who saw the goose and were curious to know what such a wonderful bird might be, and would have liked to have one of its golden feathers.

The eldest thought, " I shall soon find an opportunity of pulling out a feather," and as soon as Dummling had gone out she seized the goose by the wing, but her finger and hand remained sticking fast to it.

The second came soon afterwards, thinking only of how she might get a feather for herself, but she had scarcely touched her sister than she was held fast.

At last the third also came with the like intent, and the others screamed out, " Keep away ; for goodness' sake keep away ! " But she did not understand why she was to keep away. " The others are there," she thought, " I may as well be there too," and ran to them ; but as soon as she had touched her sister, she remained sticking fast to her. So they had to spend the night with the goose.

The next morning Dummling took the goose under his arm and set out, without troubling himself about the three girls who were hanging on to it. They were obliged to run after him continually, now left now right, just as he was inclined to go.

In the middle of the fields the parson met them, and when he saw the procession he said, " For shame, you good-for-nothing girls, why are you running across the fields after this young man ? is that seemly ? " At the same time he seized the youngest by the hand in order to pull her away, but as soon as he touched her he likewise stuck fast, and was himself obliged to run behind.

Before long the sexton came by and saw his master, the parson, running on foot behind three girls. He was astonished at this and called out, " Hi ! your reverence, whither away so quickly ? do not forget that we have a christening to-day ! " and running after him he took him by the sleeve, but was also held fast to it.

Whilst the five were trotting thus one behind the other, two labourers came with their hoes from the fields ; the parson called out to them and begged that they would set him and the sexton free. But they had scarcely touched the sexton when they were held fast, and now there were seven of them running behind Dummling and the goose.

Soon afterwards he came to a city, where a king ruled who had a daughter who was so serious that no one could make her laugh. So he had put forth a decree that whosoever should be able to make her laugh should marry her. When Dummling heard this, he went with his goose and all her train before the King's daughter, and as soon as she saw the seven people running on and on, one behind the other, she began to laugh quite loudly, and as if she would never leave off. Thereupon Dummling asked to have her for his wife, and the wedding was celebrated. After the King's death Dummling inherited the kingdom, and lived a long time contentedly with his wife.

THE PEASANT AND THE DEVIL

THERE was once on a time a far-sighted, crafty peasant whose tricks were much talked about. The best story is, however, how he once got hold of the Devil, and made a fool of him. The peasant had one day been working in his field, and as twilight had set in, was making ready for the journey home, when he saw a heap of burning coals in the middle of his field, and when, full of astonishment, he went up to it, a little black devil was sitting on the live coals. " Thou dost indeed sit upon a treasure ! " said the peasant. " Yes, in truth," replied the Devil, " on a treasure which contains more gold and silver than thou hast ever seen in thy life ! " " The treasure lies in my field and belongs to me," said the peasant. " It is thine," answered the Devil, " if thou wilt for two years give me the half of everything thy field produces. Money I have enough of, but I have a desire for the fruits of the earth." The peasant agreed to the bargain. " In order, however, that no dispute may arise about the division," said he, " everything that is above ground shall belong to thee, and what is under the earth to me." The Devil was quite satisfied with that, but the cunning peasant had sown turnips.

Now when the time for harvest came, the Devil appeared and wanted to take away his crop ; but he found nothing but the yellow withered leaves, while the peasant, full of delight, was digging up his turnips. " Thou hast had the best of it for once," said the Devil,

" but the next time that won't do. What grows above ground shall be thine, and what is under it, mine." " I am willing," replied the peasant ; but when the time came to sow, he did not again sow turnips, but wheat. The grain became ripe, and the peasant went into the field and cut the full stalks down to the ground. When the Devil came, he found nothing but the stubble, and went away in a fury down into a cleft in the rocks. " That is the way to cheat the Devil," said the peasant, and went and fetched away the treasure.

THE DOG AND THE SPARROW

A SHEPHERD's dog had a master who took no care of him, but often let him suffer the greatest hunger. At last he could bear it no longer; so he took to his heels, and off he ran in a very sad and sorrowful mood. On the road he met a sparrow that said to him, " Why are you so sad, my friend ? " " Because," said the dog, " I am very very hungry, and have nothing to eat." " If that be all," answered the sparrow, " come with me into the next town, and I will soon find you plenty of food." So on they went together into the town : and as they passed by a butcher's shop, the sparrow said to the dog, " Stand there a little while till I peck you down a piece of meat." So the sparrow perched upon the shelf and having first looked carefully about her to see if any one was watching her, she pecked and scratched at a steak that lay upon the edge of the shelf, till at last down it fell. Then the dog snapped it up, and scrambled away with it into a corner, where he soon ate it all up. " Well," said the sparrow, " you shall have some more if you will ; so come with me to the next shop, and I will peck you down another steak." When the dog had eaten this too, the sparrow said to him, " Well, my good friend, have you had enough now ? " " I have had plenty of meat," answered he, " but I should like to have a piece of bread to eat after it." " Come with me then," said the sparrow, " and you shall soon have that too." So she took him to a baker's shop, and pecked at two rolls that lay in the window, till they fell down : and as the dog still wished for more, she took him to another shop and pecked down some more for him. When that was eaten, the sparrow asked him whether he had had enough now. " Yes," said he ; " and now let us take a walk a little way out of the town." So they both went out upon the high road ; but as the weather was warm, they had not gone far before the dog said, " I am very much tired,—I should like to take a nap." " Very well," answered the sparrow, " do so, and in the mean time I will perch upon that bush." So the dog stretched himself out on the road, and fell fast asleep. Whilst he slept, there came by a carter with a cart drawn by three horses, and loaded with two casks of wine. The sparrow, seeing that the carter did not turn out of the way, but would go on in the track in which the dog lay, so as to drive over him, called out, " Stop ! stop ! Mr. Carter, or it shall be the worse for you." But the carter, grumbling to himself, " You make it the worse for me, indeed ! what can you do ? " cracked his whip, and drove his cart over the poor dog, so that the wheels crushed him to death. " There," cried the sparrow, " thou cruel villain, thou hast killed my friend the dog. Now mind what I say. This deed of thine shall cost thee all that thou hast." " Do your worst, and welcome," said the brute, " what harm can you do me ? " and passed on. But the sparrow crept under the tilt of the cart, and pecked at the bung of one of the casks till she loosened it ; and then all the wine ran out, without the carter seeing it. At last he looked round, and saw that the cart was dripping, and the cask quite empty. " What an unlucky wretch I am ! " cried he. " Not wretch enough yet ! " said the sparrow, as she alighted upon the head of one of the horses, and pecked at him till he reared up and kicked. When the carter saw this, he drew out his hatchet and aimed a blow at the sparrow, meaning to kill her ; but she flew away, and the blow fell upon the poor horse's head with such force, that he fell down dead. " Unlucky wretch that I am ! " cried he. " Not wretch enough yet ! " said the sparrow. And as the carter went on with the other two horses, she again crept under the tilt of the cart, and pecked out the bung of the second cask, so that all the wine ran out. When the carter saw this, he again cried out, " Miserable wretch that I am ! " But the sparrow answered, " Not wretch enough yet ! " and perched on the head of the second horse, and pecked at him too. The carter ran up and struck at her again with his hatchet ; but away she flew, and the blow fell upon the second horse and killed him on the spot. " Unlucky wretch that I am ! " said he. " Not wretch enough yet ! " said the sparrow ; and perching upon the third horse, she began to peck him too. The carrier was mad with fury ; and without looking about him, or caring what he was about, struck again at the sparrow ; but killed his third horse as he had done the other two. " Alas ! miserable wretch that I am ! " cried he. " Not wretch enough yet ! " answered the sparrow as she flew away ; " now will I plague and punish thee at thy own house." The carter was forced at last to leave his cart behind him, and to go home overflowing with rage and vexation. " Alas ! " said he to his wife, " what ill luck has befallen me !—my wine is all spilt, and my horses all three dead." " Alas ! husband," replied she, " and a wicked bird has come into the house, and has brought with her all the birds in the world, I am sure, and they have fallen upon our corn in the loft, and are eating it up at such a rate ! " Away ran the husband upstairs, and saw thousands of birds sitting upon the floor eating up his corn, with the sparrow in the midst of them. " Unlucky wretch that I am ! " cried the carter ; for he saw that the corn was almost all gone. " Not wretch enough yet ! " said the sparrow ; " thy cruelty shall cost thee thy life yet ! " and away she flew.

The carter seeing that he had thus lost all that he had, went down into his kitchen ; and was still not sorry for what he had done, but sat himself angrily and sulkily in the chimney corner. But the sparrow sat on the outside of the window, and cried " Carter ! thy cruelty shall cost thee thy life ! " With that he jumped up in a rage, seized his hatchet, and threw it at the sparrow ; but it missed her, and only broke the window. The sparrow now hopped in, perched upon the window-seat, and cried, " Carter ! it shall cost thee thy life ! " Then he became mad and blind with rage, and struck the window-seat with

such force that he cleft it in two : and as the sparrow flew from place
to place, the carter and his wife were so furious, that they broke all
their furniture, glasses, chairs, benches, the table, and at last the walls,
without touching the bird at all.   In the end, however, they caught
her : and the wife said, " Shall I kill her at once ? " " No," cried he,
" that is letting her off too easily : she shall die a much more cruel
death ; I will eat her."   But the sparrow began to flutter about, and
stretched out her neck and cried, " Carter ! it shall cost thee thy life
yet ! "   With that he could wait no longer : so he gave his wife the
hatchet, and cried, " Wife, strike at the bird and kill her in my hand."
And the wife struck ; but she missed her aim, and hit her husband on
the head so that he fell down dead, and the sparrow flew quietly home
to her nest.

FRITZ AND HIS FRIENDS

HONEST Fritz had worked hard all his life, but ill luck befell him ; his cattle died, his barns were burned, and he lost almost all his money. So at last he said, " Before it is all gone I will buy goods, and go out into the world, and see whether I shall have the luck to mend my fortune."

The first place he came to was a village, where the boys were running about, crying and shouting. " What is the matter ? " asked he. " See here ! " said they, " we have got a mouse that we make dance to please us. Do look at him ; what a droll sight it is ! how he jumps about ! " But the man pitied the poor little thing, and said, " Let the poor mouse go, and I will give you money." So he gave them some money, and took the mouse and let it run : and it soon jumped into a hole that was close by, and was out of their reach.

Then he travelled on and came to another village : and there the boys had got an ass, that they made stand on its hind legs, and tumble and cut capers. Then they laughed and shouted, and gave the poor beast no rest. So the good man gave them too some of his money, to let the poor thing go away in peace.

At the next village he came to, the young people were leading a bear, that had been taught to dance, and were plaguing the poor thing sadly. Then he gave them too some money, to let the beast go ; and Master Bruin was very glad to get on his four feet, and seemed quite at his ease and happy again.

But now our traveller found that he had given away all the money he had in the world, and had not a shilling in his pocket. Then said he to himself, " The King has heaps of gold in his strong box that he never uses ; I cannot die of hunger : so I hope I shall be forgiven if I borrow a little from him, and when I get rich again I will repay it all."

So he managed to get at the King's strong box, and took a very little money ; but as he came out the guards saw him, and said he was a thief, and took him to the judge. The poor man told his story ; but the judge said that sort of borrowing could not be suffered, and that those who took other people's money must be punished ; so the end of his trial was that Fritz was found guilty, and doomed to be thrown into the lake, shut up in a box. The lid of the box was full of holes to let in air ; and one jug of water and one loaf of bread were given him.

Whilst he was swimming along in the water very sorrowfully, he heard something nibbling and biting at the lock. All on a sudden it fell off, the lid flew open, and there stood his old friend the little mouse, who had done him this good turn. Then came the ass and the bear too, and pulled the box ashore ; and all helped him because he had been kind to them.

But now they did not know what to do next, so they began to put their heads together, when suddenly a wave threw on the shore a pretty white stone, that looked like a egg. Then the bear said, " That's a lucky thing ! this is the wonderful stone ; whoever has it needs only to wish, and everything he wishes for comes to him at once." So Fritz went and picked up the stone, and wished for a palace and a garden, and a stud of horses, and his wish was fulfilled as soon as he had made it. And there he lived in his castle and garden, with fine stables and horses, and all was so grand and beautiful, that he never could wonder and gaze at it enough.

After some time some merchants passed by that way. " See," said they, " what a princely palace ! The last time we were here it was nothing but a desert waste." They were very eager to know how all this had happened, and went in and asked the master of the palace how it had been so quickly raised. " I have done nothing myself," said he ; " it is the wonderful stone that did all." " What a strange stone that must be ! " said they. Then he asked them to walk in, and showed it to them.

They asked him whether he would sell it, and offered him all their goods for it ; and the goods seemed so fine and costly, that he quite forgot that the stone would bring him in a moment a thousand better and richer things ; and he agreed to make the bargain. Scarcely was the stone, however, out of his hands before all his riches were gone, and poor Fritz found himself sitting in his box in the water, with his jug of water and loaf of bread by his side.

However, his grateful friends, the mouse, the ass, and the bear, came quickly to help him ; but the mouse found she could not nibble off the lock this time, for it was a great deal stronger than before. Then the bear said, " We must find the wonderful stone again, or all we can do will be fruitless."

The merchants, meantime, had taken up their abode in the palace ; so away went the three friends, and when they came near, the bear said, " Mouse, go in and look through the keyhole, and see where the stone is kept : you are small, nobody will see you." The mouse did as she was told, but soon came back and said, " Bad news ! I have looked in, and the stone hangs under the looking-glass by a red silk string, and on each side of it sits a great black cat with fiery eyes, watching it."

Then the others took counsel together, and said, " Go back again, and wait till the master of the palace is in bed asleep ; then nip his nose and pull his hair." Away went the mouse, and did as they told her ; and the master jumped up very angrily, and rubbed his nose, and cried, " Those rascally cats are good for nothing at all ; they let the mice bite my very nose, and pull the hair off my head." Then he hunted them out of the room ; and so the mouse had the best of the game.

Next night, as soon as the master was asleep, the mouse crept in again ; and (the cats being gone) she nibbled at the red silken string to which the stone hung, till down it dropped. Then she rolled it along to the door ; but when it got there the poor little mouse was quite tired, and said to the ass, " Put in your foot, and lift it over the threshold." This was soon done ; and they took up the stone, and set off for the waterside. Then the ass said, " How shall we reach the box ? " " That is easily managed, my friend," said the bear : " I can swim very well ; and do you, donkey, put your fore feet over my shoulders ;—mind and hold fast, and take the stone in your mouth ;—as for you, mouse, you can sit in my ear."

Thus all was settled, and away they swam. After a time, Bruin began to brag and boast : " We are brave fellows, are not we ? " said he ; " what do you think, donkey ? " But the ass held his tongue, and said not a word. " Why don't you answer me ? " said the bear ; " you must be an ill-mannered brute not to speak when you are spoken to." When the ass heard this, he could hold no longer ; so he opened his mouth, and out dropped the wonderful stone. " I could not speak," said he ; " did not you know I had the stone in my mouth ? Now it is lost, and that is your fault." " Do but hold your tongue and be easy ! " said the bear ; " and let us think what is to be done now."

Then another council was held : and at last they called together all the frogs, their wives and families, kindred and friends ; and said, " A great foe of yours is coming to eat you all up ; but never mind, bring us up plenty of stones, and we will build a strong wall to guard you." The frogs hearing this were dreadfully frightened, and set to work, bringing up all the stones they could find. At last came a large fat frog, pulling along the wonderful stone by the silken string ; and when the bear saw it he jumped for joy, and said, " Now we have found what we wanted." So he set the old frog free from his load, and told him to tell his friends they might now go home to their dinners as soon as they pleased.

Then the three friends swam off again for the box, and the lid flew open, and they found they were but just in time, for the bread was all eaten and the jug of water almost empty. But as soon as honest Fritz had the stone in his hand, he wished himself safe in his palace again ; and in a moment he was there, with his garden, and his stables, and his horses ; and his three faithful friends lived with him, and they all spent their time happily and merrily together as long as they lived. And thus the good man's kindness was rewarded ; and so it ought, for—One good turn deserves another.

THE VALIANT LITTLE TAILOR

ONE summer's morning a little tailor was sitting on his table by the window ; he was in good spirits, and sewed with all his might. Then came a peasant woman down the street crying, " Good jams, cheap ! Good jams, cheap ! " This rang pleasantly in the tailor's ears ; he stretched his delicate head out of the window, and called, " Come up here, dear woman ; here you will get rid of your goods." The woman came up the three steps to the tailor with her heavy basket, and he made her unpack the whole of the pots for him. He inspected all of them, lifted them up, put his nose to them, and at length said, " The jam seems to me to be good, so weigh me out four ounces, dear woman, and if it is a quarter of a pound that is of no consequence." The woman who had hoped to find a good sale, gave him what he desired, but went away quite angry and grumbling. " Now, God bless the jam to my use," cried the little tailor, " and give me health and strength ; " so he brought the bread out of the cupboard, cut himself right across the loaf and spread the jam over it. " This won't taste bitter," said he, " but I will just finish the jacket before I take a bite." He laid the bread near him, sewed on, and in his joy, made bigger and bigger stitches. In the meantime the smell of the sweet jam ascended so to the wall, where the flies were sitting in great numbers, that they were attracted and descended on it in hosts. " Hola ! who invited you ? " said the little tailor, and drove the unbidden guests away. The flies, however, who understood no English, would not be turned away but came back again in ever-increasing companies. Then the little tailor at last lost all patience, and got a bit of cloth from the hole under his work-table, and saying, " Wait, and I will give it to you," struck it mercilessly on them. When he drew it away and counted, there lay before him no fewer than seven, dead and with legs stretched out. " Art thou a fellow of that sort ? " said he, and could not help admiring his own bravery. " The whole town shall know of this ! " And the little tailor hastened to cut himself a girdle, stitched it, and embroidered on it in large letters, " Seven at one stroke ! " " What, the town ? " he continued, " The whole world shall hear of it ! " and his heart wagged with joy

like a lamb's tail. The tailor put on the girdle, and resolved to go forth into the world, because he thought his workshop was too small for his valour. Before he went away, he sought about in the house to see if there was anything which he could take with him ; however, he found nothing but an old cheese, and that he put in his pocket. In front of the door he observed a bird which had caught itself in the thicket. It had to go into his pocket with the cheese. Now he took to the road boldly, and as he was light and nimble, he felt no fatigue. The road led him up a mountain, and when he had reached the highest point of it, there sat a powerful giant looking about him quite comfortably. The little tailor went bravely up, spoke to him, and said, " Good day, comrade, so thou art sitting there overlooking the wide-spread world ! I am just on my way thither, and want to try my luck. Hast thou any inclination to go with me ? " The giant looked contemptuously at the tailor, and said, " Thou ragamuffin ! Thou miserable creature ! "

" Oh, indeed ? " answered the little tailor, and unbuttoned his coat, and showed the giant the girdle, " There mayst thou read what kind of a man I am ! " The giant read, " Seven at one stroke," and thought that they had been men whom the tailor had killed, and began to feel a little respect for the tiny fellow. Nevertheless, he wished to try him first, and took a stone in his hand and squeezed it together so that water dropped out of it. " Do that likewise," said the giant, " if thou hast strength ? " " Is that all ? " said the tailor, " that is child's play with us ! " and put his hand into his pocket, brought out the soft cheese, and pressed it until the liquid ran out of it. " Faith," said he, " that was a little better, wasn't it ? " The giant did not know what to say, and could not believe it of the little man. Then the giant picked up a stone and threw it so high that the eye could scarcely follow it. " Now, little mite of a man, do that likewise." " Well thrown," said the tailor, " but after all the stone came down to earth again ; I will throw you one which shall never come back at all," and he put his hand into his pocket, took out the bird, and threw it into the air. The bird, delighted with its liberty, rose, flew away and did not come back. " How does that shot please you, comrade ? " asked the tailor. " Thou canst certainly throw," said the giant, " but now we will see if thou art able to carry anything properly."

He took the little tailor to a mighty oak tree which lay there felled on the ground, and said, " If thou art strong enough, help me to carry the tree out of the forest." " Readily," answered the little man ; " take thou the trunk on thy shoulders, and I will raise up the branches and twigs ; after all, they are the heaviest." The giant took the trunk on his shoulder, but the tailor seated himself on a branch, and the giant who could not look around, had to carry away the whole tree, and the little tailor into the bargain : he behind, was quite merry and happy, and whistled the song, " Three tailors rode forth from the gate," as if carrying the tree were child's play. The giant, after he had dragged the heavy burden part of the way, could go no further, and cried, " Hark you, I shall have to let the tree fall ! " The tailor sprang nimbly down, seized the tree with both arms as if he had been carrying it, and said to the giant, " Thou art such a great fellow, and yet canst not even carry the tree ! "

They went on together, and as they passed a cherry-tree, the giant laid hold of the top of the tree where the ripest fruit was hanging, bent it down, gave it into the tailor's hand, and bade him eat. But the little tailor was much too weak to hold the tree, and when the giant let it go, it sprang back again, and the tailor was hurried into the air with it. When he had fallen down again without injury, the giant said, " What is this ? Hast thou not strength enough to hold the weak twig ? " " There is no lack of strength," answered the little tailor. " Dost thou think that could be anything to a man who has struck down seven at one blow ? I leapt over the tree because the hunts-men are shooting down there in the thicket. Jump as I did, if thou canst do it." The giant made the attempt, but could not get over the tree, and remained hanging in the branches, so that in this also the tailor had the better of him.

The giant said, " If thou art such a valiant fellow, come with me into our cavern and spend the night with us." The little tailor was willing, and followed him. When they went into the cave, other giants were sitting there by the fire, and each of them had a roasted sheep in his hand and was eating it. The little tailor looked round and thought, " It is much more spacious here than in my workshop." The giant showed him a bed, and said he was to lie down in it and sleep. The bed was, however, too big for the little tailor ; he did not lie down in it, but crept into a corner. When it was midnight, and the giant thought that the little tailor was lying in a sound sleep, he got up, took a great iron bar, cut through the bed with one blow, and thought he had given the grasshopper his finishing stroke. With the earliest dawn the giants went into the forest, and had quite forgotten the little tailor, when all at once he walked up to them quite merrily and boldly. The giants were terrified, they were afraid that he would strike them all dead, and ran away in a great hurry.

The little tailor went onwards, always following his own pointed nose. After he had walked for a long time, he came to the court-yard of a royal palace, and as he felt weary, he lay down on the grass and fell asleep. Whilst he lay there, the people came and inspected him on all sides, and read on his girdle, "Seven at one stroke." "Ah!" said they, "What does the great warrior here in the midst of peace? He must be a mighty lord." They went and announced him to the King, and gave it as their opinion that if war should break out, this would be a weighty and useful man who ought on no account to be allowed to depart. The counsel pleased the King, and he sent one of his courtiers to the little tailor to offer him military service when he awoke. The ambassador remained standing by the sleeper, waited until he stretched his limbs and opened his eyes, and then conveyed to him this proposal. "For this very reason have I come here," the tailor replied, "I am ready to enter the King's service." He was therefore honourably received, and a separate dwelling was assigned him.

The soldiers, however, were set against the little tailor, and wished him a thousand miles away. "What is to be the end of this?" they said amongst themselves. "If we quarrel with him, and he strikes about him, seven of us will fall at every blow; not one of us can stand against him." They came therefore to a decision, betook themselves in a body to the King, and begged for their dismissal. "We are not prepared," said they, "to stay with a man who kills seven at one stroke." The King was sorry that for the sake of one he should lose all his faithful servants, wished that he had never set eyes on the tailor, and would willingly have been rid of him again. But he did not venture to give him his dismissal, for he dreaded lest he should strike him and all his people dead, and place himself on the royal throne.

He thought about it for a long time, and at last found good counsel. He sent to the little tailor and caused him to be informed that as he was such a great warrior, he had one request to make to him. In a forest of his country lived two giants, who caused great mischief with their robbing, murdering, ravaging, and burning, and no one could approach them without putting himself in danger of death. If the tailor conquered and killed these two giants, he would give him his only daughter to wife, and half of his kingdom as a dowry, likewise one hundred horsemen should go with him to assist him. " That would indeed be a fine thing for a man like me ! " thought the little tailor. " One is not offered a beautiful princess and half a kingdom every day of one's life ! " " Oh, yes," he replied, " I will soon subdue the giants, and do not require the help of the hundred horsemen to do it ; he who can hit seven with one blow, has no need to be afraid of two."

The little tailor went forth, and the hundred horsemen followed him. When he came to the outskirts of the forest, he said to his followers, " Just stay waiting here, I alone will soon finish off the giants." Then he bounded into the forest and looked about right and left. After a while he perceived both giants. They lay sleeping under a tree, and snored so that the branches waved up and down. The little tailor, not idle, gathered two pocketsful of stones, and with these climbed up the tree. When he was half-way up, he slipped down by a branch, until he sat just above the sleepers, and then let one stone after another fall on the breast of one of the giants. For a long time the giant felt nothing, but at last he awoke, pushed his comrade, and said, " Why art thou knocking me ? " " Thou must be dreaming," said the other, " I am not knocking thee." They laid themselves down to sleep again, and then the tailor threw a stone down on the second. " What is the meaning of this ? " cried the other. " Why art thou pelting me ? " " I am not pelting thee," answered the first, growling. They disputed about it for a time, but as they were weary they let the matter rest, and their eyes closed once more. The little tailor began his game again, picked out the biggest stone, and threw it with all his might on the breast of the first giant. " That is too bad ! " cried he, and sprang up like a madman, and pushed his companion against the tree until it shook. The other paid him back in the same coin, and they got into such a rage that they tore up trees and belaboured each other so long, that at last they both fell down dead on the ground at the same time. Then the little tailor leapt down. "It is a lucky thing," said he, "that they did not tear up the tree on which I was sitting, or I should have had to spring on to another like a squirrel ; but we tailors are nimble." He drew out his sword and gave each of them a couple of stabs in the heart, and then went out to the horsemen and said, "The work is done ; I have given both of them their finishing stroke, but it was hard work ! They tore up trees in their sore need, and defended themselves with them but all that is to no purpose when a man like myself comes, who can kill seven at one blow." "But are you not wounded ?" asked the horsemen. "You need not concern yourself about that," answered the tailor, "They have not hurt one hair of me." The horseman would not believe him, and rode into the forest ; there they found the giants swimming in their blood, and all round about lay the torn-up trees.

The little tailor demanded of the King the promised reward ; he, however, repented of his promise, and again bethought himself how he could get rid of the hero. "Before thou receivest my daughter, and the half of my kingdom," said he to him, "thou must perform one more heroic deed. In the forest roams a unicorn which does great harm, and thou must catch it first." "I fear one unicorn still less than two giants. Seven at one blow is my kind of affair." He took a rope and an axe with him, went forth into the forest, and again bade those who were sent with him to wait outside. He had not to seek long. The unicorn soon came towards him, and rushed directly on the tailor, as if it would split him on its horn without more ceremony. "Softly, softly ; it can't be done as quickly as that," said he, and stood still waiting until the animal was quite close, and then sprang nimbly behind the tree. The unicorn ran against the tree with all its strength, and struck its horn so fast in the trunk that it had not strength enough to draw it out again, and thus it was caught. "Now I have him safe !" said the tailor, and came out from behind the tree and put the rope round its neck, and then with his axe he hewed the horn out of the tree, and when all was ready he led the beast away and took it to the King.

The King still would not give him the promised reward, and made a third demand. Before the wedding the tailor was to catch him a wild boar that made great havoc in the forest, and the huntsmen should give him their help. " Willingly," said the tailor, " that is child's play ! " He did not take the huntsmen with him into the forest, and they were well pleased that he did not, for the wild boar had several times received them in such a manner that they had no inclination to lie in wait for him. When the boar perceived the tailor, it ran on him with foaming mouth and whetted tusks, and was about to throw him to the ground, but the active hero sprang into a chapel which was near, and up to the window at once, and in one bound out again. The boar ran in after him, but the tailor ran round outside and shut the door behind it, and then the raging beast, which was much too heavy and awkward to leap out of the window, was caught. The little tailor called the huntsmen thither that they might see the prisoner with their own eyes. The hero, however, went to the King, who was now, whether he liked it or not, obliged to keep his promise, and gave him his daughter and the half of his kingdom. Had he known that it was no warlike hero, but a little tailor who was standing before him, it would have gone to his heart still more than it did. The wedding was held with great magnificence and small joy, and out of a tailor a king was made.

After some time the young Queen heard her husband say in his dreams at night, " Boy, make me the doublet, and patch the pantaloons, or else I will rap the yard-measure over thine ears." Then she discovered in what state of life the young lord had been born, and next morning complained of her wrongs to her father, and begged him to help her to get rid of her husband, who was nothing else but a tailor. The King comforted her and said, " Leave thy bed-room door open this night, and my servants shall stand outside, and when he has fallen asleep shall go in, bind him, and take him on board a ship which shall carry him into the wide world." The woman was satisfied with this ; but the King's armour-bearer, who had heard all, was friendly with the young King, and informed him of the whole plot. " I'll put a screw into that business," said the little tailor. At night he went to bed with his wife at the usual time, and when she thought that he had fallen asleep, she got up, opened the door, and then lay down again. The little tailor, who was only pretending to be asleep, began to cry out in a clear voice, " Boy, make me the doublet and patch me the pantaloons, or I will rap the yard-measure over thine ears. I smote seven at one blow. I killed two giants, I brought away one unicorn, and caught a wild boar, and am I to fear those who are standing outside the room." When these men heard the tailor speaking thus, they were overcome by a great dread, and ran as if the wild huntsman were behind them, and none of them dared to plot any more against him. So the little tailor was a king and remained one, to the end of his life.

THE TOM-TIT AND THE BEAR

ONCE in summer-time the bear and the wolf were walking in the forest, and the bear heard a bird singing so beautifully that he said, " Brother wolf, what bird is it that sings so well ? " " That is the King of the birds," said the wolf, " before whom we must bow down." It was, however, in reality the Tom-tit. " If that's the case," said the bear, " I should very much like to see his royal palace ; come, take me thither." " That is not as easy as you seem to think," said the wolf ; " you must wait until the Queen comes." Soon afterwards, the Queen arrived with some food in her beak, and the lord King came too, and they began to feed their young ones. The bear would have liked to go at once, but the wolf held him back by the sleeve, and said, " No, you must wait until the lord and lady Queen have gone away again." So they observed the hole in which was the nest, and trotted away. The bear, however, could not rest until he had seen the royal palace,

and when a short time had passed, again went to it. The King and Queen had just flown out, so he peeped in and saw five or six young ones lying in it. " Is that the royal palace ? " cried the bear ; " it is a wretched hole, and you are not King's children, you are but base-born brats ! " When the young tom-tits heard that, they were frightfully angry, and screamed, " No, that we are not ! Our parents are honest people ! Bear, thou wilt have to pay for that ! "

The bear and the wolf grew uneasy, and turned back and went into their holes. The young tom-tits, however, continued to cry and scream, and when their parents again brought food they said, " We will not as much as touch one fly's leg, no, not if we were dying of hunger, until you have settled whether we are respectable children or not ; the bear has been here and has insulted us ! " Then the old King said, " Be easy, he shall be punished," and he at once flew with the Queen to the bear's cave, and called in " Old Growler, why hast thou insulted my children ? Thou shalt suffer for it—we will punish thee by a bloody war." Thus war was announced to the bear, and all four-footed animals were summoned to take part in it, oxen, asses, cows, deer, and every other animal the earth contained. And the tom-tit summoned everything which flew in the air, not only birds, large and small, but midges, and hornets, bees and flies had to come.

When the time came for the war to begin, the tom-tit sent out spies to discover who was the enemy's commander-in-chief. The gnat, who was the most crafty, flew into the forest where the enemy was assembled, and hid herself beneath a leaf of the tree where the watch-word was to be given. There stood the bear, and he called the fox before him and said, " Fox, thou art the most cunning of all animals, thou shalt be general and lead us." " Good," said the fox, " but what signal shall we agree upon ? " No one knew that, so the fox said, " I have a fine long bushy tail, which almost looks like a plume of red feathers. When I lift my tail up quite high, all is going well, and you must charge ; but if I let it hang down, run away as fast as you can." When the gnat had heard that, she flew away again, and revealed everything, with the greatest minuteness, to the tom-tit. When day broke, and the battle was to begin, all the four-footed animals came running up with such a noise that the earth trembled. The

tom-tit also came flying through the air with his army with such
a humming, and whirring, and swarming that every one was uneasy
and afraid, and on each side they advanced against each other. But

the tom-tit sent down the hornet, with orders to get beneath the fox's tail, and sting it with all his might. When the fox felt the first sting, he started so that he drew up one leg, with the pain, but he bore it, and still kept his tail high in the air ; at the second sting, he was forced to put it down for a moment ; at the third, he could hold out no longer, and screamed out and put his tail between his legs. When the animals saw that they thought all was lost, and began to fly, each into his hole and the birds had won the battle.

Then the King and Queen flew home to their children and cried, " Children, rejoice, eat and drink to your heart's content, we have won the battle ! " But the young tom-tits said, " We will not eat yet, the bear must come to the nest, and beg for pardon and say that we are honourable children, before we will do that." Then the tom-tit flew to the bear's hole and cried, " Growler, thou art to come to the nest to my children, and beg their pardon, or else every rib of thy body shall be broken." So the bear crept thither in the greatest fear, and begged their pardon. And now at last the young tom-tits were satisfied, and sat down together and ate and drank, and made merry till quite late into the night.

GIANT GOLDEN-BEARD

In a country village, over the hills and far away, lived a poor man, who had an only son born to him. Now this child was born under a lucky star, and was therefore what the people of that country call a Luck's-child ; and those who told his fortunes said, that in his fourteenth year he would marry no less a lady than the king's own daughter.

It so happened that the king of that land, soon after the child's birth, passed through the village in disguise, and stopping at the blacksmith's shop, asked what news was stirring. " Good news ! " said the people. " Master Brock, down that lane, has just had a child born to him that they say is a Luck's-child ; and we are told that, when he is fourteen years old, he is fated to marry our noble king's daughter." This did not please the king ; so he went to the poor child's parents, and asked them whether they would sell him their son ? " No," said they. But the stranger begged very hard, and said he would give a great deal of money : so as they had scarcely bread to eat, they at last agreed, saying to themselves, " He is a Luck's-child ; all, therefore, is no doubt for the best—he can come to no harm."

The king took the child, put it into a box, and rode away ; but when he came to a deep stream he threw it into the current, and said to himself, " That young gentleman will never be my daughter's husband." The box, however, floated down the stream. Some kind fairy watched over it, so that no water reached the child ; and at last, about two miles from the king's chief city, it stopped at the dam of a mill. The miller soon saw it, and took a long pole and drew it towards the shore, and finding it heavy, thought there was gold inside ; but when he opened it he found a pretty little boy that smiled upon him merrily. Now the miller and his wife had no children, and they therefore rejoiced to see their prize, saying, " Heaven has sent it to us ; " so they treated it very kindly, and brought it up with such care that everyone liked and loved it.

About thirteen years passed over their heads, when the same king came by chance to the mill, and seeing the boy, asked the miller if that was his son. " No," said he, " I found him, when a babe, floating down the river in a box into the mill-dam." " How long ago ? " asked the king. " Some thirteen years," said the miller. " He is a fine fellow," said the king ; " can you spare him to carry a letter to the queen ? It will please me very much, and I will give him two pieces of gold for his trouble." " As your majesty pleases," said the miller.

Now the king had guessed at once that this must be the child he had tried to drown, so he wrote a letter by him to the queen saying, " As soon as the bearer of this reaches you, let him be killed and buried so that all may be over before I come back."

The young man set out with this letter but missed his way, and came in the evening to a dark wood. Through the gloom he saw a light afar off, to which he bent his steps, and found that it came from a little cottage. There was no one within except an old woman, who was frightened at seeing him, and said, " Why do you come hither, and whither are you going ? " " I am going to the queen, to whom I was to have given a letter ; but I have lost my way, and shall be glad if you will give me a night's rest." " You are very un- lucky," said she, " for this a robbers' hut ; and if the band come back while you are here it may be worse for you." " I am so tired, however," replied he, " that I must take my chance, for I can go no further ; " so he laid the letter on the table, stretched himself out upon a bench, and fell asleep.

When the robbers came home and saw him, they asked the old woman who the strange lad was. " I have given him shelter for charity," said she ; " he had a letter to carry to the queen, and lost his way." The robbers took up the letter, broke it open, and read the orders which were in it to murder the bearer. Then their leader was very angry at the king's trick ; so he tore his letter, and wrote a fresh one, begging the queen, as soon as the young man reached her, to marry him to the princess. Meantime they let him sleep on till morning broke, and then showed him the right way to the queen's palace ; where, as soon as she had read the letter, she made all ready for the wedding : and as the young man was very handsome, the princess was very dutiful, and took him then and there for a husband.

After a while the king came back ; and when he saw that this Luck's-child was married to the princess, notwithstanding all the art and cunning he had used to thwart his luck, he asked eagerly how all this had happened, and what were the orders which he had given. "Dear husband," said the queen, "here is your own letter—read it for yourself." The king took it, and seeing that an exchange had been made, asked his son-in-law what he had done with the letter he gave him to carry. "I know nothing of it," said he ; "if it is not the one you gave me, it must have been taken away in the night, when I slept." Then the king was very wroth and said, "No man shall have my daughter who does not go down into the wonderful cave and bring me three golden hairs from the beard of the giant king who reigns there ; do this, and you shall have my free leave to be my daughter's husband." "I will soon do that," said the youth ; so he took leave of his wife, and set out on his journey.

At the first city that he came to, the guard at the gate stopped him and asked what trade he followed, and what he knew. "I know everything," said he. "If that be so," said they, "you are just the man we want ; be so good as to find out why our fountain in the market-place is dry, and will give no water. Tell us the cause of that, and we will give you two asses loaded with gold." "With all my heart," said he, "when I come back."

Then he journeyed on, and came to another city, and there the guard also asked him what trade he followed, and what he understood. "I know everything," answered he. "Then pray do us a good turn," said they ; "tell us why a tree, which always before bore us golden apples, does not even bear a leaf this year." "Most willingly," said he, "as I come back."

At last his way led him to the side of a great lake of water, over which he must pass. The ferryman soon began to ask, as the others had done, what was his trade, and what he knew. "Everything," said he. "Then," said the other, "pray tell me why I am forced for ever to ferry over this water, and have never been able to get my freedom ; I will reward you handsomely." "Ferry me over," said the young man, "and I will tell you all about it as I come home."

When he had passed the water, he came to the wonderful cave. It looked very black and gloomy ; but the wizard king was not at

home, and his grandmother sat at the door in her easy chair. "What do you want?" said she. "Three golden hairs from the giant's beard," answered he. "You will run a great risk," said she, "when he comes home; yet I will try what I can do for you." Then she changed him into an ant, and told him to hide himself in the folds of her cloak. "Very well," said he: "but I want also to know why the city fountain is dry; why the tree that bore golden apples is now leafless; and what it is that binds the ferryman to his post." "You seem fond of asking puzzling things," said the old dame; "but lie still, and listen to what the giant says when I pull the golden hairs, and perhaps you may learn what you want." Soon night set in, and the old gentleman came home. As soon as he entered he began to snuff

up the air, and cried, " All is not right here : I smell man's flesh."
Then he searched all round in vain, and the old dame scolded, and
said, " Why should you turn everything topsy-turvy ? I have just
set all straight." Upon this he laid his head in her lap, and soon fell
asleep. As soon as he began to snore, she seized one of the golden hairs
of his beard and pulled it out. " Mercy ! " cried he, starting up :
" what are you about ? " " I had a dream that roused me," said she,
" and in my trouble I seized hold of your hair. I dreamt that the
fountain in the market-place of the city was become dry, and would
give no water ; what can be the cause ? " " Ah ! if they could find
that out they would be glad," said the giant : " under a stone in the
fountain sits a toad ; when they kill him, it will flow again."

This said, he fell asleep, and the old lady pulled out another hair.
" What would you be at ? " cried he in a rage. " Don't be angry,"
said she, " I did it in my sleep ; I dreamt that I was in a great kingdom
a long way off, and that there was a beautiful tree there, that used
to bear golden apples, but that now has not even a leaf upon it ;
what is the meaning of that ? " " Aha ! " said the giant, " they
would like very well to know that. At the root of the tree a mouse
is gnawing ; if they were to kill him, the tree would bear golden
apples again : if not, it will soon die. Now do let me sleep in peace ;
if you wake me again, you shall rue it."

Then he fell once more asleep ; and when she heard him snore
she pulled out the third golden hair, and the giant jumped up and
threatened her sorely ; but she soothed him, and said, " It was a
very strange dream I had this time : methought I saw a ferryman,
who was bound to ply backwards and forwards over a great lake,
and could never find out how to set himself free ; what is the charm
that binds him ? " " A silly fool ! " said the giant : " if he were to
give the rudder into the hand of any passenger that came, he would
find himself free, and the other would be forced to take his place.
Now pray let me sleep."

In the morning the giant arose and went out ; and the old woman
gave the young man the three golden hairs, reminded him of the three
answers, and sent him on his way.

He soon came to the ferryman, who knew him again, and asked
for the answer which he had said he would give him. " Ferry me

over first," said he, " and then I will tell you." When the boat reached the other side, he told him to give the rudder to the first passenger that came, and then he might run away as soon as he pleased. The next place that he came to was the city where the barren tree stood : " Kill the mouse," said he, " that is gnawing the tree's root, and you will have golden apples again." They gave him a rich gift for this news, and he journeyed on to the city where the fountain had dried up ; and the guard asked him how to make the water flow. So he told them how to cure that mischief, and they thanked him, and gave him the two asses laden with gold.

And now at last this Luck's-child reached home, and his wife was very glad to see him, and to hear how well everything had gone with him. Then he gave the three golden hairs to the king, who could no longer deny him, though he was at heart quite as spiteful against his son-in-law as ever. The gold, however, astonished him, and when he saw all the treasure, he cried out with joy, " My dear son, where did you find all this gold ? " " By the side of a lake," said the youth, " where there is plenty more to be had." " Pray tell me where it lies," said the king, " that I may go and get some too." " As much as you please," replied the other. " You must set out and travel on and on, till you come to the shore of a great lake : there you will see a ferryman ; let him carry you across, and when once you are over, you will see gold as plentiful as sand upon the shore."

Away went the greedy king ; and when he came to the lake he beckoned to the ferryman, who gladly took him into his boat ; and as soon as he was there gave the rudder into his hand and sprang ashore, leaving the old king to ferry away, as a reward for his craftiness and treachery.

" And is his majesty plying there to this day ? " You may be sure of that, for nobody will trouble himself to take the rudder out of his hands.

THE THREE SPINNERS

THERE was once a girl who was idle and would not spin, and let her mother say what she would, she could not bring her to it. At last the mother was so overcome with anger and impatience, that she beat her, on which the girl began to weep loudly. Now at this very moment the Queen drove by, and when she heard the weeping she stopped her carriage, went into the house and asked the mother why she was beating her daughter so that the cries could be heard out on the road? Then the woman was ashamed to reveal the laziness of her daughter and said, " I cannot get her to leave off spinning. She insists on spinning all day long, and I am poor, and cannot buy the flax." Then answered the Queen, " There is nothing that I like better to hear than spinning, and I am never happier than when the wheels are humming. Let me have your daughter with me in the palace, I have flax enough, and there she shall spin as much as she likes." The mother was heartily satisfied with this, and the Queen took the girl with her. When they had arrived at the palace, she led her up into three rooms which were filled from the bottom to the top with the finest flax. " Now spin me this flax," said she, " and when thou hast done it, thou shalt have my eldest son for a husband, even if thou art poor. I care nothing for that, thy wonderful industry is dowry enough." The girl was secretly terrified, for she could not have spun the flax, no, not if she had lived till she was three hundred years old, and had sat at it every day from morning till night. When she was left alone she began to weep and sat thus for three days without moving a finger. On the third day came the Queen, and when she saw that nothing had been spun yet, she was surprised ; but the girl excused herself by saying that she had not been able to begin because of her great distress at leaving her mother's house. The Queen was satisfied with this, but said when she was going away, " To-morrow thou must begin to work."

When the girl was alone again, she did not know what to do, and in her distress went to the window. Then she saw three women coming towards her, the first of whom had a broad flat foot, the second had such a great underlip that it hung down over her chin, and the third had a broad thumb. They remained standing before the window, looked up, and asked the girl what was amiss with her ?

She complained of her trouble, and then they offered her their help and said, " If thou wilt invite us to the wedding, not be ashamed of us, and wilt call us thine aunts, and likewise wilt place us at thy table, we will spin the flax for thee, and that in a very short time." " With all my heart," she replied, " do but come in and begin the work at once." Then she let in the three strange women, and cleared a place in the first room, where they seated themselves and began their spinning. The one drew the thread and trod the wheel, the other wetted the thread, the third twisted it, and struck the table with her finger, and as often as she struck it, a skein of thread fell to the ground that was spun in the finest manner possible. The girl concealed the three spinners from the Queen, and showed her whenever she came the great quantity of spun thread, until the latter could not praise her enough. When the first room was empty she went to the second, and at last to the third, and that too was quickly cleared. Then the three women took leave and said to the girl, " Do not forget what thou has promised us,—it will make thy fortune."

When the maiden showed the Queen the empty rooms, and the great heap of yarn, she gave orders for the wedding, and the bridegroom rejoiced that he was to have such a clever and industrious wife, and praised her mightily. " I have three aunts," said the girl, " and as they have been very kind to me, I should not like to forget them in my good fortune ; allow me to invite them to the wedding, and let them sit with us at table." The Queen and the bridegroom said, " Why should we not allow that ? " Therefore when the feast began, the three women entered in strange apparel, and the bride said, " Welcome, dear aunts." " Ah," said the bridegroom, " how comest thou by these hideous friends ? " Thereupon he went to the one with the broad flat foot, and said " How do you come by such a broad foot ? " " By treading," she answered, " by treading." Then the bridegroom went to the second, and said, " How do you come by your wide lip ? " " By licking," she answered, " by licking." Then he asked the third, " How do you come by your broad thumb ? " " By twisting the thread," she answered, " by twisting the thread." On this the King's son was alarmed and said, " Neither now nor ever shall my beautiful bride touch a spinning-wheel." And thus she got rid of the hateful flax-spinning.

THE WHITE SNAKE

A LONG time ago there lived a king who was famed for his wisdom through all the land. Nothing was hidden from him, and it seemed as if news of the most secret things was brought to him through the air. But he had a strange custom ; every day after dinner, when the table was cleared, and no one else was present, a trusty servant had to bring him one more dish. It was covered, however, and even the servant did not know what was in it, neither did any one know, for the King never took off the cover to eat of it until he was quite alone.

This had gone on for a long time, when one day the servant, who took away the dish, was overcome with such curiosity that he could not help carrying the dish into his room. When he had carefully locked the door, he lifted up the cover, and saw a white snake lying on the dish. But when he saw it he could not deny himself the pleasure of tasting it, so he cut off a little bit and put it into his mouth. No sooner had it touched his tongue than he heard a strange whispering of little voices outside his window. He went and listened, and then noticed that it was the sparrows who were chattering together, and telling one another of all kinds of things which they had seen in the fields and woods. Eating the snake had given him power of understanding the language of animals.

Now it so happened that on this very day the Queen lost her most beautiful ring, and suspicion of having stolen it fell upon this trusty servant, who was allowed to go everywhere. The King ordered the man to be brought before him, and threatened with angry words that unless he could before the morrow point out the thief, he himself should be looked upon as guilty and executed. In vain he declared his innocence ; he was dismissed with no better answer.

In his trouble and fear he went down into the courtyard and took thought how to help himself out of his trouble. Now some ducks were sitting together quietly by a brook and taking their rest ; and, whilst they were making their feathers smooth with their bills, they were having a confidential conversation together. The servant stood by and listened. They were telling one another of all the places where they had been waddling about all the morning, and what good food they had found ; and one said in a pitiful tone, " Something lies heavy on my stomach ; as I was eating in haste I swallowed a ring which lay under the Queen's window." The servant at once seized her by the neck, carried her to the kitchen, and said to the cook, " Here is a fine duck ; pray kill her." " Yes," said the cook, and weighed her in his hand ; " she has spared no trouble to fatten herself, and has been waiting to be roasted long enough." So he cut off her head, and as she was being dressed for the spit, the Queen's ring was found inside her.

The servant could now easily prove his innocence ; and the King, to make amends for the wrong, allowed him to ask a favour, and promised him the best place in the court that he could wish for. The servant refused everything, and only asked for a horse and some money for travelling, as he had a mind to see the world and go about a little.

When his request was granted he set out on his way, and one day came to a pond, where he saw three fishes caught in the reeds and gasping for water. Now, though it is said that fishes are dumb, he heard them lamenting that they must perish so miserably, and, as he had a kind heart, he got off his horse and put the three prisoners back into the water. They quivered with delight, put out their heads, and cried to him, " We will remember you and repay you for saving us ! "

He rode on, and after a while it seemed to him that he heard a voice in the sand at his feet. He listened, and heard an ant-king complain, " Why cannot folks, with their clumsy beasts, keep off our bodies ? That stupid horse, with his heavy hoofs, has been treading down my people without mercy ! " So he turned on to a side path and the ant-king cried out to him, " We will remember you—one good turn deserves another ! "

The path led him into a wood, and there he saw two old ravens standing by their nest, and throwing out their young ones. " Out with you, you idle, good-for-nothing creatures ! " cried they ; " we cannot find food for you any longer ; you are big enough, and can provide for yourselves." But the poor young ravens lay upon the ground flapping their wings, and crying, " Oh, what helpless chicks we are ! We must shift for ourselves, and yet we cannot fly ! What can we do, but lie here and starve ? " So the good young fellow alighted and killed his horse with his sword, and gave it to them for food. Then they came hopping up to it, satisfied their hunger, and cried, " We will remember you—one good turn deserves another ! "

And now he had to use his own legs, and when he had walked a long way, he came to a large city. There was a great noise and crowd in the streets, and a man rode up on horseback, crying aloud, "The King's daughter wants a husband; but whoever sues for her hand must perform a hard task, and if he does not succeed he will forfeit his life." Many had already made the attempt, but in vain; nevertheless when the youth saw the King's daughter he was so overcome by her great beauty that he forgot all danger, went before the King, and declared himself a suitor.

So he was led out to the sea, and a gold ring was thrown into it, in his sight; then the King ordered him to fetch this ring up from the bottom of the sea, and added, "If you come up again without it you will be thrown in again and again until you perish amid the waves." All the people grieved for the handsome youth; then they went away, leaving him alone by the sea.

He stood on the shore and considered what he should do, when suddenly he saw three fishes come swimming towards him, and they were the very fishes whose lives he had saved. The one in the middle held a mussel in its mouth, which it laid on the shore at the youth's feet, and when he had taken it up and opened it, there lay the gold ring in the shell. Full of joy he took it to the King, and expected that he would grant him the promised reward.

But when the proud princess perceived that he was not her equal in birth, she scorned him, and required him first to perform another task. She went down into the garden and strewed with her own hands ten sacks-full of millet-seed on the grass: then she said, "To-morrow morning before sunrise these must be picked up, and not a single grain be wanting."

The youth sat down in the garden and considered how it might be possible to perform this task, but he could think of nothing, and there he sat sorrowfully awaiting the break of day, when he should be led to death. But as soon as the first rays of the sun shone into the garden he saw all the ten sacks standing side by side, quite full, and not a single grain was missing. The ant-king had come in the night with thousands and thousands of ants, and the grateful creatures had by great industry picked up all the millet-seed and gathered them into the sacks.

Presently the King's daughter herself came down into the garden,

and was amazed to see that the young man had done the task she had given him. But she could not yet conquer her proud heart, and said, "Although he has performed both the tasks, he shall not be my husband until he has brought me an apple from the Tree of Life."

The youth did not know where the Tree of Life stood, but he set out, and would have gone on for ever, as long as his legs would carry him, though he had no hope of finding it. After he had wandered through three kingdoms, he came one evening to a wood, and lay down under a tree to sleep. But he heard a rustling in the branches, and a golden apple fell into his hand. At the same time three ravens flew down to him, perched themselves upon his knee, and said, " We are the three young ravens whom you saved from starving ; when we had grown big, and heard that you were seeking the Golden Apple, we flew over the sea to the end of the world, where the Tree of Life stands, and have brought you the apple." The youth, full of joy, set out homewards, and took the Golden Apple to the King's beautiful daughter, who had now no more excuses left to make. They cut the Apple of Life in two and ate it together ; and then her heart became full of love for him, and they lived in undisturbed happiness to a great age.

THE GOLD-CHILDREN

THERE was once a poor man and a poor woman who had nothing but a little cottage, and who earned their bread by fishing, and always lived from hand to mouth. But it came to pass one day when the man was sitting by the water-side, and casting his net, that he drew out a fish entirely of gold. As he was looking at the fish, full of astonish-ment, it began to speak and said, " Hark you, fisherman, if you will throw me back again into the water, I will change your little hut into a splendid castle." Then the fisherman answered, " Of what use is a castle to me, if I have nothing to eat ? " The gold fish continued,

" That shall be taken care of, there will be a cupboard in the castle in which, when you open it, shall be dishes of the most delicate meats, and as many of them as you can desire." " If that be true," said the man, " then I can well do you a favour." " Yes," said the fish, " there is, however, the condition that you shall disclose to no one in the world, whosoever he may be, whence your good luck has come, if you speak but one single word, all will be over." Then the man threw the wonderful fish back again into the water, and went home. But where his hovel had formerly stood, now stood a great castle. He opened wide his eyes, entered, and saw his wife dressed in beautiful clothes, sitting in a splendid room, and she was quite delighted, and said, " Husband, how has all this come to pass? It suits me very well." " Yes," said the man, " it suits me too, but I am frightfully hungry, just give me something to eat." Said the wife, " But I have got nothing and don't know where to find anything in this new house." " There is no need of your knowing," said the man, " for I see yonder a great cupboard, just unlock it." When she opened it, there stood cakes, meat, fruit, wine, quite a bright prospect.

Then the woman cried joyfully, " What more can you want, my dear?" and they sat down, and ate and drank together. When they had had enough, the woman said, " But, husband, whence come all these riches?" " Alas," answered he, " do not question me about it, for I dare not tell you anything ; if I disclose it to any one, then all our good fortune will fly." " Very good," said she, " if I am not to know anything, then I do not want to know anything." However, she was not in earnest ; she never rested day or night, and she goaded her husband until in his impatience he revealed that all was owing to a wonderful golden fish which he had caught, and to which in return he had given its liberty. And as soon as the secret was out, the splendid castle with the cupboard immediately disappeared, they were once more in the old fisherman's hut, and the man was obliged to follow his former trade and fish. But fortune would so have it, that he once more drew out the golden fish. " Listen," said the fish, " if you will throw me back into the water again, I will once more give you the castle with the cupboard full of roast and boiled meats ; only be firm, for your life's sake don't reveal from whom you have it, or you will lose it all again !" " I will take good care," answered the fisherman,

196

and threw the fish back into the water. Now at home everything was once more in its former magnificence, and the wife was overjoyed at their good fortune, but curiosity left her no peace, so that after a couple of days she began to ask again how it had come to pass, and how he had managed to secure it. The man kept silence for a short time, but at last she made him so angry that he broke out, and betrayed the secret. In an instant the castle disappeared, and they were back again in their old hut. "Now you have got what you want," said he ; "and we can gnaw at a bare bone again." "Ah," said the woman, "I had rather not have riches if I am not to know from whom they come, for then I have no peace."

The man went back to fish, and after a while he chanced to draw out the gold fish for a third time. "Listen," said the fish, "I see very well that I am fated to fall into your hands, take me home and cut me into six pieces ; give your wife two of them to eat, two to your horse and bury two of them in the ground, then they will bring you a blessing." The fisherman took the fish home with him, and did as it had bidden him. It came to pass, however, that from the two pieces that were buried in the ground two golden lilies sprang up, that the horse had two golden foals, and the fisherman's wife bore two children who were made entirely of gold. The children grew up, became tall and handsome, and the lilies and horses grew likewise. Then they said, "Father, we want to mount our golden steeds and travel out in the world." But he answered sorrowfully, "How shall I bear it if you go away, and I know not how it fares with you ? " Then they said, "The two golden lilies remain here. By them you can see how it is with us ; if they are fresh, then we are in health ; if they are withered, we are ill ; if they perish, then we are dead." So they rode forth and came to an inn, in which were many people, and when they perceived the gold-children they began to laugh, and jeer. When one of them heard the mocking he felt ashamed and would not go out into the world, but turned back and went home again to his father. But the other rode forward and reached a great forest. As he was about to enter it, the people said, "It is not safe for you to ride through, the wood is full of robbers who would treat you badly. You will fare ill, and when they see that you are all of gold, and your horse likewise, they will assuredly kill you."

But he would not allow himself to be frightened, and said, " I must and will ride through it." Then he took bear-skins and covered himself and his horse with them, so that the gold was no more to be seen, and rode fearlessly into the forest. When he had ridden onward a little he heard a rustling in the bushes, and heard voices speaking together. From one side came cries of, " There is one," but from the other, " Let him go, 'tis an idle fellow, as poor and bare as a church-mouse, what should we gain from him ? "

So the gold-child rode joyfully through the forest, and no evil befell him. One day he entered a village wherein he saw a maiden, who was so beautiful that he did not believe that any more beautiful than she, existed in the world. And as such a mighty love took possession of him, he went up to her and said, " I love thee with my whole heart, wilt thou be my wife ? " He, too, pleased the maiden so much that she agreed and said, " Yes, I will be thy wife, and be true to thee thy whole life long." Then they were married, and just as they were in the greatest happiness, home came the father of the bride, and when he saw that his daughter's wedding was being celebrated, he was astonished, and said, " Where is the bridegroom ? " They showed him the gold-child, who, however, still wore his bear-skins. Then the father said wrathfully, " A vagabond shall never have my daughter ! " and was about to kill him. Then the bride begged as hard as she could, and said, " He is my husband, and I love him with all my heart ! " until at last he allowed himself to be appeased. Nevertheless the idea never left his thoughts, so that next morning he rose early, wishing to see whether his daughter's husband was a common ragged beggar. But when he peeped in, he saw a magnificient golden man in the bed, and the cast-off bear-skins lying on the ground. Then he went back and thought, " What a good thing it was that I restrained my anger ! I should have committed a great crime." But the gold-child dreamed that he rode out to the chase of a splendid stag, and when he awoke in the morning, he said to his wife, " I must go out hunting." She was uneasy, and begged him to stay there, and said, " You might easily meet with a great misfortune," but he answered, " I must and will go."

Thereupon he got up, and rode forth into the forest, and it was not long before a fine stag crossed his path exactly according to his dream. He aimed and was about to shoot it, when the stag ran away. He gave chase over hedges and ditches for the whole day without feeling tired, but in the evening the stag vanished from his sight, and when the gold-child looked round him, he was standing before a little house, wherein was a witch. He knocked, and a little old woman came out and asked, " What are you doing so late in the midst of the great forest ? " " Have you not seen a stag ? " " Yes," answered she, " I know the stag well," and thereupon a little dog which had come out of the house with her, barked at the man violently. " Wilt thou be silent, thou odious toad," said he, " or I will shoot thee dead." Then the witch cried out in a passion, " What ! will you slay my little dog ? " and immediately transformed him, so that he lay like a stone, and his bride awaited him in vain, and thought, " That which I so greatly dreaded, which lay so heavily on my heart, has come upon him ! " But at home the other brother was standing by the gold-lilies, when one of them suddenly drooped. " Good heavens ! " said he, " my brother has met with some great misfortune ! I must away to see if I can possibly rescue him." Then the father said, " Stay here, if I lose you also, what shall I do ? " But he answered, " I must and will go forth ! "

Then he mounted his golden horse, and rode forth and entered the great forest, where his brother lay turned to stone. The old witch came out of her house and called him, wishing to entrap him also, but he did not go near her, but said, " I will shoot you, if you will not bring my brother to life again." She touched the stone, though very unwillingly, with her forefinger, and he was immediately restored to his human shape. But the two gold-children rejoiced, when they saw each other again, kissed and caressed each other, and rode away together out of the forest, the one home to his bride, the other to his father. The father then said, " I knew well that you had rescued your brother, for the golden lily suddenly rose up and blossomed out again." Then they lived happily, and all prospered with them until their death.

THE POOR MILLER'S BOY AND THE CAT

IN a certain mill lived an old miller who had neither wife nor child, and three apprentices served under him. As they had been with him several years, he one day said to them, " I am old, and want to sit in the chimney-corner, go out, and whichsoever of you brings me the best horse home, to him will I give the mill, and in return for it he shall take care of me till my death." The third of the boys was, however, the drudge, who was looked on as foolish by the others : they begrudged the mill to him, and determined he should not have it. Then all three went out together, and when they came to the village, the two said to stupid Hans, " Thou mayst just as well stay here, as long as thou livest thou wilt never get a horse." Hans, however, went with them, and when it was night they came to a cave in which they lay down to sleep. The two sharp ones waited until Hans had fallen asleep, then they got up, and went away leaving him where he was. And they thought they had done a very clever thing, but it was certain to turn out ill for them. When the sun arose, and Hans woke up, he was lying in a deep cavern. He looked around on every side and exclaimed, " Oh, heavens, where am I ? " Then he got up and clambered out of the cave, went into the forest, and thought, " Here I am quite alone and deserted, how shall I obtain a horse now ? " Whilst he was thus walking full of thought, he met a small tabby-cat which said quite kindly, " Hans, where are you going ? " " Alas, thou canst not help me." " I well know your desire," said the cat. " You wish to have a beautiful horse. Come with me, and be my faithful servant for seven years long, and then I will give you one more beautiful than any you have ever seen in your whole life." " Well, this is a wonderful cat ! " thought Hans, " but I am determined to see if she is telling the truth." So she took him with her into her enchanted castle, where there were nothing but cats who were her servants. They leapt nimbly upstairs and downstairs, and were merry and happy. In the evening when they sat down to dinner, three of them had to make music. One played the bassoon, the other the fiddle, and the third put the trumpet to his lips, and blew out his cheeks as much as he possibly could. When they had dined, the table

was carried away, and the cat said, " Now, Hans, come and dance with me." " No," said he, " I won't dance with a pussy cat. I have never done that yet." " Then take him to bed," said she to the cats. So one of them lighted him to his bed-room, one pulled his shoes off, one his stockings, and at last one of them blew out the cnadle. Next morning they returned and helped him out of bed, one put his stockings on for him, one tied his garters, one brought his shoes, one washed him, and one dried his face with her tail. " That feels very soft ! " said Hans. He, however, had to serve the cat, and chop some wood every day, and to do that he had an axe of silver, and the wedge and saw were of silver and the mallet of copper. So he chopped the wood small ; stayed there in the house and had good meat and drink, but never saw any one but the tabby-cat and her servants. Once she said to him, " Go and mow my meadow, and dry the grass," and gave him a scythe of silver, and a whetstone of gold, but bade him deliver them up again carefully. So Hans went thither, and did what he was bidden, and when he had finished the work, he carried the scythe, whetstone, and hay to the house, and asked if it was not yet time for her to give him his reward. " No," said the cat, " you must first do something more for me of the same kind, there is timber of silver, carpenter's axe, square, and everything that is needful, all of silver, with these build me a small house." Then Hans built the small house, and said that he had now done everything, and still he had no horse. Nevertheless, the seven years had gone by with him as if they were six months. The cat asked him if he would like to see her horses ? " Yes," said Hans. The she opened the door of the small house, and when she had opened it, there stood twelve horses,—such horses, so bright and shining, that his heart rejoiced at the sight of them. And now she gave him to eat and to drink, and said, " Go home, I will not give thee thy horse to take with thee ; but in three days' I will follow thee and bring it." So Hans set out, and she showed him the way to the mill. She had, however, never once given him a new coat, and he had been obliged to keep on his dirty old smock-frock, which he had brought with him, and which during the seven years had every-where become too small for him. When he reached home, the two other apprentices were there again as well, and each of them certainly had brought a horse with him, but one of them was a blind one, and the other lame. They asked Hans where his horse was? " It will follow me in three days' time." Then they laughed and said, " Indeed, stupid Hans, where wilt thou get a horse? It will be a fine one !" Hans went into the parlour, but the miller said he should not sit down to table, for he was so ragged and torn, that they would all be ashamed of him if any one came in. So they gave him a mouthful of food outside, and at night, when they went to rest, the two others would not let have a bed, and at last he was forced to creep into the goose-house, and lie down on a little hard straw. In the morning when he awoke, the three days had passed, and a coach came with six horses and they shone so bright that it was delightful to see them !—and a servant brought a seventh as well, which was for the poor miller's boy. And a magnificent princess alighted from the coach and went into the mill, and this princess was the little tabby-cat whom poor Hans had served for seven years. She asked the miller where the miller's boy and drudge was? Then the miller said, " We cannot have him here in the mill, for he is so ragged ; he is lying in the goose-house." Then the King's daughter said that they were to bring him immediately. So they brought him out, and he had to hold his little smock-frock together to cover himself. The servants unpacked splendid garments, and washed him and dressed him, and when that was done, no King could have looked more handsome. Then the maiden desired to see the horses which the other apprentices had brought home with them, and one of them was blind and the other lame. So she ordered the servant to bring the seventh horse, and when the miller saw it, he said that such a horse as that had never yet entered his yard. " And that is for the third miller's-boy," said she. " Then he must have the mill," said the miller, but the King's daughter said that the horse was there, and that he was to keep his mill as well, and took her faithful Hans and set him in the coach, and drove away with him. They first drove to the little house which he had built with the silver tools, and behold it was a great castle, and everything inside it was of silver and gold ; and then she married him, and he was rich, so rich that he had enough for all the rest of his life. After this, let no one ever say that any one who is silly can never become a person of importance.

LITTLE BRIAR-ROSE

A LONG time ago there were a King and Queen who said every day, " Ah, if only we had a child ! " but they never had one. But it happened that once when the Queen was bathing, a frog crept out of the water on to the land, and said to her, " Your wish shall be fulfilled ; before a year has gone by you shall have a daughter."

What the frog had said came true, and the Queen had a little girl who was so pretty that the King could not contain himself for joy, and ordered a great feast. He invited not only his kindred, friends and acquaintance, but also the Wise Women, in order that they might be kind and well-disposed towards the child. There were thirteen of them in his kingdom, but, as he had only twelve golden plates for them to eat out of, one of them had to be left at home.

The feast was held with all manner of splendour, and when it came to an end the Wise Women bestowed their magic gifts upon the baby : one gave virtue, another beauty, a third riches, and so on with everything in the world that one can wish for.

When eleven of them had made their promises, suddenly the thirteenth came in. She wished to avenge herself for not having been invited, and without greeting, or even looking at any one, she cried with a loud voice, " The King's daughter shall in her fifteenth year prick herself with a spindle and fall down dead." And without saying a word more she turned round and left the room.

They were all shocked ; but the twelfth, whose good wish still remained unspoken, came forward, and as she could not undo the evil sentence, but only soften it, she said, " It shall not be death, but a deep sleep of a hundred years, into which the princess shall fall."

The King, who would fain keep his dear child from the misfortune, gave orders that every spindle in the whole kingdom should be burnt. Meanwhile the gifts of the Wise Women were plenteously fulfilled on the young girl, for she was so beautiful, modest, good-natured, and wise, that every one who saw her was bound to love her.

It happened that on the very day when she was fifteen years old, the King and Queen were not at home, and the maiden was left in the palace quite alone. So she went round into all sorts of places, looked into rooms and bed-chambers just as she liked, and at last came to an old tower. She climbed up the narrow winding-staircase, and reached a little door. A rusty key was in the lock, and when she turned it the door sprang open, and there in a little room sat an old woman with a spindle, busily spinning her flax.

"Good day, old dame," said the King's daughter; "what are you doing there?" "I am spinning," said the old woman, and nodded her head. "What sort of thing is that, that rattles round so merrily?" said the girl, and she took the spindle and wanted to spin too. But scarcely had she touched the spindle when the magic decree was fulfilled, and she pricked her finger with it.

And, in the very moment when she felt the prick, she fell down upon the bed that stood there, and lay in a deep sleep. And this sleep extended over the whole palace; the King and Queen who had just come home, and had entered the great hall, began to go to sleep, and the whole of the court with them. The horses, too, went to sleep in the stable, the dogs in the yard, the pigeons upon the roof, the flies on the wall; even the fire that was flaming on the hearth became quiet and slept, the roast meat left off frizzling, and the cook, who was just going to pull the hair of the scullery boy, because he had forgotten something, let him go, and went to sleep. And the wind fell, and on the trees before the castle not a leaf moved again.

But round about the castle there began to grow a hedge of thorns, which every year became higher, and at last grew close up round the castle and all over it, so that there was nothing of it to be seen, not even the flag upon the roof. But the story of the beautiful sleeping "Briar-rose," for so the princess was named, went about the country, so that from time to time kings' sons came and tried to get through the thorny hedge into the castle.

But they found it impossible, for the thorns held fast together, as if they had hands, and the youths were caught in them, could not get loose again, and died a miserable death.

After long, long years a King's son came again to that country, and heard an old man talking about the thorn-hedge, and that a castle was said to stand behind it in which a wonderfully beautiful princess, named Briar-rose, had been asleep for a hundred years; and that the King and Queen and the whole court were asleep likewise. He had heard, too, from his grandfather, that many kings' sons had already come, and had tried to get through the thorny hedge, but they had remained sticking fast in it, and had died a pitiful death. Then the youth said, " I am not afraid, I will go and see the beautiful Briar-rose." The good old man might dissuade him as he would, he did not listen to his words.

But by this time the hundred years had just passed, and the day had come when Briar-rose was to awake again. When the King's son came near to the thorn-hedge, it was nothing but large and beautiful flowers, which parted from each other of their own accord, and let him pass unhurt, then they closed again behind him like a hedge. In the castle-yard he saw the horses and the spotted hounds lying asleep ; on the roof sat the pigeons with their heads under their wings. And when he entered the house, the flies were asleep upon the wall, the cook in the kitchen was still holding out his hand to seize the boy, and the maid was sitting by the black hen which she was going to pluck.

He went on farther, and in the great hall he saw the whole of the court lying asleep, and up by the throne lay the King and Queen.

Then he went on still farther, and all was so quiet that a breath could be heard, and at last he came to the tower, and opened the door into the little room where Briar-rose was sleeping. There she lay, so beautiful that he could not turn his eyes away ; and he stooped down and gave her a kiss. But as soon as he kissed her, Briar-rose opened her eyes and awoke, and looked at him sweetly.

Then they went down together, and the King awoke, and the Queen, and the whole court, and looked at each other in great astonishment. And the horses in the court-yard stood up and shook themselves ; the hounds jumped up and wagged their tails ; the pigeons upon the roof pulled out their heads from under their wings, looked round, and flew into the open country ; the flies on the wall crept again ; the fire in the kitchen burned up and flickered and cooked the meat ; the joint began to turn and frizzle again, and the cook gave the boy such a box on the ear that he screamed, and the maid plucked the fowl ready for roasting. And then the marriage of the King's son with Briar-rose was celebrated with all splendour, and they lived contented to the end of their days.

THE SINGING, SOARING LARK

THERE was once on a time a man who was about to set out on a long journey, and on parting he asked his three daughters what he should bring back with him for them. Whereupon the eldest wished for pearls, the second wished for diamonds, but the third said, "Dear father, I should like a singing, soaring lark." The father said, "Yes, if I can get it, you shall have it," kissed all three, and set out. Now when the time had come for him to be on his way home again, he had brought pearls and diamonds for the two eldest, but he had sought everywhere in vain for a singing, soaring lark for the youngest, and he was very unhappy about it, for she was his favourite child. Then his road lay through a forest, and in the midst of it was a splendid castle, and near the castle stood a tree, but quite on the top of the tree, he saw a singing, soaring lark. "Aha, you come just at the right moment !" he said, quite delighted, and called to his servant to climb up and catch the little creature. But as he approached the tree, a lion leapt from beneath it, shook himself, and roared till the leaves on the tree trembled. "He who tries to steal my singing, soaring lark," he cried, "will I devour." Then the man said, "I did not know that the bird belonged to thee. I will make amends for the wrong I have done and ransom myself with a large sum of money, only spare my life." The lion said, "Nothing can save thee, unless thou wilt promise to give me for mine own what first meets thee on thy return home ; but if thou wilt do that, I will grant thee thy life, and thou shalt have the bird for thy daughter, into the bargain." But the man hesitated and said, "That might be my youngest daughter, she loves me best, and always runs to meet me on my return home." The servant, however, was terrified and said, "Why should your daughter be the very one to meet you, it might as easily be a cat or dog ?" Then the man allowed himself to be over-persuaded, took the singing, soaring lark, and promised to give the lion whatsoever should first meet him on his return home.

When he reached home and entered his house, the first who met him was no other than his youngest and dearest daughter, who came running up, kissed and embraced him, and when she saw that he had brought with him a singing, soaring lark, she was beside herself with joy. The father, however, could not rejoice, but began to weep, and said, " My dearest child, I have bought the little bird dear. In return for it, I have been obliged to promise thee to a savage lion, and when he has thee he will tear thee in pieces and devour thee," and he told her all, just as it had happened, and begged her not to go there, come what might. But she consoled him and said, " Dearest father, indeed your promise must be fulfilled. I will go thither and soften the lion, so that I may return to thee safely." Next morning she had the road pointed out to her, took leave, and went fearlessly out into the forest. The lion, however, was an enchanted prince and was by day a lion, and all his people were lions with him, but in the night they resumed their natural human shapes. On her arrival she was kindly received and led into the castle. When night came, the lion turned into a handsome man, and their wedding was celebrated with great magnificence. They lived happily together, remained awake at night, and slept in the daytime. One day he came and said, " To-morrow there is a feast in thy father's house, because thy eldest sister is to be married, and if thou art inclined to go there, my lions shall conduct thee." She said, " Yes, I should very much like to see my father again," and went thither, accompanied by the lions. There was great joy when she arrived, for they had all believed that she had been torn in pieces by the lion, and had long ceased to live. But she told them what a handsome husband she had, and how well off she was, remained with them while the wedding-feast lasted, and then went back again to the forest. When the second daughter was about to be married, and she was again invited to the wedding, she said to the lion, " This time I will not be alone, thou must come with me." The lion, however, said that it was too dangerous for him, for if when there a ray from a burning candle fell on him, he would be changed into a dove, and for seven years long would have to fly about with the doves. She said, " Ah, but do come with me, I will take great care of thee, and guard thee from all light." So they went away together, and took with them their little child as well. She had a chamber built there, so strong and thick that no ray could pierce through it ; in this he was to shut himself up when the candles were lit for the wedding-feast. But the door was made of green wood which warped and left a little crack which no one noticed. The wedding was celebrated with magnificence, but when the procession with all its candles and torches came back from church, and passed by this apartment, a ray about the breadth of a hair fell on the King's son, and when this ray touched him, he was transformed in an instant, and when she came in and looked for him, she did not see him, but a white dove was sitting there. The dove said to her, "For seven years must I fly about the world, but at every seventh step that thou takest I will let fall a drop of red blood and a white feather, and these will show thee the way, and if thou followest the trace thou canst release me." Thereupon the dove flew out at the door, and she followed him, and at every seventh step a red drop of blood and a little white feather fell down and showed her the way.

So she went continually further and further in the wide world, never looking about her or resting, and the seven years were almost past ; then she rejoiced and thought that they would soon be delivered, and yet they were so far from it ! Once when they were thus moving onwards, no little feather and no drop of red blood fell, and when she raised her eyes the dove had disappeared. And as she thought to herself, "In this no man can help thee," she climbed up to the sun, and said to him, "Thou shinest into every crevice, and over every peak, hast not thou seen a white dove flying ? " " No," said the sun, "I have seen none, but I present thee with a casket, open it when thou art in sorest need." Then she thanked the sun, and went on until evening came and the moon appeared ; she then asked her, "Thou shinest the whole night through, and on every field and forest, hast thou not seen a white dove flying ? " " No," said the moon, "I have seen no dove, but here I give thee an egg, break it when thou art in great need." She thanked the moon, and went on until the night wind came up and blew on her, then she said to it, "Thou blowest over every tree and under every leaf, hast thou not seen a white dove flying ? " " No," said the night wind, " I have seen none, but I will ask the three other winds, perhaps they have seen it." The east wind and the west wind came, and had seen nothing, but the south wind said, " I have seen the white dove, it has flown to the Red Sea, there it has become a lion again, for the seven years are over, and the lion is there fighting with a dragon ; the dragon, however, is an

enchanted princess." The night wind then said to her, " I will advise thee ; go to the Red Sea, on the right bank are some tall reeds, count them, break off the eleventh, and strike the dragon with it, then the lion will be able to subdue it, and both then will regain their human form. After that, look round and thou wilt see the griffin which is by the Red Sea ; swing thyself, with thy beloved, on to his back, and the bird will carry you over the sea to your own home. Here is a nut for thee, when thou art above the centre of the sea, let the nut fall, it will immediately shoot up, and a tall nut-tree will grow out of the water on which the griffin may rest ; for if he cannot rest, he will not be strong enough to carry you across, and if thou forgettest to throw down the nut, he will let you fall into the sea."

Then she went thither, and found everything as the night wind had said. She counted the reeds by the sea, and cut off the eleventh, struck the dragon therewith, whereupon the lion overcame it, and immediately both of them regained their human shapes. But when the princess, who had before been the dragon, was delivered from enchantment, she took the youth by the arm, seated herself on the griffin, and carried him off with her. There stood the poor maiden who had wandered so far and was again forsaken. She sat down and cried, but at last she took courage and said, " Still I will go as far as the wind blows and as long as the cock crows, until I find him," and she went forth by long, long roads, until at last she came to the castle where both of them were living together ; there she heard that soon a feast was to be held, in which they would celebrate their wedding, but she said, " God still helps me," and opened the casket that the sun had given her. A dress lay therein as brilliant as the sun itself. So she took it out and put it on, and went up into the castle, and every-one, even the bride herself, looked at her with astonishment. The dress pleased the bride so well that she thought it might be for her wedding-dress, and asked if it was for sale ? " Not for money or land," answered she, " but for flesh and blood." The bride asked her what she meant by that, then she said, " Let me sleep one night in the room where the bridegroom sleeps." The bride would not, yet wanted very much to have the dress ; at last she consented, but the page was to give the prince a sleeping-draught. When it was night, therefore, and the youth was already asleep, she was led into the chamber ;

she seated herself on the bed and said, " I have followed after thee for seven years. I have been to the sun and the moon, and the four winds, and have enquired for thee, and have helped thee against the dragon ; wilt thou, then, quite forget me ? " But the prince slept so soundly that it only seemed to him as if the wind were whistling outside in the fir-trees. When therefore day broke, she was led out again, and had to give up the golden dress. And as that even had been of no avail, she was sad, went out into a meadow, sat down there, and wept. While she was sitting there, she thought of the egg which the moon had given her ; she opened it, and there came out a clucking hen with twelve chickens all of gold, and they ran about chirping, and crept again under the old hen's wings ; nothing more beautiful was ever seen in the world ! Then she arose, and drove them through the meadow before her, until the bride looked out of the window. The little chickens pleased her so much that she immediately came down and asked if they were for sale. " Not for money or land, but for flesh and blood ; let me sleep another night in the chamber where the bridegroom sleeps." The bride said, " Yes," intending to cheat her as on the former evening. But when the prince went to bed he asked the page what the murmuring and rustling in the night had been ? On this the page told all ; that he had been forced to give him a sleeping-draught, because a poor girl had slept secretly in the chamber, and that he was to give him another that night. The prince said, " Pour out the draught by the bedside." At night, she was again led in, and when she began to relate how ill all had fared with her, he immediately recognized his beloved wife by her voice, sprang up and cried, " Now I really am released ! I have been as it were in a dream, for the strange princess has bewitched me so that I have been compelled to forget thee, but God has delivered me from the spell at the right time." Then they both left the castle secretly in the night, for they feared the father of the princess, who was a sorcerer, and they seated themselves on the griffin which bore them across the Red Sea, and when they were in the midst of it, she let fall the nut. Immediately a tall nut-tree grew up, whereon the bird rested, and then carried them home, where they found their child, who had grown tall and beautiful, and they lived thenceforth happily until their death.

THE GRAVE-MOUND

A RICH farmer was one day standing in his yard inspecting his fields and gardens. The corn was growing up vigorously and the fruit-trees were heavily laden with fruit. The grain of the year before still lay in such immense heaps on the floors that the rafters could hardly bear it. Then he went into the stable, where were well-fed oxen, fat cows, and horses bright as looking-glass. At length he went back into his sitting-room, and cast a glance at the iron chest in which his money lay.

Whilst he was thus standing surveying his riches, all at once there was a loud knock close by him. The knock was not at the door of his room, but at the door of his heart. It opened, and he heard a voice which said to him, " Hast thou done good to thy family with it ? Hast thou considered the necessities of the poor ? Hast thou shared thy bread with the hungry ? Hast thou been contented with what thou hast, or didst thou always desire to have more ? " His heart was not slow in answering, " I have been hard and pitiless, and have never shown any kindness to my own family. If a beggar came, I turned away my eyes from him. I have not troubled myself about God, but have thought only of increasing my wealth. If everything which the sky covers had been mine own, I should still not have had enough."

When he was aware of this answer he was greatly alarmed, his knees began to tremble, and he was forced to sit down.

Then there was another knock, but the knock was at the door of his room. It was his neighbour, a poor man who had a number of children whom he could no longer satisfy with food. " I know," thought the poor man, " that my neighbour is rich, but he is as hard as he is rich. I don't believe he will help me, but my children are crying for bread, so I will venture it." He said to the rich man, " You do not readily give away anything that is yours, but I stand here like one who feels the water rising above his head. My children are starving, lend me four measures of corn." The rich man looked at him long, and then the first sunbeam of mercy began to melt away some of the ice of his greediness. " I will not lend thee four measures," he answered, " but I will make thee a present of eight, but thou must fulfil one condition." " What am I to do ? " said the poor man. " When I am dead, thou shalt watch for three nights by my grave." The peasant was disturbed in his mind at this request, but in the need in which he was, he would have consented to anything ; he accepted, therefore, and carried the corn home with him.

It seemed as if the rich man had foreseen what was about to happen, for when three days were gone by, he suddenly dropped down dead. No one knew exactly how it came to pass, but no one grieved for him. When he was buried, the poor man remembered his promise ; he would willingly have been released from it, but he thought, " After all, he acted kindly by me. I have fed my hungry children with his corn, and even if that were not the case, where I have once given my promise I must keep it." At nightfall he went into the churchyard, and seated himself on the grave-mound. Everything was quiet, only the moon appeared above the grave, and frequently an owl flew past and uttered her melancholy cry. When the sun rose, the poor man betook himself in safety to his home, and in the same manner the second night passed quietly by. On the evening of the third day he he felt a strange uneasiness, it seemed to him that something was about to happen. When he went out he saw, by the churchyard-wall, a man whom he had never seen before. He was no longer young, had scars on his face, and his eyes looked sharply and eagerly around. He was entirely covered with an old cloak, and nothing was visible but his great riding-boots. " What are you looking for here ? " the peasant asked. " Are you not afraid of this lonely place ? "

" I am looking for nothing," he answered, " and I am afraid of nothing ! I am like the youngster who went forth to learn how to shiver, and had his labour for his pains, but got the King's daughter to wife and great wealth with her, only I have remained poor. I am nothing but a paid-off soldier, and I mean to pass the night here, because I have no other shelter." " If you are without fear," said the peasant, " stay with me, and help me to watch that grave there."

" To keep watch is a soldier's business," he replied, " whatever we fall in with here, whether it be good or bad, we will share it between us." The peasant agreed to this, and they seated themselves on the grave together.

All was quiet until midnight, when suddenly a shrill whistling was heard in the air, and the two watchers perceived the Evil One standing bodily before them. " Be off, you ragamuffins ! " cried he to them, " the man who lies in that grave belongs to me ; I want to take him, and if you don't go away I will wring your necks ! " " Sir with the red cloak," said the soldier, " you are not my captain, I have no need to obey you, and I have not yet learned how to fear. Go away, we shall stay sitting here."

The Devil thought to himself, " Money is the best thing with which to get hold of these two vagabonds." So he began to play a softer tune, and asked quite kindly, if they would not accept a bag of money, and go home with it ? " That is worth listening to," answered the soldier, " but one bag of gold won't serve us, if you will give as much as will go into one of my boots, we will quit the field for you and go away."

" I have not so much as that about me," said the Devil, " but I will fetch it. In the neighbouring town lives a money-changer who is a good friend of mine, and will readily advance it to me." When the Devil had vanished the soldier took his left boot off, and said, " We will soon pull that black fellow's nose for him, just give me your knife, comrade." He cut the sole off the boot, and put it in the high grass near the grave on the edge of a hole that was half over-grown. " That will do," said he : " now the chimney-sweep may come."

They both sat down and waited, and it was not long before the Devil returned with a small bag of gold in his hand. " Just pour it in," said the soldier, raising up the boot a little, " but that won't be enough."

The Black One shook out all that was in the bag ; the gold fell through, and the boot remained empty. " Stupid thing," cried the soldier, " it won't do ! Didn't I say so at once ? Go back again, and bring more." The Devil shook his head, went, and in an hour's time came with a much larger bag under his arm. " Now pour it in," cried the soldier, " but I doubt the boot won't be full." The gold clinked as it fell, but the boot remained empty. The Devil looked in himself with his burning eyes, and convinced himself of the truth. " You have shamefully big calves to your legs ! " cried he, and made a wry face. " Did you think," replied the soldier, " that I had a cloven foot like you ? Since when have you been so stingy ? See that you get more gold together, or our bargain will come to nothing ! " The Wicked One went off again. This time he stayed away longer, and when at length he appeared he was panting under the weight of a sack which lay on his shoulders. He emptied it into the boot, which was just as far from being filled as before. He became furious, and was just going to tear the boot out of the soldier's hands, but at that moment the first ray of the rising sun broke forth from the sky, and the Evil Spirit fled away with loud shrieks, so the poor soul was saved.

The peasant wished to divide the gold, but the soldier said, " Give what falls to my lot to the poor, I will come with thee to thy cottage, and together we will live in rest and peace on what remains, as long as God is pleased to permit."

THE OLD WOMAN IN THE WOOD

A POOR servant-girl was once travelling with the family with which she was in service, through a great forest, and when they were in the midst of it, robbers came out of the thicket, and murdered all they found. All perished together except the girl, who had jumped out of the carriage in a fright, and hidden herself behind a tree. When the robbers had gone away with their booty, she came out and beheld the great disaster. Then she began to weep bitterly, and said, " What can a poor girl like me do now ? I do not know how to get out of the forest, no human being lives in it, so I must certainly starve." She walked about and looked for a road, but could find none. When it was evening she seated herself under a tree, gave herself into God's keeping, and resolved to sit waiting there and not go away, let what might happen. When, however, she had sat there for a while, a white dove came flying to her with a little golden key in its mouth. It put the little key in her hand, and said, " Dost thou see that great tree, therein is a little lock, it opens with the tiny key, and there thou wilt find food enough, and suffer no more hunger." Then she went to the tree and opened it, and found milk in a little dish, and white bread to break into it, so that she could eat her fill. When she was satisfied, she said, " It is now the time when the hens at home go to roost, I am so tired I could go to bed too." Then the dove flew to her again, and brought another golden key in its bill, and said, " Open that tree there, and thou wilt find a bed." So she opened it, and found a beautiful white bed, and she prayed God to protect her during the night, and lay down and slept. In the morning the dove came for the third time, and again brought a little key, and said, " Open that tree there, and thou wilt find clothes." And when she opend it, she found garments beset with gold and with jewels, more splendid than those of any king's daughter. So she lived there for some time, and the dove came every day and provided her with all she needed, and it was a quiet good life.

Once, however, the dove came and said, " Wilt thou do something my sake ? " " With all my heart," said the girl. Then said the little dove, " I will guide thee to a small house ; enter it, and inside it, an old woman will be sitting by the fire and will say, ' Good-day.' But on thy life give her no answer, let her do what she will, but pass by her on the right side ; further on, there is a door, which open, and thou wilt enter into a room where a quantity of rings of all kinds are lying, amongst which are some magnificent ones with shining stones ; leave them, however, where they are, and seek out a plain one, which must likewise be amongst them, and bring it here to me as quickly as thou canst." The girl went to the little house, and came to the door. There sat an old woman who stared when she saw her, and said, " Good day, my child." The girl gave her no answer, and opened the door. " Whither away," cried the old woman, and seized her by the gown, and wanted to hold her fast, saying, " That is my house ; no one can go in there if I choose not to allow it." But the girl was silent, got away from her, and went straight into the room. Now there lay on the table an enormous quantity of rings, which gleamed and glittered before her eyes. She turned them over and looked for the plain one, but could not find it. While she was seeking, she saw the old woman and how she was stealing away, and wanting to get off with the bird-cage which she had in her hand. So she went after her and took the cage out of her hand, and when she raised it up and looked into it, a bird was inside which had the plain ring in its bill. Then she took the ring, and ran quite joyously home with it, and thought the little white dove would come and get the ring, but it did not. Then she leant against a tree and determined to wait for the dove, and, as she thus stood, it seemed just as if the tree was soft and pliant, and was letting its branches down. And suddenly the branches twined around her, and were two arms, and when she looked round, the tree was a handsome man, who embraced and kissed her heartily, and said, " Thou hast delivered me from the power of the old woman, who is a wicked witch. She had changed me into a tree, and every day for two hours I was a white dove, and so long as she possessed the ring I could not regain my human form." Then his servants and his horses, who had likewise been changed into trees, were freed from the enchantment also, and stood beside him. And he led them forth to his kingdom, for he was a King's son, and they married, and lived happily.

ONE-EYE, TWO-EYES, AND THREE-EYES

THERE was once a woman who had three daughters, the eldest of whom was called One-eye, because she had only one eye in the middle of her forehead, and the second, Two-eyes, because she had two eyes like other folks, and the youngest, Three-eyes, because she had three eyes ; and her third eye was also in the centre of her forehead. However, as Two-eyes saw just as other human beings did, her sisters and her mother could not endure her. They said to her, " Thou, with thy two eyes, art no better than the common people ; thou dost not belong to us ! " They pushed her about, and threw old clothes to her, and gave her nothing to eat but what they left, and did everything that they could to make her unhappy. It came to pass that Two-eyes had to go out into the fields and tend the goat, but she was still quite hungry, because her sisters had given her so little to eat. So she sat down on a ridge and began to weep, and so bitterly that two streams ran down from her eyes. And once when she looked up in her grief, a woman was standing beside her, who said, " Why art thou weeping, little Two-eyes ? " Two-eyes answered, " Have I not reason to weep, when I have two eyes like other people, and my sisters and mother hate me for it, and push me from one corner to another, throw old clothes at me, and give me nothing to eat but the scraps they leave ? To-day they have given me so little that I am still quite hungry." Then the wise woman said, " Wipe away thy tears, Two-eyes, and I will tell thee something to stop thee ever suffering from hunger again ; just say to thy goat,

> " *Bleat, my little goat, bleat,*
> *Cover the table with something to eat,*"

and then a clean well-spread little table will stand before thee, with the most delicious food upon it of which thou mayst eat as much as thou art inclined for, and when thou hast had enough, and hast no more need of the little table, just say,

> " *Bleat, my little goat, I pray,*
> *And take the table quite away,*"

and then it will vanish again from thy sight." Hereupon the wise woman departed. But Two-eyes thought, "I must instantly make a trial, and see if what she said is true, for I am far too hungry," and she said,

> " *Bleat, my little goat, bleat,*
> *Cover the table with something to eat,*"

and scarcely had she spoken the words than a little table, covered with a white cloth, was standing there, and on it was a plate with a knife and fork, and a silver spoon ; and the most delicious food was there also, warm and smoking as if it had just come out of the kitchen. Then Two-eyes said the shortest prayer she knew, " Lord God, be with us always, Amen," and she helped herself to some food, and enjoyed it. And when she was satisfied, she said, as the wise woman had taught her,

> " *Bleat, my little goat, I pray,*
> *And take the table quite away,*"

and immediately the little table and everything on it was gone again. "That is a delightful way of keeping house ! " thought Two-eyes, and was quite glad and happy.

In the evening, when she went home with her goat, she found a small earthenware dish with some food, which her sisters had set ready for her, but she did not touch it. Next day she again went out with her goat, and left the few bits of broken bread which had been handed to her, lying untouched. The first and second time that she did this, her sisters did not remark it at all, but as it happened every time, they did observe it, and said, " There is something wrong about Two-eyes, she always leaves her food untasted, and she used to eat up everything that was given her ; she must have discovered other ways of getting food." In order that they might learn the truth, they resolved to send One-eye with Two-eyes when she went to drive her goat to the pasture, to observe what Two-eyes did when she was there, and whether any one brought her anything to eat and drink. So when Two-eyes set out the next time, One-eye went to her and said, " I will go with you to the pasture, and see that the goat is well taken care of, and driven where there is food." But Two-eyes knew what was in One-eye's mind, and drove the goat into high grass and said,

" Come, One-eye, we will sit down, and I will sing something to you."
One-eye sat down and was tired with the unaccustomed walk and the
heat of the sun, and Two-eyes sang constantly,

> *" One eye, wakest thou ?*
> *One eye, sleepest thou ? "*

until One-eye shut her one eye, and fell asleep, and as soon as Two-eyes
saw that One-eye was fast asleep, and could discover nothing, she
said,

> *" Bleat, my little goat, bleat,*
> *Cover the table with something to eat,"*

and seated herself at her table, and ate and drank until she was
satisfied, and then she again cried,

> *" Bleat, my little goat, I pray,*
> *And take the table quite away,"*

and in an instant all was gone. Two-eyes now awakened One-eye, and
said, " One-eye, you want to take care of the goat, and go to sleep
while you are doing it, and in the meantime the goat might run all
over the world. Come, let us go home again." So they went home,
and again Two-eyes let her little dish stand untouched, and One-
eye could not tell her mother why she would not eat it, and to excuse
herself said, " I fell asleep when I was out."

Next day the mother said to Three-eyes, " This time thou shalt go
and observe if Two-eyes eats anything when she is out, and if any
one fetches her food and drink, for she must eat and drink in secret."
So Three-eyes went to Two-eyes, and said, " I will go with you and
see if the goat is taken proper care of, and driven where there is food."
But Two-eyes knew what was in Three-eyes' mind, and drove the
goat into high grass and said, " We will sit down, and I will sing
something to you, Three-eyes." Three-eyes sat down and was tired
with the walk and with the heat of the sun, and Two-eyes began the
same song as before, and sang,

> *" Three eyes, are you waking ? "*

but then, instead of singing,

> *" Three eyes, are you sleeping ? "*

as she ought to have done, she thoughtlessly sang,

> " *Two eyes, are you sleeping ?* "

and sang all the time,

> " *Three eyes, are you waking ?*
> *Two eyes, are you sleeping ?* "

Then two of the eyes which Three-eyes had, shut and fell asleep, but the third, as it had not been named in the song, did not sleep. It is true that Three-eyes shut it, but only in her cunning, to pretend it was asleep too, but it blinked, and could see everything very well. And when Two-eyes thought that Three-eyes was fast asleep, she used her little charm,

> " *Bleat, my little goat, bleat,*
> *Cover the table with something to eat.*"

and ate and drank as much as her heart desired, and then ordered the table to go away again,

> " *Bleat, my little goat, I pray,*
> *And take the table quite away,*"

and Three-eyes had seen everything. Then Two-eyes came to her, waked her and said, " Have you been asleep, Three-eyes ? You are a good care-taker ! Come, we will go home." And when they got home, Two-eyes again did not eat, and Three-eyes said to the mother, " Now, I know why that high-minded thing there does not eat. When she is out, she says to the goat,

> " *Bleat, my little goat, bleat,*
> *Cover the table with something to eat,*"

and then a little table appears before her covered with the best of food, much better than any we have here, and when she has eaten all she wants, she says,

> " *Bleat, my little goat, I pray,*
> *And take the table quite away,*"

223

and all disappears. I watched everything closely. She put two of my eyes to sleep by using a certain form of words, but luckily the one nearest to her kept awake." Then the envious mother cried, " Dost thou wish to fare better than we do ? The desire shall pass away," and she fetched a butcher's knife and thrust it into the heart of the goat, which fell down dead.

When Two-eyes saw that, she went out full of trouble, seated herself on the ridge of grass at the edge of the field, and wept bitter tears. Suddenly the wise woman once more stood by her side, and said, " Two-eyes, why art thou weeping ? " " Have I not reason to weep ? " she answered. " The goat which covered the table for me every day when I spoke your charm, has been killed by my mother, and now I shall again have to bear hunger and want." The wise woman said, " Two-eyes, I will give thee a piece of good advice ; ask thy sisters to give thee the heart of the slaughtered goat, and bury it in the ground in front of the house, and thy fortune will be made." Then she vanished, and Two-eyes went home and said to her sisters, " Dear sisters, do give me some part of my goat ; I don't wish for what is good, but give me the heart." Then they laughed and said, " If that's all you want, you can have it." So Two-eyes took the heart and buried it quietly in the evening, in front of the house-door, as the wise woman had counselled her to do.

Next morning, when they all awoke, and went to the house-door, there stood a strangely magnificent tree with leaves of silver, and fruit of gold hanging among them, so that in all the wide world there was nothing more beautiful or precious. They did not know how the tree could have come there during the night, but Two-eyes saw that it had grown up out of the heart of the goat, for it was standing on the exact place where she had buried it. Then the mother said to One-eye, " Climb up, my child, and gather some of the fruit of the tree for us." One-eye climbed up, but when she was about to get hold of one of the golden apples, the branch escaped from her hands, and that happened each time, so that she could not pluck a single apple, let her do what she might. Then said the mother, " Three-eyes, do you climb up ; you with your three eyes can look about you better than One-eye." One-eye slipped down, and Three-eyes climbed up. Three-eyes was not more skilful, and might search as she liked, but the golden apples always escaped her. At length the mother grew impatient, and climbed up herself, but could get hold of the fruit no better than One-eye and Three-eyes, for she always clutched empty air. Then said Two-eyes, " I will just go up, perhaps I may succeed better." The sisters cried, " You indeed, with your two eyes, what can you do ? " But Two-eyes climbed up, and the golden apples did not get out of her way, but came into her hand of their own accord, so that she could pluck them one after the other, and brought a whole apronful down with her. The mother took them away from her, and instead of treating poor Two-eyes any better for this, she and One-eye and Three-eyes were only envious, because Two-eyes alone had been able to get the fruit, and they treated her still more cruelly.

It so befell that once when they were all standing together by the tree, a young knight came up. " Quick, Two-eyes," cried the two sisters, " creep under this, and don't disgrace us ! " and with all speed they turned an empty barrel which was standing close by the tree over poor Two-eyes, and they pushed the golden apples which she had been gathering, under it too. When the knight came nearer he was a handsome lord who stopped and admired the magnificent gold and silver tree, and said to the two sisters, " To whom does this fine tree belong ? Any one who would bestow one branch of it on me might in return for it ask whatsoever he desired." Then One-eye and Three-eyes replied that the tree belonged to them, and that they would give him a branch. They both took great trouble, but they were not able to do it, for the branches and fruit both moved away from them every time. Then said the knight, " It is very strange that the tree should belong to you, and that you should still not be able to break a piece off." They again asserted that the tree was their property. Whilst they were saying so, Two-eyes rolled out a couple of golden apples from under the barrel to the feet of the knight, for she was vexed with One-eye and Three-eyes, for not speaking the truth. When the knight saw the apples he was astonished, and asked where they came from. One-eye and Three-eyes answered that they had another sister, who was not allowed to show herself, for she had only two eyes like any common person. The knight, however, desired to see her, and cried, " Two-eyes, come forth." Then Two-eyes,

o

quite comforted, came from beneath the barrel, and the knight was surprised at her great beauty, and said, " Thou, Two-eyes, canst certainly break off a branch from the tree for me." " Yes," replied Two-eyes, " that I certainly shall be able to do, for the tree belongs to me." And she climbed up, and with the greatest ease broke off a branch with beautiful silver leaves and golden fruit, and gave it to the knight. Then said the knight, " Two-eyes, what shall I give thee for it ? " " Alas ! " answered Two-eyes, " I suffer from hunger and thirst, grief and want, from early morning till late night ; if you would take me with you, and deliver me from these things, I should be happy." So the knight lifted Two-eyes on to his horse, and took her home with him to his father's castle, and there he gave her beautiful clothes, and meat and drink to her heart's content, and as he loved her so much he married her, and the wedding was solemnized with great rejoicing. When Two-eyes was thus carried away by the handsome knight, her two sisters grudged her good fortune in downright earnest. " The wonderful tree, however, still remains with us," thought they, " and even if we can gather no fruit from it, still every one will stand still and look at it, and come to us and admire it. Who knows what good things may be in store for us ? " But next morning, the tree had vanished, and all their hopes were at an end. And when Two-eyes looked out of the window of her own little room, to her great delight it was standing in front of it, and so it had followed her.

Two-eyes lived a long time in happiness. Once two poor women came to her in her castle, and begged for alms. She looked in their faces, and recognized her sisters, One-eye and Three-eyes, who had fallen into such poverty that they had to wander about and beg their bread from door to door. Two-eyes, however, made them welcome, and was kind to them, and took care of them, so that they both with all their hearts repented the evil that they had done their sister in their youth.

WISE FOLKS

ONE day a peasant took his good hazel-stick out of the corner and said to his wife, " Trina, I am going across country, and shall not return for three days. If during that time the cattle-dealer should happen to call and want to buy our three cows, you may strike a bargain at once, but not unless you can get two hundred thalers for them ; nothing less, do you hear ? " " For heaven's sake just go in peace," answered the woman, " I can manage that." " You, indeed," said the man. " Let me tell you this, if you do anything foolish, I will beat you black and blue, you may rely on that." And having said that, the man went on his way.

Next morning the cattle-dealer came, and the woman had no need to say many words to him. When he had seen the cows and heard the price, he said, " I am quite willing to give that. Honestly speaking, they are worth it. I will take the beasts away with me at once." He unfastened their chains and drove them out of the byre, but just as he was going out of the yard-door, the woman clutched him by the sleeve and said, " You must give me the two hundred thalers now, or I cannot let the cows go." " True," answered the man, " but I have forgotten to buckle on my money-belt. Have no fear, however, you shall have security for my paying. I will take two cows with me and leave one, and then you will have a good pledge." The woman saw the force of this, and let the man go away with the cows, and thought to herself, " How pleased Hans will be when he finds how cleverly I have managed it ! " The peasant came home on the third day as he had said he would, and at once inquired if the cows were sold ? " Yes, indeed, dear Hans," answered the woman, " and as you said, for two hundred thalers. They are scarcely worth so much, but the man took them without making any objection." " Where is the money ? " asked the peasant. " Oh, I have not got the money," replied the woman ; " he had happened to forget his money-belt, but he will soon bring it, and he left good security behind him." " What kind of security ? " asked the man. " One of the three cows, which he shall not have until he has paid for the other two. I have managed very

227

cunningly, for I have kept the smallest, which eats the least." The man was enraged and lifted up his stick, and was just going to give her the beating he had promised her. Suddenly he let the stick fall and said, " You are the stupidest goose that ever waddled on God's earth, but I am sorry for you. I will go out into the highways and wait for three days to see if I find any one who is still stupider than you. If I succeed in doing so, you shall go scot-free, but if I do not find him, you shall receive your well-deserved reward without any discount."

He went out into the great highways, sat down on a stone, and waited for what would happen. Then he saw a peasant's waggon coming towards him, and a woman was standing upright in the middle of it, instead of sitting on the bundle of straw which was lying beside her, or walking near the oxen and leading them. The man thought to himself, " That is certainly one of the kind I am in search of," and jumped up and ran backwards and forwards in front of the waggon like one who is not very wise. " What do you want, my friend ? " said the woman to him ; " I don't know you, where do you come from ? " " I have fallen down from Heaven," replied the man, " and don't know how to get back again, couldn't you drive me up ? " " No," said the woman, " I don't know the way, but if you come from Heaven you can surely tell me how my husband, who has been there these three years, is. You must have seen him ? " " Oh, yes, I have seen him, but all men can't get on well. He keeps sheep, and the sheep give him a great deal to do. They run up the mountains and lose their way in the wilderness, and he has to run after them and drive them together again. His clothes are all torn to pieces too, and will soon fall off his body. There is no tailor there, for Saint Peter won't let any of them in, as you know by the story." " Who would have thought it ? " cried the woman, " I tell you what, I will fetch his Sunday coat which is still hanging at home in the cupboard, he can wear that and look respectable. You will be so kind as to take it with you." " That won't do very well," answered the peasant ; " people are not allowed to take clothes into Heaven, they are taken away from one at the gate." " Then hark you," said the woman, " I sold my fine wheat yesterday and got a good lot of money for it, I will send that to him. If you hide the purse in your pocket, no one will know that you have it." " If you can't manage it any other way," said the peasant, " I will do you that favour." " Just sit still where you are," said she, " and I will drive home and fetch the purse, I shall soon be back again. I do not sit down on the bundle of straw, but stand up in the waggon, because it makes it lighter for the cattle." She drove her oxen away, and the peasant thought, " That woman has a perfect talent for folly, if she really brings the money, my wife may think herself fortunate, for she will get no beating." It was not long before she came in a great hurry with the money, and with her own hands put it in his pocket. Before she went away, she thanked him again a thousand times for his courtesy.

When the woman got home again, she found her son who had come in from the field. She told him what unlooked-for things had befallen her, and then added, " I am truly delighted at having found an opportunity of sending something to my poor husband. Who would ever have imagined that he could be suffering for want of anything up in Heaven ? " The son was full of astonishment. " Mother," said he, " it is not every day that a man comes from Heaven in this way, I will go out immediately, and see if he is still to be found ; he must tell me what it is like up there, and how the work is done." He saddled the horse and rode off with all speed. He found the peasant who was sitting under a willow-tree, and was just going to count the money in the purse. " Have you seen the man who has fallen down from Heaven ? " cried the youth to him. " Yes," answered the peasant, " he has set out on his way back there, and has gone up that hill, from whence it will be rather nearer ; you could still catch him up, if you were to ride fast." " Alas," said the youth, " I have been doing tiring work all day, and the ride here has completely worn me out ; you know the man, be so kind as to get on my horse, and go and persuade him to come here." " Aha ! " thought the peasant, " here is another who has no wick in his lamp ! " " Why should I not do you this favour ? " said he, and mounted the horse and rode off in a quick trot. The youth remained sitting there till night fell, but the peasant never came back. " The man from Heaven must certainly have been in a great hurry, and would not turn back," thought he, " and the peasant has no doubt given him the horse to take to my father." He went home and told his mother what had happened, and that he had sent his father the horse so that he might not have to be always running about. " Thou hast done well," answered she, " thy legs are younger than his, and thou canst go on foot."

When the peasant got home, he put the horse in the stable beside the cow which he had as a pledge, and then went to his wife, and said " Trina, as your luck would have it, I have found two who are still sillier fools than you ; this time you escape without a beating, I will store it up for another occasion." Then he lighted his pipe, sat down in his grandfather's chair, and said, " It was a good stroke of business to get a sleek horse and a great purse full of money into the bargain, for two lean cows. If stupidity always brought in as much as that I would be quite willing to hold it in honour." So thought the peasant, but you no doubt prefer the simple and honest folks.

THE WHITE BRIDE AND THE BLACK ONE

A WOMAN was going about the unenclosed land with her daughter and her step-daughter cutting fodder, when the Lord came walking towards them in the form of a poor man, and asked, " Which is the way into the village ? " " If you want to know," said the mother, " seek it for yourself," and the daughter added, " If you are afraid you will not find it, take a guide with you." But the step-daughter said, " Poor man, I will take you there, come with me." Then God was angry with the mother and daughter, and turned his back on them, and wished that they should become as black as night and as ugly as sin. To the poor step-daughter, however, God was gracious, and went with her, and when they were near the village, he said a blessing over her, and spake, " Choose three things for thyself, and I will grant them to thee." Then said the maiden, " I should like to be as beautiful and fair as the sun," and instantly she was white and fair as day. "Then I should like to have a purse of money which would never grow empty." That the Lord gave her also, but he said, "Do not forget what is best of all." Said she, "For my third wish, I desire, after my death, to inhabit the eternal kingdom of Heaven." That also was granted unto her, and then the Lord left her. When the step-mother came home with her daughter, and they saw that they were both as black as coal and ugly, but that the step-daughter was white and beautiful, wickedness increased still more in their hearts, and they thought of nothing else but how they could do her an injury. The step-daughter, however, had a brother called Reginer, whom she loved much, and she told him all that had happened. Once on a time Reginer said to her, "Dear sister, I will take thy likeness, that I may continually see thee before mine eyes, for my love for thee is so great that I should like always to look at thee." Then she answered, "But, I pray thee, let no one see the picture." So he painted his sister and hung up the picture in his room; he, however, dwelt in the King's palace, for he was his coachman. Every day he went and stood before the picture, and thanked God for the happiness of having such a dear sister. Now it happened that the King whom he served, had just lost his wife, who had been so beautiful that no one could be found to compare with her, and on this account the King was in deep grief. The attendants about the court, however, remarked that the coachman stood daily before this beautiful picture, and they were jealous of him, so they informed the King. Then the latter ordered the picture to be brought to him, and when he saw that it was like his lost wife in every respect, except that it was still more beautiful, he fell mortally in love with it. He caused the coachman to be brought before him, and asked whom that portrait represented? The coachman said it was his sister, so the King resolved to take no one but her as his wife, and gave him a carriage and horses and splendid garments of cloth of gold, and sent him forth to fetch his chosen bride. When Reginer came on this errand, his sister was glad, but the black maiden was jealous of her good fortune, and grew angry above all measure, and said to her mother, "Of what use are all your arts to us now when you cannot procure such a piece of luck for me?" "Be quiet," said the old woman, "I will soon divert it to you"—and by her arts of witchcraft, she so troubled the eyes of the coachman that he was half-blind, and she stopped the ears of the white maiden so that she was half-deaf. Then they got into the carriage, first the bride in her noble royal apparel, then the step-mother with her daughter, and Reginer sat on the box to drive. When they had been on the way for some time the coachman cried,

> " *Cover thee well, my sister dear,*
> *That the rain may not wet thee,*
> *That the wind may not load thee with dust,*
> *That thou may'st be fair and beautiful*
> *When thou appearest before the King.*"

The bride asked, " What is my dear brother saying ? " " Ah," said the old woman, " he says that you ought to take off your golden dress and give it to your sister." Then she took it off, and put it on the black maiden, who gave her in exchange for it a shabby grey gown. They drove onwards, and a short time afterwards, the brother again cried,

> " *Cover thee well, my sister dear,*
> *That the rain may not wet thee,*
> *That the wind may not load thee with dust,*
> *That thou may'st be fair and beautiful*
> *When thou appearest before the King.*"

The bride asked, " What is my dear brother saying ? " " Ah," said the old woman, " he says that you ought to take off your golden hood and give it to your sister." So she took off the hood and put it on her sister, and sat with her own head uncovered. And they drove on farther. After a while, the brother once more cried,

> " *Cover thee well, my sister dear,*
> *That the rain may not wet thee,*
> *That the wind may not load thee with dust,*
> *That thou may'st be fair and beautiful*
> *When thou appearest before the King.*"

The bride asked, " What is my dear brother saying ? " " Ah," said the old woman, " he says you must look out of the carriage." They were, however, just on a bridge, which crossed deep water.

When the bride stood up and leant forward out of the carriage, they both pushed her out, and she fell into the middle of the water. At the same moment that she sank, a snow-white duck arose out of the mirror-smooth water, and swam down the river. The brother had observed nothing of it, and drove the carriage on until they reached the court. Then he took the black maiden to the King as his sister, and thought she really was so, because his eyes were dim, and he saw the golden garments glittering. When the King saw the boundless ugliness of his intended bride, he was very angry, and ordered the coachman to be thrown into a pit which was full of adders and nests of snakes. The old witch, however, knew so well how to flatter the

King and deceive his eyes by her arts, that he kept her and her daughter until she appeared quite endurable to him, and he really married her.

One evening when the black bride was sitting on the King's knee, a white duck came swimming up the gutter to the kitchen, and said to the kitchen-boy, " Boy, light a fire, that I may warm my feathers." The kitchen-boy did it, and lighted a fire on the hearth. Then came the duck and sat down by it, and shook herself and smoothed her feathers to rights with her bill. While she was thus sitting and enjoying herself, she asked, " What is my brother Reginer doing ? " The scullery-boy replied, " He is imprisoned in the pit with adders and with snakes." Then she asked, " What is the black witch doing in the house ? " The boy answered, " She is loved by the King and happy."

" May God have mercy on him," said the duck, and swam forth by the sink.

The next night she came again and put the same questions, and the third night also. Then the kitchen-boy could bear it no longer, and went to the King and discovered all to him. The King, however, wanted to see it for himself, and next evening went thither, and when the duck thrust her head in through the sink, he took his sword and cut through her neck, and suddenly she changed into a most beautiful maiden, exactly like the picture, which her brother had made of her. The King was full of joy, and as she stood there quite wet, he caused splendid apparel to be brought and had her clothed in it. Then she told how she had been betrayed by cunning and falsehood, and at last thrown down into the water, and her first request was that her brother should be brought forth from the pit of snakes, and when the King had fulfilled this request, he went into the chamber where the old witch was, and asked, What does she deserve who does this and that ? and related what had happened. Then was she so blinded that she was aware of nothing and said, " She deserves to be stripped naked, and put into a barrel with nails, and that a horse should be harnessed to the barrel, and the horse sent all over the world." All of which was done to her, and to her black daughter. But the King married the white and beautiful bride, and rewarded her faithful brother, and made him a rich and distinguished man.

THE JEW AMONG THORNS

THERE was once a rich man, who had a servant who served him diligently and honestly : he was every morning the first out of bed, and the last to go to rest at night ; and, whenever there was a difficult job to be done, which nobody cared to undertake, he was always the first to set himself to it. Moreover, he never complained, but was contented with everything, and always merry.

When a year was ended, his master gave him no wages, for he said to himself, " That is the cleverest way ; for I shall save something, and he will not go away, but stay quietly in my service." The servant said nothing, but did his work the second year as he had done it the first ; and when at the end of this, likewise, he received no wages, he made himself happy, and still stayed on.

When the third year also was past, the master considered, put his hand in his pocket, but pulled nothing out. Then at last the servant said, " Master, for three years I have served you honestly, be so good as to give me what I ought to have ; for I wish to leave, and look about me a little more in the world."

" Yes, my good fellow," answered the old miser ; "you have served me industriously, and, therefore, you shall be cheerfully rewarded ; " and he put his hand into his pocket but counted out only three farthings, saying, " There, you have a farthing for each year ; that is large and liberal pay, such as you would have received from few masters."

The honest servant, who understood little about money, put his fortune into his pocket, and thought, " Ah ! now that I have my purse full, why need I trouble and plague myself any longer with hard work ! " So on he went, up hill and down dale ; and sang and jumped to his heart's content. Now it came to pass that as he was going by a thicket a little man stepped out, and called to him, " Whither away, merry brother ? I see you do not carry many cares." " Why should I be sad ? " answered the servant ; " I have enough ; three years' wages are jingling in my pocket."

" How much is your treasure ? " the dwarf asked him.

" How much ? Three farthings sterling, all told."

" Look here," said the dwarf, " I am a poor needy man, give me your three farthings ; I can work no longer, but you are young, and can easily earn your bread."

And as the servant had a good heart, and felt pity for the old man, he gave him the three farthings, saying, " Take them in the name of Heaven, I shall not be any the worse for it."

Then the little man said, " As I see you have a good heart I grant you three wishes, one for each farthing, they shall all be fulfilled."

" Aha ? " said the servant, " you are one of those who can work wonders ! Well, then, if it is to be so, I wish, first, for a gun, which shall hit everything that I aim at ; secondly, for a fiddle, which when I play on it, shall compel all who hear it to dance ; thirdly, that if I ask a favour of any one he shall not be able to refuse it."

" All that shall you have," said the dwarf ; and put his hand into the bush, and only think, there lay a fiddle and gun, all ready, just as if they had been ordered. These he gave to the servant, and then said to him, " Whatever you may ask at any time, no man in the world shall be able to deny you."

" Heart alive ! What can one desire more ? " said the servant to himself, and went merrily onwards. Soon afterwards he met a Jew with a long goat's-beard, who was standing listening to the song of a bird which was sitting up at the top of a tree. " Good heavens," he was exclaiming, " that such a small creature should have such a fearfully loud voice ! if it were but mine ! if only some one would sprinkle some salt upon its tail ! "

" If that is all," said the servant, " the bird shall soon be down here ; " and taking aim he pulled the trigger, and down fell the bird into the thorn-bushes. " Go, you rogue," he said to the Jew, " and fetch the bird out for yourself ! "

" Oh ! " said the Jew, " leave out the rogue, my master, and I will do it at once. I will get the bird out for myself, as you really have hit it." Then he lay down on the ground, and began to crawl into the thicket.

When he was fast among the thorns, the good servant's humour so tempted him that he took up his fiddle and began to play. In a moment the Jew's legs began to move, and to jump into the air, and the more the servant fiddled the better went the dance. But the thorns tore his shabby coat for him, combed his beard, and pricked and plucked him all over the body. "Oh dear," cried the Jew, "what do I want with your fiddling? leave the fiddle alone, master, I do not want to dance."

But the servant did not listen to him, and thought, "You have fleeced people often enough, now the thorn-bushes shall do the same to you;" and he began to play over again, so that the Jew had to jump higher than ever, and scraps of his coat were left hanging on the thorns. "Oh, woe's me!" cried the Jew; "I will give the gentleman whatsoever he asks if only he leaves off fiddling—a purse full of gold." "If you are so liberal," said the servant, "I will stop my music; but this I must say to your credit, that you dance to it so well that it is quite an art;" and having taken the purse he went his way.

The Jew stood still and watched the servant quietly until he was far off and out of sight, and then he screamed out with all his might, "You miserable musician, you beer-house fiddler! wait till I catch you alone, I will hunt you till the soles of your shoes fall off! You ragamuffin! just put five farthings in your mouth, and then you may be worth three halfpence!" and went on abusing him as fast as he could speak. As soon as he had refreshed himself a little in this way, and got his breath again, he ran into the town to the justice.

"My lord judge," he said, "I have come to make a complaint; see how a rascal has robbed and ill-treated me on the public highway! a stone on the ground might pity me; my clothes all torn, my body pricked and scratched, my little all gone with my purse—good ducats, each piece better than the last; now pray let this man be thrown into prison!"

"Was it a soldier," said the judge, "who cut you thus with his sabre?" "Nothing of the sort!" said the Jew; "it was no sword that he had, but a gun hanging at his back, and a fiddle at his neck; the wretch may easily be known."

So the judge sent his people out after the man, and they found the good servant, who had been going quite slowly along, and they found, too, the purse with the money upon him. As soon as he was taken before the judge he said, "I did not touch the Jew, nor take his money;

he gave it to me of his own free will, that I might leave off fiddling because he could not bear my music."

" Heaven defend us ! " cried the Jew, " his lies are as thick as flies upon the wall."

But the judge also did not believe his tale, and said, " This is a bad defence, no Jew would do that." And because he had committed robbery on the public highway, he sentenced the good servant to be hanged. As he was being led away the Jew again screamed after him, " You vagabond ! you dog of a fiddler ! now you are going to receive your well-earned reward ! " The servant walked quietly with the hangman up the ladder, but upon the last step he turned round and said to the judge, " Grant me just one request before I die."

" Yes, if you do not ask your life," said the judge.

" I do not ask for life," answered the servant, " but as a last favour let me play once more upon my fiddle."

The Jew raised a great cry of " Murder ! murder ! for goodness' sake do not allow it ! Do not allow it ! " But the judge said, " Why should I not let him have this short pleasure ? it has been granted to him, and he shall have it." However, he could not have refused on account of the gift which had been bestowed on the servant.

Then the Jew cried, " Oh ! woe's me ! tie me, tie me fast ! " while the good servant took his fiddle from his neck, and made ready. As he gave the first scrape, they all began to quiver and shake, the judge, his clerk, and the hangman and his men, and the cord fell out of the hand of the one who was going to tie the Jew fast. At the second scrape all raised their legs, and the hangman let go his hold of the good servant, and made himself ready to dance. At the third scrape they all leaped up and began to dance ; the judge and the Jew being the best at jumping. Soon all who had gathered in the market-place out of curiosity were dancing with them ; old and young, fat and lean, one with another. The dogs, likewise, which had run there got up on their hind legs and capered about ; and the longer he played, the higher sprang the dancers, so that they knocked against each other's heads, and began to shriek terribly.

At length the judge cried, quite out of breath, " I will give you your life if you will only stop fiddling." The good servant thereupon had compassion, took his fiddle and hung it round his neck again, and stepped down the ladder. Then he went up to the Jew, who was lying upon the ground panting for breath, and said, " You rascal, now confess, whence you got the money, or I will take my fiddle and begin to play again." " I stole it, I stole it ! " cried he ; " but you have honestly earned it." So the judge had the Jew taken away and hanged as a thief.

FAITHFUL JOHN

AN old king fell sick ; and when he found his end drawing near, he said, " Let Faithful John come to me." Now Faithful John was the servant that he was fondest of, and was so called because he had been true to his master all his life long. Then when he came to the bed-side, the king said, " My Faithful John, I feel that my end draws nigh, and I have now no cares save for my son, who is still young, and stands in need of good counsel. I have no friend to leave him but you ; if you do not pledge yourself to teach him all he should know, and to be a father to him, I shall not shut my eyes in peace." Then John said, " I will never leave him, but will serve him faithfully even though it should cost me my life." And the king said, " I shall now die in peace ; after my death, show him the whole palace ; all the rooms and vaults, and all the treasures and stores which lie there ; but take care how you show him one room,—I mean the one where hangs the picture of the daughter of the king of the golden roof. If he sees it, he will fall deeply in love with her, and will then be plunged into great dangers on her account : guard him in this peril." And when Faithful John had once more pledged his word to the old king, he laid his head on his pillow, and died in peace.

Now when the old king had been carried to his grave, Faithful John told the young king what had passed upon his death-bed, and said, " I will keep my word truly, and be faithful to you as I was always to your father, though it should cost me my life." And the young king wept, and said, " Neither will I ever forget your faithfulness."

The days of mourning passed away, and then Faithful John said to his master, " It is now time that you should see your heritage ; I will show you your father's palace." Then he led him about every-where, up and down, and let him see all the riches and all the costly rooms ; only one room, where the picture stood, he did not open. Now the picture was so placed, that the moment the door opened, you could see it, and it was so beautifully done, that one would think it breathed and had life, and that there was nothing more lovely in the whole world. When the young king saw that Faithful John always went by this door, he said, " Why do you not open that room ? " " There is something inside," he answered, " which would frighten you." But the king said, " I have seen the whole palace, and I must also see what is in there " ; and he went and began to force open the door : but Faithful John held him back, and said, " I gave my word to your father before his death, that I would take heed how I showed you what stands in that room, lest it should lead you and me into great trouble." " The greatest trouble to me," said the young king, " will be not to go in and see the room ; I shall have no peace by day or by night until I do ; so I shall not go hence until you open it."

Then Faithful John saw that with all he could do or say the young king would have his way ; so, with a heavy heart and many fore-boding sighs, he sought for the key out of his great bunch ; and he opened the door of the room, and entered in first, so as to stand between the door of the room, and the picture, hoping he might not see it : but he raised himself upon tiptoes, and looked over John's shoulders ; and as soon as he saw the likeness of the lady, so beautiful, and shining with gold, he fell down upon the floor senseless. Then Faithful John lifted him up in his arms, and carried him to his bed, and was full of care, and thought to himself, " This trouble has come upon us ; O Heaven ! what will come of it ? "

At last the king came to himself again ; but the first thing that he said was, "Whose is that beautiful picture?" "It is the picture of the daughter of the king of the golden roof," said Faithful John. But the king went on, saying, "My love towards her is so great that if all the leaves on the trees were tongues, they could not speak it ; I care not to risk my life to win her ; you are my faithful friend, you must aid me."

Then John thought for a long time what was now to be done ; and at last said to the king, "All that she has about her is of gold : the tables, stools, cups, dishes, and all the things in her house are of gold ; and she is always seeking new treasures. Now in your stores there is much gold ; let it be worked up into every kind of vessel, and into all sorts of birds, wild beasts, and wonderful animals ; then we will it take and try our fortunes." So the king ordered all the goldsmiths to be sought for ; and they worked day and night, until at last the most beautiful things were made ; and Faithful John had a ship loaded with them, and put on a merchant's dress, and the king did the same, that they might not be known.

When all was ready they put to sea, and sailed till they came to the coast of the land where the king of the golden roof reigned. Faithful John told the king to stay in the ship, and wait for him ; "for perhaps," said he, "I may be able to bring away the king's daughter with me : therefore take care that everything be in order ; let the golden vessels and ornaments be brought forth, and the whole ship be decked out with them." And he chose out something of each of the golden things to put into his basket, and got ashore, and went towards the king's palace. And when he came to the castle yard, there stood by the well side a beautiful maiden, who had two golden pails in her hand, drawing water. And as she drew up the water, which was glittering with gold, she turned herself round, and saw the stranger, and asked him who he was. Then he drew near, and said, "I am a merchant," and opened his basket, and let her look into it ; and she cried out, "Oh! what beautiful things!" and set down her pails, and looked at one after the other. Then she said, "The king's daughter must see all these ; she is so fond of such things, that she will buy all of you." So she took him by the hand, and led him in ; for she was one of the waiting-maids of the daughter of the king.

When the princess saw the wares, she was greatly pleased, and said, " They are so beautiful that I will buy them all." But Faithful John said, " I am only the servant of a rich merchant ; what I have here is nothing to what he has lying in yonder ship : there he has the finest and most costly things that ever were made in gold." The princess wanted to have them all brought ashore ; but he said, " That would take up many days, there are such a number ; and much more rooms would be wanted to place them in than are in the greatest house." But her wish to see them grew still greater, and at last she said, " Take me to the ship, I will go myself, and look at your master's wares."

Then Faithful John led her joyfully to the ship, and the king, when he saw her, thought that his heart would leap out of his breast ; and it was with the greatest trouble that he kept himself still. So she got into the ship, and the king led her down ; but Faithful John stayed behind with the steersman, and ordered the ship to put off : " Spread all your sail," cried he, " that she may fly over the waves like a bird through the air."

And the king showed the princess the golden wares, each one singly : the dishes, cups, basins, and the wild and wonderful beasts : so that many hours flew away, and she looked at every thing with delight, and was not aware that the ship was sailing away. And after she had looked at the last, she thanked the merchant, and said she would go home ; but when she came upon the deck, she saw that the ship was sailing far away from land upon the deep sea, and that it flew along at full sail. " Alas ! " she cried out in her fright, " I am betrayed ; I am carried off, and have fallen into the power of a roving trader ; I would sooner have died." But then the king took her by the hand, and said, " I am not a merchant, I am a king, and of as noble birth as you. I have taken you away by stealth, but I did so because of the very great love I have for you ; for the first time I saw your face, I fell on the ground in a swoon." When the daughter of the king of the golden roof heard all, she was comforted, and her heart soon turned towards him, and she was willing to become his wife.

But it so happened, that whilst they were sailing on the deep sea, Faithful John, as he sat on the prow of the ship playing on his lute, saw three ravens flying in the air towards him. Then he left off playing, and listened to what they said to each other, for he understood their tongue. The first said, "There he goes! he is bearing away the daughter of the king of the golden roof; let him go!" "Nay," said the second, "there he goes, but he has not got her yet." And the third said, "There he goes; he surely has her, for she is sitting by his side in the ship." Then the first began again, and cried out, "What boots it to him? See you not that when they come to land, a horse of a foxy-red colour will spring towards him; and then he will try to get upon it, and if he does, it will spring away with him into the air, so that he will never see his love again." "True! true!" said the second, "but is there no help?" "Oh! yes, yes!" said the first; "if he who sits upon the horse takes the dagger which is stuck in the saddle and strikes him dead, the young king is saved; but who knows that? and who will tell him, that he who thus saves the king's life will turn to stone from the toes of his feet to his knee?" Then the second said, "True! true! but I know more still; though the horse be dead, the king loses his bride; when they go together into the palace, there lies the bridal dress on the couch, and looks as if it were woven of gold and silver, but it is all brimstone and pitch; and if he puts it on, it will burn him, marrow and bones." "Alas! alas! is there no help?" said the third. "Oh! yes, yes!" said the second, "if some one draws near and throws it into the fire, the young king will be saved. But what boots that? who knows and will tell him, for if he does, his body from the knee to the heart will be turned to stone?" "More! more! I know more," said the third; "were the dress burnt, still the king loses his bride. After the wedding when the dance begins, and the young queen dances on, she will turn pale, and fall as though she were dead; and if some one does not draw near and lift her up, and immediately take from her three drops of blood, she will surely die. But if any one knew this, we would tell him, that if he does do so, his body will turn to stone, from the crown of his head to the tip of his toe."

Then the ravens flapped their wings, and flew on; but Faithful John, who had understood it all, from that time was sorrowful, and did not tell his master what he had heard; for he saw if he told him, he must himself lay down his life to save him: at last he said to himself, "I will be faithful to my word, and save my master, if it costs me my life."

243

Now when they came to land, it happened just as the ravens had foretold ; for there sprang out a fine foxy-red horse. " See," said the king, " he shall bear me to my palace " : and he tried to mount, but Faithful John leaped before him, and swung himself quickly upon it, drew the dagger, and smote the horse dead. Then the other servants of the king, who were jealous of Faithful John, cried out, " What a shame to kill the fine beast that was to take the king to his palace ! " But the king said, " Let him alone, it is my Faithful John ; who knows but that he did it for some good end ? "

Then they went on to the castle, and there stood a couch in one room, and a fine dress lay upon it, that shone with gold and silver ; and the young king went up to it to take hold of it, but Faithful John cast it on the fire, and burnt it. And the other servants began again to grumble, and said, " See, now he is burning the wedding dress." But the king said, " Who knows what he does it for ? let him alone ! he is my faithful servant John."

Then the wedding feast was held, and the dance began, and the bride also came in ; but Faithful John took good heed, and looked in her face ; and on a sudden she turned pale, and fell as though she were dead upon the ground. But he sprung towards her quickly, lifted her up, and took her and laid her upon a couch, and drew three drops of blood from her. And at last she breathed again, and came to herself. But the young king had seen all, and did not know why Faithful John had done it ; so he was very angry at his boldness, and said, " Throw him into prison."

The next morning Faithful John was led forth, and stood upon the gallows, and said, " May I speak out before I die ? " and when the king answered " It shall be granted thee," he said, " I am wrongly judged, for I have always been faithful and true " : and then he told what he heard the ravens say upon the sea, and how he meant to save his master, and had therefore done all these things.

When he had told all, the king called out, " Oh my most faithful John ! pardon ! pardon ! take him down ! " But Faithful John had fallen down lifeless at the last word he spoke, and lay as a stone : and the king and queen mourned over him ; and the king said, " Oh, how ill have I rewarded thy truth ! " And he ordered the stone figure to be taken up, and placed in his own room near to his bed ; and as often as he looked at it he wept, and said, " Oh that I could bring thee back to life again, my Faithful John ! "

After a time, the queen had two little sons, who grew up, and were her great joy. One day, when she was at church, the two children stayed with her father ; and as they played about, he looked at the stone figure, and sighed, and cried out, " O that I could bring thee back to life, my Faithful John ! " Then the stone began to speak, and said, " O king ! thou canst bring me back to life if thou wilt give up for my sake what is dearest to thee." But the king said, " All that I have in the world would I give up for thee." " Then," said the stone, " cut off the heads of thy children, sprinkle their blood over me, and I shall live again." Then the king was greatly shocked : but he thought how Faithful John had died for his sake, and because of his great truth towards him ; and rose up and drew his sword as if to cut off his children's heads and do as he had been bid ; but the moment he drew his sword Faithful John was alive again, and stood before his face, and said, " Your truth is rewarded." And the children sprang about and played as happily as ever.

Then the king was full of joy : and when he saw the queen coming, to try her, he put Faithful John and the two children in a large closet ; and when she came in he said to her, " Have you been at church ? " " Yes," said she, " but I could not help thinking of Faithful John, who was so true to us." " Dear wife," said the king, " we can bring him back to life again, but it will cost us both our little sons, and we must give them up for his sake." When the queen heard this, she turned pale and was frightened in her heart ; but she said, " Let it be so ; we owe him all, for his great faith and truth." Then he rejoiced because she thought as he had thought, and went in and opened the closet, and brought out the children and Faithful John, and said, " Heaven be praised ! he is ours again, and we have our sons safe too." So he told her the whole story ; and all lived happily together the rest of their lives.

THE FOX AND THE HORSE

A PEASANT had a faithful horse which had grown old and could do no more work, so his master would no longer give him anything to eat and said, " I can certainly make no more use of thee, but still I mean well by thee ; if thou provest thyself still strong enough to bring me a lion here, I will maintain thee, but now take thyself away out of my stable," and with that he chased him into the open country. The horse was sad, and went to the forest to seek a little protection there from the weather. Then the fox met him and said, " Why dost thou hang thy head so, and go about all alone ? " " Alas," replied the horse, " avarice and fidelity do not dwell together in one house. My master has forgotten what services I have performed for him for so many years, and because I can no longer plough well, he will give me no more food, and has driven me out." " Without giving thee a chance ? " asked the fox. " The chance was a bad one. He said, if I were still strong enough to bring him a lion, he would keep me, but he well knows that I cannot do that." The fox said, " I will help thee, just lay thyself down, stretch thyself out, as if thou wert dead, and do not stir." The horse did as the fox desired, and the fox went to the lion, who had his den not far off, and said, " A dead horse is lying outside there, just come with me, thou canst have a rich meal." The lion went with him, and when they were both standing by the horse the fox said, " After all it is not very comfortable for thee here—I tell thee what—I will fasten it to thee by the tail, and then thou canst drag it into thy cave, and devour it in peace."

This advice pleased the lion : he lay down, and in order that the fox might tie the horse fast to him, he kept quite quiet. But the fox tied the lion's legs together with the horse's tail, and twisted and fastened all so well and so strongly that no strength could break it. When he had finished his work, he tapped the horse on the shoulder and said " Pull, white horse, pull." Then up sprang the horse at once, and drew the lion away with him. The lion began to roar so that all the birds in the forest flew out in terror, but the horse let him roar, and drew him and dragged him over the country to his master's door. When the master saw the lion, he was of a better mind, and said to the horse, " Thou shalt stay with me and fare well," and he gave him plenty to eat until he died.

THE BOOTS OF BUFFALO-LEATHER

A SOLDIER who is afraid of nothing, troubles himself about nothing. One of this kind had received his discharge, and as he had learnt no trade and could earn nothing, he travelled about and begged alms of kind people. He had an old waterproof on his back, and a pair of riding-boots of buffalo-leather which were still left to him. One day he was walking he knew not where, straight out into the open country, and at length came to a forest. He did not know where he was, but saw sitting on the trunk of a tree which had been cut down, a man who was well dressed and wore a green shooting-coat. The soldier shook hands with him, sat down on the grass by his side, and stretched out his legs. " I see thou hast good boots on, which are well blacked," said he to the huntsman ; " but if thou hadst to travel about as I have, they would not last long. Look at mine, they are of buffalo-leather, and have been worn for a long time, but in them I can go through thick and thin." After a while the soldier got up and said, " I can stay no longer, hunger drives me onwards ; but, Brother Bright-boots, where does this road lead to ? " " I don't know that myself," answered the huntsman, " I have lost my way in the forest," " Then thou art in the same plight as I," said the soldier ; " birds of a feather flock together, let us remain together, and seek our way." The huntsman smiled a little, and they walked on further and further, until night fell. " We do not get out of the forest," said the soldier, " but there in the distance I see a light shining, which will help us to something to eat." They found a stone house, knocked at the door, and an old woman opened it. " We are looking for quarters for the night," said the soldier, " and some lining for our stomachs, for mine is as empty as an old knapsack." " You cannot stay here," answered the old woman ; " this is a robber's house, and you would do wisely to get away before they come home, or you will be lost." " It won't be so bad as that," answered the soldier, " I have not had a mouthful for two days, and whether I am murdered here or die of hunger in the forest is all the same to me. I shall risk it." The huntsman would not follow, but the soldier drew him in with him by the sleeve. " Come, my dear brother, we shall not come to an end so quickly as that ! "

The old woman had pity on them and said, " Creep in here behind the stove, and if they leave anything, I will give it to you on the sly when they are asleep." Scarcely were they in the corner before twelve robbers came bursting in, seated themselves at the table which was already laid and shouted fiercely for supper. The old woman brought in some great dishes of roast meat, and the robbers enjoyed that thoroughly. When the smell of the food reached the nostrils of the soldier, he said to the huntsman, " I cannot hold out any longer, I shall seat myself at the table, and eat with them." " Thou wilt bring us to destruction," said the huntsman, and held him back by the arm. But the soldier began to cough loudly. When the robbers heard that, they threw away their knives and forks, leapt up, and discovered the two who were behind the stove. " Aha, gentlemen, are you in the corner ? " cried they, " What are you doing here ? Have you been sent as spies ? Wait a while, and you shall learn how we treat our enemies." " But do be civil." said the soldier, " I am hungry, give me something to eat, and then you can do what you like with me." The robbers were astonished, and the captain said, " I see that thou hast no fear ; well, thou shalt have some food, but after that thou must die." " We shall see," said the soldier, and seated himself at the table, and began to cut away valiantly at the roast meat. " Brother Brightboots, come and eat," cried he to the huntsman ; " thou must be as hungry as I am, and cannot have better roast meat at home," but the huntsman would not eat. The robbers looked at the soldier in astonishment, and said, " He makes himself at home ! " After a while he said, " I have had enough food, now get me something good to drink." The captain was in the mood to humour him in this also, and called to the old woman, " Bring a bottle out of the cellar, and mind it is of the best." The soldier drew out the cork with a loud noise, and then went with the bottle to the huntsman and said, " Pay attention, brother, and thou shalt see something that will surprise thee ; I am now going to drink the health of the whole clan." Then he brandished the bottle over the heads of the robbers, and cried, " Long life to you all, but with your mouths open and your right hands lifted up," and then he drank a hearty draught. Scarcely were the words said than they all sat motionless as if made of stone, and their mouths were open and their right hands stretched up in the air.

The huntsman said to the soldier, " I see that thou art acquainted with tricks of another kind, but now come and let us go home." " Oho, my dear brother, but that would be marching away far too soon ; we have conquered the enemy, and must first take the booty. Those men there are sitting fast, and are opening their mouths with astonishment, but they will not be allowed to move until I permit them. Come, eat and drink." The old woman had to bring another bottle of the best wine, and the soldier would not stir until he had eaten enough to last for three days. At last when day came, he said, " Now it is time to get on our way, and that our march may be a short one, the old woman shall show us the nearest way to the town." When they had arrived there he went to his old comrades, and said, " Out in the forest I have found a nest full of gallows' birds, come with me and we will take it." The soldier led them, and said to the huntsman, " Thou must go back again with me to see how they shake when we seize them by the feet." He placed the men round about the robbers, and then he took the bottle, drank a mouthful, brandished it above them, and cried, " Live again." Instantly they all regained the power of movement, but were thrown down and bound hand and foot with cords. Then the soldier ordered them to be thrown into a cart as if they had been so many sacks, and said, " Now drive them straight to prison." The huntsman, however, took one of the men aside and gave him another commission besides. " Brother Bright-boots," said the soldier, " we have safely routed the enemy and been well fed, now we will quietly walk behind them as if we were stragglers ! " When they approached the town, the soldier saw pouring through the gate of the town a crowd of people who were raising loud cries of joy, and waving green boughs in the air. Then he saw that the entire body-guard was coming up. " What can this mean ? " said he to the huntsman. " Dost thou not know ? " he replied, " that the King has for a long time been absent from his kingdom, and that to-day he is returning, and every one is going to meet him." " But where is the King ? " said the soldier, " I do not see him." " Here he is," answered the huntsman, " I am the King, and have announced my arrival." Then he opened his huntingcoat, and his royal garments were visible. The soldier was alarmed, and fell on his knees and begged him to forgive him for having in his ignorance treated him as an equal, and spoken to him by such a name.   But the King shook hands with him, and said, "Thou art a brave soldier, and hast saved my life.   Thou shalt never again be in want, I will take care of thee.   And if ever thou wouldst like to eat a piece of roast meat, as good as that in the robber's house, come to the royal kitchen.   But if thou wouldst drink a health, thou must first ask my permission."

DOCTOR KNOWALL

THERE was once on a time a poor peasant called Crabb, who drove with two oxen a load of wood to the town, and sold it to a doctor for two thalers.   When the money was being counted out to him, it so happened that the doctor was sitting at table, and when the peasant saw how daintily he ate and drank, his heart desired what he saw, and he would willingly have been a doctor too.   So he remained standing a while, and at length inquired if he too could not be a doctor.   "Oh, yes," said the doctor, "that is soon managed."   "What must I do?" asked the peasant.   "In the first place, buy thyself an A B C book of the kind which has a cock on the frontispiece; in the second, turn thy cart and thy two oxen into money, and get thyself some clothes, and whatsoever else pertains to medicine; thirdly, have a sign painted for thyself with the words, 'I am Doctor Knowall,' and have that nailed up above thy house-door."   The peasant did everything that he had been told to do.   When he had doctored people awhile, but not long, a rich and great lord had some money stolen.   Then he was told about Doctor Knowall who lived in such and such a village, and must know what had become of the money.   So the lord had the horses put in his carriage, drove out to the village, and asked Crabb if he were Doctor Knowall?   Yes, he was, he said.   Then he was to go with him and bring back the stolen money.   "Oh, yes, but Grethe, my wife, must go too."   The lord was willing, and let both of them have a seat in the carriage, and they all drove away together.   When they came to the nobleman's castle, the table was spread, and Crabb was told to sit down and eat. " Yes, but my wife, Grethe, too," said he, and he seated himself with her at the table. And when the first servant came with a dish of delicate soup, the peasant nudged his wife, and said, " Grethe, that was the first," meaning that was the servant who brought the first dish. The servant, however, thought he intended by that to say, " That is the first thief," and as he actually was so, he was terrified, and said to his comrade outside, " The Doctor knows all : we shall fare ill, he said I was the first." The second did not want to go in at all, but was forced. So when he went in with his dish, the peasant nudged his wife, and said, " Grethe, that is the second." This servant was just as much alarmed, and left quickly. The third did not fare better, for the peasant again said, " Grethe, that is the third." The fourth had to carry in a dish of roasted *crab*-apples that was covered, and the lord told the Doctor that he was to show his skill, and guess what was beneath the cover. The doctor looked at the dish, had no idea what to say, and cried, " Oh, poor Crabb." When the lord heard that, he cried, " There ! he knows ; and he knows who has the money ! "

On this the servants looked uneasy, and winked at the Doctor, meaning that they wished him to go out for a moment. When he did so, all four of them confessed to him that they had stolen the money, and said that they would willingly restore it and give him a large sum into the bargain if he would not denounce them, for if he did they would be killed. They led him to the spot where the money was concealed. With this the Doctor was satisfied, and returned to the hall, sat down to the table, and said, " My lord, now will I search in my book where the gold is hidden." The fifth servant, secretly crept into the stove to hear if the doctor knew still more. The Doctor, however, sat still and opened his A B C book, turned the pages backwards and forwards, and looked for the cock. As he could not find it immediately he said, " I know you are there, so you had better show yourself." Then the fellow in the stove thought that the doctor meant him, and full of terror, sprang out crying, " That man knows everything ! " Then Doctor Knowall showed the lord where the money was, but did not say who had stolen it, and received from both sides much money in reward, and became a famous man.

MASTER PFRIEM

MASTER PFRIEM was a short, thin, but lively man, who never rested a moment. He had a turned-up nose, his hair was grey and shaggy, his eyes small, but they glanced perpetually about on all sides. He saw everything, criticised everything, knew everything best, and was always in the right. When he went into the streets, he moved his arms about as if he were rowing; and once he struck the pail of a girl, who was carrying water, so high in the air that he himself was wetted all over by it. "Stupid thing," cried he to her, while he was shaking himself, "couldst thou not see that I was coming behind thee?" By trade he was a shoemaker, and when he worked he pulled his thread out with such force that he drove his fist into every one who did not keep far enough off. No apprentice stayed more than a month with him, for he had always some fault to find with the very best work. At one time it was that the stitches were not even, at another that one shoe was too long, or one heel higher than the other, or the leather not cut large enough. "Wait," said he to his apprentice, "I will soon show thee how we make skins soft," and he brought a strap and gave him a couple of strokes across the back. He called them all sluggards. He himself did not turn much work out of his hands, for he never sat still for a quarter of an hour. If his wife got up very early in the morning and lighted the fire, he jumped out of bed, and ran bare-footed into the kitchen, crying, "Wilt thou burn my house down for me? That is a fire one could roast an ox by! Does wood cost nothing?" If the servants were standing by their wash-tubs and laughing, and telling each other all they knew, he scolded them, and said, "There stand the geese cackling, and forgetting their work, to gossip! And why fresh soap? Disgraceful extravagance and shameful idleness into the bargain! They want to save their hands, and not rub the things properly!" And out he would run and knock a pail full of soap and water over, so that the whole kitchen was flooded. Some one was building a new house, so he hurried to the window to look on. "There, they are using that red sand-stone again that never dries!" cried he. "No one will ever be healthy in that house! and just look how badly the fellows are laying the stones! Besides, the mortar is good for nothing! It ought to have gravel in it, not sand. I shall live to see that house tumble down on the people who are in it." He sat down, put a couple of stitches in, and then jumped up again, unfastened his leather-apron, and cried, "I will just go out, and appeal to those men's consciences." He stumbled on the carpenters. "What's this?" cried he, "you are not working by the line! Do you expect the beams to be straight?

one wrong will put all wrong." He snatched an axe out of a carpenter's hand and wanted to show him how he ought to cut ; but as a cart loaded with clay came by, he threw the axe away, and hastened to the peasant who was walking by the side of it : " You are not in your right mind," said he, " who yokes young horses to a heavily-laden cart ? The poor beasts will die on the spot." The peasant did not give him an answer, and Pfriem in a rage ran back into his workshop. When he was setting himself to work again, the apprentice reached him a shoe. " Well, what's that again ? " screamed he, " Haven't I told you you ought not to cut shoes so broad ? Who would buy a shoe like this, which is hardly anything else but a sole ? I insist on my orders being followed exactly." " Master," answered the apprentice, " you may easily be quite right about the shoe being a bad one, but it is the one which you yourself cut out, and yourself set to work at. When you jumped up a while since, you knocked it off the table, and I have only just picked it up. An angel from heaven, however, would never make you believe that."

One night Master Pfriem dreamed he was dead, and on his way to heaven. When he got there, he knocked loudly at the door. " I wonder," said he to himself, " that they have no knocker on the door—one knocks one's knuckles sore." The apostle Peter opened the door, and wanted to see who demanded admission so noisily. " Ah, it's you, Master Pfriem ; " said he, " well, I'll let you in, but I warn you that you must give up that habit of yours, and find fault with nothing you see in heaven, or you may fare ill." " You might have spared your warning," answered Pfriem. " I know already what is seemly, and here, God be thanked, everything is perfect, and there is nothing to blame as there is on earth." So he went in, and walked up and down the wide expanses of heaven. He looked around him, to the left and to the right, but sometimes shook his head, or muttered something to himself. Then he saw two angels who were carrying away a beam. It was the beam which some one had had in his own eye whilst he was looking for the splinter in the eye of another. They did not, however, carry the beam lengthways, but slanting. " Did any one ever see such a piece of stupidity ? " thought Master Pfriem ; but he said nothing, and seemed satisfied with it. " It comes to the same thing after all, whichever way they carry the beam, straight or crooked, if they only get along with it, and truly I do not see them knock against anything." Soon after this he saw two angels who were drawing water out of a well into a bucket, but at the same time he observed that the bucket was full of holes, and that the water was running out of it on every side. They were watering the earth with rain. "Hang it," he exclaimed; but happily recollected himself, and thought, "Perhaps it is only a pastime. If it is an amusement, then it seems they can do useless things of this kind even here in heaven, where people, as I have already noticed, do nothing but idle about." He went farther and saw a cart which had stuck fast in a deep hole. "It's no wonder," said he to the man who stood by it "who would load so unreasonably? what have you there?" "Good wishes," replied the man. "I could not go along the right way with it, but still I have pushed it safely up here, and they won't leave me sticking here." In fact an angel did come and harnessed two horses to it. "That's quite right," thought Pfriem, "but two horses won't get that cart out, it must at least have four to it." Another angel came and brought two more horses; she did not, however, harness them in front of it, but behind. That was too much for Master Pfriem, "Clumsy creature," he burst out with, "what are you doing there? Has any one ever since the world began seen a cart drawn in that way? But you, in your conceited arrogance, think that you know everything best." He was going to say more, but one of the inhabitants of heaven seized him by the throat and pushed him forth with irresistible strength. Beneath the gateway Master Pfriem turned his head round to take one more look at the cart, and saw that it was being raised into the air by four winged horses.

At this moment Master Pfriem awoke. "Things are certainly arranged in heaven otherwise than they are on earth," said he to himself, "and that excuses much; but who can see horses harnessed both behind and before with patience; to be sure they had wings, but who could know that? It is, besides, great folly to fix a pair of wings to a horse that has four legs to run with already! But I must get up, or else they will make nothing but mistakes for me in my house. It is a lucky thing for me though, that I am not really dead."

THE WISHING-TABLE, THE GOLD-ASS, AND THE CUDGEL IN THE SACK

THERE was once upon a time a tailor who had three sons, and only one goat. But as the goat supported the whole of them with her milk, she was obliged to have good food, and to be taken every day to pasture. The sons, therefore, did this, in turn. Once the eldest took her to the churchyard, where the finest herbs were to be found, and let her eat and run about there. At night when it was time to go home he asked, " Goat, hast thou had enough ? " The goat answered,

> " *I am satisfied quite,*
> *No more can I bite.*"

" Come home, then," said the youth, and took hold of the cord round her neck, led her into the stable and tied her up securely. " Well," said the old tailor, " has the goat had as much food as she ought ? " " Oh," answered the son, " she has eaten so much, not a leaf more she'll touch." But the father wished to satisfy himself, and went down to the stable, stroked the dear animal and asked, " Goat, art thou satisfied ? " The goat answered,

> " *About the little graves I played*
> *And could not find a single blade.*"

" What do I hear ? " cried the tailor, and ran upstairs and said to the youth, " Hollo, thou liar ; thou saidst the goat had had enough, and hast let her hunger ! " and in his anger he took the yard-measure from the wall, and drove him out with blows.

Next day it was the turn of the second son, who looked out for a place in the fence of the garden, where nothing but good herbs grew, and the goat cleared them all off. At night when he wanted to go home, he asked, " Goat, art thou satisfied ? " The goat answered,

> " *I have eaten so much,*
> *Not a leaf more I'll touch, meh ! meh !* "

" Come home, then," said the youth, and led her home, and tied her up in the stable. " Well," said the old tailor, " has the goat had as

Q

much food as she ought ? " " Oh," answered the son, " she has eaten so much, not a leaf more she'll touch," The tailor would not rely on this, but went down to the stable and said, " Goat, hast thou had enough ? " The goat answered,

> " *How should I be satisfied ?*
> *Among the graves I leapt about,*
> *And found no food, so went without, meh ! meh ! "*

" The wicked wretch ! " cried the tailor, " to let such a good animal hunger," and he ran up and drove the youth out of doors with the yard-measure.

Now came the turn of the third son, who wanted to do the thing well, and sought out some bushes with the finest leaves, and let the goat devour them. In the evening when he wanted to go home, he asked, " Goat, hast thou had enough ? " The goat answered,

> " *I have eaten so much,*
> *Not a leaf more I'll touch, meh ! meh ! "*

" Come home, then," said the youth, and led her into the stable, and tied her up. " Well," said the old tailor, " has the goat had a proper amount of food ? " " She has eaten so much, not a leaf more she'll touch." The tailor did not trust to that, but went down and asked, " Goat, hast thou had enough ? " The wicked beast answered,

> " *How should I be satisfied ?*
> *Among the graves I leapt about,*
> *And found no leaves, so went without, meh ! meh ! "*

" Oh, the brood of liars ! " cried the tailor, " each as wicked and forgetful of his duty as the other ! Ye shall no longer make a fool of me," and, quite beside himself with anger, he ran upstairs and be-laboured the poor young fellow so vigorously with the yard-measure that he sprang out of the house.

The old tailor was now alone with his goat. Next morning he went down into the stable, caressed the goat and said, " Come, my dear little animal, I will take thee to feed myself." He took her by the rope and conducted her to green hedges, and amongst milfoil, and whatever else goats like to eat. " There thou mayest for once eat to thy heart's content," said he to her, and let her browse till evening. Then he asked, " Goat, art thou satisfied ? " she replied,

> " I have eaten so much,
> Not a leaf more I'll touch, meh ! meh ! "

" Come home, then," said the tailor, and led her into the stable, and tied her fast. When he was going away, he turned round again and said, " Well, art thou satisfied for once ? " But the goat did not behave better to him, and cried,

> " How should I be satisfied ?
> Among the graves I leapt about,
> And found no leaves, so went without, meh ! meh ! "

When the tailor heard that, he was shocked, and saw clearly that he had driven away his three sons without cause. " Wait, thou un-grateful creature," cried he, " it is not enough to drive thee forth, I will mark thee so that thou wilt no more dare to show thyself amongst honest tailors." In great haste he ran upstairs, fetched his razor, lathered the goat's head, and shaved her as clean as the palm of his hand. And as the yard-measure would have been too good for her, he brought the horsewhip, and gave her such cuts with it that she ran away in violent haste.

When the tailor was thus left quite alone in his house he fell into great grief, and would gladly have had his sons back again, but no one knew whither they were gone. The eldest had apprenticed himself to a joiner, and learnt industriously and indefatigably, and when the time came for him to go home again, his master presented him with a little table which had no particular appearance, and was made of common wood, but it had one good property ; if any one set it out, and said, " Little table, spread thyself," the good little table was at once covered with a clean little cloth, and a plate was there, and a knife and fork beside it, and dishes with boiled meats and roasted meats, as many as there was room for, and a great glass of red wine shone so that it made the heart glad. The young journeyman thought, " With this thou hast enough for thy whole life," and went joyously about the world and never troubled himself at all whether an inn was good or bad, or if anything was to be found in it or not. When it suited him he did not enter an inn at all, but either in the plain, in a wood, a meadow, or wherever he fancied, he took his little table off his back, set it down before him, and said, " Cover thyself," and then everything appeared that his heart desired. At length he took it into his head to go back to his father, whose anger would now be appeased, and who would now willingly receive him with his wishing-table. It came to pass that on his way home, he came one evening to an inn which was filled with guests. They bade him welcome, and invited him to sit and eat with them, for otherwise he would have difficulty in getting anything. " No," answered the joiner, " I will not take the few bites out of your mouths ; rather than that, you shall be my guests." They laughed, and thought he was jesting with them ; he, however, placed his wooden table in the middle of the room, and said, " Little table, cover thyself." Instantly it was covered with food, so good that the host could never have procured it, and the smell of it ascended pleasantly to the nostrils of the guests. " Fall to, dear friends," said the joiner ; and the guests when they saw that he meant it, did not need to be asked twice, but drew near, pulled out their knives and attacked it valiantly. And what surprised them the most was that when a dish became empty, a full one instantly took its place of its own accord. The innkeeper stood in one corner and watched the affair ; he did not at all know what to say, but thought, " Thou couldst easily find a use for such a cook as that in thy kitchen." The joiner and his comrades made merry until late into the night ; at length they lay down to sleep, and the young apprentice also went to bed, and set his magic table against the wall. The host's thoughts, however, let him have no rest ; it occurred to him that there was a little old table in his lumber-room, which looked just like the apprentice's, and he brought it out quite softly, and exchanged it for the wishing-table. Next morning, the joiner paid for his bed, took up his table, never thinking that he had got a false one, and went his way. At mid-day he reached his father, who received him with great joy. " Well, my dear son, what hast thou learnt ? " said he to him. " Father, I have become a joiner."

" A good trade," replied the old man ; " but what hast thou brought back with thee from thy apprenticeship ? " " Father, the best thing which I have brought back with me is this little table." The tailor inspected it on all sides and said, " Thou didst not make a masterpiece when thou mad'st that ; it is a bad old table." " But it is a table which furnishes itself," replied the son. " When I set it out, and tell it to cover itself, the most beautiful dishes stand on it, and a wine also, which gladdens the heart. Just invite all our relations and friends, they shall refresh and enjoy themselves for once, for the table will give them all they require." When the company was assembled, he put his table in the middle of the room and said, " Little table, cover thyself," but the little table did not bestir itself, and remained just as bare as any other table which did not understand language. Then the poor apprentice became aware that his table had been changed, and was ashamed at having to stand there like a liar. The relations, however, mocked him, and were forced to go home without having eaten or drunk. The father brought out his patches again, and went on tailoring, but the son went to a master in the craft.

The second son had gone to a miller and had apprenticed himself to him. When his years were over, the master said, " As thou has conducted thyself so well, I give thee an ass of a peculiar kind, which neither draws a cart nor carries a sack." " To what use is he put, then ? " asked the young apprentice. " He lets gold drop from his mouth," answered the miller. " If thou settest him on a cloth and says ' Bricklebrit,' the good animal will drop gold pieces for thee." " That is a fine thing," said the apprentice, and thanked the master, and went out into the world. When he had need of gold, he had only to say " Bricklebrit " to his ass, and it rained gold pieces, and he had nothing to do but pick them off the ground. Wheresoever he went, the best of everything was good enough for him, and the dearer the better, for he had always a full purse. When he had looked about the world for some time, he thought, " Thou must seek out thy father, if thou goest to him with the gold-ass he will forget his anger, and receive thee well." It came to pass that he came to the same public-house in which his brother's table had been exchanged. He led his ass by the bridle, and the host was about to take the animal from him and tie him up, but the young apprentice said, " Don't trouble yourself, I will take my grey horse into the stable, and tie him up myself too, for I must know where he stands." This struck the host as odd, and he thought that a man who was forced to look after his ass himself, could not have much to spend ; but when the stranger put his hand in his pocket and brought out two gold pieces, and said he was to provide something good for him, the host opened his eyes wide, and ran and sought out the best he could muster. After dinner the guest asked what he owed. The host did not see why he should not double the reckoning, and said the apprentice must give two more gold pieces. He felt in his pocket, but his gold was just at an end. " Wait an instant, sir host," said he, " I will go and fetch some money ; " but he took the table-cloth with him. The host could not imagine what this could mean, and being curious, stole after him, and as the guest bolted the stable-door, he peeped through a hole left by a knot in the wood. The stranger spread out the cloth under the animal and cried, " Bricklebrit," and immediately the beast began to let gold pieces fall, so that it fairly rained down money on the ground. " Eh, my word," said the host, " ducats are quickly coined here ! A purse like that is not amiss." The guest paid his score, and went to bed, but in the night the host stole down into the stable, led away the master of the mint, and tied up another ass in his place. Early next morning the apprentice travelled away with his ass, and thought that he had his gold-ass. At mid-day he reached his father, who rejoiced to see him again, and gladly took him in. " What hast thou made of thyself, my son ? " asked the old man. " A miller, dear father," he answered. " What hast thou brought back with thee from thy travels ? " " Nothing else but an ass." " There are asses enough here," said the father, " I would rather have had a good goat." " Yes," replied the son, " but it is no common ass, but a gold-ass, when I say ' Bricklebrit,' the good beast opens its mouth and drops a whole sheetful of gold pieces. Just summon all our relations hither, and I will make them rich folks." " That suits me well," said the tailor, " for then I shall have no need to torment myself any longer with the needle," and ran out himself and called the relations together. As soon as they were assembled, the miller bade them make way, spread out his cloth, and brought the ass into the room. " Now watch," said he, and cried, " Bricklebrit," but no gold pieces fell, and it was clear that the animal knew nothing of the art, for every ass does not attain such perfection. Then the poor miller pulled a long face, saw that he was betrayed, and begged pardon of the relatives, who went home as poor as they came.

There was no help for it, the old man had to betake him to his needle once more, and the youth hired himself to a miller.

The third brother had apprenticed himself to a turner, and as that is skilled labour, he was the longest in learning. His brothers, however, told him in a letter how badly things had gone with them, and how the inn-keeper had cheated them of the beautiful wishing-gifts on the last evening before they reached home. When the turner had served his time, and had to set out on his travels, as he had conducted himself so well, his master presented him with a sack and said, "There is a cudgel in it." "I can put on the sack," said he, "and it may be of good service to me, but why should the cudgel be in it? It only makes it heavy." "I will tell thee why," replied the master; "if any one has done anything to injure thee, do but say, 'Out of the sack, Cudgel!' and the cudgel will leap forth among the people, and play such a dance on their backs that they will not be able to stir or move for a week, and it will not leave off until thou sayest, 'Into the sack, Cudgel!'" The apprentice thanked him, put the sack on his back, and when any one came too near him, and wished to attack him, he said, "Out of the sack, Cudgel!" and instantly the cudgel sprang out, and dusted the coat or jacket of one after the other on their backs, and never stopped until it had stripped it off them, and it was done so quickly, that before any one was aware, it was already his own turn. In the evening the young turner reached the inn where his brothers had been cheated. He laid his sack on the table before him and began to talk of all the wonderful things which he had seen in the world. "Yes," said he, "people may easily find a table which will cover itself, a gold-ass, and things of that kind—extremely good things which I by no means despise—but these are nothing in comparison with the treasure which I have won for myself, and am carrying about with me in my sack there." The inn-keeper pricked up his ears, "What in the world can that be?" thought he; "the sack must be filled with nothing but jewels; I ought to get them cheap too, for all good things go in threes." When it was time for sleep, the guest stretched himself on the bench, and laid his sack beneath him for a pillow. When the inn-keeper thought his guest was lying in a sound sleep, he went to him and pushed and pulled quite gently and carefully at the sack to see if he could possibly draw it away and lay another in its place. The turner had, however, been waiting for this for a long time, and now just as the inn-keeper was about to give a hearty tug, he cried, " Out of the sack, Cudgel ! " Instantly the little cudgel came forth, and fell on the inn-keeper, and gave him a sound thrashing.

The host cried for mercy ; but the louder he cried, so much the more heavily the cudgel beat the time on his back, until at length he fell to the ground exhausted. Then the turner said, " If thou dost not give back the table which covers itself, and the gold-ass, the dance shall begin afresh." " Oh, no," cried the host, quite humbly, " I will gladly prduce everything, only make the accursed goblin creep back into the sack." Then said the apprentice, " I will let mercy take the place of justice, but beware of getting into mischief again ! " So he cried, " Into the sack, Cudgel ! " and let him have rest.

Next morning the turner went home to his father with the wishing-table, and the gold-ass. The tailor rejoiced when he saw him once more, and asked him likewise what he had learned in foreign parts. " Dear father," said he, " I have become a turner." " A skilled trade," said the father. " What hast thou brought back with thee from thy travels ? "

" A precious thing, dear father," replied the son, " a cudgel in the sack."

" What ! " cried the father, " a cudgel ! That's worth thy trouble, indeed ! From every tree thou canst cut thyself one." " But not one like this, dear father. If I say ' Out of the sack, Cudgel ! ' the cudgel springs out and leads any one who means ill with me a weary dance, and never stops until he lies on the ground and prays for fair weather. Look you, with this cudgel have I got back the wishing-table and the gold-ass which the thievish inn-keeper took away from my brothers. Now let them both be sent for, and invite all our kinsmen. I will give them to eat and to drink, and will fill their pockets with gold into the bargain." The old tailor would not quite believe, but nevertheless got the relatives together. Then the turner spread a cloth in the room and led in the gold-ass, and said to his brother, " Now, dear brother, speak to him." The miller said, " Bricklebrit," and instantly the gold pieces fell down on the cloth like a thunder-shower, and the ass did not stop until every one of them had so much that he could carry no more. (I can see in thy face that thou also wouldst have liked to be there.)

Then the turner brought the little table, and said, " Now, dear brother, speak to it." And scarcely had the carpenter said, " Table, cover thyself," than it was spread and amply covered with the most exquisite dishes. Then such a meal took place as the good tailor had never yet known in his house, and the whole party of kinsmen stayed together till far in the night, and were all merry and glad. The tailor locked away needle and thread, yard-measure and all, in a press, and lived with his three sons in joy and splendour.

(What, however, has become of the goat who was to blame for the tailor driving out his three sons ? That I will tell thee. She was ashamed that she had a bald head, and ran to a fox's hole and crept into it. When the fox came home, he was met by two great eyes shining out of the darkness, and was terrified and ran away. A bear met him, and as the fox looked quite disturbed, he said, " What is the matter with thee, brother Fox, why dost thou look like that ? " " Ah," answered Redskin, " a fierce beast is in my cave and stared at me with its fiery eyes." " We will soon drive him out," said the bear, and went with him to the cave and looked in, but when he saw the fiery eyes, fear seized on him likewise ; he would have nothing to do with the furious beast, and took to his heels. The bee met him, and as she saw that he was ill at ease, she said, " Bear, thou art really pulling a very pitiful face ; what has become of all thy gaiety ? " " It is all very well for thee to talk," replied the bear, " a furious beast with staring eyes is in Redskin's house, and we can't drive him out." The bee said, " Bear, I pity thee, I am a poor weak creature whom thou wouldst not turn aside to look at, but still, I believe, I can help thee." She flew into the fox's cave, lighted on the goat's smoothly-shorn head, and stung her so violently, that she sprang up, crying " Meh, meh," and ran forth into the world as if mad, and to this hour no one knows where she has gone.)

TWO SAD STORIES ABOUT SNAKES

THERE was once a little child whose mother gave her every afternoon a small bowl of bread and milk, and the child would sit in the yard with it. One day, when she began to eat, a snake came creeping out of a crevice in the wall, dipped its little head in the dish, and ate with her. This delighted the child, and when she was sitting there with her little dish and the snake did not come at once, she cried,

> *" Snake, snake, swiftly come,*
> *Hither come, thou little thing,*
> *Thou shalt have thy crumbs of bread,*
> *Thou shalt feed thyself with milk."*

Then the snake came in haste, and enjoyed its food. Moreover it showed gratitude, for it brought the child all kinds of pretty things from its hidden treasures, bright stones, pearls, and golden playthings. The snake, however, only drank the milk, and left the bread-crumbs alone. Then one day the child took its little spoon and tapped the snake gently on its head with it, and said, " Eat the bread-crumbs as well, little thing." The mother, who was standing in the kitchen, heard the child talking to some one, and when she saw that she was striking a snake with her spoon, ran out with a log of wood, and killed the good little creature.

From that time forth, a change came over the child. As long as the snake had eaten with her, she had grown tall and strong, but now she lost her pretty rosy cheeks and wasted away. It was not long before the little owls began to cry in the night, and the redbreast to collect little branches and leaves for a funeral garland, and soon afterwards the child lay on her bier.

SECOND STORY

An orphan child was sitting and spinning on the town walls when she saw a snake coming out of a hole low down in the wall. Quickly she spread out one of the blue silk handkerchiefs which snakes have such a strong liking for, and which are the only things they will creep on. As soon as the snake saw this, it went back, returned, bringing with it a small golden crown, laid it on the handkerchief, and then went away again. The girl took up the crown, which was made of glittering golden filigree. It was not long before the snake came back for the second time, but when it no longer saw the crown, it crept up to the wall, and in its grief smote its little head against it as long as it had strength to do so, until at last it lay there dead. If the girl had only left the crown where it was, the snake would certainly have brought still more of its treasures out of the hole.

THE ROBBER BRIDEGROOM

THERE was once on a time a miller, who had a beautiful daughter, and as she was grown up, he wished that she was provided for, and well married. He thought, " If any good suitor comes and asks for her, I will give her to him." Not long afterwards, a suitor came, who appeared to be very rich, and as the miller had no fault to find with him, he promised his daughter to him. The maiden, however, did not like him quite so much as a girl should like the man to whom she is engaged, and had no confidence in him. Whenever she saw, or thought of him, she felt a secret horror. Once he said to her, " Thou art my betrothed, and yet thou hast never once paid me a visit." The maiden replied, " I know not where thy house is." Then said the bridegroom, " My house is out there in the dark forest." She tried to excuse herself, and said she could not find the way there. The bridegroom said, " Next Sunday thou must come out there to me ; I have already invited the guests, and I will strew ashes in order that thou mayst find thy way through the forest." When Sunday came, and the maiden had to set out on her way, she became very uneasy, she herself knew not exactly why, and to mark her way she filled both her pockets full of peas and lentils. Ashes were strewn at the entrance of the forest, and these she followed, but at every step she threw a couple of peas on the ground. She walked almost the whole day until she reached the middle of the forest, where it was the darkest, and there stood a solitary house, which she did not like, for it looked so dark and dismal. She went inside it, but no one was within, and the most absolute stillness reigned. Suddenly a voice cried,

> " *Turn again, bonny bride,*
> *Turn again home :*
> *Haste from the robber's den*
> *Haste away home !* "

The maiden looked up, and saw that the voice came from a bird, which was hanging in a cage on the wall. Again it cried,

> " *Turn again, bonny bride,*
> *Turn again home :*
> *Haste from the robber's den*
> *Haste away home !* "

Then the young maiden went on farther from one room to another, and walked through the whole house, but it was entirely empty and not one human being was to be found. At last she came to the cellar, and there sat an extremely aged woman, whose head shook constantly. " Can you not tell me," said the maiden, " if my betrothed lives here ? "

" Alas, poor child," replied the old woman, " whither hast thou come ? Thou art in a murderer's den. Thou thinkest thou art a bride soon to be married, but thou wilt keep thy wedding with death. Look, I have been forced to put a great kettle on there, with water in it, and when they have thee in their power, they will cut thee to pieces without mercy, will cook thee, and eat thee, for they are eaters of human flesh. If I do not have compassion on thee, and save thee, thou art lost."

So then the old woman led her behind a great wine-cask where she could not be seen. " Be as still as a mouse," said she, " do not make a sound, or move, or all will be over with thee. At night, when the robbers are asleep, we will escape ; I have long waited for an opportunity." Hardly was this done, than the wicked crew came home. They dragged with them another young girl. They were drunk, and paid no heed to her screams and lamentations. They gave her wine to drink, three glasses full, one glass of white wine, one glass of red, and a glass of yellow, and with this her heart burst in twain. The poor bride behind the cask trembled and shook, for she saw right well what fate the robbers had destined for her. One of them noticed a golden ring on the little finger of the dead girl, and as it would not come off at once, he took an axe and cut the finger off, but it sprang up in the air, away over the cask and fell straight into the bride's lap. The robber took a candle and wanted to look for it, but could not find it. Then another of them said, " Hast thou looked behind the great wine-cask ? " But the old woman cried, " Come and get something to eat, and leave off looking till the morning, the finger won't run away from you."

Then the robbers said, " The old woman is right," and gave up their search, and sat down to eat, and the old woman poured a sleeping-draught in their wine, so that they soon lay down in the cellar, and slept and snored. When the bride heard that, she came out from behind the wine-cask, and had to step over the sleepers, for they lay in rows on the ground, and great was her terror lest she should waken one of them. But God helped her, and she got safely over. The old woman went up with her, opened the doors, and they hurried out of the murderers' den with all the speed in their power. The wind had blown away the strewn ashes, but the peas and lentils had sprouted and grown up, and showed them the way in the moonlight. They walked the whole night, until in the morning they arrived at the mill, and then the maiden told her father everything exactly as it had happened.

When the day came when the wedding was to be celebrated, the bridegroom appeared, and the Miller had invited all his relations and friends. As they sat at table, each was bidden to relate something. The bride sat still, and said nothing. Then said the bridegroom to the bride, " Come, my darling, dost thou know nothing? Relate a tale to us like the rest." She replied, " Then I will tell you a dream. I was walking alone through a wood, and at last I came to a house, in which no living soul was, but on the wall there was a bird in a cage which cried,

> " *Turn again, bonny bride,*
> *Turn again home :*
> *Haste from the robber's den*
> *Haste away home !* "

And this it cried once more. My darling, it was only a dream. Then I went through all the rooms, and they were all empty, and there was something so horrible about them ! At last I went down into the cellar, and there sat a very, very old woman, whose head shook ; I asked her, ' Does my bridegroom live in this house ? ' She answered, ' Alas, poor child, thou hast got into a murderers' den, thy bridegroom does live here, but he will kill thee." My darling, it was only a dream. But the old woman hid me behind a great wine-cask, and scarcely was I hidden, when the robbers came home, dragging a maiden with them, to whom they gave three kinds of wines to drink, white, red and yellow, with which her heart broke in twain. My darling, it was only a dream. And one of the robbers saw that there was still a ring on her little finger, and as it was hard to draw off, he took an axe and cut it off, but the finger sprang up in the air, and sprang behind the great wine-cask, and fell in my lap. And there is the finger with the ring!" And with these words she drew it forth, and showed it to those present.

The robber, who had during this story become as pale as ashes, leapt up and wanted to escape, but the guests held him fast, and delivered him over to justice. Then he and his whole troop were executed for their wicked deeds.

THE MASTER-THIEF

ONE day an old man and his wife were sitting in front of a miserable house resting a while from their work. Suddenly a splendid carriage with four black horses came driving up, and a richly-dressed man descended from it. The peasant stood up, went to the great man, and asked what he wanted, and in what way he could be useful to him? The stranger stretched out his hand to the old man, and said, " I want nothing but to enjoy for once a country dish ; cook me some potatoes, in the way you always have them, and then I will sit down at your table and eat them with pleasure." The peasant smiled and said, " You are a count or a prince, or perhaps even a duke ; noble gentlemen often have such fancies, but you shall have your wish." The wife went into the kitchen, and began to wash and rub the potatoes, and to make them into balls, as they are eaten by the country-folks. Whilst she was busy with this work, the peasant said to the stranger, " Come into my garden with me for a while,

I have still something to do there." He had dug some holes in the garden, and now wanted to plant some trees in them. "Have you no children," asked the stranger, "who could help you with your work?" "No," answered the peasant, "I had a son, it is true, but it is long since he went out into the world. He was a ne'er-do-well; sharp, and knowing, but he would learn nothing and was full of bad tricks, at last he ran away from me, and since then I have heard nothing of him."

The old man took a young tree, put it in a hole, drove in a post beside it, and when he had shovelled in some earth and had trampled it firmly down, he tied the stem of the tree above, below, and in the middle, fast to the post by a rope of straw. "But tell me," said the stranger, "why you don't tie that crooked knotted tree, which is lying in the corner there, bent down almost to the ground, to a post also that it may grow straight, as well as these?" The old man smiled and said, "Sir, you speak according to your knowledge, it is easy to see that you are not familiar with gardening. That tree there is old, and mis-shapen, no one can make it straight now. Trees must be trained while they are young." "That is how it was with your son," said the stranger, "if you had trained him while he was still young, he would not have run away; now he too must have grown hard and mis-shapen." "Truly it is a long time since he went away," replied the old man, "he must have changed." "Would you know him again if he were to come to you?" asked the stranger. "Hardly by his face," replied the peasant, "but he has a mark about him, a birth-mark on his shoulder, that looks like a bean." When he had said that the stranger pulled off his coat, bared his shoulder, and showed the peasant the bean. "Well-a-day!" cried the old man, thou art really my son!" and love for his child stirred in his heart. "But," he added, "how canst thou be my son, thou hast become a great lord and livest in wealth and luxury? How hast thou contrived to do that?" "Ah, father," answered the son, "the young tree was bound to no post and has grown crooked, now it is too old, it will never be straight again. How have I got all that? I have become a thief, but do not be alarmed, I am a master-thief. For me there are neither locks nor bolts, whatsoever I desire is mine. Do not imagine that I steal like a common thief, I only take some of the superfluity of the rich. Poor people are safe, I would rather give to them than take anything from them. It is the same with anything which I can have without trouble, cunning and dexterity—I never touch it." " Alas, my son," said the father, " it still does not please me, a thief is still a thief, I tell thee it will end badly." He took him to his mother, and when she heard that was her son, she wept for joy, but when he told her that he had become a master-thief, two streams flowed down over her face. At length she said, " Even if he has become a thief, he is still my son, and my eyes have beheld him once more." They sat down to table, and once again he ate with his parents the wretched food which he had not eaten for so long. The father said, " If our Lord, the count up there in the castle, learns who thou art, and what trade thou followest, he will not take thee in his arms and cradle thee in them as he did when he held thee at the font, but will cause thee to swing from a halter." " Be easy, father, he will do me no harm, for I understand my trade. I will go to him myself this very day." · When evening drew near, the master-thief seated himself in his carriage, and drove to the castle. The count received him civilly, for he took him for a distinguished man. When, however, the stranger made himself known, the count turned pale and was quite silent for some time. At length he said, " Thou art my godson, and on that account mercy shall take the place of justice, and I will deal leniently with thee. Since thou pridest thyself on being a master-thief, I will put thy art to the proof, but if thou dost not stand the test, thou must marry the rope-maker's daughter, and the croaking of the raven must be thy music on the occasion." " Lord count," answered the master-thief, " Think of three things, as difficult as you like, and if I do not perform your tasks, do with me what you will." The count reflected for some minutes, and then said, " Well, then, in the first place, thou shalt steal the horse I keep for my own riding, out of the stable ; in the next, thou shalt steal the sheet from beneath the bodies of my wife and myself when we are asleep, without our observing it, and the wedding-ring of my wife as well ; thirdly and lastly, thou shalt steal away out of the church, the parson and clerk. Mark what I am saying, for thy life depends on it."

The master-thief went to the nearest town ; there he bought the clothes of an old peasant woman, and put them on. Then he stained his face brown, and painted wrinkles on it as well, so that no one could have recognized him. Then he filled a small cask with old Hungary wine in which was mixed a powerful sleeping-drink. He put the cask in a basket, which he took on his back, and walked with slow and tottering steps to the count's castle. It was already dark when he arrived. He sat down on a stone in the court-yard and began to cough, like an asthmatic old woman, and to rub his hands as if he were cold. In front of the door of the stable some soldiers were lying round a fire ; one of them observed the woman, and called out to her, " Come nearer, old mother, and warm thyself beside us. After all, thou hast no bed for the night, and must take one where thou canst find it." The old woman tottered up to them, begged them to lift the basket from her back, and sat down beside them at the fire. " What hast thou got in thy little cask, old lady ? " asked one. " A good mouthful of wine," she answered. " I live by trade, for money and fair words I am quite ready to let you have a glass." " Let us have it here, then," said the soldier, and when he had tasted one glass he said, " When wine is good, I like another glass," and had another poured out for himself, and the rest followed his example. " Hallo, comrades," cried one of them to those who were in the stable, " here is an old goody who has wine that is as old as herself ; take a draught, it will warm your stomachs far better than our fire." The old woman carried her cask into the stable. One of the soldiers had seated himself on the saddled riding-horse, another held its bridle in his hand, a third had laid hold of its tail. She poured out as much as they wanted until the spring ran dry. It was not long before the bridle fell from the hand of the one, and he fell down and began to snore, the other left hold of the tail, lay down and snored still louder. The one who was sitting in the saddle, did remain sitting, but bent his head almost down to the horse's neck, and slept and blew with his mouth like the bellows of a forge. The soldiers outside had already been asleep for a long time, and were lying on the ground motionless, as if dead. When the master-thief saw that he had succeeded, he gave the first a rope in his hand instead of the bridle, and the other who had been holding the tail, a wisp of straw, but what was he to do with the one who was sitting on the horse's back ? He did not want to throw him down, for he might have awakened and have uttered a cry. He had a good idea, he unbuckled the girths of the saddle, tied a couple of ropes which were hanging to a ring on the wall fast to the saddle, and drew the sleeping rider up into the air on it, then he twisted the rope round the posts, and made it fast. He soon unloosed the horse from the chain, but if he had ridden over the stony pavement of the yard they would have heard the noise in the castle. So he wrapped the horse's hoofs in old rags, led him carefully out, leapt upon him, and galloped off.

When day broke, the master galloped to the castle on the stolen horse. The count had just got up, and was looking out of the window. "Good morning, Sir Count," he cried to him, "here is the horse, which I have got safely out of the stable! Just look, how beautifully your soldiers are lying there sleeping; and if you will but go into the stable, you will see how comfortable your watchers have made it for themselves." The count could not help laughing, then he said, "For once thou hast succeeded, but things won't go so well the second time, and I warn thee that if thou comest before me as a thief, I will handle thee as I would a thief." When the countess went to bed that night, she closed her hand with the wedding-ring tightly together, and the count said, "All the doors are locked and bolted, I will keep awake and wait for the thief, but if he gets in by the window, I will shoot him." The master-thief, however, went in the dark to the gallows, cut a poor sinner who was hanging there down from the halter, and carried him on his back to the castle. Then he set a ladder up to the bedroom, put the dead body on his shoulders, and began to climb up. When he had got so high that the head of the dead man showed at the window, the count who was watching in his bed, fired a pistol at him, and immediately the master let the poor sinner fall down, and hid himself in one corner. The night was sufficiently lighted by the moon, for the master to see distinctly how the count got out of the window on to the ladder, came down, carried the dead body into the garden, and began to dig a hole in which to lay it. "Now," thought the thief, "the favourable moment has come," stole nimbly out of his corner, and climbed up the ladder straight into the countess's bedroom. "Dear wife," he began in the count's voice, "the thief is dead, but, after all, he is my godson, and has been more of a scape-grace than a villain. I will not put him to open shame ; besides, I am sorry for the parents. I will bury him myself before daybreak, in the garden that the thing may not be known, so give me the sheet, I will wrap up the body in it, and bury him under a tree and no one will know." The countess gave him the sheet. " I tell you what," continued the thief, " I have a fit of magnanimity on me, give me the ring too—the unhappy man risked his life for it, so he may take it with him into his grave." She would not gainsay the count, and although she did it unwillingly she drew the ring from her finger, and gave it to him. The thief made off with both these things, and reached home safely before the count in the garden had finished his work of burying.

What a long face the count made when the master came the next morning, and brought him the sheet and the ring. " Art thou a wizard ? " said he, " Who has fetched thee out of the grave in which I myself laid thee, and brought thee to life again ? " " You did not bury me," said the thief, " but the poor sinner on the gallows," and he told him exactly how everything had happened, and the count was forced to own to him that he was a clever, crafty thief. " But thou hast not reached the end yet," he added, " thou hast still to perform the third task, and if thou dost not succeed in that, all is of no use." The master smiled and returned no answer.

When night had fallen he went with a long sack on his back, a bundle under his arms, and a lantern in his hand to the village-church. After this he put on a long black garment that looked like a monk's cowl, and stuck a grey beard on his chin. When at last he was quite unrecognizable, he took the sack and the lighted lantern, went into the church, and ascended the pulpit. The clock in the tower was just striking twelve ; when the last stroke had sounded, he cried with a loud and piercing voice, " Hearken, sinful men, the end of all things has come ! The last day is at hand ! Hearken ! Hearken ! Whosoever wishes to go to heaven with me must creep into the sack. I am Peter, who opens and shuts the gate of Heaven. Into the sack ! The world is ending ! " The cry echoed through the whole village. The parson and clerk who lived nearest to the church, heard it first, and they observed that something unusual was going on, and went into the church. They listened to the sermon for a while, and then the clerk nudged the parson and said, " It would not be amiss if we were to use the opportunity together, and before the dawning of the last day, find an easy way of getting to heaven." " To tell the truth," answered the parson, " that is what I myself have been thinking, so if you are inclined, we will set out on our way." " Yes," answered the clerk, " but you, the pastor, have the precedence, I will follow." So the parson went first, and ascended the pulpit where the master opened his sack. The parson crept in first, and then the clerk. The master immediately tied up the sack tightly, seized it by the middle, and dragged it down the pulpit-steps, and whenever the heads of the two fools bumped against the steps, he cried, " We are going over the mountains." Then he drew them through the village in the same way, and when they were passing through puddles, he cried, " Now we are going through wet clouds," and when at last he was dragging them up the steps of the castle, he cried, " Now we are on the steps of heaven, and will soon be in the outer court." When he had got to the top, he pushed the sack into the pigeon-house, and when the pigeons fluttered about, he said, " Hark how glad the angels are, and how they are flapping their wings ! " Then he bolted the door upon them, and went away.

Next morning he went to the count, and told him that he had performed the third task also, and had carried the parson and clerk out of the church. " Where hast thou left them ? " asked the lord. " They are lying upstairs in a sack in the pigeon-house, and imagine that they are in heaven." The count went up himself, and convinced himself that the master had told the truth. When he had delivered the parson and clerk from their captivity, he said, " Thou art an arch-thief, and hast won thy wager. For once thou escapest with a whole skin, but see that thou leavest my land, for if ever thou settest foot on it again, thou shalt not escape punishment." The Master-thief took leave of his parents, once more went forth into the wide world, and no one has ever heard of him since.

SEVEN LITTLE STORIES

1. THE WISE SERVANT

How fortunate is the master, and how well all goes in his house, when he has a wise servant who listens to his orders and does not obey them, but prefers following his own wisdom. A clever John of this kind was once sent out by his master to seek a lost cow. He stayed away a long time, and the master thought, "Faithful John does not spare any pains over his work!" As, however, he did not come back at all, the master was afraid lest some misfortune had befallen him, and set out himself to look for him. He had to search a long time, but at last he perceived the boy who was running up and down a large field. " Now, dear John," said the master when he had got up to him, " hast thou found the cow which I sent thee to seek ? " " No, master," he answered, " I have not found the cow, but then I have not looked for it." " Then what hast thou looked for, John ? " " Something better, and that luckily I have found." " What is that, John ? " " Three blackbirds," answered the boy. " And where are they ? " asked the master. " I see one of them, I hear the other, and I am running after the third," answered the wise boy.

Take example by this, do not trouble yourselves about your masters or their orders, but rather do what comes into your head and pleases you, and then you will act just as wisely as prudent John.

---

2. Brides on their Trial

THERE was once a young shepherd who wished much to marry, and was acquainted with three sisters who were all equally pretty, so that it was difficult to him to make a choice, and he could not decide to give the preference to any of them. Then he asked his mother for advice, and she said, " Invite all three, and set some cheese before them, and watch how they eat it." The youth did so ; the first, however, swallowed the cheese with the rind on ; the second hastily cut the rind off the cheese, but she cut it so quickly that she left much good cheese with it, and threw that away also ; the third peeled the rind off carefully, and cut neither too much nor too little. The shepherd told all this to his mother, who said, " Take the third for thy wife." This he did, and lived contentedly and happily with her.

3. SWEET PORRIDGE

THERE was a poor but good little girl who lived alone with her mother, and they no longer had anything to eat. So the child went into the forest, and there an aged woman met her who was aware of her sorrow, and presented her with a little pot, which when she said, " Cook, little pot, cook," would cook good, sweet porridge, and when she said, " Stop, little pot," it ceased to cook. The girl took the pot home to her mother, and now they were freed from their poverty and hunger, and ate sweet porridge as often as they chose. Once on a time when the girl had gone out, her mother said, " Cook, little pot, cook." And it did cook and she ate till she was satisfied, and then she wanted the pot to stop cooking, but did not know the word. So it went on cooking and the porridge rose over the edge, and still it cooked on until the kitchen and whole house were full, and then the next house, and then the whole street, just as if it wanted to satisfy the hunger of the whole world, and there was the greatest distress, but no one knew how to stop it. At last when only one single house remained, the child came home and just said, " Stop, little pot," and it stopped and gave up cooking, and whosoever wished to return to the town had to eat his way back.

---

4. A RIDDLING TALE

THREE women were changed into flowers which grew in the field, but one of them was allowed to be in her own home at night. Then once when day was drawing near, and she was forced to go back to her companions in the field and become a flower again, she said to her husband, " If thou wilt come this afternoon and gather me, I shall be set free and henceforth stay with thee." And he did so. Now the question is, how did her husband know her, for the flowers were exactly alike, and without any difference ? Answer : as she was at her home during the night and not in the field, no dew fell on her as it did on the others, and by this her husband knew her.

5. Odds and Ends

THERE was once on a time a maiden who was pretty, but idle and negligent. When she had to spin she was so out of temper that if there was a little knot in the flax, she at once pulled out a whole heap of it, and strewed it about on the ground beside her. Now she had a servant who was industrious and gathered together the bits of flax which were thrown away, cleaned them, span them fine, and had a beautiful gown made out of them for herself. A young man had wooed the lazy girl, and the wedding was to take place. On the eve of the wedding, the industrious one was dancing merrily about in her pretty dress, and the bride said,—

" Ah, how that girl does jump about, dressed in my odds and ends."

The bridegroom heard that, and asked the bride what she meant by it. Then she told him that the girl was wearing a dress made of the flax which she had thrown away. When the bridegroom heard that, and saw how idle she was, and how industrious the poor girl was, he gave her up and went to the other, and chose her as his wife.

---

6. The Peasant in Heaven

ONCE on a time a poor pious peasant died, and arrived before the gate of heaven. At the same time a very, very rich lord came there who also wanted to get into heaven. Then Saint Peter came with the key, and opened the door and let the great man in but apparently did not see the peasant, and shut the door again. And now the peasant outside heard how the great man was received in heaven with all kinds of rejoicing, and how they were making music and singing within. At length all became quiet again, and Saint Peter came and opened the gate of heaven and let the peasant in. The peasant, however, expected that they would make music and sing when he went in also, but all remained quite quiet ; he was received with great affection, it is true, and the angels came to meet him, but no one sang.

Then the peasant asked Saint Peter how it was that they did not sing for him as they had done when the rich man went in, and said that it seemed to him that there in heaven things were done with just as much unfairness as on earth. Then said Saint Peter, " By no means, thou art just as dear to us as any one else, and wilt enjoy every heavenly delight that the rich man enjoys, but poor fellows like thee come to heaven every day, but a rich man like this does not come more than once in a hundred years ! "

---

7. THE EAR OF CORN

IN former times, when God himself still walked the earth, the fruitfulness of the soil was much greater that it is now ; then, the ears of corn did not bear fifty or sixty, but four or five hundred-fold. Then the corn grew from the bottom to the very top of the stalk, and according to the length of the stalk was the length of the ear. Men however are so made, that when they are too well off they no longer value the blessings which come from God, but grow indifferent and careless. One day a woman was passing by a corn-field when her little child, who was running beside her, fell into a puddle, and dirtied her frock. On this the mother tore up a handful of the beautiful ears of corn, and cleaned the frock with them.

When the Lord, who just then came by, saw that, he was angry, and said, " Henceforth shall the stalks of corn bear no more ears ; men are no longer worthy of heavenly gifts." The by-standers who heard this, were terrified, and fell on their knees and prayed that he would still leave something on the stalks, even if the people were undeserving of it, for the sake of the innocent birds which would otherwise have to starve. The Lord, who foresaw their suffering, had pity on them and granted the request. So the ears were left as they now grow.

THE FOUR SKILFUL BROTHERS

THERE was once a poor man who had four sons, and when they were grown up, he said to them, " My dear children, you must now go out into the world, for I have nothing to give you, so set out, and go to some distance and learn a trade, and see how you can make your way." So the four brothers took their sticks, bade their father farewell and went through the town-gate together. When they had travelled about for some time, they came to a cross-way which branched off in four different directions. Then said the eldest, " Here we must separate, but on this day four years, we will meet each other again at this spot, and in the meantime we will seek our fortunes."

Then each of them went his way, and the eldest met a man who asked him where he was going, and what he was intending to do ? " I want to learn a trade." he replied. Then the other said, " Come with me, and be a thief." " No," he answered, " that is no longer regarded as a reputable trade, and the end of it is that one has to swing on the gallows." " Oh," said the man, " you need not be afraid of the gallows ; I will only teach you to get such things as no other man could ever lay hold of, and no one will ever detect you." So he allowed himself to be talked into it, and while with the man became an accomplished thief, and so dexterous that nothing was safe from him, if he once desired to have it. The second brother met a man who put the same question to him—what he wanted to learn in the world. " I don't know yet," he replied. " Then come with me, and be an astronomer ; there is nothing better than that, for nothing is hid from you." He liked the idea, and became such a skilful astronomer that when he had learnt everything, and was about to travel onwards, his master gave him a telescope and said to him, " With that canst thou see whatsoever takes place either on earth, or in heaven, and nothing can remain concealed from thee." A huntsman took the the third brother into training, and gave him such excellent instruction in everything which related to huntsmanship, that he became an experienced hunter. When he went away, his master gave him a gun and said, " It will never fail you ; whatsoever you aim at, you are certain to hit." The youngest brother also met a man who spoke to him, and required what his intentions were. " Would you not like to be a tailor ? " said he. " Not that I know of," said the youth ; " sitting doubled up from morning till night, driving the needle and the goose backwards and forwards, is not to my taste." " Oh, but you are speaking in ignorance," answered the man ; " with me you would learn a very different kind of tailoring, which is respectable and proper, and for the most part very honourable." So he let himself be persuaded, and went with the man, and learnt his art from the very beginning. When they parted, the man gave the youth a needle, and said, " With this you can sew together whatever is given you, whether it is as soft as an egg or as hard as steel ; and it will all become one piece of stuff, so that no seam will be visible."

When the appointed four years were over, the four brothers arrived at the same time at the cross-roads, embraced and kissed each other, and returned home to their father. " So now," said he, quite delighted, " the wind has blown you back again to me." They told him of all that had happened to them, and that each had learnt his own trade. Now they were sitting just in front of the house under a large tree, and the father said, " I will put you all to the test, and see what you can do." Then he looked up and said to his second son, " Between two branches up at the top of this tree, there is a chaffinch's nest, tell me how many eggs there are in it ? " The astronomer took his glass, looked up, and said, " There are five." Then the father said to the eldest, " Fetch the eggs down without disturbing the bird which is sitting hatching them." The skilful thief climbed up, and took the five eggs from beneath the bird, which never observed what he was doing, and remained quietly sitting where she was, and brought them down to his father. The father took them, and put one of them on each corner of the table, and the fifth in the middle, and said to the huntsman, " With one shot thou shalt shoot me the five eggs in two, through the middle." The huntsman aimed, and shot the eggs, all five as the father had desired, and that at one shot. He certainly must have had some of the powder for shooting round corners. " Now it's your turn," said the father to the fourth son ; " you shall sew the eggs together again, and the young birds that are inside them as well, and you must do it so that they are not hurt by the shot." The tailor brought his needle, and sewed them as his father wished. When he had done this the thief had to climb up the tree again, and carry them to the nest, and put them back again under the bird without her being aware of it. The bird sat her full time, and after a few days the young ones crept out, and they had a red line round their necks where they had been sewn together by the tailor.

"Well," said the old man to his sons, "I begin to think you are all worth more than you look; you have used your time well, and learnt something good. I can't say which of you deserves the most praise. That will be proved if you have but an early opportunity of using your talents." Not long after this, there was a great uproar in the country, for the King's daughter was carried off by a dragon. The King was full of trouble about it, both by day and night, and caused it to be proclaimed that whosoever brought her back should have her to wife. The four brothers said to each other, "This would be a fine opportunity for us to show what we can do!" and resolved to go forth together and liberate the King's daughter. "I will soon know where she is," said the astronomer, and looked through his telescope and said, "I see her already, she is far away from here on a rock in the sea, and the dragon is beside her watching her." Then he went to the King, and asked for a ship for himself and his brothers, and sailed with them over the sea until they came to the rock. There the King's daughter was sitting, and the dragon was lying asleep on her lap. The huntsman said, "I dare not fire, I should kill the beautiful maiden at the same time." "Then I will try my art," said the thief, and he crept thither and stole her away from under the dragon, so quietly and dexterously, that the monster never remarked it, but went on snoring. Full of joy, they hurried off with her on board ship, and steered out into the open sea; but the dragon, who when he awoke had found no princess there, followed them, and came snorting angrily through the air. Just as he was circling above the ship, and about to descend on it, the huntsman shouldered his gun, and shot him to the heart. The monster fell down dead, but was so large and powerful that his fall shattered the whole ship. Fortunately, however, they laid hold of a couple of planks, and swam about the wide sea. Then again they were in great peril, but the tailor, who was not idle, took his wondrous needle, and with a few stitches sewed the planks together, and they seated themselves upon them, and collected together all the fragments of the vessel. Then he sewed these so skilfully together, that in a very short time the ship was once more seaworthy, and they could go home again in safety.

When the King once more saw his daughter, there were great rejoicings. He said to the four brothers, " One of you shall have her to wife, but which of you it is to be you must settle among yourselves." Then a warm contest arose among them, for each of them preferred his own claim. The astronomer said, " If I had not seen the princess, all your arts would have been useless, so she is mine." Then thief said, " What would have been the use of your seeing, if I had not got her away from the dragon ? so she is mine." The huntsman said, " You and the princess, and all of you, would have been torn to pieces by the dragon if my ball had not hit him, so she is mine." The tailor said, " And if I, by my art, had not sewn the ship together again, you would all of you have been miserably drowned, so she is mine." Then the King uttered this saying, " Each of you has an equal right, and as all of you cannot have the maiden, none of you shall have her, but I will give to each of you, as a reward, half a kingdom." The brothers were pleased with this decision, and said, " It is better thus than that we should be at variance with each other." Then each of them received half a kingdom, and they lived with their father in the greatest happiness as long as it pleased God.

SNOW-WHITE AND THE SEVEN DWARFS

ONCE upon a time in the middle of winter, when the flakes of snow were falling like feathers from the sky, a queen sat at a window sewing, and the frame of the window was made of black ebony. And whilst she was sewing and looking out of the window at the snow, she pricked her finger with the needle, and three drops of blood fell upon the snow. And the red looked pretty upon the white snow, and she thought to herself, " Would that I had a child as white as snow, as red as blood, and as black as the wood of the window-frame."

Soon after that she had a little daughter, who was as white as snow, and as red as blood, and her hair was as black as ebony ; and she was therefore called Little Snow-white. And when the child was born, the Queen died.

After a year had passed the King took to himself another wife. She was a beautiful woman, but proud and haughty, and she could not bear that any one else should surpass her in beauty. She had a wonderful mirror, and when she stood in front of it and looked at herself in it, and said—

> " *Mirror, Mirror, on the wall,*
> *Who is the fairest one of all ?* "

the mirror answered—

> " *Thou, O Queen, art the fairest of all !* "

Then she was satisfied, for she knew that the mirror spoke the truth.

But Snow-white was growing up, and grew more and more beautiful ; and when she was seven years old she was as beautiful as the day, and more beautiful than the Queen herself. And once when the Queen asked her mirror—

> " *Mirror, Mirror on the wall,*
> *Who is the fairest one of all ?* "

it answered—

> " *Thou, Queen mayst fair and beautous be,*
> *But Snow-white is lovelier far than thee.*"

Then the Queen was shocked, and turned yellow and green with envy. From that hour, whenever she looked at Snow-white, her heart heaved in her breast, she hated the girl so much.

And envy and pride grew higher and higher in her heart like a weed, so that she had no peace day or night. She called a huntsman and said, " Take the child away into the forest ; I will no longer have her in my sight. Kill her, and bring me back her heart as a token." The huntsman obeyed, and took her away ; but when he had drawn his knife, and was about to pierce Snow-white's innocent heart, she began to weep, and said, " Ah, dear huntsman, leave me my life ! I will run away into the wild forest, and never come home again."

And as she was so beautiful the huntsman had pity on her and said, " Run away, then, you poor child." " The wild beasts will soon have devoured you," thought he, and yet it seemed as if a stone

had been rolled from his heart since it was no longer needful for him to kill her. And as a young boar just then came running by he stabbed it, and cut out its heart and took it to the Queen as a proof that the child was dead.

But now the poor child was all alone in the great forest, and so terrified that she looked at every leaf of every tree, and did not know what to do. Then she began to run, and ran over sharp stones and through thorns, and the wild beasts ran past her, but did her no harm.

She ran as long as her feet would go until it was almost evening; then she saw a little cottage and went into it to rest herself. Everything in the cottage was small, but neater and cleaner than can be told. There was a table on which was a white cover, and seven little plates, and on each plate a little spoon; moreover, there were seven little knives and forks, and seven little mugs. Against the wall stood seven little beds side by side, and covered with snow-white counterpanes.

Little Snow-white was so hungry and thirsty that she ate some vegetables and bread from each plate and drank a drop of wine out of each mug, for she did not wish to take all from one only. Then, as she was so tired, she laid herself down on one of the little beds, but none of them suited her; one was too long, another too short, but at last she found that the seventh one was right, and so she remained in it, said a prayer and went to sleep.

When it was quite dark the owners of the cottage came back; they were seven dwarfs who dug and delved in the mountains for ore. They lit their seven candles, and as it was now light within the cottage they saw that some one had been there, for everything was not in the same order in which they had left it.

The first said, " Who has been sitting on my chair ? "
The second, " Who has been eating off my plate ? "
The third, " Who has been taking some of my bread ? "
The fourth, " Who has been eating my vegetables ? "
The fifth, " Who has been using my fork ? "
The sixth, " Who has been cutting with my knife ? "
The seventh, " Who has been drinking out of my mug ? "

Then the first looked round and saw that there was a little hole on his bed, and he said, " Who has been getting into my bed ? " The others came up and each called out, " Somebody has been lying in my bed too." But the seventh when he looked at his bed saw little Snow-white, who was lying asleep therein. And he called the others, who came running up, and they cried out with astonishment, and brought their seven little candles and let the light fall on little Snow-white. "Oh, heavens! oh, heavens!" cried they, "what a lovely child!" and they were so glad that they did not wake her up, but let her sleep on in the bed. And the seventh dwarf slept with his companions, one hour with each, and so got through the night.

When it was morning little Snow-white awoke, and was frightened when she saw the seven dwarfs. But they were friendly and asked her what her name was. "My name is Snow-white," she answered. "How have you come to our house?" said the dwarfs. Then she told them that her step-mother had wished to have her killed, but that the huntsman had spared her life, and that she had run for the whole day, until at last she had found their dwelling. The dwarfs said, "If you will take care of our house, cook, make the beds, wash, sew, and knit, and if you will keep everything neat and clean, you can stay with us and you shall want for nothing," "Yes," said Snow-white, "with all my heart," and she stayed with them. She kept the house in order for them; in the mornings they went to the mountains and looked for copper and gold, in the evenings they came back, and then their supper had to be ready. The girl was alone the whole day, so the good dwarfs warned her and said, "Beware of your step-mother, she will soon know that you are here; be sure to let no one come in."

But the Queen, believing that she had killed Snow-white, could not but think that she was again the first and most beautiful of all; and she went to her mirror and said—

> " *Mirror, Mirror on the wall,*
> *Who is the fairest one of all?* "

and the mirror answered—

> " *Thou, Queen art fairest in all this land,*
> *But over the hills, in the greenwood shade*
> *Where the seven dwarfs their dwelling have made,*
> *There Snow-white is hiding her head, and she*
> *Is lovelier far, O Queen, than thee.*"

Then she was astounded, for she knew that the mirror never spoke falsely, and she knew that the huntsman had betrayed her, and that little Snow-white was still alive.

And so she thought and thought again how she might kill her, for so long as she was not the fairest in the whole land, envy let her have no rest. And when she had at last thought of something to do, she painted her face, and dressed herself like an old pedlar-woman, and no one could have known her. In this disguise she went over the seven mountains to the seven dwarfs, and knocked at the door and cried, " Pretty things to sell, very cheap, very cheap." Little Snow-white looked out of the window and called out, " Good-day, my good woman, what have you to sell ? " " Good things, pretty things," she answered ; " stay-laces of all colours," and she pulled out one which was woven of bright-coloured silk. " I may let the worthy old woman in," thought Snow-white, and she unbolted the door and bought the pretty laces. " Child," said the old woman, " what a fright you look ; come, I will lace you properly for once." Snow-white had no suspicion, but stood before her, and let herself be laced with the new laces. But the old woman laced so quickly and laced so tightly that Snow-white lost her breath and fell down as if dead. " Now I am the most beautiful," said the Queen to herself, and ran away.

Not long afterwards, in the evening, the seven dwarfs came home, but how shocked they were when they saw their dear little Snow-white lying on the ground, and that she neither stirred nor moved, and seemed to be dead. They lifted her up, and, as they saw that she was laced too tightly, they cut the laces ; then she began to breathe a little, and after a while came to life again. When the dwarfs heard what had happened they said, " The old pedlar-woman was no one else than the wicked Queen ; take care and let no one come in when we are not with you."

But the wicked woman when she had reached home went in front of the mirror and asked—

> " *Mirror, Mirror on the wall,*
> *Who is the fairest one of all ?* "

and it answered as before—

> *" Thou, Queen art fairest in all this land,*
> *But over the hills, in the greenwood shade,*
> *Where the seven dwarfs their dwelling have made,*
> *There Snow-white is hiding her head, and she*
> *Is lovier far, O Queen, than thee."*

When she heard that, all her blood rushed to her heart with fear, for she saw plainly that little Snow-white was again alive. " But now," she said, " I will think of something that shall put an end to you," and by the help of witchcraft, which she understood, she made a poisonous comb. Then she disguised herself and took the shape of another old woman. So she went over the seven mountains to the seven dwarfs, knocked at the door, and cried, " Good things to sell, cheap, cheap ! " Little Snow-white looked out and said, " Go away ; I cannot let any one come in." " I suppose you can look," said the old woman, and pulled the poisonous comb out and held it up. It pleased the girl so well that she let herself be beguiled, and opened the door. When they had made a bargain the old woman said, " Now I will comb you properly for once." Poor little Snow-white had no suspicion, and let the old woman do as she pleased, but hardly had she put the comb in her hair than the poison in it took effect, and the girl fell down senseless. " You paragon of beauty," said the wicked woman, " you are done for now," and she went away.

But fortunately it was almost evening, when the seven dwarfs came home. When they saw Snow-white lying as if dead upon the ground they at once suspected the step-mother, and they looked and found the poisoned comb. Scarcely had they taken it out when Snow-white came to herself, and told them what had happened. Then they warned her once more to be upon her guard and to open the door to no one.

The Queen, at home, went in front of the mirror and said—

> *" Mirror, Mirror on the wall,*
> *Who is the fairest one of all ? "*

then it answered as before—

> *" Thou, Queen art fairest in all this land,*
> *But over the hills, in the greenwood shade*
> *Where the seven dwarfs their dwelling have made,*
> *There Snow-white is hiding her head, and she*
> *Is lovelier far, O Queen, than thee."*

When she heard the mirror speak thus she trembled and shook with rage. " Snow-white shall die," she cried, " even if it costs me my life ! "

Thereupon she went into a quite secret, lonely room, where no one ever came, and there she made a very poisonous apple. Outside it looked pretty, golden with a red cheek, so that every one who saw it longed for it ; but whoever ate a piece of it must surely die.

When the apple was ready she painted her face, and dressed herself up as a country-woman, and so she went over the seven mountains to the seven dwarfs. She knocked at the door. Snow-white put her head out of the window and said, " I cannot let any one in ; the seven dwarfs have forbidden me." " It is all the same to me," answered the woman, " I shall soon get rid of my apples. There, I will give you one."

" No," said Snow-white, " I dare not take anything." " Are you afraid of poison ? " said the old woman ; " look, I will cut the apple in two pieces ; you eat the red cheek, and I will eat the yellow." The apple was so cunningly made that only the red cheek was poisoned. Snow-white longed for the fine apple, and when she saw that the woman ate part of it she could resist no longer, and stretched out her hand and took the poisonous half. But hardly had she a bit of it in her mouth than she fell down dead. Then the Queen looked at her with a dreadful look, and laughed aloud and said, " White as snow, red as blood, black as ebony-wood ! this time the dwarfs cannot wake you up again."

And when she asked of the mirror at home—

> *" Mirror, Mirror on the wall,*
> *Who is the fairest one of all ? "*

it answered at last—

" Oh, Queen, in this land thou art fairest of all."

Then her envious heart had rest, so far as an envious heart can have rest.

The dwarfs, when they came home in the evening, found Snow-white lying upon the ground ; she breathed no longer and was dead. They lifted her up, looked to see whether they could find anything poisonous, unlaced her, combed her hair, washed her with water and wine, but it was all of no use ; the poor child was dead, and remained dead. They laid her upon a bier, and all seven of them sat round it and wept for her, and wept three days long.

Then they were going to bury her, but she still looked as if she were living, and still had her pretty red cheeks. They said, " We could not bury her in the dark ground," and they had a transparent coffin of glass made, so that she could be seen from all sides, and they laid her in it, and wrote her name upon it in golden letters, and that she was a king's daughter. Then they put the coffin out upon the mountain, and one of them always stayed by it and watched it. And birds came too, and wept for Snow-white ; first an owl, then a raven, and last a dove.

And now Snow-white lay a long, long time in the coffin, and she did not change, but looked as if she were asleep ; for she was as white as snow, as red as blood, and her hair was as black as ebony.

It happened, however, that a king's son came into the forest, and went to the dwarfs' house to spend the night. He saw the coffin on the mountain, and the beautiful Snow-white within it, and read what was written upon it in golden letters. Then he said to the dwarfs, " Let me have the coffin, I will give you whatever you want for it." But the dwarfs answered, " We will not part with it for all the gold in the world." Then he said, " Let me have it as a gift, for I cannot live without seeing Snow-white. I will honour and prize her as my dearest possession." As he spoke in this way the good dwarfs took pity upon him, and gave him the coffin.

And now the King's son had it carried away by his servants on their shoulders. And it happened that they stumbled over a tree-stump, and with the shock the poisonous piece of apple which Snow-white had bitten off came out of her throat. And before long she opened her eyes, lifted up the lid of the coffin, sat up, and was once more alive. " Oh, heavens, where am I ? " she cried. The King's son, full of joy, said, " You are with me," and told her what had happened, and said, " I love you more than everything in the world ; come with me to my father's palace, you shall be my wife."

And Snow-white was willing, and went with him, and their wedding was held with great show and splendour. But Snow-white's wicked step-mother was also bidden to the feast. When she had arrayed herself in beautiful clothes she went before the mirror, and said—

> " Mirror, Mirror on the wall,
> Who is the fairest one of all ? "

the mirror answered—

> " Thou, lady, art loveliest here, I ween,
> But lovelier far is the new made Queen."

Then the wicked woman uttered a curse, and was so wretched, so utterly wretched, that she knew not what to do. At first she would not go to the wedding at all, but she had no peace, and must go to see the young Queen. And when she went in she knew Snow-white ; and she stood still with rage and fear, and could not stir. But iron slippers had already been put upon the fire, and they were brought in with tongs, and set before her. Then she was forced to put on the red-hot shoes, and dance until she dropped down dead.

ASHPUTTEL, OR CINDERELLA

THE wife of a rich man fell sick, and as she felt that her end was drawing near, she called her only daughter to her bedside and said, " Dear child, be good and pious, and then the good God will always protect thee, and I will look down on thee from heaven and be near thee." Thereupon she closed her eyes and departed. Every day the maiden went out to her mother's grave and wept, and she remained pious and good. When winter came the snow spread a white sheet over the grave, and when the spring sun had drawn it off again, the man had taken another wife.

The woman had brought two daughters into the house with her, who were beautiful and fair of face, but vile and black of heart. Now began a bad time for the poor step-child. " Is the stupid goose to sit in the parlour with us?" said they. "He who wants to eat bread must earn it; out with the kitchen-wench." They took her pretty clothes away from her, put an old grey gown on her, and gave her wooden shoes. "Just look at the proud princess, how decked out she is!" they cried, and laughed, and led her into the kitchen. There she had to do hard work from morning till night, get up before daybreak, carry water, light fires, cook and wash. Besides this, the sisters did her every imaginable injury—they mocked her and emptied her peas and lentils into the ashes, so that she was forced to sit and pick them out again. In the evening when she had worked till she was weary she had no bed to go to, but had to sleep by the fireside in the ashes. And as on that account she always looked dusty and dirty, they called her Cinderella. It happened that the father was once going to the fair, and he asked his two step-daughters what he should bring back for them. "Beautiful dresses," said one, "Pearls and jewels," said the second. "And thou, Cinderella," said he, "what wilt thou have?" "Father, break off for me the first branch which knocks against your hat on your way home." So he bought beautiful dresses, pearls and jewels for his two step-daughters, and on his way home, as he was riding through a green thicket, a hazel twig brushed against him and knocked off his hat. Then he broke off the branch and took it with him. When he reached home he gave his step-daughters the things which they had wished for, and to Cinderella he gave the branch from the hazel-bush. Cinderella thanked him, went to her mother's grave and planted the branch on it, and wept so much that the tears fell down on it and watered it. It grew, however, and became a handsome tree. Thrice a day Cinderella went and sat beneath it, and wept and prayed, and a little white bird always came on the tree, and if Cinderella expressed a wish, the bird threw down to her what she had wished for.

It happened, however, that the King appointed a festival which was to last three days, and to which all the beautiful young girls in the country were invited, in order that his son might choose himself a bride. When the two step-sisters heard that they too were to appear among the number, they were delighted, called Cinderella and said, "Comb our hair for us, brush our shoes and fasten our buckles, for we are going to the festival at the King's palace." Cinderella obeyed, but wept, because she too would have liked to go with them to the dance, and begged her step-mother to allow her to do so. " Thou go, Cinderella ! " said she ; " Thou art dusty and dirty, and wouldst go to the festival ? Thou hast no clothes and shoes, and yet wouldst dance ! " As, however, Cinderella went on asking, the step-mother at last said, " I have emptied a dish of lentils into the ashes for thee, if thou hast picked them out again in two hours, thou shalt go with us." The maiden went through the back-door into the garden, and called, " You tame pigeons, you turtle-doves, and all you birds beneath the sky, come and help me to pick

> " *The good into the pot,*
> *The bad into the crop.*"

Then two white pigeons came in by the kitchen-window, and afterwards the turtle-doves, and at last all the birds beneath the sky, came whirring and crowding in, and alighted amongst the ashes. And the pigeons nodded with their heads and began pick, pick, pick, pick, and the rest began also pick, pick, pick, pick, and gathered all the good grains into the dish. Hardly had one hour passed before they had finished, and all flew out again. Then the girl took the dish to her step-mother, and was glad, and believed that now she would be allowed to go with them to the festival. But the step-mother said, " No, Cinderella, thou hast no clothes and thou canst not dance ; thou wouldst only be laughed at." And as Cinderella wept at this, the step-mother said, " If thou canst pick two dishes of lentils out of the ashes for me in one hour, thou shalt go with us." And she thought to herself, " That she most certainly cannot do." When the step-mother had emptied the two dishes of lentils amongst the ashes, the maiden went through the back-door into the garden and cried, " You tame pigeons, you turtle-doves, and all you birds under heaven, come and help me to pick

> " *The good into the pot,*
> *The bad into the crop.*"

Then two white pigeons came in by the kitchen-window, and afterwards the turtle-doves, and at length all the birds beneath the sky, came whirring and crowding in, and alighted amongst the ashes.

And the doves nodded with their heads and began pick, pick, pick, pick, and the others began also pick, pick, pick, pick, and gathered all the good seeds into the dishes, and before half an hour was over they had already finished, and all flew out again. Then the maiden carried the dishes to the step-mother and was delighted, and believed that she might now go with them to the festival. But the step-mother said, " All this will not help thee ; thou goest not with us, for thou hast no clothes and canst not dance ; we should be ashamed of thee ! " On this she turned her back on Cinderella, and hurried away with her two proud daughters.

As no one was now at home, Cinderella went to her mother's grave beneath the hazel-tree, and cried,

> " *Shiver and quiver, little tree,*
> *Silver and gold throw over me.*"

Then the bird threw a gold and silver dress down to her, and slippers embroidered with silk and silver. She put on the dress with all speed, and went to the festival. Her step-sisters and the step-mother however did not know her, and thought she must be a foreign princess, for she looked so beautiful in the golden dress. They never once thought of Cinderella, and believed that she was sitting at home in the dirt, picking lentils out of the ashes. The prince went to meet her, took her by the hand and danced with her. He would dance with no other maiden, and never left loose of her hand, and if any one else came to invite her, he said, " This is my partner."

She danced till it was evening, and then she wanted to go home. But the King's son said, " I will go with thee and bear thee company," for he wished to see to whom the beautiful maiden belonged. She escaped from him, however, and sprang into the pigeon-house. The King's son waited until her father came, and then he told him that the stranger maiden had leapt into the pigeon-house. The old man thought, " Can it be Cinderella ? " and they had to bring him an axe and a pickaxe that he might hew the pigeon-house to pieces, but no one was inside it. And when they got home Cinderella lay in her dirty clothes among the ashes, and a dim little oil-lamp was burning on the mantel-piece, for Cinderella had jumped quickly down from the back of the pigeon-house and had run to the little hazel-tree, and there she had taken off her beautiful clothes and laid them on the grave, and the bird had taken them away again, and then she had placed herself in the kitchen amongst the ashes in her grey gown.

Next day when the festival began afresh, and her parents and the step-sisters had gone once more, Cinderella went to the hazel-tree and said—

> " *Shiver and quiver, my little tree,*
> *Silver and gold throw over me.*"

Then the bird threw down a much more beautiful dress than on the preceding day. And when Cinderella appeared at the festival in this dress, every one was astonished at her beauty. The King's son had waited until she came, and instantly took her by the hand and danced with no one but her. When others came and invited her, he said, " She is my partner." When evening came she wished to leave, and the King's son followed her and wanted to see into which house she went. But she sprang away from him, and into the garden behind the house. Therein stood a beautiful tall tree on which hung the most magnificent pears. She clambered so nimbly between the branches like a squirrel, that the King's son did not knew where she was gone. He waited until her father came, and said to him, " The stranger-maiden has escaped from me, and I believe she has climbed up the pear-tree." The father thought, " Can it be Cinderella ? " and had an axe brought and cut the tree down, but no one was on it. And when they got into the kitchen, Cinderella lay there amongst the ashes, as usual, for she had jumped down on the other side of the tree, had taken the beautiful dress to the bird on the little hazel-tree, and put on her grey gown.

On the third day, when the parents and sisters had gone away, Cinderella once more went to her mother's grave and said to the little tree—

> " *Shiver and quiver, my little tree,*
> *Silver and gold throw over me.*"

And now the bird threw down to her a dress which was more splendid and magnificent than any she had yet had, and the slippers were golden. And when she went to the festival in the dress, no one knew how to speak for astonishment. The King's son danced with her only, and if any one invited her to dance, he said, " She is my partner."

When evening came, Cinderella wished to leave, and the King's son was anxious to go with her, but she escaped from him so quickly that he could not follow her. The King's son had, however, used a stratagem, and had caused the whole staircase to be smeared with pitch, and there, when she ran down, had the maiden's left slipper remained sticking. The King's son picked it up, and it was small and dainty, and all golden. Next morning, he went with it to the father, and said to him, " No one shall be my wife but she whose foot this golden slipper fits." Then were the two sisters glad, for they had pretty feet. The eldest went with the shoe into her room and wanted to try it on, and her mother stood by. But she could not get her big toe into it, and the shoe was too small for her. Then her mother gave her a knife and said, " Cut the toe off; when thou art Queen thou wilt have no more need to go on foot." The maiden cut the toe off, forced the foot into the shoe, swallowed the pain, and went out to the King's son. Then he took her on his horse as his bride and rode away with her. They were, however, obliged to pass the grave, and there, on the hazel-tree, sat the two pigeons and cried,

> " *Turn and peep, turn and peep,*
> *There's blood within the shoe,*
> *The shoe it is too small for her,*
> *The true bride waits for you.*"

Then he looked at her foot and saw how the blood was streaming from it. He turned his horse round and took the false bride home again, and said she was not the true one, and that the other sister was to put the shoe on. Then this one went into her chamber and got her toes safely into the shoe, but her heel was too large. So her mother gave her a knife and said, " Cut a bit off thy heel; when thou art Queen thou wilt have no more need to go on foot." The maiden cut a bit off her heel, forced her foot into the shoe, swallowed the pain, and went out to the King's son. He took her on his horse as his bride, and rode away with her, but when they passed by the hazel-tree, two little pigeons sat on it and cried,

> *" Turn and peep, turn and peep,*
> *There's blood within the shoe,*
> *The shoe it is too small for her,*
> *The true bride waits for you."*

He looked down at her foot and saw how the blood was running out of her shoe, and how it had stained her white stocking. Then he turned his horse and took the false bride home again. " This also is not the right one," said he, " have you no other daughter ? " " No," said the man. " There is still a little kitchen-wench which my late wife left behind her, but she cannot possibly be the bride." The King's son said he was to send her up to him ; but the mother answered, " Oh no, she is much too dirty, she cannot show herself ! " He absolutely insisted on it, and Cinderella had to be called. She first washed her hands and face clean, and then went and bowed down before the King's son, who gave her the golden shoe. Then she seated herself on a stool, drew her foot out of the heavy wooden shoe, and put it into the slipper, which fitted like a glove. And when she rose up and the King's son looked at her face he recognized the beautiful maiden who had danced with him and cried, " That is the true bride ! " The step-mother and the two sisters were terrified and became pale with rage ; he, however, took Cinderella on his horse and rode away with her. As they passed by the hazel-tree, the two white doves cried,

> *" Turn and peep, turn and peep,*
> *No blood is in the shoe,*
> *The shoe is not too small for her,*
> *The true bride rides with you,"*

and when they had cried that, the two came flying down and placed themselves on Cinderella's shoulders, one on the right, the other on the left, and remained sitting there.

THE GOLDEN KEY

In the winter time, when deep snow lay on the ground, a poor boy was forced to go out with a sledge to fetch wood. When he had gathered it together and piled it he wished, as he was so frozen with cold, not to go home at once but to light a fire and warm himself a little. So he scraped away the snow and as he was thus clearing the ground, he found a tiny gold key. So he thought that where the key was the lock must be too, and dug in the ground and found an iron chest. " If only the key fits it ! " thought he ; " no doubt there are precious things in that little box." He searched, but no keyhole was there. At last he discovered one, but so small that it was hardly visible. He tried it, and the key fitted it exactly. Then he turned it once round, and now we must wait until he has quite unlocked it and opened the lid, and then we shall learn what wonderful things were inside that box.

First published in 1946 by Eyre & Spottiswoode (Publishers) Ltd, London
This edition published in 2012 by
The British Library
96 Euston Road
London NW1 2DB

British Library Cataloguing in Publication Data
A catalogue record for this publication is available from
The British Library

ISBN 978-0-7123-5858-3

Printed in Hong Kong by Great Wall Printing Co. Ltd